D1147471

Denise Mina is the author of nine critically acclaimed novels including *Garnethill*, which won the John Creasey Memorial Prize for best first crime novel. Passionate about all aspects of the genre, she also writes short stories, graphic novels, and is a regular contributor to both TV and radio. Denise lives in Glasgow with her husband and two children. Find out more at www.denisemina.co.uk

By Denise Mina

Garnethill
Exile
Resolution
Sanctum
The Field of Blood
The Dead Hour
The Last Breath
Still Midnight
The End of the Wasp Season

RESOLUTION

Denise Mina

An Orion paperback

First published in Great Britain in 2001
by Bantam Press,
a division of Transworld Publishers
This paperback edition published in 2011
by Orion Books Ltd,
Orion House, 5 Upper St Martin's Lane,
London WC2H 9EA

An Hachette UK company

A CIP catalogue record for this book
is available from the British Library.

Typeset by Input Data Services Ltd, Bridgwater, Somerset

Printed and bound by CPI Group (UK) Ltd, Croydon, CR0 4YY

The Orion Publishing Group's policy is to use papers
that are natural, renewable and recyclable products and
made from wood grown in sustainable forests. The logging
and manufacturing processes are expected to conform to
the environmental regulations of the country of origin.

www.orionbooks.co.uk

For Amy and Sam.
Three cheers for the Purples!

Acknowledgements

Many, many thanks to Gerry Considine for explaining the Scottish legal system and for handing me plot twists on a plate. Also to Tommy Smith and a nameless officer of the Crown for explaining the ins and outs of the High Court. The Media and Information Service of the Strathclyde Police Department also helped. Thanks again to Selina Walker, Rachel Calder and Katrina Whone, all of whom love attention and will be thrilled at a mention. Particular thanks are due to Stephen Evans for Kilty's joke about the shark documentary, among many, many other things.

I'd like to thank all the kind souls who, over the course of this series, have, uncomplainingly, let me steal their jokes. Those who did complan will be dealt with forthwith, future jokes notwithstanding. You know who you are. Start running.

I

Angus Farrell

It was quiet in the grey corridor. High summer shone through the consecutive windows, lighting the lazy dust; window bars cast chilly shadows on to cracked plaster. They were waiting in the corridor-in-between for the door to be opened to the visitors' block. The police were out there. Angus didn't know what they were going to charge him with yet. He guessed the murders and not the rapes. They didn't have any good witnesses for the rapes. A guard at the far end watched them lethargically, standing on one leg.

The sour smell of disinfectant was making Angus's battered sinuses ache again; he was sure he had a fragment of bone stuck in there. He sat forward suddenly, hanging his head between his knees. Henry, the burly nurse sitting next to him, shifted his legs out of splatter range.

'Are you gonnae be sick?' he asked.

'No,' said Angus, bending lower. 'My head hurts.'

Henry grunted. 'Tell them at meds.'

Medication was four hours away. 'Thanks, Henry,' said Angus, 'I will.'

He looked between his legs. The wooden bench was bolted to the wall, the mysterious point of attachment plastered over so that no one could wrench it off and use it as a weapon. Angus had understood the rationale of institutional vigilance during his career as a psychologist. It wasn't until he became a patient that he began to appreciate the psychic impact of static furniture, of lukewarm food and

I

blunt knives. The minor amendments caught his attention every time, making him speculate about the behaviour being deterred.

Henry shifted his weight forward, straining the bench from the wall. He had deodorant on, an acrid, hollow smell. Angus shut his eyes and remembered. It had been so dark outside the window that night. His most searing sensual memory was a light lemony aftershave billowing out towards him as Douglas opened the front door of Maureen O'Donnell's flat. He'd whispered angrily to Angus, asking him what he wanted, what was he doing there. Angus had stepped into the hallway, clicked the door shut behind him and, in a single fluid movement, grabbed Douglas by the hair and pulled him down, kneeing him sharply on the chin, knocking him off his feet. He held on to him by the hair, letting him down slowly to the floor, dropping him quietly. There was so much blood at the end, running off the rim of the chair. Angus had stood at the bedroom door, looking in at her through the crack in the door. Maureen was snoring lightly and it made him smile. Her clothes were on the floor by the bed, a stepped-out-of dress, kicked-off shoes. So much blood. Angus couldn't remember the first cut properly, just the build-up and the outcome. Disappointed, he sighed.

'Don't worry,' said Henry. 'You'll be fine.'

Angus sat upright, making a brave face and nodding.

'They're just going to charge ye,' said Henry. 'They're not even going to question ye today.'

Angus had been here for almost a year. For the first eight months he had been deluded and terrified, hadn't known where he was, what was real or imagined. Reality came in snippets at first and he began quickly to yearn for the alien confusion. The noise and the smell of the hospital were unbearable. Two men on his block were nocturnal, a moaner and an idiot who tapped on the pipes all night. Angus listened for two months, using his experience of crosswords, trying to decipher the message. There was no message, just a rhythm, over and over, as if the man was trying to tell a careful listener that he was still alive and almost sentient.

Henry was picking his nose. It was a straightforward, unceremonious hoick, an index finger rammed up his nostril, searching for congealed mucus. The doctors here picked at their arses, nurses swore, domestic staff stared with open-mouthed amusement at the patients and stopped working when supervisors left the room. It didn't matter how many social conventions they breached, they still felt better than their charges because state mental patients were credited with no opinions, no judgement. They were empty vessels. Angus knew that being in here superseded every-thing else he had ever been.

No one had thought that he might be familiar with the criminal justice process, not his lawyer, not Dr Heikle, his psychiatrist, not even the police. It astonished him. He had worked in the health service for seventeen years but he'd also done court reports and diversions. They had forgotten his career because he was a patient now, a nothing.

He looked up and down the bleak corridor. Maureen O'Donnell had brought him to this and she was going to get him out.

2

Polis

Hugh McAskill and Joe McEwan sat side by side on Maureen O'Donnell's settee. They were tall men. Joe would have been attractive if he hadn't been such a prick. He had blond hair, turning white in the recent wave of sunshine, a deep tan, and he was always smartly dressed, in chinos and well-fitting shirts and jumpers. When Maureen first met Joe, his tan looked as if he'd just come back from a nice holiday somewhere Mediterranean. In the past year the tan had become more orange and sunbed-ish but it might have been her jaundiced view of him: they had an unhappy history. Hugh looked far more Scottish. His hair was a russet red, flecked with silver at the temples. His eyes were blue and his skin flushed red or white depending on the season. The living room window was pushed right up and the evening was cooler than the day but the men were still sweating into their collars.

Usually, Glasgow's weather vacillates between freezing rain and not-so-freezing rain but sometimes, on a five-to ten-year cycle, the weather turns and the city doesn't know itself. This was such a time. Unconditional sunshine had arrived one week ago. Virulent, fecund plant life had sprung up everywhere: trees and bushes were heavy with deep green leaves, growth appeared on buildings, between cracks in the pavement, on bins. The city burst into life and everyone began to farm their skin. Water-white cheeks and necks withered and puckered with relentless exposure. Casualty departments heaved under the strain of sunburn and heat stroke. Everyone in the unaccustomed city was dressing as if they'd woken up naked in a bush and had to borrow clothes to get home: old women wore young women's summer dresses, vest tops were stretched over belly rolls, short sleeves showed off straps from industrial bras. Every night felt like Friday night and parties went on too long. Fantastic blood-alcohol levels were attained by con-scientious individuals. Everyone was dangerously out of character.

Hugh sipped the coffee and Joe lit a super-low-tar cig-arette.

'Are ye sure I can't get you anything, Joe?' said Maureen.

'Just sit down,' said Joe impatiently. 'We need to talk to you.'

'I'll just go to the loo,' she said, and Joe rolled his eyes.

Maureen sat on the toilet and held her head in her hands. The timing couldn't have been worse. Her big sister Una was expecting a baby any day now, her father Michael was back in Glasgow, floating around like a toxic cloud, and the dreams and flashbacks were getting worse and worse. When she thought of Michael in her city, the air caught in her throat, the light stung her skin and scratched her eyes. She would rather have been dead than share the air with him. And now Joe and Hugh were back up at her door asking about Angus Farrell again.

Joe had never liked her much but he treated her with frank contempt now. She'd lied about Angus writing to her from the hospital and had kept all the letters back from them for as long as she could. She couldn't hand over those letters. Angus had written them to make the police think he was insane, to give himself a defence, but she read between the lines and knew that he wasn't. The irrationality was too ordered, too carefully set. Angus had a plan. He'd hinted at what had happened between himself and Maureen in almost every letter, hinted that she had drugged him with acid. If she handed over the letters she'd be damning herself and giving him evidence for an insanity defence. The police had searched her house, got hold of them anyway and Joe had loathed her ever since. However much she tried to convince herself that it didn't matter because she didn't like him either, it was hard to be in his company.

She dug her nails into her scalp, deep into the skin, promising herself a cigarette if she went back into the living room. She stood up and flushed the toilet for authenticity, lifting the lid so it was loud enough for Joe and Hugh to hear.

They had their elbows on their knees, their ankles crossed, mirroring one another.

'This place looks pretty empty,' said Joe, glancing around the sparse living room. 'Are you moving?'

'No,' she said, sitting cross-legged on the floor. 'I'm just chucking stuff out.'

She was emptying the room gradually and had recently given away all her precious books and chucked out the broken video. The books were a big step. She wasn't sure why she was doing it, but the house felt better without the clutter. She felt as if she was stripping the set, getting ready to leave with no idea of where she was moving to.

Joe looked at the far wall. 'Where's all the books?'

She shrugged and lit a cigarette. 'I gave them away to a charity shop.'

'If you're moving you need to tell us.'

'I'm not moving, Joe.'

'We need to get in touch with ye.'

'I'm not moving, Joe.'

A man with the merest smattering of manners would have let it go at that but Joe didn't care if he offended or bored or annoyed her. 'You look as if you're moving.'

Maureen sighed and shrugged helplessly. Hugh reached into his jacket pocket and pulled out a notebook. Joe was looking unhappily around the room, at the portable television balanced on a kitchen chair and the blood-stained floorboards. 'Ye might have painted over that,' he said, flinching.

Maureen looked at the bloody mess. It was a flattened stain, squashed out of shape because the carpet had been over it when Douglas, her boyfriend, was murdered. She looked back at Joe. 'Are you an interior decorator now?'

'Maureen,' said Hugh, butting in before they got started, 'we need to ask you some questions about Angus Farrell.'

She nodded.

'You know his trial is coming up, don't you?'

Maureen sat up straight. 'No,' she said, 'I thought he'd had a trial already.'

'That was just a preliminary hearing. This is the full trial. He's mentioned you in his defence and we need to ask you what you're going to say in court.'

'I had to go and see his lawyer yesterday. Was that about the same thing?'

'Yeah,' said Hugh.

'He kept asking about my brother.' She smiled nervously. 'D'you think they'll ask about him? I won't have to be a witness in court, will I?'

Unable to give her a blanket assurance, Hugh looked at his notebook. 'Maybe not. Wait and see.'

'Did you drug Farrell in Millport?' said Joe suddenly.

'No,' she lied. 'I didn't.'

'Did you tie him up?'

'No, I never touched him.'

'Have you ever even been to Millport?' he asked sarcastically. The previous winter the papers had carried a large

7

photograph of her with a tricycle on Millport seafront.

'I have been to Millport in the past,' she said.

'Did you go there at any point last September?' asked Hugh.

'No.'

Hugh made a note and spoke again. 'That fifteen grand Douglas paid into your bank account, what was that about?'

Maureen shrugged. 'I never did find out. An apology, maybe.'

'For what?' said Joe.

She was going to tell him that when Douglas found out that Angus had been raping patients it had made him look at his own behaviour, that he had probably found it hard to square having an affair with Maureen when she was a patient at his clinic, but she knew Joe'd say something nasty. 'I don't know,' she said. A thought struck her and she cringed. 'D'ye think they'll ask me about being in hospital?'

'Yeah,' said Joe unkindly. 'I think your stay in a mental hospital might be material.'

Hugh glanced at his boss's knee, and Maureen had had enough. 'Fuck off, Joe,' she snapped. 'You're a cheeky bitch.'

He was on his feet and pointing at her. 'Don't you talk to me like that.'

And suddenly she was up and angry and couldn't be arsed being nice about two big men coming into her house looking for a fight. 'Why did you come here?' she shouted at him.

'You're *legally obliged* to co-operate with us,' yelled Joe.

She turned on Hugh. 'Why did you bring him up here? What's he doing here?'

'I can come here if I want.'

'You're a cheeky bugger and you're here making trouble.'

'Don't you swear at me.'

They were head to head, Joe a foot and a half taller than her. They hesitated. They had escalated the fight too fast.

Now would be the moment to start punching each other and neither of them was about to do that.

'Sit down,' said Hugh, sounding tired, 'and we'll continue.'

They backed off. Joe glanced behind him to check the settee was still there before sitting down and Maureen lurched forward, as if she was making him sit down. Joe stood up again and they both heard Hugh muttering, 'Forfucksake,' under his breath. The anger passed and it all seemed ridiculous to Maureen. She smiled as she sat down on the floor and Joe took offence, which made her smile all the more. It felt as if they had all known each other for ever. The only person she fought with like that was her brother. 'Okay,' she said. 'I'm sorry, Hugh. Ask me anything you want.'

Hugh held up a hand and spoke to both of them. 'I'm not refereeing.'

'Sorry,' said Maureen, and Joe sat on the settee. She didn't know anything about the police but she knew that Joe was too senior to be here. He had chosen to come, knowing it would be incendiary, knowing it would affect the quality of information Hugh could get for the prosecution. 'Sorry,' she said again. 'I'll be good. Ask me anything.'

'I was gonnae,' said Hugh flatly, letting her know that he didn't need her permission.

'Well, go on, then.' She smiled, getting the last word.

'When I'm ready,' said Hugh, grinning at his notes.

Maureen nodded at his notebook. 'Shoot,' she said.

On the way out she stopped Hugh by the door, letting Joe jog down the stairs ahead of him. 'Hugh,' she said, 'what are the chances Angus'll get off?'

'Oh,' Hugh frowned, 'hard to say until the defence case is submitted.'

'If he does get off,' she said quietly, 'he'll come for me, won't he?'

'If he gets out we'll protect you,' said Hugh seriously. 'Don't worry about that. If he gets off the murder charge we'll get him on the rapes.'

Downstairs Joe pulled the close door open to the street and called back up to Hugh to come on.

'If it goes to a rape case,' said Maureen, 'would Siobhain McCloud need to give evidence?'

'Sorry. She may not be a good witness but she's the best we've got,' Hugh replied.

Siobhain was one of the patients Angus had raped in the Northern Psychiatric Hospital. Maureen had been with Siobhain when she was questioned about it by the police. She hadn't talked for days afterwards – she could hardly walk from the station to the taxi. Hugh saw how downcast Maureen looked. 'Listen, there'll be fifty policemen in this close if he gets out. We'd have to protect you because of the threats in his letters.' He reached forward and rubbed her arm. 'If he gets out, I promise we'll be here.'

Maureen sat alone on the settee. They were going to bring up Liam's history of drug-dealing in court. If the university found out they might even chuck him out. She wouldn't tell him. She'd wait and see what happened. Everything was coming to an end.

Sunshine lingered in the living room, puddled in a corner of the bay window. It was ten o'clock and the sun would be going down soon. Taking a glass from the kitchen, she stood by the living room window and poured herself a large whisky, rolling it in her mouth before swallowing. The sunshine gilded the city below. Shards of glass in the yellow and burgundy sandstone glinted against a blue sky backdrop. In the street below, excited midges caught the sun, shimmering like animated flecks of gold.

She watched the high summer sun set quickly, like an orange rolling off a table, and suddenly found herself sitting in a blue gloom, holding an empty glass, looking out over the street at closing time. Dispensing with formalities, she drank straight from the whisky bottle, the tiny vacuum in the neck kissing the tip of her tongue. At the foot of the dark bill a string of orange street-lights flickered awake. It was a beautiful city and Maureen was glad she had lived here.

3
Ella McGee

'No,' said Cindy, watching her lift the upright hoover out of the cupboard.

Ella McGee ignored her, unwound the flex and carried the plug to the wall socket.

'I said no.'

Ella crouched down and punched the plug into the wall.

'She's right, Mrs G,' said Kevin. 'He said not tae.'

'Well,' Ella smiled up at the bouncer, 'I think I know a wee bit more about cleaning than he does.'

'Look, you,' Cindy came around the desk and stomped towards her, moving gracelessly in her high heels and miniskirt, 'don't fucking . . .' She tried to bend down to take out the plug but her tight skirt stopped her so she shouted instead, 'Not when there's punters here, ya daft old cow. He's fuckin' telt ye.'

And it was then that Ella made the worst mistake of her life. She elbowed Cindy in the leg, hitting her hard on the shin. Cindy reached for the desk on her way down, pulling the cheap table over, knocking the phone on the floor. Ella stood up and looked at her. Her skirt had ripped at the side, showing her baggy off-white knickers. Ella had never liked her – she thought she was something.

Cindy looked up at the old woman in the tracksuit, grinning down at her. 'You fucking cunt,' she screamed. Kevin stepped towards them. 'Girls, enough.'

They heard steps on the stairs and Si appeared from the

basement, hurrying up to the hallway when he saw Cindy on the floor. He helped her to her feet, saw the ripped skirt and sent her off to get another one.

'I want paid for it,' said Cindy, looking at Ella.

'You'll get paid for it,' he said. 'Go to the back office and see if Cath's got one.'

Cindy tottered down the hallway, huffing as if she'd hurt herself. Si righted the desk and picked up the phone, sitting the receiver in the cradle. He wouldn't look her in the eye and Ella knew it was bad. 'Put that Hoover away,' he said.

'That carpet needs going over, it's a right state.'

Margaret's head appeared at the mouth of the stairs to the basement. She looked at her brother and Si turned to Ella. 'Look, we need to talk to you.'

It was his own office, not the place's office, and no one was allowed in but Margaret and Si. It annoyed Ella. She'd tried to get in to clean it a couple of times, once when he was there and once when he was out. He wouldn't let her in and Cindy swore she didn't have a key. It wasn't anything special, just a dark room at the back of the basement, bars on the window, a fire escape leading to the alley, a desk with an open newspaper on it and a locked safe he must keep the money in. He could have trusted her, she would hardly have robbed him.

Margaret sat on the desk and Si took the chair. They seemed quite tense, the two of them, glancing at each other and looking away quickly, as if they'd been discussing her. Sometimes she felt she didn't know them at all. 'That daft cow,' she said. 'She was trying to pull the plug out of the wall and she fell over. Did ye see her, Magret? Split her skirt right up her arse, so she did.'

Margaret ignored her and looked at her brother. He

sighed at the desk. 'Look, Mum,' he said heavily, 'ye can't work here any more.'

Ella was stunned. 'How no?'

''Cause you're a fucking trouble-causer,' sneered Margaret. She'd a nasty, coarse manner about her sometimes.

Si touched his sister's arm, telling her to shut up. 'Mum, ye can't get on with any of them, you're always doing things we ask you not to do.' He had a nicer voice, a cultured voice.

'Like what do I do?' said Ella.

Si pointed up to the ceiling. 'Like hoovering when there are men in—'

'That carpet was a state.' She nodded adamantly. 'Ye want the place to have a bit of class, don't ye?'

'You don't listen,' he said, shutting his eyes. '*You don't listen to me.*'

'Simon,' Ella laughed indignantly, 'I don't need you to tell me when a carpet needs cleaned—'

'Get out now,' said Margaret flatly.

'I will not get out,' said Ella, looking to her son for support. Si blinked, cutting her off, and when he opened his eyes again, he was looking at the paper. Ella poked a finger at him. 'You owe me my wages.'

'Don't fucking pay her,' said Margaret, and turned back to her mother. 'Get out.'

'I won't leave till yees give me what I'm owed.'

'Don't fucking pay her, she's a waste of money.'

Margaret and her brother looked at each other, smiling a little, enjoying humiliating their old mother, even now, in their thirties, savouring the power shift.

'I'll tell the polis about ye,' said Ella, casting up a familiar threat they had used against her when they were children.

Si and his sister sniggered at her impotence. 'They know about us,' he said. 'We've got a licence for this place. D'ye

14

think they really believe we're giving saunas until three in the morning?'

'They don't know about they foreign women, do they?' said Ella, and their smug faces fell. 'They don't know ye keep them locked up through the wall there, do they?' She had expected them to react, maybe shout at her, but when she saw Margaret's hand coming out and the overhead light glint on the shaft of metal she knew she'd overplayed her hand by a mile. She lifted her hand to defend herself and the knife caught on her palm, sliding easily through the bridge of skin between her thumb and forefinger.

It was a deep cut, right through the flesh on her hand. Margaret laughed and watched Ella's hand bleeding on to the desk. Si pulled the newspaper under it, protecting the desk. Without saying sorry or even offering Ella her money, Si took down the first-aid box, covered the cut in cotton wool and wrapped a bandage round it. When he had finished he told her it would be best if she went home.

Cindy smirked at the appointments book as Ella walked past the desk. She had a red miniskirt on now, with zips up the side, and looked as cheap as the rest of them. She'd put the Hoover away and the carpet was still filthy. Kevin muttered that he was sorry as he opened the door for her. She kept it together until she got out into the dark street, and then Ella McGee cried all the way home.

4
Hot

Outside the kitchen window the morning sky was as clear as a baby's conscience. Below, at the base of Garnethill, the slip-road to the motorway was clogging up and the heat began to rise from the dawning city. Maureen sipped her coffee and shuddered compulsively, remembering the sleepy vagueness in her limbs just before the alarm. She looked out at the blackened silhouette on the horizon. It was the jagged tower of an old fever hospital, built a mile away from the city. Around it, peering over the shoulder of the hill, she saw the smashed onion domes on the smaller buildings, looking like caved-in heads.

Maureen had been dreaming about her stomach splitting open again, about Michael being in the room, touching her with razor fingers, making her bleed between her legs. It was getting worse – it was getting worse because he was out there somewhere. Acknowledging the fear tripped her mind to the image of Michael lying on the floor.

She kept thinking of a dark room. She shut her eyes. He was lying on his side ten yards from her, his breathing laboured. Maureen's face was sore down one side, smarting from a punch or fall. She walked over to him, raised an arm for balance and brought the heel of her boot down on his head, again and again, felt the cracking of bone shudder up her leg, again and again, until Michael was dead.

She opened her eyes and looked at her trembling hands.

She could try to imagine what it would feel like, to see if she could do it, but she would never know before the time came. She stopped herself, rubbing her eyes hard, reminding herself that there had been no phone call in the night: her sister Una's baby wasn't born yet. She had one more day of grace before the wars.

She took her coffee into the living room and put the telly on to drown out the noise in her head. An earnest local news reporter was standing in a park, sweating in a heavy woollen suit. He warned the public to stay indoors or use a high-factor sun cream. The piece must have been filmed at lunchtime. The grassy hillside behind him was carpeted with pink and red bodies slathered in baby oil. Over his left shoulder a team of sunburnt topless men, lying on the grass, raised their lager cans to the camera, waving fags and laughing, the living embodiment of a uniquely Scottish cavalier disregard for health.

As she watched the morning news, Maureen's bare feet felt the powdery dust on the floorboards and her toes re-coiled, pressing the flaking grit against the soft skin. She had left the stains from his blood unpainted, hoping somehow that it would help her assimilate Douglas's death. It hadn't. Before she could begin to take in what had happened she was forgetting Douglas's face and his manner, forgetting what she'd seen in him, forgetting everything but the shock and revulsion when she found his body. His eyes were the last image to slip her memory. When she saw him now, smiling and blinking slowly, she didn't know if she was remembering him or the memory of him. The heat was lifting his blood out of the wood, forming a brown dust that gathered in the still corners. Everything that was ever Douglas was slithering away.

In the bedroom, she pulled on a fresh T-shirt and a pair of baggy jungle shorts that hung low on her hips, pressing and wriggling her blood-dusty feet into a pair of trainers. Hearing her brother's soft, familiar knock at the door, she walked out to the hall. Liam would be the first to know if the baby was born and, although she was expecting him, she looked out through the spy-hole for clues about Una. Liam was standing on the landing, his sports bag in one hand and his college bag in the other. His shades couldn't hide a face still puffy with sleep. She opened the door and let him in.

'All right, Mauri?' he said, his voice taut with sleep and flecks of morning phlegm. He pulled off his glasses and followed her through to the kitchen, sitting the sports bag on the table.

'D'ye want a coffee?' she asked.

'Naw,' he said, 'I'm going to the library. I'll just sort ye out and go.'

Unzipping the bag, he lifted six boxes of duty-free Embassy Regal cigarettes on to the table. 'I haven't got any Superkings just now but I'll bring some tomorrow.'

Maureen nodded. 'This sleeve's a bit battered,' she said, lifting one box and looking at the smashed corner.

He took it back and tutted at it. 'Fuckers,' he said lethargically. 'They shouldn't give me shit like that. If ye can't use them, give them back to me on Monday and I'll refund the difference.'

'No, no, don't worry,' said Maureen, conscious that she was already getting the cigarettes at cost price as a special favour. 'I'll smoke them. When's your exam?'

'Tuesday morning,' he said, taking out a cigarette and lighting up.

'That's handy, then, because the wedding's on Wednesday.'

'Oh, God, yeah,' he said. 'I forgot about that.'

He pulled some blue pouches of rolling tobacco out of

his bag but Maureen waved them back in. 'We've got loads of those. There's a guy up the lane selling them fifty pence cheaper.'

'How can he afford that?'

'Well,' said Maureen, 'he's not on a stall, he's got no overheads.'

'He's a wee bastard whatever his story is,' said Liam.

Tired, they gave each other token smiles.

'No word about Una, then?' said Maureen quietly.

'No,' said Liam, clamping the cigarette between his teeth as he zipped up the bag and walked out to the hall.

'Do you want that table?' she said, pointing to the telephone table by the door. It wasn't nice, the wood was cheap and the varnish was chipped, but it was tall and thin and perfect for a telephone in an unobtrusive corner.

Liam tilted his head and looked at it. 'What's wrong with it?'

'Nothing. There's just too much stuff in here.'

'Ye sure?'

'Aye.' Maureen lifted the phone on to the floor and kicked the dusty phone books out of the way.

Liam hooked his arm underneath, lifted the table and struggled backwards out of the front door. The leg got caught in a stray strap from the sports bag and yanked it off his shoulder. He climbed over the bag, smashing the table off the doorframe. The sharp sound ricocheted off the close walls.

'Keep it down,' whispered Maureen. 'It's only half eight.'

'Sorry.' Liam smiled, closing an eye against the stream of smoke from his cigarette. He bent down to lift the bag and cracked the leg off the concrete floor. 'Shit. I'll see ye later,' he said, and walked down the stairs, inadvertently banging the table top off the iron banisters, leaving a trail of smoke behind him.

Back in the kitchen she finished her coffee and filled her cycle bag with the sleeves of cigarettes. She packed in as many as she could and hoped it would be a busy day at the market. Maureen needed to sell a lot of sleeves: she owed the Inland Revenue six thousand pounds' inheritance tax.

The day before he died Douglas had deposited fifteen thousand pounds in her bank account. Their brief and pointless affair had weighed heavily on him and the money was a tainted apology. It was an uncomfortable legacy, making Maureen feel like Douglas's deepest regret. She had spent it as quickly as she could, buying clothes and take-aways, handing lumps of it to anyone who'd take it and finally paying off a chunk of her mortgage. She was down to her last grand when Douglas's wife, Elsbeth, got in touch. She was settling his estate, and because it had been given within the seven years before his death, the money was liable to inheritance tax. Elsbeth wasn't about to pay it for Maureen. If Maureen didn't pay the six thousand, the tax man could sell her house from under her. In the two months they had been selling the cigarettes Maureen had managed to save two and a half thousand quid. They'd have made more if they weren't smoking so much of the stock.

An irresponsible driver out in the street hooted the horn three times, waking up anyone not keeping time to their clock. Maureen nipped into the kitchen, looked out of the window and saw a dirty white van in the street. Leslie was riding the clutch impatiently, sliding the van up and down the hill. Maureen picked up the cycle bag, pocketed her fags and sunglasses and locked the front door on the way out.

The close was quiet and cool. Radios and televisions

murmured behind the doors as everyone breakfasted and got ready to meet the day. Maureen pulled the close door open and a wall of heat hit her, making her hair prickle to attention. She slid on her shades. They were a cheap Ray-Bans imitation and sat so close to her face that her eyelashes brushed the glass. She opened the back door of the van and put the bag in, slamming the door shut and pausing to make sure it didn't fall open again. Then she clambered into the front seat and did up her belt, tying the long strap and the short strap together in a knot. It was an old van. 'Hiya,' she said chirpily.

Leslie was miserable, the pink tinge to her eyes exacerbated by the rose-tinted glass on her sad-eye shades. 'Hiya,' she said, scratching her cheek with her thumbnail and looking as if she might cry.

Leslie was dressed in a pair of pink denim cut-offs and a green running shirt. She rarely drove her motorbike now that they had the van. Maureen was used to seeing her in her leathers all the time and she'd forgotten Leslie's flair for throwing on horrible clothes and making them look like a daring statement. She had thick black hair, cut short, with a life and will of its own, large dark eyes and the righteous air of a very angry mother taking on the school bullies. She had perfect shoulders, fat-free arms, and radiant skin that made Maureen secretly jealous.

'I've ... I've split up with Cammy,' she said, and sighed at the wheel.

Maureen was finding it hard to keep acting surprised. Leslie and Cammy had split up three times this month alone. 'Really?' She tried to think of something to say that she hadn't already said about it. 'How's he taking it?'

Leslie nodded indignantly at the wheel. 'Well, he knows I'm serious this time, that's for sure.'

'Are ye serious this time?'

'Maureen,' rebuked Leslie, 'I'm doing my best here.'

'I know,' said Maureen, 'I know.'

Leslie wrestled the wheel left and pulled out. 'And I'm not bringing him to Kilty's brother's wedding either,' she said. 'I've told him.'

'Oh,' said Maureen, secretly pleased. 'Have you told Kilty?'

'No, but I will.'

'Because it's about fifty quid a head at Cameron House.'

'I'll tell her, I'll phone her. Anyway, tonight,' said Leslie, stopping at the lights, 'we're sorting his stuff out and he's giving me the keys back.'

'God, that serious, is it?' said Maureen, trying to sound encouraging.

'That serious. He's suffocating me, I can't stand it any more. If I'm in the loo too long he thinks I'm having an affair.'

Maureen didn't like Cammy and the feeling was mutual. They snipped at each other when they were in company and sat in a chilly, stubborn silence when they were left alone. Cammy was a contrary little shit. He blamed his bullying temper on the oppression of the Irish Catholic working man. Leslie was Protestant and, although not a natural candidate for ancestral guilt, she believed him. Maureen and Liam were Catholic and told her that Cammy's patter was a load of paranoid rubbish, that their generation were untouched by anti-Catholic prejudice, and sectarianism was nothing more than a football fan's accessory now. Still, Cammy maintained that history had dealt him a cruel blow. Maureen was sure that Leslie would have finished with him long ago if she had still had her job at the Scottish Women's Shelters. Being a house manager had

22

given her a focus, a role to play in the good fight, and she was restless and unfulfilled since being sacked.

Behind the van the driver of a red truck hooted.

'Keep your hair on, ya postie bastard,' said Leslie, and jerked the old van into first gear.

5
Paddy's

Beyond the designer shops and glass cathedral shopping malls of Glasgow city centre, across a broad and windy car park stood the ancient flea market called Paddy's. Anything could be bought there, from secondhand underpants to office furniture. Trapped between the river and a high railway viaduct, it made the shoddiest car-boot sale look as orchestrated as Disneyland. The market consisted of a ramshackle series of stalls set up in the dark tunnels under the disused railway line. In good weather hawkers would set up in the uneven alleyway outside, some on trestle tables, some spreading their goods over blankets laid out on the cobbles. It was a lawless place and the decency of the hawkers set the standards. Duty-free fags and cheap drink were okay, as was out-of-date mayonnaise and sectarian regalia. Hard-core pornography had to be kept hidden and, whatever they were selling, the junkie dealers were hedged in at the end of the lane by the river, away from everyone else.

Paddy's was named in honour of the last major wave of itinerant immigrants to Glasgow and operated as a cultural port of entry with each new group of incomers coming to buy cheap goods or make a small living. As they became known at the market and introduced their own customs and marketing opportunities, gradually, usually grudgingly, they became integrated.

In times past the market had been much bigger but the

railway above was disused now and three of the tunnels had been shut down because of galloping damp. The spare ground in front of the lane, where the poorest hawkers gathered, had been clawed back by the council for an extension to the High Court. The council tax had risen and everyone knew that Paddy's was dying. The council were proposing to lift the cobbles from the lane and sell them to a new development. The flea market was being asset-stripped.

Leslie eased the rickety van slowly down the cobbled lane at the back of the market, climbed out and knocked on the big wooden door three times. After a short pause, red-faced Peter, an obese man with a heart condition, swung the door wide, pinning it open. Maureen and Leslie lifted the cardboard boxes of cleaning products from the back of the van and carried them to their stall.

It was just inside the back door, across the tunnel from fat Peter and wee Lenny. Peter sold batteries, crockery and second-hand videotapes. Lenny was a TV repairman who'd been sacked from Radio Rentals on the ground that he was, indeed, radio rental. He took his smelly dog, Elsie Tanner, everywhere with him. Lenny had found Elsie in Ruchill Park, just behind the Co-op, hungry and homeless. She just ran out of a bush at him and he had no choice but to take her home with him. It didn't trouble Lenny that a hungry dog was unlikely to hang about in a little-used public park when there were bins aplenty fifty feet away. It was obvious to everyone but Lenny that he had stolen someone's dog.

Maureen set up, arranging the bleach, the squeezy and the dusters on the stall. They hardly ever sold any of the cleaning products: they were just a cover for the duty-free fags – the bleach bottles were getting dusty, a sure giveaway. Maureen opened a packet of dusters and gave the bottles a wipe, shielding Leslie from view. Leslie opened the cycle bag, took out the sleeves of cigarettes and placed them carefully in the green council wheelie bin that always sat near the back door. If the police found the cigarettes they could deny all knowledge of them: the worst that would happen was that their stock would be confiscated.

The tunnel seemed particularly damp today, contrasting bitterly with the warmth of the sunny lane outside. Leslie went off to park the van. When she came back in she found Maureen wiping down bottles of Toilet Duck and singing along to the cheeky, staccato beat of 'It's A Kind Of Magic'.

'It's a Home Gran Gotcha.' Leslie handed over one of the jerseys they kept in the cab for damp days in the tunnel.

'God,' said Maureen, realizing she had been singing. 'I don't even know I'm doing it.'

Together, they peered accusingly down the tunnel to the tapes stall. The woman standing behind it was a white-haired sixty-year-old with gold sovereign rings on every finger. She dressed in trainers and one of the rustling, baggy Kappa tracksuits all the kids were wearing. Giving her age away, she drew brown, single-line arched eyebrows high on her forehead above the frames of her glasses like Joan Crawford. She sold bootlegged tapes of CD albums on a stall financed by her well-to-do son and played tapes on her ghetto-blaster all day long. They were mediocre mainstream ballads and rock anthems, songs the listener didn't realize they loved until they heard them out of context, without the prejudice of packaging or association. Maureen and Leslie found themselves singing along to Jim Diamond, Queen and the Quo, knowing all the words, feeling uplifted until they realized who it was.

Maureen and Leslie unfolded their little canvas picnic stools and sat, Maureen facing the entrance to the tunnel and Leslie the wheelie bin, watching for robbers. Leslie kept her sad-eye shades on to hide her sad eyes. Maureen gave them a squashed Regal each and took out her chrome oval lighter. The flint jammed and she had to pull the backside off the lighter, unscrew the spring and put the flint back in before she could get a light. The strip-down and rebuild took thirty seconds because she'd done it so often.

Leslie kicked her ankle and made a sad face when she looked up. 'Oh,' she said pathetically, 'I think I'd feel a bit better if I had a fried-egg roll.'

Maureen laughed. 'You go,' she said. 'I'm always going.'

'But I'm having a trauma.'

'So am I.'

'What's your trauma?'

'My pal's bossing me around.'

'That's not as sad as a relationship failure,' said Leslie. 'It could result in a relationship failure,' said Maureen seriously.

Leslie looked away wistfully. 'If only someone cared.'

Maureen stood up. 'All right, but you're going tomorrow.'

She was walking towards the mouth of the tunnel, checking her pocket for change, when a hand shot out and grabbed her roughly by the shoulder, spinning her round. Home Gran was behind her, peering down her bifocals. Maureen had never seen her so close up before. The puff of white hair had a yellow nicotine smudge at the front and the cross-hatched wrinkles on her cheeks looked like duelling scars. Today she was modelling a beige tracksuit with black trim. 'You,' she said and took Maureen's hand. Surprisingly strong, she swung Maureen between the stalls to behind her tape counter, manoeuvring her by twisting her wrist like a rudder. 'You've got a degree, haven't ye?'

'Yeah,' said Maureen, 'but it's only in history of art.'

'Don't care about that.' Home Gran pointed Maureen on to a rickety kitchen stool, gave her a pen and an official-looking form. 'I need this filled out.' It was a form to start a case in the small-claims court. The agile old woman squatted down to sit on the stall's cross-bar, five inches off the ground.

'I haven't got anything to lean on,' said Maureen.

Home Gran reached underneath the stall and pulled out a rough scrap of hardboard. She had a bandage on her right hand, wrapped tightly around her wrist and her thumb.

Maureen had never really had a conversation with Home Gran but she knew the other stallholders were wary of her. Peter and Lenny had told Leslie that Home Gran was a retired prostitute. Her son had been a scholarship boy at a posh private school. The Parish Mothers had organized a petition against the place going to her boy because she was a street-walker but, to the school's credit, they kept him on and he went to university and studied management, no less. Maureen had heard of Home Gran walloping light-fingered shoppers across the head with the lid of her change tray. Sometimes she did it to innocent young guys on suspicion, prompting widespread disapproval: no one would come to the market if they thought they might get battered just for looking. But it was a slow day and Maureen had nothing else to do but go outside and dodge the sunshine. 'Okay, then,' she said, pulling the lid off the biro. 'What's your name?'

'Ella McGee.'

'Address?'

'Fifty-four, flat 12 D, Benny Lynch Court, G1.'

The Gorbals had recently been renamed and rebranded for the third time in a century but the area had yet to lose its heroin-plague and slasher-gang reputation. The high flats were a reminder of a simpler time, when the area was a repository for the most difficult and troubled families in the city. Maureen had heard that the janny's office was fitted with bullet-proof glass. Ella muttered, 'It's not like ye think.'

28

Maureen moved on swiftly. 'And who're ye bringing the case against?'

Maureen waited, pen poised, but Ella didn't answer. She looked up to find Ella with her bandaged hand raised, ready to give a slap. '*One word to anyone*,' she said, but it sounded as if she was begging.

Maureen shrugged casually. 'No odds to me,' she said, and pointed at Ella's hand, 'but raise your hand to me again and I'm off.' She went back to waiting to fill out the form and, out of the corner of her eye, saw Ella's hand drop to her knee.

'Okay. It's my son, Si.' She waited for a reaction but Maureen kept a straight face.

'Si McGee,' said Maureen. Is that his full name?'

'No,' said Ella.

'Well, we should put his full name down.'

'Simon Alan Egbert McGee.'

'Egbert, is that a confirmation name?'

'Aye.'

Maureen hadn't figured Home Gran for a Pape at all but now she looked at her and saw the heavy gold crucifix at her neck in a slightly less Versace light.

'Egbert.' Ella smiled weakly. 'Silly bugger, eh?'

'There's dafter names in the canon,' said Maureen, letting Ella know that she was Catholic too. Liam's confirmation name, Mortimer, had been chosen out of a hat in collusion with four pals at school. It could have been worse: the other options were Crispin, Ado and Mary. Maureen marvelled once again at the idiocy of allowing hysterical children to choose their own confirmation names. She left Egbert out of Si McGee's name and moved on to the address box. She looked up at Ella expectantly, pointing at the page. Ella was watching her face. 'Well?' said Maureen. 'Where does he stay, then?'

'Twelve Bentynck Street, Bearsden,' said Ella.

'That's a swanky address. Is there that much money in tapes?'

'Naw, he's got different businesses,' Ella pointed to the tray of tapes above her head. 'There's not a lot of money in this. He just set me up to keep me out of the way of the buses.'

Maureen turned back to the form, pointing to the amount box. Ella was staring at her face again, trying to read something in it. She seemed determined not to look at the form. Maureen tapped the page with the pen and looked at her expectantly. Ella blinked and raised her drawn-on eyebrows.

'How much does he owe ye?' asked Maureen finally.

'Seven hundred pound.'

'How come?'

Crouched down on the cross-bar, Ella looked like a withered child, hiding from angry adults. She lowered her voice. 'Don't tell?' Maureen shook her head and Ella looked at the floor, resting her chin on her knee as she drew a finger through the dust. 'He hasnae been paying me,' she said softly.

'For working here?' whispered Maureen.

'Aye, and my cleaning I do for him in his shop.'

'Has he got money worries?'

'Nut. The shops are doing well. He's not short, he just thinks there's nothing I can do if he doesn't pay me.' Uncomfortably, she gestured an elaborate rolling circle with her finger and stopped. 'I'm getting benefit. If they knew I worked ...'

Maureen had seen tourists hounded out of the flea market for raising a camera and knew that Ella's position was not unique. 'Ye'd hardly get a balloon and a badge for that here, would ye?' she said, wondering why Ella was confiding all of this information in her at all. They didn't know each other. She must have had closer friends in the market. Maureen wrote 'loan' in the box, trying to keep her writing tidy. The hardboard she was leaning on was still gritty and she felt the pen crunch through dust, pitting the back of the page. She looked up and Ella was still drawing zigzags on the dusty floor. 'What does your son sell in his shops?'

'This and that,' Ella waved her hand, 'houses, and wholesale stuff, ye know.'

'He's an estate agent?'

'Aye, and other things.'

'Well, what business address should I put in here?'

Ella thought about it for a moment, looking at the floor. Her face contracted slowly, her lips tightened, eyes narrowed. 'Park Circus Health Club, ninety-three Becci Street, Kelvingrove.'

'I didn't know there was a health club there,' said Maureen, writing it down.

When she looked up again Ella was suddenly ancient. Maureen imagined her without the tracksuit, without the gold rings and the eyebrows and her glasses, and realized she must be much older than sixty. She was at least seventy. 'And that's where you clean, is it?'

'Aye.'

It wasn't part of the form but Maureen was keen to know. 'Why don't ye just keep back the money from the stall?'

Ella harrumphed. 'Wouldn't cover it.'

'So you're still handing over the money ye make here?'

'I've kept my side of the bargain.'

'Is he just avoiding ye, then?'

'Nut,' said Ella, turning her mouth down at the corners. 'He's threatened me.'

'With violence?'

'What else would he threaten me with – a holiday?'

Maureen dropped the board on to her lap and leaned

forward. 'Ella, that's appalling,' she said seriously. 'Did ye have a fall-out?'

Ella nodded quietly. 'Over a foreign woman. Not even a Scottish woman,' she said, as if that made a difference to the fight-worthiness of anyone.

'A girlfriend?'

Ella chewed the inside of her cheek.

'Have ye got any other kids?'

'A daughter.'

'Could she not talk to him for ye?'

Ella ignored her and sat up, straightening her back and pointing at Maureen. 'Ye know what? Fuck them, I'll go to court if I need to.'

Maureen thought back to her time working at the Scottish Women's Shelters, remembered how unusual it was for family members to go all the way to court over anything, much less a small debt and a point of pride. 'Up to you. Ye just need to sign this.' She held out the form but Ella shoved the hardboard back at her.

'You do it.'

'Well, it says here *you* have to sign it.' Maureen pointed to the box.

'Oh, Christ,' said Ella, getting flustered, 'you fucking do it.' She stood up and turned away, busying herself with the tapes.

Maureen stood up behind her uncertainly. 'You've to sign it, you're bringing the case. I can't sign for you.'

Ella McGee looked at her as if she were stupid. 'Aye, ye can.'

Maureen stood up next to her. 'Are ye afraid to sign it, Ella?'

'No,' she said emphatically, patting the Phil Collins tapes into a tidy row.

Maureen watched her turn away, looked at the back of

her wrinkled neck and realized why Ella had confided in her. Ella couldn't fill in the form herself because Ella couldn't write. It would have been shaming to ask anyone else for help but Maureen was a newcomer to the market and Maureen didn't count.

'Will I sign it, then?' said Maureen.

'Aye, you do that.'

Maureen considered signing Ella's name but thought it might be fraudulent. She put down her own name and address. 'Um, you'll need to write an envelope and send it to the Sheriff's office.'

'You can do that, can't ye?'

They looked at each other and Maureen nodded. 'Aye, no bother, I'll do it.'

She folded the form and went to brush past her, but Home Gran caught her by the flesh on her upper arm. 'And you'll come to the court with me, eh?' she said anxiously. 'If it comes to that.'

Maureen didn't want to. She had more than enough psychos in her own life without a man who'd threatened his seventy-year-old mother. They wouldn't go to court, families don't go to court. 'Might not come to it,' said Maureen, squeezing past her.

'Aye, might not,' said Ella unconvincingly. 'Eh, Pat by the river got raided yesterday.'

Maureen would have heard it from someone else anyway but she knew Ella telling her was a friendship gesture.

'Took all his fags away,' said Ella, 'and he still needs to pay Sammy for them.'

'Nightmare. Thanks, Ella.'

'No bother,' said Ella, as if she'd done Maureen the favour. 'By the way, wee Trish showed me your picture in the paper this morning. Ye look nice.'

'In the what?'

'You're in the paper.'

Maureen bolted for the mouth of the tunnel and the bright sunshine.

The newspaper-seller was hiding in the shadow of the high tunnel over the road, hollering headlines unintelligibly. The poster on the front of his stall read: 'Brady Trial Exclusive'. She bought the paper and read the front page. Angus Farrell had been declared fit for trial and had been charged with the murders of his colleague Douglas Brady and a hospital porter. The porter, Martin Donegan, had been twice the man Douglas ever was but his name wasn't mentioned because his mother wasn't famous. An old file photograph showed Carol Brady, the ex-MEP and victim's mother, snarling into the camera. Mrs Brady was quoted: 'I am heartbroken,' claimed Brady. 'He must never get out of Sunnyfields.' Maureen had had an uncomfortable lunch with Carol Brady a year ago and knew her patterns of speech. Either she'd had a stroke in the interim or the journalist was making it up. A small inset photograph showed Maureen's building from the outside, the black and gold Mars Bar advert above Mr Padda's shop visible in the corner. The close door was propped open in the picture, showing how insecure it was. Inside, on page five, they'd reprinted the photograph of Maureen on holiday in Millport. She was wearing a 'Never Mind The Bollocks' T-shirt and shades, grinning as she held on to a rented tricycle. Liam and Leslie had taken her to the seaside for a holiday just after she got out of hospital. She was painfully thin but still recognizable. Any nutter with the price of a paper had her face, her name, a picture of her house and its approximate position in the city. Siobhain might see that headline, and God knew what it would do to her. Maureen felt the fight go out of her. It was too much, the baby and the trial at the same time. She leaned against the wall under the high arch, standing in the dark, pretending to read as she tried to get her nerve together. Angus Farrell was twice as smart as she was. He scared the shit out of her.

She leaned her bare shoulder against the crumbling cold wall and looked at the guddle of the market. Joe the Hawk was selling car stereos with the wires still hanging out the back. Lenny's daft wee dog, Elsie Tanner, was sniffing a blanket someone had left in a gutter. Milling crowds gathered around stalls selling tights and biscuits, curling tongs and bits of stereos. Everyone was sunburned in a snapshot trace of their activities the day before: red necks and shoulders from gardening, red forearms with inside elbows cadaverous white where they'd been reading a book or sipping cups of tea. The true religious had full-on red faces and white garrotte rings around their necks. Gordon Go-A-Bike waved to her from his perch and she waved back. Gordon sold greetings cards in the lane. He had something wrong with his legs and rather than stand still all day and make his condition worse he sat on an old exercise bike and worked his knees while he shouted at the passers-by to get their cards here.

Maureen looked at the busy crowds of good people, looking for bargains and just the very thing. Not yet. None of it had happened yet. She dropped the paper to the ground. There was time enough for grief, she told herself, without rehearsing it for weeks in advance.

She stopped at Gordon-Go-A-Bike's stall, bought a packet of big brown envelopes and he gave her a loan of a stamp. She addressed one, as the form instructed, to the Clerk of the Sheriff Court and nipped out to the street to post it. When she came back with the egg rolls Leslie asked her what Home Gran had been saying.

'She wanted me to fill out a form for her.'

'What form was it?'

'Um, the council tax,' said Maureen, because she'd promised not to tell.

'Aye,' said Leslie. 'It's a bugger that form.'

'Aye,' said Maureen. 'It's nice and cold in here.'

She lowered herself on to the wee stool and they sat complaining about their achy-breaky knees, staring at each other, and smoked the day away in their dark tunnel as another scorcher blazed across the city.

6

Broken

They were in the square waiting room next to the interview cubicles. Across the room a stocky prison officer nodded slowly to the guard sitting next to Angus Farrell, letting him know that he was watching.

It was an old part of the asylum building, refurbished with soundproof walls and remote-control security doors. The white strip-lights embedded in the ceiling were painfully bright and in each corner of the room red-eyed, whirring cameras watched every movement. Some patients could only be interviewed in the containment rooms, held behind a window while their lawyer shouted reassurance through toughened safety glass. Some were interviewed across a normal table. Whichever Angus got would give him a clue as to whether his lawyer trusted him. He had no other way of knowing. He was waiting for the man to arrive. In the past he'd had to wait here for up to an hour, poring over the events of last autumn.

He thought back to the Northern Psychiatric Hospital, to all those mute girls, provocative, defenceless, and their goading blank eyes. His dick warmed and twitched. He almost hoped the lawyer would talk about them, show him pictures of the cupboard or the girls or something. He blinked and remembered the sluice cupboard, the grimy darkness and stinging air, thick with the smell of urine. The lawyer wouldn't talk about the rapes, they hadn't charged him with the rapes, just the murders. It would be better to go to prison as a murderer. The rapes would give him a shorter sentence but he'd be held in segregation and would be afraid for his life most of the time. Labels matter most on the margins. The ideal outcome would be no conviction at all.

At the far end of the room a door buzzed. An officer pushed through it and the tone rose to an urgent whine until the lock clicked shut behind him. The door was made of yellow pine with small glass windows, like an outside door, sturdier than Maureen O'Donnell's close door.

The door beside Angus opened and Alan Grace looked out, inviting him into the room with a raised eyebrow and a forced smile. Grace was a thin man, bald, his uneven pate glinting under the fluorescent light, the hair too long at the sides. The guard stood up and nodded deferentially, standing Angus up with an authoritative pat to his elbow, guiding him with a hand on his shoulder forward into the room. Angus glanced up just once. It was a small room, painted two shades of grey, dark to shoulder height, lighter above. There was no partition, just a table bolted to the floor and two chairs. In two of the high corners black cameras watched, hungry for action. The officer stopped at the door behind him as if he was waiting for a tip. 'Will I come in with yees?'

'I think we'll be fine,' said Grace, and the guard left, shutting the door after him. 'Perhaps you might like to sit, Mr Farrell.' Grace always maintained a cheery voice. It sounded less like conviviality than egging himself through an unpleasant task. 'We can start to go over what happened to you yesterday.'

As Angus sat down the legs on the chair splayed beneath him, thin plastic that wouldn't snap or give an edge. Behind Grace's head an air vent hummed softly, wafting the fringe of hair back and forth over his ears. He seemed very young. Young but tired.

'Are you well, Mr Farrell?' Grace was trying to catch his eye.

'Fine.'

'They treating you all right?'

'Fine.'

Grace nodded. 'I understand you had a visit from the Crown Office yesterday,' he said quietly, 'at which they charged you with the murders of Mr Douglas Brady and Mr Martin Donegan.'

Angus stared at the table. 'I don't know what they're talking about,' he whispered urgently.

Grace looked at his notes. 'You know who Mr Brady is?'

'Of course I know him,' said Angus, sitting up and coming alive. His accent was clipped and clear. 'I worked with him for years. They interviewed all of us in the clinic about it. He died in Maureen O'Donnell's living room. But the porter, Martin, I didn't even know he was dead until yesterday.'

Grace made a consolatory face. 'You have been ill for quite some time, I'm afraid.'

'Dr Heikle tells me I was given a massive dose of LSD.'

'So it would seem. He's surprised that you recovered. Do you remember anything about the time leading up to your admission here?'

Angus looked at him. 'I remember nothing,' he breathed, his eyes flickering around the grey table top as if he was trying to reassemble the events. 'I told the police yesterday that I remember meeting the woman, Maureen O'Donnell. She's an ex-patient of mine. We had coffee together in my office. After that I remember nothing but fire and being scared and being here.' He stabbed the table, as if his presence in this room was the only thing he had been sure

39

about for a very long time. 'I remember being here. I don't know what happened to me to get me *here*.'

Grace paused, writing a note to himself in his pad. 'Did you know,' he said eventually, 'that Miss O'Donnell was having an affair with Mr Brady?'

'The police told me. I was disappointed in Douglas for that.'

'Did you know that O'Donnell's brother is a drug-dealer?'

Angus sat forward, and the broken veins on his nose came into focus. 'No, I didn't know that. She could have given me the LSD. Can you do that with coffee?'

'I don't know, we'll find out. But it does suggest a knowledge of drugs and a potential source. Incidentally, you were writing threatening letters to Miss O'Donnell while you were still … under the influence. Do you remember that?'

Angus cringed and sat back, sliding his flat palms back across the table, his fingers leaving snail trails of sweat on the scarred grey plastic. 'Vaguely.' He shrugged apologetically. 'She's my last memory before I went under. Maybe I got stuck …'

Grace sat forward, tapping the table with his pen. 'Can you pinpoint the date on which Miss O'Donnell came to see you with the coffee?'

Angus shook his head. 'I was at the clinic in the morning, briefly. She came in to see me after Douglas's death.'

'Would that be the last day you went into the clinic before disappearing?'

Angus sat back as if startled by his acumen. 'I expect it was. I honestly have no idea.'

Grace scribbled something on his pad. 'We can check that out.' He looked up. 'The evidence they have links you to the murder of Mr Donegan. They have only circumstantial evidence linking you to the murder of Douglas Brady. Realistically they would have to prove the second case to get a conviction on the first.'

'What evidence do they have?'

'Your bloody fingerprints on the back of Mr Donegan's neck.' Grace dropped his voice in embarrassment. 'He was stabbed . . . in the face.'

Angus shrank. 'Could I have done that?' he muttered urgently.

'The evidence suggests that you did, Mr Farrell.'

'How could I?' he whispered, and let his head drop to his chest. 'Why would I do such a thing?'

'I really don't know,' said Grace, and turned back to his notes. He seemed uncomfortable.

'Is there any hope at all?' whispered Angus, wondering as he did so whether he was overplaying it. He was suddenly overcome by the desire to smile. He covered his face with his hands, and slipped his fingers under the lenses of his glasses, rubbing his eyes roughly with his fingertips. His specs jiggled up and down.

Grace cleared his throat. 'I don't want you to get too excited about this,' he said seriously, 'but we have a potential defence. It's speculative at the moment.' He spoke slowly. 'It would be very difficult for the prosecution to get a conviction on the Brady charges without a guilty on the Donegan charge. Let's just say that you were under the influence of LSD at the time of the Donegan murder, yes?' Grace waited, and Angus looked at him and nodded that he understood.

'Yes,' he said.

'And if we can show that someone else gave you the LSD, yes?'

Grace waited again. Angus considered bludgeoning him with the chair but nodded instead.

'Yes?' said Grace. 'Well, we can plead that while you

41

physically did the act you were not *mentally* responsible for it.'

Angus decided that he had shown enough interest in the plea. He crumpled his chin at the table. 'Did I do it?' he asked.

'It would seem so. But we may be able to argue that you didn't have the mental intent to do it, if you were given the drugs without your knowledge.'

'What does mental intent mean?'

'Well, if you didn't mean to do it,' said Grace patiently, slipping into Ladybird law-book language, 'even if you did the physical actions, then the law says you're not guilty. We'll have to check the sightings of you, make sure the dates match and so on. If the plea is successful – there are a lot of conditions on that, I should stress – well, you'll be going home, Mr Farrell.'

'But did I do it?' muttered Angus.

'It would seem so, Mr Farrell,' repeated Grace.

Angus Farrell rubbed his eyes hard again and his mouth dropped open. The crooked lower teeth were worn down to dark, ringed stubs from the months he had spent grinding them when he first came here. His head ached all the time. He rubbed his eyes harder. 'God almighty,' he whispered. 'I did it, didn't I?'

7
Sheila

It was a warm evening but the room felt damp. It always felt damp. The grey carpet squares were beginning to curdle in protest. Ten group members were sitting in a circle, sipping tea and coffee from Styrofoam cups and nibbling at the lovely chocolate biscuits Liz bought from Marks & Spencer every week.

Sheila, a tall woman in her fifties with an eating disorder, was the Incest Survivor Group's convenor. She wore her greying brown hair up in a leather clasp and dressed in shapeless shirts and long skirts, as if trying to deny that she had a body. She raised her elegant English voice and cut across the chatter. 'Let's convene this week's meeting with a reminder.' She held up the laminated page and read through it. It was a poetic rendition of a series of group rules. No directional advice would be given by members of the group unless requested, no one would interrupt another member while they were sharing.

Maureen zoned out and took out a cigarette.

'I want to speak tonight.' Colin leaned forward into the circle as he ran a hand through his hair. Behind him, tall Alex sighed and folded his arms. Colin always wanted to speak first. He spoke every week, and every week he said the same thing: he wasn't coping. His ex-wife wanted him to look after their child but he couldn't. Colin had only realized that his abuse was still a live issue when his son reached seven. When he got angry he wanted to hurt the boy. He could control the urges if he saw him during the day and didn't spend too long with him. His ex-wife wanted him to take his son for weekends. If he told her why he couldn't do it she'd stop him seeing the child altogether. He stared at the carpet, wringing his hands, the anxious sweat on his palms smacking noisily, making him even less likeable. He was going to have to stop seeing him, he knew that, he was afraid for him. He loved him. That was all he had to say. Any advice would be welcome.

When she was sure he had finished, Sheila thanked him and asked whether someone else would like to come in. Tall Alex lunged forward and began his tirade against whoever had pissed him off that week. He was angry. The focus of his fury changed from week to week but the content was always the same. Everyone was picking on him, they underestimated him, he wasn't going to stand for it. Every week he had a new revenge fantasy, he was going to show them. The revenge was always small, a slight or a slap, spreading a rumour. A blind dog in a drunken stupor with no clinical training could have identified the pattern: Alex was just angry and he was angry because he was afraid, but no one was allowed to say that. Every week he finished by saying that advice would not be welcome. If anyone attempted to talk to him afterwards he'd speak from the body of the hall the next week, railing against know-all bastards, glancing pointedly at the offender, threatening petty Armageddon.

Hugh McAskill had told her about the group during the investigation into Douglas's death. She hadn't really understood why he was so kind to her at the time; it was only afterwards when she came to the group that she realized how much his experience matched hers. She didn't associate Hugh the policeman with Hugh the responsible group member. The damp room felt separate somehow, like a grubby grey antechamber to real life where each member's darkest moments could be touched on and safely left behind, lingering in the smell of mouldy dust, waiting for next week.

Although the group was composed predominantly of women, the men always spoke first. The usual form was that Hugh would speak next, calming everyone down with his soft voice and sad demeanour, talk about aspects of his own struggle that reflected the previous speakers', but Hugh wasn't there tonight. The silence lasted longer than was comfortable and they began to look around at each other expectantly. No one wanted to come in before Hugh had set the atmosphere right.

'Anyone else?' asked Sheila, and sat back.

The meeting room was on the second storey of a small outhouse, abutting a large red sandstone chapel in Partick. The outbuildings had developed chaotically, and twenty feet across the lane a newer hall had been built. It was used on Thursdays for Irish dancing classes and they could hear a skirl of tinny music through the open fire exit. All of a sudden, a hundred tiny feet simultaneously stamped about the distant pine floor.

'Surely someone else wants to speak tonight?' said Sheila.

Maureen found herself coming in. 'I'll speak, Sheila,' she said, and Sheila sat back gratefully, giving her the floor.

Maureen hadn't thought about what she was going to say and it all fell out in a jumble. 'I've been trying to enjoy the weather today,' she said, following Hugh's style of sharing and starting with something positive, in the present. 'I've been working really hard at enjoying everything I can. Feeling good, happy, spending time in the house and at my work and not being sad or frightened.'

She had wanted to say that she was happy and coping, that she was getting on with her life, but knew she sounded miserable and confused, as if she was lying to herself. 'I'm getting the money together for my debts because I don't want to leave debts . . .' She hadn't meant to say that. She sounded as if she was going to die. 'Not that I'm leaving.' Trying to lighten up, she let out a hollow, lonely laugh that smarted off the damp walls. She looked around but no one was looking back at her: they were nodding at their laps, picking their nails, everyone frowning heavily except Alex, who was watching her with his arms crossed, sucking his cheeks in, looking amused.

'I dreamed about my dad last night. It was the same dream and I was sweating.' She wasn't thinking about suicide, she should make that clear. She looked up. 'I'm not going to kill myself,' she said. Sheila looked worried. Alex sniggered because someone else was making a tit of themselves. Maureen gave up the attempt at sounding cheerful and her chin sank to her chest. 'I think bad things are about to happen,' she said, and her hot eyes dripped tears, her face slackened. 'Now my dad's back in Glasgow, I can't think about anything else. Nothing else seems real or . . .' She sat forward, letting her tears fall on to the soiled carpet. The group had heard it all before but she couldn't stop saying the same things. 'When my sisters brought him back from London I couldn't believe it. They paid for him to come here even though they knew, even though I'd told them what he did.' Her chin crumpled and she couldn't speak. She breathed in, fighting the pressure from her heavy heart to sob. 'They don't believe me. I can cope with that. But Una, she's having a baby soon, next few days. She's chucked her husband out. She'll give the baby to Michael, to prove that she believes him, to prove I'm wrong. I'm the only one who can do anything about it. No one else is going to do anything. I feel as if I'm dying.'

She covered her face, feeling like a histrionic arsehole, wishing she could control herself, but her nose was dripping on to her lip and she couldn't catch her breath. She didn't want to cry, especially not in front of Alex, and in the effort to suppress it she let go a high-pitched, piggy squeal. Across the lane the tap-dancing children clattered their way to an untidy climax. The group was waiting for Maureen to wrap up but she couldn't speak. She put a hand to her head and dug her nails into her scalp, dragging them back on her head, and the clear, searing pain drew the breath back into her body. She sat up and managed a wobbly smile. 'So, I'm trying to enjoy these last few days. Trying to savour things. Enjoy things.' She licked a hot tear from her lip. 'Any advice would be welcome.'

She sat back, drawing tremulously on her cigarette, and the group looked away from her. It was like the reaction Colin got every week. There was no solution to the problem, there was nothing to say. They'd pat her shoulder on the way out. A couple of them would hug her awkwardly. Liz the Christian would promise to pray for her, and they'd all go home. Sheila asked for another speaker and Alice came in to talk about her insomnia. She was wearing a long-sleeved top despite the hot weather, pulling the cuffs down over her hands as she spoke, and they all guessed that she had been cutting herself again. She didn't mention it.

Sheila chaired through another three speakers, but Maureen wasn't listening. She hadn't meant to say any of that. She finished her fag and stubbed it out in a filthy tin ashtray, swirling the compressed ash from a hundred dead cigarettes, releasing the sick, thick smell of stale smoke. Enjoy the days, she told herself, just enjoy. It didn't matter that she'd made an arse of herself. She wished Hugh were here, that he could talk to her afterwards and make it all right.

When the meeting was finished they stood downstairs, chatting and smoking and making arrangements for the following week. Sheila threw the cups into the bin, made sure the urn was off and wiped down the worktop and sink. 'Okay, everybody,' she said, clapping her hands, 'let's go.'

They shuffled out to the lane. In the new hall the dancing class was finishing too. The fire exit had been left open to let the air in. Past the blur of yellow light came the noise of children screaming and chasing each other. Sheila stopped Maureen. 'Let me give you a lift home,' she said quietly.

'Naw,' said Maureen, still embarrassed, 'I'm fine, I'll walk.'

'I'll drive you home,' said Sheila, and turned to lock the door.

The others called goodbye and made their way out to the street, saying final goodbyes as they reached the pavement before dispersing into the bright evening. Most of the group were friends and phoned one another during the week for support. Maureen had managed to attend for two months without making a single firm friend. She liked it that way, liked keeping it separate from the rest of her life.

'Look, it's all right,' she said, 'I'd really like to walk.'

'No,' said Sheila, holding up her hand to avert further protest, 'I'll drive you.'

Maureen actually did want to walk. Her house was two pleasant miles away and she liked walking in the fading light, when she could think and talk to herself without feeling self-conscious. Maybe Sheila needed to talk. Maureen climbed into the estate car and Sheila turned to her. 'Have you got time for a cup of tea?' she asked.

Maureen didn't really want to go with her. Sheila was very nice but she was hard to listen to. She had a tendency to talk like a vague, new-age self-help book that Maureen couldn't quite understand "Kay.' She shrugged, hoping it wouldn't take long.

Sheila started the car and drove up the hill, through the

posher areas of Hyndland and over to the high flats at Broomhill.

Michael had disappeared when Maureen was ten. She had no memory of him leaving the family home, just of him being there and then not being there, that before was the darkness and after was the light. He had locked Maureen in the cupboard under the stairs when he left but she didn't remember that either. Una and Marie did: they were there when their mother, Winnie, crowbarred the door open and pulled Maureen out. They remembered the blood between her legs and her limp, blank compliance as they all gave her a bath to wash it away. Winnie said she'd fallen on her bottom. They knew instinctively not to talk about it or mention it outside the family. Maureen grew up into a strange young woman.

Crippling fears haunted her at school and university. Bizarre stimuli could floor her for days: a figure in a door with the light behind them, the sound of a man breathing through a blocked nose, the smell of gin and orange on someone's breath, certain types of brown shoes or hair cut razor-straight along the neckline. She had bad dreams that stayed with her for days. She often found it hard to eat and swallow. Winnie's livid alcoholism and the graphic fights with her new husband, George, didn't exactly create a healing atmosphere in the house.

As Maureen approached the end of her degree things began to get worse. The panic attacks grew more frequent, sometimes blurring together at their ragged edges into hour-long frenzies. She began to barricade her bedroom door at night and sleep in the corner, watching the bed. She read obsessively, tracing the same lines and paragraphs over and over. She had to have a book with her at all times. If she found herself with nothing to read she'd grab a menu, read a leaflet or a bus timetable. She knew she was going down. The prospect of a bleak future wasn't a shocking disappointment. Coming from a war-torn family she had never had very high expectations – none of the O'Donnells did. Secretly and individually they all dreamed of peace and quiet. Maureen told no one what was happening. She got the first job she saw advertised, in a theatre ticket office, and bought the poky flat in Garnethill.

A year and a half after graduating she disappeared. The ticket-office manager phoned Winnie and told her that Maureen had been missing for three days. It was Liam who found her, hiding in the hall cupboard in Garnethill. It was Liam who wrapped her up in a blanket and took her to hospital, carrying her to his car, whispering that she was fine, still safe, be brave. Her forehead was damp with his tears, she remembered.

When she came to it was summer, and she spent it with Pauline Doyle in the grounds of the Northern Psychiatric Hospital. They sat in the gardens and smoked fags, did pottery classes and gossiped about the other patients and the staff. The family came to see her, Una and her husband, Alistair, standing stiff at the end of her bed. Her eldest sister, Marie, was too busy to visit but sent a message from London that Maureen remembered as a wish that she wasn't sick. Winnie came, drunk and drunker, attracting pitying glances from the other patients and falling out with the doctors. Liam and Leslie came to see her and be with her, reminding her of who she had been and what she might be again. She couldn't start to make sense of it until Alistair came on his own and told the doctors what Una had told him about Michael and the bleeding.

Winnie never forgave Alistair for telling. She used to phone him when she was drunk and tell him what a shit he was. She behaved as if all the O'Donnells' troubles were caused by his loose mouth. Years later, when Una discovered Alistair was having an affair with the upstairs neighbour, Winnie took it as confirmation of everything she had ever believed about him.

What Alistair had told the doctor made sense of everything. Maureen began to piece together the dreams and flashbacks, reassembling the story, remembering and making sense of her life. Michael had left because of the blood. She remembered him seeing it, the shock on his face and the sudden anger. He must have had a ragged nail and cut her inside. She dreamed about the blood and pain, always a sharp, ripping pain in the dreams. Dr Paton suggested a joint session with Winnie to clear up the dates and details of what had happened. During the session it became clear that Winnie didn't believe Michael had abused anyone. She started crying and ran away to the toilet with her handbag, coming back drunk and argumentative. Michael had loved Winnie. He didn't want Maureen, he wanted Winnie, he loved her. She seemed to think they'd been having an affair.

Maureen got better regardless. She remembered the rest of the summer as afternoons in the hospital gardens with Pauline Doyle, the anorexic from her ceramics class. Liam and Leslie visited every day and she counted herself lucky to have such good friends.

When she left hospital Dr Paton had referred her to a psychiatrist with cold killer eyes. She stopped going to see him and applied to the Rainbow Clinic's outreach scheme for victims of sexual abuse instead. She only saw Angus Farrell twice but he was wonderful. Helpful and kind, he concentrated on helping her get on with her life and taught her usable techniques for dealing with intrusive thoughts. She thought about it afterwards, wondering why he was so good for her, why she would see a future after just two sessions with him. Angus was a pragmatist. Instead of empathizing or getting her to talk about it, he asked what the worst effects were and suggested solutions to panic attacks and nightmares, changing the way she perceived flashback stimuli. By the time he referred her to Louisa at the Albert Hospital she had already started her hopeless affair with Douglas, his colleague at the Rainbow.

Maureen didn't want to go back to the Northern hospital after she got out. Slowly, she stopped phoning Pauline. She had nothing to say to her and wanted to distance herself. Six months later Pauline killed herself in a wood near her parents' house: she had told the hospital staff that her father and one of her brothers had been anally raping her since she was young but couldn't bring herself to tell her mother – she thought it would break her heart. Her housing application had fallen through and she had been released back to the parental home. She was found in the wood, dead two days from an overdose, with dried spunk on her back.

Michael had been missing for fifteen years when Marie's diligent work paid off and she found him. She had been looking since Maureen was admitted to hospital. They found him living in a council flat in south London, with nothing but a bed and lager cans for furniture. Una paid for him to come home. When Maureen looked out of the window of her flat at the city she knew that he was out there somewhere. On bad days she knew that he was everywhere, watching.

The Broomhill flats were among the most coveted council flats in Glasgow. Built on a sharp escarpment high above the river Clyde, the tower promised a view over the sprawling Govan shipyards. They were well tended and near to the trendy West End. Picking her way among the modest cars, Sheila backed deftly into a tiny space. 'This is us,' she said.

Maureen looked up at the grey front of the tower block. Warm yellow lights shone from the box homes, competing with the fading evening. The only clue that the flats were council-owned was the peeling paint on the concrete exterior and big blue by-law notices everywhere prohibiting ball games, parking, loitering and rubbish. 'This is lovely,' she said, noticing that there were no people hanging around outside.

'They don't allow kids,' said Sheila, opening her door. 'Plus, most of us have had to work full-time for years to get moved in here so everyone's very precious about it. You need about eighty points.'

The lobby was quiet and the lift came immediately.

'What do you have to do to get eighty points?' Maureen asked.

Sheila stepped into the lift and pressed the button for the eleventh floor. 'Be homeless for a decade,' she said, as the lift took off. 'Have at least one breakdown, be a victim of crime and cry in the housing office every day for six months.'

Maureen puffed out her cheeks. 'Harsh,' she said.

'Hardest work I've ever done,' said Sheila.

The doors opened and they stepped out, following the broad corridor along to Sheila's door.

'I don't bring many people here,' said Sheila, wiggling the key into the lock. 'It's my sanctuary.'

The hall was painted pale grey and led into a white, rectangular living room with low beige corduroy chairs and a glass coffee table with a pile of green pebbles on it. Maureen glanced out of the window and was disappointed to see that the flat looked over the roofs of red stone tenements.

'No,' said Sheila, as she dropped her keys into a brass dish on a hall table. 'It doesn't look out over the river.'

'Aw, well, it's still lovely.'

Sheila smiled. 'It is, isn't it?' She hesitated and blushed a little. 'I don't think about it much. I suppose I should.'

'If you don't bring many people up here why did you invite me?'

'Let's have a cup of tea.'

In the narrow galley kitchen the kettle hissed to a boil. Sheila took a packet of biscuits from a cupboard and put some on a plate. Maureen was surprised that someone with such a bad eating disorder would have biscuits in her house. When she tasted one, it was soggy and old. There was no food in the kitchen, Maureen realized, no bread left out, no wrappings sitting on the side. When Sheila opened the fridge to get the skimmed milk Maureen saw that the shelves were empty apart from three large bowls of jelly with spoonfuls missing. 'I take it black, thanks,' said Maureen. 'Sheila, is there something you want to talk about?'

Sheila picked up the kettle. 'I heard you tonight,' she said. 'Don't do it.'

Maureen cast her mind back over what she had said. 'Don't do what?' she said.

'We've all thought about it, you're not special.' She poured the hot water into the cups, squeezed out the teabags and put them into the bin carefully. 'Come next door.'

They sat next to each other on the low chairs, their knees converging, and looked out of the window at the powder blue sky. Maureen didn't want to ask her what she meant. Sheila sipped her tea. 'I think if abusers are absent it's easy to see things in black and white. They're not there to cloud the issues,' she said. Maureen looked a bit confused. 'Abusers come to personalize the damage they've done. You think that if you kill him, you'll undo the damage he's done, but you won't.'

She was exactly right. It was one of the bizarre aspects of

being in the group: other people would know what Maureen was thinking, sometimes before she articulated it to herself. It felt a little uncomfortable, like hanging about with a bunch of psychics, several of whom she didn't like very much.

'I haven't decided to do anything yet,' she said quietly.

Sheila watched calmly as Maureen pulled out a packet of cigarettes and lit one, sucking down the sense of wild panic. The fag scratched her throat as she inhaled. She liked it and inhaled again, making herself light-headed.

'My grandfather,' Sheila waved her hand to the past, 'he got my mum as well. No one talked about such things then. She had an eating problem, drink and drugs. Dead at thirty-eight. I wanted to kill him for her because she never had a chance.'

'But you didn't,' said Maureen, knowing full well that the old man had died in a nursing home at the ripe old age of eighty-eight, surrounded by family and friends. His funeral had been well attended, his obituary had been in all the local papers and one national paper because of his position on the board of a charity for blind people.

Sheila ignored her. 'It's a fairly typical gut response, you know, but you have to unpack it, look at what's in there, look at your real motives for doing it. You mentioned your sister's pregnant?'

Maureen nodded.

'Baby's important,' said Sheila, 'but probably not as important as it seems. It might be an excuse, you know, to do what you want to do anyway. If you don't value yourself enough to make a stand but you're still angry you might be channelling it into saving someone else. It's easy to confuse what's good for Baby and what you want. People do that all the time. Have you phoned Social Services about Baby?'

'If I do they'll tell the police,' said Maureen, uncomfortable with Sheila's reference to the child as if it were Lord High-muck-a-muck.

'Is that out of the question? Filing a report doesn't mean you go to court.'

'I've had trouble with the police,' said Maureen.

Sheila looked at the tip of her cigarette and Maureen could tell she was wondering whether to say it.

'I know Hugh's a policeman,' said Maureen. 'I've been interviewed by the police and it was fucking horrible. You know how hard it is to talk about it. The very last thing I ever want to do is to try and explain it all to them.'

Sheila nodded. 'Maureen,' she said, 'think about this. You're more than the sum of his actions, much more. Look, you haven't been in the group that long but we do make progress. We can recover. He's already stolen your childhood, don't give him your adulthood as well.'

Maureen was dismayed that Sheila didn't understand. 'Sheila, he's got my adulthood. I see him everywhere, I feel him everywhere. I can't have a relationship with a man because of it, I can't hold down a job. I don't know why my friends stay with me, I can't even look at myself in a normal mirror. D'ye understand? I have to use a magnifying mirror because I can't stand looking at more than a wee fragment of my face at a time.'

Sheila waited for her to calm down. 'You know,' she said softly, 'people who haven't been abused have trouble with those things too. They're bloody hard, probably the hardest things there are in life.'

She smiled and Maureen smiled back. Sheila's eyes were creamy brown and her voice was kind. 'Think of the life you could have if you used all this energy to get over it. But if you do this thing, you'll be making him the most important event in your life, ever. Whether you go to jail or not, he'll define every aspect of your life. Every time you look in the mirror you'll see him.'

Spitefully, Maureen thought about pointing out the irony of an anorexic with a fridge full of low-cal jelly giving motivational speeches. She stubbed out her cigarette in the ashtray. 'Sometimes it's right to put yourself aside,' she said. 'It's not always about a lack of self-esteem or destructive patterns of behaviour. Someone needs to be responsible.'

Sheila sat back in her chair and looked at her. 'Yes, but it doesn't need to be you, Maureen. It doesn't always need to be you.'

Maureen got Sheila to drop her around the corner from her house. Her flat was at the top of Garnethill, the highest hill in the city. The views were spectacular but the possibility of subsidence kept the property prices low and the steep hill meant that few outsiders wandered into it. It was an island state in the heart of the city. She waved back to Sheila as she walked up Rose Street, heading for Mr Padda's licensed grocery around the corner. She heard the dread clatter of metal shutters being pulled down and ran faster. Mr Padda saw her sprinting towards him and smiled.

Inside the shop Mr Padda Junior was playing behind the counter, stroking the kittenish bum-fluff on his cheeks and chin. He had recently graduated from watching telly in the cupboard at the back of the shop to working behind the counter but he found it dull. As Maureen approached he spun round, narrowly stopping himself from falling over by catching the counter, one shoulder up, the other hand raised in surprise as if he was in a Bollywood musical.

'Very good,' Maureen said.

'The usual?' he asked, pointing at her and pulling the trigger.

Maureen nodded. Padda Junior did a demi-spin, singing

under his breath, caught a bottle of cheap whisky off the shelf, spun back into place and stabbed at the till buttons like Liberace on a camp day. Delighted with the overall effect, he grinned to himself. 'You fairly knock it back, don't ye?'

She made a mental note to use another offy in future.

As she climbed the stairs to her front door she promised herself that if there was no message on her machine about the baby she wasn't going to think about it or Sheila or Michael tonight. She'd have a long, calm evening alone. She should savour the time while she had it.

'Well, bonjourno, Maureen.'

Her creepy neighbour, Jim Maliano, was standing on the landing above her, a large red suitcase on the landing in front of him, his tan deep and flush. He was a small man with a little round belly that he accentuated by tucking his jumpers into his jeans. He did something odd with his hair so that it changed texture and quality over his crown. It was as if he was trying to hide a bald patch but Maureen had seen his crown and it wasn't bald. It looked like a tiny yarmulke-toupee.

'Jim.' Maureen climbed the last few stairs. 'You're back.'

'Aye.' Jim was dressed like an Italian spiv in a cream and salmon striped shirt, grey slip-on loafers and beige slacks held up with a white plastic belt. He went to see his extended family every year for a month and every year he came back more Italian, less able to articulate in English, more hand-wavy, more punchable. He was always pleased to see her and Maureen didn't know why. She was never very nice to him. 'I had a marvellous time, as usual.' He took a step towards her. 'It really is so beautiful over there. You should go. The heat makes you relax and the food is fabulous—'

'And how's the family?' interrupted Maureen, sliding her key into the lock and opening the door.

'Aye, the family's all well,' he said, smiling and nodding as if she knew them and cared. 'I brought you some amaretti biscuits.'

'Ah, great, I'll get them from ye later. Welcome home,' she said, and shut the door on his hopeful face.

There were no messages on the machine. The baby might come tomorrow and tonight would be her final happy night. It was to be a night of drunkenness and a long look over the city.

She lit a cigarette and looked at the chrome lighter. It was Vik's lighter, Vik the almost-boyfriend. It was a birthday gift from the guys in his band with 'Let's Get the Rock Out of Here' inscribed on it in sentimental italics. He had left it in her house the last time he came to see her, when they'd had the big fight. For months afterwards she told herself that he had left it deliberately, that he meant to come back and get it. He never had. He had left her because she wasn't very nice to him; she didn't know how to be. She wondered if Sheila was right, if it could be her petulance and selfishness that made the relationship seem impossible. She'd always assumed it was the abuse. And then she thought about what Sheila had said about her motives and Michael and the baby. She stopped herself. Not tonight. Tonight she was alone and none of it had happened yet. Flicking back to the previous thought but one, she remembered Vik. She remembered his shoulders, the musty smell of his chest and his dark eyelashes. The memory made her skin bristle for him, but she did what she had been doing for three months and turned it round. She was glad she'd known him. He was a nice man.

Someone knocked on the door, not a polite knock but a slow, aggressive rapping. Knowing it would be Jim Maliano, angry and holding a packet of unwelcome broken biscuits, Maureen tiptoed out to the hall She leaned into the spy-hole from the side, so that if he pushed the packet of biscuits through the postbox he wouldn't be looking at her feet.

It wasn't Jim. It was an unfamiliar woman with cropped blonde hair and a waistcoat over a T-shirt. She looked tired and utterly pissed off. She sighed and reeled round to the stairs, walking down them heavily, speeding up as she got further away from the door as if she was glad no one had been in. The corner of a business card was sticking in the hinged postbox. Maureen waited until she heard the close door slam shut and pulled the card out. Her name was Aggie Grey and she was a journalist for a sleazy Sunday tabloid. She'd written 'call me re ££s' on the back of the card. Maureen threw it on the floor.

8

Doyle

The ringing phone cut urgently through the still morning. Maureen prised open her puffy eyes and felt her heart quicken. She threw back the duvet, fell on to her feet and staggered out to the hall. 'Hello, Liam.'

'What?' said Leslie.

'Leslie?'

'Aye, it's me.'

'I thought you were Liam.'

'No.'

Maureen rubbed her eyes open. Liam would phone her himself, she was sure, he wouldn't get Leslie to call her. 'Why are you phoning me?'

'I'm going to be late today,' said Leslie.

A wave of relief washed over Maureen. 'Aw, Leslie,' she said fondly, 'don't worry about that.' She stopped, realizing from the flattened tone of Leslie's voice that she was lying down. 'Wait a minute, are you in your bed?'

'Aye,' said Leslie. 'I'm gonnae be late.'

'Have you just phoned me', she said indignantly, 'and got me out my bed to tell me you're having a lie-in?'

'I suppose I did.' Leslie sounded miserable. 'I've had a shit night.'

'Fucksake!' Maureen tutted and was about to hang up when she lifted the receiver to her mouth again. 'When are ye coming then?'

"Bout half nine.'

'Fucksake,' said Maureen, and hung up. She knew she wouldn't be able to get back to sleep. 'Fucksake.'

She tramped down the hall to the bathroom, filling the sink with warm water as she sat on the loo, splashing her face and wetting her hair to wake herself up. She was angry until it occurred to her that it was good: the baby wasn't born.

Cammy was refusing to go quietly and Leslie was distraught. He'd been crying all night, telling Leslie that he couldn't go on without her, that he'd get a job, make friends with her friends, do anything to make it all right again. She'd said it was over and he'd said he loved her, as if that was an answer, as if that would change her mind. She put him out. She never wanted to see him again but he'd come back to the house at four in the morning, crying and banging on the door.

They arrived at the market and Leslie pulled the van over to the side, slumping over the wheel, staring at the cobbles ahead and looking desperate. Maureen hugged her, rubbing her back, giving her an emotional winding. Beyond the dirty windscreen a figure approached, a middle-aged man with his hands in his pockets, swinging his shoulders, his grey head down. He looked up and for a searing moment Maureen saw Michael's face. She blinked. The man's features melted, resolving themselves into another face, utterly unfamiliar. He glanced into the cab as he walked past. Leslie peeled herself away and looked at her hands. 'Mauri, are you going through the change or something?' She sniffed. 'You're covered in sweat.'

'Fine, I'm fine.'

When Peter opened the door to the tunnel they saw four regular punters already waiting for them. Leslie served them, attracting an even larger crowd of customers who had been hanging about at the doors, getting the sun while they waited. Any one of them might be Michael. Maureen felt herself start to sweat again. She did as Angus had taught her, brushing away the intrusive thoughts by bringing herself back to the present. She took the money, getting into the swing of the day. They had sold a quarter of their stock before they had even set up the stall. Leslie cocked her head. 'No tunes,' she said.

Maureen looked down to Ella's stall. It was empty and an old cardboard box had been abandoned on it, suggesting that it hadn't been set up at all today.

'Peter?' said Maureen. 'Where's the lady that sells the tapes today?'

'She's in hospital,' said Peter.

'How come?'

He shrugged. 'Dunno. Wee Trish told me.'

'I'll not be long,' said Maureen, and left before Leslie answered.

Wee Trish had a holy stall selling nylon first-communion dresses, fake mother-of-pearl prayer books, plastic rosaries and twenty sizes and styles of crucifixes. Trish herself looked like a Cairn terrier. Her hair was streaked blonde and wiry, cut so short that it stood up whatever she put on it. Her sharp features and leathery skin were accentuated by a short chin and a top lip that curled upwards when in repose, showing her teeth, so that she looked as if she was growling.

'Trish, where's Ella?'

Trish looked wary. 'D'you even know Ella?' she asked.

'Aye,' said Maureen. 'Peter said she was in hospital.'

'Aye,' said Trish, still unsure of her. 'She got taken in last night.'

'What's wrong with her?'

Trish thought about it. Obviously no one else had

63

bothered to ask for details. 'Dunno. The ambulance came and took her from the house. I heard she fell and hurt her face.'

'She fell?' said Maureen incredulously.

'She's old,' Wee Trish said defensively.

Maureen wanted to say that a woman able to crouch on a cross-bar for twenty minutes was unlikely to topple over spontaneously in her living room. 'D'ye know what hospital she's in?' she asked.

'I dunno. Somewhere with a casualty ward? The Albert probably.'

Leslie was waiting for her when she got back to the stall and Maureen told her what Trish had said. 'Poor thing,' said Leslie. She was very pale and her lips were turning blue.

'Have you eaten anything since that roll yesterday?'

'No,' said Leslie, and looked as if she might cry again.

'Poor wee henny-hen,' said Maureen, wrapping a jumper around Leslie's shoulders and sitting her down on her stool. 'You stay here and I'll go and get you a roll 'n' sausage and a juice.'

Leslie nodded miserably at the floor, wrapping her arms around her stomach.

'Peter,' said Maureen, 'keep your eye on her.'

Peter pointed at Maureen uncertainly. 'Seen ye,' he said, surprised and respectful. Maureen frowned at him. He thumbed over his shoulder. 'In the paper yesterday. Good for you.'

She didn't understand why people were so impressed. No one seemed to have read the story or clocked that she'd been having an affair with a married man and was a suspect when he was brutally mutilated in her living room. Everyone seemed pleased for her anyway.

At the back of the tunnel nearest the river, through a rickety green door, was the café. It was owned and run by Blonde Mary and her daughter Lara, who added a glamorous touch to the market. Both women were tall and slim with honey-blonde hair and soft voices. They cooked and took the money behind a shallow counter, frying on an open griddle and serving mince and potatoes and peas from a well-stocked steaming bain-marie, universally referred to as the 'bamburri'. Inside, the tunnel was dripping with damp and would probably be next to be shut down and bricked up. The café looked like a well-tended cave: they had disguised the damp ceiling with tastefully draped silver tarpaulin and faded Formica tables were scattered across the uneven floor.

'Two rolls and sausage and two tins of cola, please,' said Maureen.

'Onion on both?' said Lara, sliding two squares of sausage on to the spitting hot griddle.

'Aye, please,' said Maureen, counting out her change.

As she stood waiting, Maureen gradually became conscious of a looming presence at her shoulder. Mark Doyle was standing behind her, dressed in an incongruous black overcoat, buttoned up to the neck as though he had just come in from the rain. 'Fuck, you gave me a scare.' She grinned and clasped her hand to her chest. 'What are you doing here?'

'I'm on my way home. I wanted a roll.'

Maureen caught Lara's eye. 'And a roll as well.' She turned back to Doyle. 'Is that all ye want? D'ye not want sausage on it?'

'Naw, just a roll and butter.'

'Not want bacon?'

'Naw, just the roll,' said Doyle quietly. His eczema was so extreme that he looked as if he was rotting. Patches of raw and dried skin marred what might have been a handsome face.

'What are you doing up at this time in the morning?'

'Havenae been home. Been out,' he said, and looked away.

Doyle wasn't drunk and he wasn't stoned. Wherever he had spent the evening it hadn't been at a party. Maureen suspected that he gambled and lost but she didn't know what he did with his time. He travelled a lot and she had noticed only recently that his shoes were expensive but badly looked after, with dusty black uppers and pale leather soles. It made her smile when she thought about it. He might be an eccentric millionaire for all she knew, jet-setting around the world, and leaving his conservatory of rare orchids to come to Paddy's and nag her. He looked tired today. 'You should look after yourself better,' she said.

Doyle seemed a little bewildered by her concern. 'How?' he said.

'Well,' she said, 'get sleep and eat better.'

He scratched his head, covering his face and his embarrassment at being fussed over. 'I eat fine,' he said sulkily.

'I only ever see you when there's no one else here,' she said, and smiled.

He didn't smile back. She could tell she had offended him by talking about his diet. He thought she was blaming him for the eczema, as if fruit would have stopped his skin trying to fall away from him. His thick dark hair was always clotted with white lumps lifting from his scalp. Maureen saw Mary and Lara stealing sneaky glances. As if he could feel their eyes on him, he turned away and sat at a table, gesturing for Maureen to join him.

Mark Doyle had met Maureen at his sister's cremation. Pauline's funeral had been a grim, harrowing affair, as

66

suicide endings always are. Pauline's father stood next to his unknowing wife in the pew, squeezing her shoulder and keeping his eyes down. Her two brothers stood side by side and hurried outside as the coffin slid away, missing the line-up by the door in their eagerness to have a fag. When they followed the other mourners over the motorway bridge to a dark pub they spoke to no one but each other and even then said little. They were both tall and broad across the shoulders, drank fast and smoked without pleasure.

It was years later when she saw Doyle again. They were in a grimy pub, looking for a friend of Leslie's, and he approached them, asking where he knew Maureen from. His skin had got a lot worse since the funeral. He had a brutalized aura about him, war-veteran eyes and scars on his knuckles. He drawled his words like a hard man and when he looked at Maureen, his gaze fell short, settling on her cheek, her nose, her chin but never meeting her eyes. As she looked at him in the pub she firmly believed he'd been the brother who'd raped Pauline, maybe even wanked on to her back as she lay dying. She'd wanted to hurt him for Pauline and run away from the scarred eyes and the raw skin.

It wasn't until she was in London, being dragged down Brixton High Street by a man with fists like mallets, that she began to doubt it. Doyle came out of nowhere, knocked the guy down and picked her up, carrying her through the fruit market and taking her to safety in his attic bedsit. As they sat and talked in the bare room Doyle told her that his father and brother were dead. He wouldn't talk about what had happened to them, wouldn't openly admit that he had killed them, but Maureen knew. He said it brought him no peace.

She'd tried to be a friend to him but Doyle didn't want

a friend. He never wanted to talk about himself or what he did or how he lived. His sole purpose in seeing Maureen was to dissuade her from doing anything to Michael. It was all he ever talked about. He was adamant about it. Maureen tried to imagine how it must have been for him, growing up in a house with two men raping and assaulting his twelve-year-old wee sister, but she couldn't. She couldn't imagine the recrimination or the self-loathing but she knew he was trying to avert another disaster, trying to stop her killing Michael and becoming like him. Sheila said it was easier to save other people. Maureen looked at him, hunched over the far table, his back to the crowd, hiding himself and she felt for him. He was half dead already.

'Three roll, two 'n' sausage,' said Lara, handing over the cans and a brown paper bag, one corner already clear with grease.

Maureen paid and walked over to the table, reaching into the bag for Doyle's roll. 'Here ye are.'

Doyle took the roll and bit it automatically, keeping his eye on the door as if he was watching for someone.

'I'll need to go,' said Maureen, holding up the bag. 'I've got my pal's roll.'

Doyle looked at her as if remembering she was there. He nodded her closer to him. 'What's happening?' he muttered.

'About Michael?'

Doyle nodded. The oil from the bag was burning Maureen's hand but she held on to it tightly. 'Baby's due any day,' she said, and thought of Sheila.

Doyle picked up a plastic sauce bottle and squeezed watery red juice on to his roll, pressing the bottle too hard with his big hand, causing a little hiss from beneath the lid. 'Promise,' he said, 'you'll tell me before you do anything.' He ate and watched her, waiting for her to nod assent. He reached into his overcoat pocket and pulled out a scrap of paper. Awkwardly, he handed it to her. It had a long number written on it, pressed twice into the paper where the biro had dried out and been replaced. 'Phone me before.'

Maureen folded her arms and looked at him reproachfully. 'Mark,' he almost flinched at her use of his name, as if he couldn't bear to hear it, 'we've talked about this. If I'm gonnae do it, I'm gonnae do it.'

Doyle finished his roll and slipped his hands into the pocket of his overcoat. 'Just phone me, okay?'

'Once I make my mind up, you're not going to convince me otherwise,' she said quietly.

Doyle rubbed his forehead with his open hand. It sounded like sandpaper over parchment. He looked terribly sad for her. 'Please phone.' He stood up and ducked through the low doorway without looking back at her.

She watched him go, the hot oil nibbling her skin. The baby seemed suddenly very real and imminent. The hairs on the back of her neck shimmered awake. She shut her eyes, lifting her face to the sagging silver ceiling and, rolling her head from side to side, bullied the hairs back into place. The baby wasn't born yet, not just yet. She turned round to face the tunnel and put it out of her mind.

Back at the stall Leslie was still slumped on her stool, blinking hard to stay awake. Peter's eyes lit up when he spied the greasy parcel Maureen was carrying. 'Is that rolls and sausage?'

Leslie took the bag from Maureen and held it away from Peter as if he might pounce at it. 'Away and eat a pear, sick boy,' she said. 'You want to be careful.'

'I've ruined myself already,' said Peter, watching Leslie take out the roll and bite into it. A trickle of salty oil escaped from the side of her mouth and she grinned at him as she licked it back. 'It's you who should be careful,' he said. 'Hear about the A-level results? The girls getting better results than the boys?'

Peter had discovered through no particular intellectual effort that Leslie was a feminist and he liked to wind her up. Maureen could tell that he liked Leslie and meant to flirt and tease her. Leslie could not.

'It's not right, is it?' he said, smiling to himself. 'What's the point in letting them do exams? They're just going to sit at home eating Milk Tray and watching the telly.'

'You know, Peter,' Leslie raised her voice and her tired eyes flushed red at the rims: Maureen could tell she was getting disproportionately angry, 'I doubt whether you've ever satisfied a full grown woman.'

Peter frowned. 'I've never had any complaints,' he muttered.

'But do ye have an effective complaints procedure?' said Maureen, trying to lighten the tone.

'Do ye hate women?' said Leslie aggressively.

'No,' said Peter, disconcerted. 'No, I love women.'

'Is that right?' said Leslie. 'D'ye love everything about us, or d'ye just like us when we're sitting about in our knickers waiting for a shag?'

Peter smiled nervously at Maureen. Leslie stood up and sidled over to him, looking around as if she was about to confide in him. 'Peter,' she said slowly, her mouth a couple of inches from his ear, 'I'm menstruating. *Heavily.*'

Peter shut his eyes and shuddered with disgust as Leslie swaggered back to her seat. He looked at her as if she'd hit him and turned his back, pretending to have an interesting and engaging conversation with Lenny, as if such a thing were possible.

Leslie lowered herself on to her stool. 'What d'ye do that for?' said Maureen.

'I like scaring them with our big leaky bodies.' Leslie grinned. 'That's cheered me right up.'

'Yeah, well, good one,' said Maureen. 'Let's attack all the men with chronic angina. That'll learn 'em.'

Leslie liked to put up an aggressive front but she was a bit cowardly, really. When they had lured Angus to Miliport she had crapped it and stayed downstairs with Siobhain while Maureen went to meet him. It was a sore point. They'd argued about it but never talked about it and Maureen had noticed that knowing she was impotent had made Leslie even more aggressive.

'So,' said Maureen as she sat down, 'ye'd a bad night?'

'Aye,' Leslie hung her head and rubbed the back of her neck, 'it was fucking terrible. He wouldn't go away.'

'Ye know, ye could do the deed and move in with me for a couple of weeks. Let him cool off a bit.' Maureen hoped she wouldn't need to. Leslie was hard work at the best of times and this wasn't the best of times.

'Yeah. He's convinced I'm seeing someone else so he wants us to have a kid.'

'How do those two things fit together?'

'He doesn't want kids at all, he just wants to tie me down and control me. It's a twenty-year commitment for me and he's a guy so he can piss off and come back when it suits him.'

'I think you're right.'

'What a situation to bring a wee life into. He's not working, I'm here and God knows how long that'll last for.' They nodded to each other. 'And he wants a family. I said to him, I said, "Cammy, fuck off."'

Maureen chuckled to herself. 'You're a great negotiator, Leslie.'

'Yeah, well, he can fuck off. Tell ye what else: it sharpens the mind when ye think about someone else listening to the

"Fields of fucking Athenrye" five times a week.' She smiled at Maureen. 'I'll think about moving in, if that's all right?'

'Any time,' said Maureen, and lit a cigarette to mask her reluctance.

9
Mobile

Angus Farrell sipped his cold tea, closing his eyes tight, trying to shake the sore head that had plagued him since breakfast. He had taken a painkiller bought from the trustee the night before because he wanted a sleep but there had been something wrong with it – maybe it clashed with his other medication. A shrill, hot pain had been flaring up behind his eyes since morning. Drug-taking was the central recreation of the ward but he couldn't give himself to it. He pushed aside the sandwich.

A clatter against the metal door made him jump, and as the door swung open into the bright, sunny corridor Angus sat upright, straightening his face, getting ready to be seen by the warden. 'Solicitor's here,' said the officer. 'You're going through to Alpha block.'

Angus picked up his cup of tea and the food tray with the uneaten sandwich on it and stood, looking at the guard.

'Is that you ready?' said the guard.

'Aye,' said Angus.

'Ye not eating your lunch?'

'Not hungry.'

The guard hesitated. 'Well, look, leave it down,' he said, gesturing to the bed, 'and I'll give it in to Hungry George down the row.'

Angus turned and placed the tray on the bed. They would be in here when he was away, searching. He was glad he'd taken the pill the night before. They wouldn't find anything

73

in his room. He stood up again and the guard stepped away from the door, let him pass. They walked the length of the corridor, passing door after door, hearing men strain to shit or talking to themselves. The warmth in the corridor heightened the acrid smells of unwashed men, of faeces and piss, and the flashing pain behind Angus's eyes made him flinch again. Davie, the trustee, looked at his feet as he rolled the trolley by and banged on the next door, calling for the trays back.

The strip-lights and high whirr of the cameras burrowed behind his eyes and he leaned forward to make it worse so that when he sat up it would feel like a relief. The pain started to recede, to feel like a flashback to pain from another time, pain from Maureen O'Donnell. In his mind, Angus looked around the little room in Millport: twin beds with matching covers, a sink in the corner and the terrible heat, his hand cuffed to the bed and his legs bare, trousers somewhere else, Maureen O'Donnell standing in front of him, her outline watery through the hot air. He told her she'd been having the dreams because her father had raped her and she'd head-butted him, breaking his nose. He liked making her do that to him. He smiled to himself and sat up slowly, folding his hands in his lap as he looked around the waiting room. Maureen's pale blue eyes, livid and angry, panic at the edges, hoping to God that he was wrong about her father.

He imagined a court room. A witness box with Maureen in it, dressed in cheap clothes – she always wore cheap clothes. Hair tidied, some makeup on. If he was near to her he would smell cigarettes from her clothes, smell her shampoo, see her never-quite-clean finger nails. No, he rewound, he'd be across the room. They'd put the witness box far from the dock. A witness box with Maureen in it, dressed in cheap clothes, she always wore cheap clothes.

He'd look at her, let his eyes fall to her tits and she'd get that look again, panic at the edges of her pale blue eyes.

He had written to Maureen from hospital, when he first came out of the acid haze. A volley of letters, nonsensical notes that only she would understand about her father and the bleeding. He liked to imagine her getting each letter and opening it, reading it and her first reaction, avoiding the letter during the day and rereading it at night, reviving the revulsion. He had sent the letters through the official post. They couldn't stop him writing to her because she wasn't part of his case and she wouldn't complain: he'd mentioned Millport often enough to make it tricky for her. He'd known all along that the hospital censor read the mail and would have notified the police. They'd have traced the letters to Maureen, and her reluctance to hand them over would only serve to convince them that he was sincere.

He looked around the waiting room. The guard next to him was yawning repeatedly because the room was airless. Angus closed his eyes. A witness box with Maureen in it, dressed in cheap clothes, she always wore cheap clothes. Hair tidied, some makeup on. She'd have to point him out, have to look at him. He imagined her being calm and denying giving him the acid-laced coffee. She was a bad witness, had a history of mental illness, a problem with authority, but she could be quite together sometimes. She had a university degree and a pleasant manner. He remembered her coming into his office, smiling for him, asking after him in her heavy, smoky voice, her dark ringlet hair falling over her face. Angus opened his eyes. She couldn't be like that at the trial. She couldn't be credible at his trial. None of it would work if she was.

Grace sat at the table and talked through the details he had gleaned from the police statements. Times and places, Maureen's known movements and when she came to the clinic. 'She's got to be a rotten witness,' said Angus. 'She's got a history of hospitalization, and I'm a trained psychologist.'

Grace looked up at him, the fringe of hair fell back over his ears. 'We want to avoid bringing evidence about her personal reputation if we can.'

'Why?'

'Because if we do that,' said Grace quietly, 'then they can bring evidence about your reputation.'

Angus shrugged nonchalantly. 'So?'

'They'll bring evidence about the rape allegations at the Northern Psychiatric Hospital,' said Grace. Just for a moment Angus saw a shiver in his eyes, saw what he really thought about him. 'You realize, Mr Farrell, that if this case fails they'll be bringing a rape case against you?'

Angus frowned, as if he hadn't known that, as if he hadn't orchestrated the whole play himself. 'That's a ludicrous allegation,' he said nervously. 'The Northern Hospital rapes were nearly a decade ago now. Certainly I worked there but that doesn't make me guilty. They can't have any witnesses.'

'They do have one witness,' said Grace softly.

Angus drummed his nails on the table. He looked at Grace and laughed abruptly. 'Do you know what I'm really worried about?'

Grace shook his head.

'I'm worried about what I'm going to wear.' He snorted. 'My mum's got my suit in the dry-cleaner's. I haven't got any phone calls left to tell her to get it out and bring it.'

'Well,' said Grace, reaching into his inside pocket, 'that's one problem I can alleviate.' He pulled out a mobile phone and flicked it open. Angus watched him hand it over the table and he smiled. He knew the number by heart, tapped it in and grinned up at Grace as he listened to it ring, pressing it tight to his ear so that Grace couldn't hear it. It rang twice. 'Mum, it's me, you know my suit and shirt and things?' he said to the ringing, pausing for breath as the operator picked up and asked him for his message. 'Send them now.'

'Is that all, sir?' asked the operator.

Angus hung up. 'Left a message on her pager,' he said, knowing Grace might get an itemized bill and check the call. He handed back the phone. 'Thanks for that, you've really helped me.'

10

Si

The Albert Hospital was a blackened Victorian monstrosity. It stood alone at the head of the town, dwarfing the squat medieval cathedral. Eight storeys high, the sheer facade had suffered attempts at ornamentation but the pilasters and banding on the brick were as effective as false eyelashes on an elephant. Maureen had been here many times, first on her regular visits to see Louisa, the psychiatrist to whom Angus had referred her, then one last time to see her school-friend Benny after Liam broke his jaw.

Ducking across the busy slip-road from the motorway, Maureen waited at the lights. The warm sun and the exhaust fumes formed a gritty haze over the road, catching on her chest. Above her, overlooking the road, wards ended in long balconies furnished with seats for the smokers who were too sick to get downstairs to a designated area.

The reception area was an open two-storey space with a mezzanine and a newsagent's and flower stall near the door. She bought a bunch of big, tired daisies padded out with ferns, and followed the signs for Ward G. The lift doors slid back and Maureen stepped in. An elderly man in a felt cap and summer jacket was taking charge of the controls and asked her which floor, pressed the button with a flourish and smiled at her when the doors closed.

Down a number of corridors with polished lino floors and muted echoes, Maureen finally found Ward G. It consisted of a long room with ten beds on either side and three separate rooms for jumpy trauma victims. High windows trapped the warm, fetid air. At the head of the big room, just before the corridor entrance, a small room served as the nurses' station. A young male nurse with a naval beard was sitting at the desk looking depressed and tired. He didn't stand up but swivelled towards her on his chair and hung his head lethargically to the side when Maureen asked after Ella. Apparently, she had contusions to both eyes, a broken thigh and bruising to her arms. He pointed her through to one of the private rooms off the ward. 'Her son's already here,' he said.

Ella was propped up against some pillows but seemed to have slipped down the bed. Her eyes were a terrifying red mess of burst vessels, clashing with the blue irises. The left side of her face was black and green and her eyebrows were missing, making her forehead look bald and barren. The sheet, pulled up to her chin, had somehow slipped over her mouth. Under the blankets a small tent held it away from her legs. Her right hand lay on top of the covers, a clear plastic tube taped to the back, a small plaster cupping the flesh between her thumb and forefinger where the bandage had been.

In front of her sat a middle-aged man, dressed in blue slacks and a pale blue shirt. He turned to look at her and Maureen could see traces of Ella everywhere, in the thin lips, the gold-rimmed glasses and the small blue eyes, but Ella's son was not a bonny boy. His eyes were slightly splayed, not enough to constitute a squint but enough to be disconcerting. His chin was so weak it looked as if he was recoiling from the world in disgust. He was not pleased to meet Maureen. He looked her up and down, hiding his resentment behind heavy hooded eyes.

The atmosphere between mother and son was strained and shocked, as if Ella had just revealed the truth about crop circles and he had countered with pictures of Elvis working as an interpreter at the UN.

'Hiya, Ella,' said Maureen, pretending not to notice the peculiar atmosphere. 'We were all worried about ye at the market so I was sent up to see ye.'

From her reclining position Ella nodded faintly, making the sheet slip off her mouth and shoulder. She was wearing a blue paper nightdress.

'I brought ye these flowers but I can see we've been outdone.' Maureen gestured at the bedside cabinet and a big bunch of long-stem red roses hanging wildly out of a short vase. The man smiled a little, his lips sliding open over his teeth, his eyes remaining static as he wondered who the hell she was. Ella looked down at the tent blanket over her feet.

'How are ye feeling?' said Maureen.

Ella looked at Si for a moment and he leaned forward, giving her a light slap on her elbow. 'You can speak,' he said disdainfully. 'Go on, answer her.' His accent was middle class and he smiled an apology for his ignorant old mother at Maureen.

Maureen felt her gorge rise. 'I'm Maureen from Paddy's,' she said, and shoved out her hand.

He stood up and shook it. His palm was damp and she had the impression that he didn't want to shake hands or introduce himself but courtesy compelled him. 'Si McGee,' he said quickly. 'She's been very quiet today. Maybe you should come back tomorrow.'

Ella looked up at her with startled red eyes and Maureen pulled over a chair. 'Aye, well, I'm here now.' She set the chair upstream of Si and sat down. 'What's the food like here?' she asked, for something to say.

Ella seemed to shrink under the sheet a little.

80

Maureen tried again. 'What happened to get you in this state, then?'

Ella wasn't about to answer. Maureen turned to Si. 'She fell over in the house,' he said, annoyed that she was still here, 'and hurt herself.'

Maureen looked to Ella for confirmation but she wasn't talking. Behind the bloody eyes she looked absent and afraid. If Ella had fallen she would have had to land on both eyes and on the side of her head as well. Barring the possibility of a bizarre trampolining incident, Ella's injuries hadn't been caused by a fall. 'Is she on medication?'

'Aye, painkillers,' said Si, adding unnecessarily, 'for the pain.'

Maureen nodded as though she were a surgeon and understood. She turned back to Ella. 'Can I bring ye anything up? D'ye want rollers for your hair or anything?'

Ella's eyes didn't move. She was staring over Maureen's shoulder at her son.

Maureen patted her hand and promised to come up again the next day. When she stood up and bent forward to move the chair back behind her, she could see the bottom half of Si's face. His mouth was a wizened line. She stood up quickly to catch him, but he anticipated her and took her hand in both of his, squeezing a little too hard as he pumped it and thanked her for coming. 'I'll get you out,' he said.

'No, it's all right,' said Maureen. 'I know the way.'

'I'm leaving anyway.' He stood up and smiled at her, trying to seem friendly. 'I've got the car outside. I'll drive you home, if you like.'

Maureen glanced at Ella but Ella was staring at her son. 'Thanks, but I'm fine, someone's picking me up.'

Si smiled with cold eyes. 'It's no trouble,' he said. 'I'd like to.'

'No, someone's picking me up.'

In the lift Si kept catching her eye and trying to smile. 'Where is it you stay?' he said, sliding along the metal wall towards her.

Maureen slid along the wall in the opposite direction, distancing herself. She didn't want to tell him anything about herself. 'West End,' she lied.

'That figures,' he said. 'Trendy wee thing like you.'

Maureen looked him in the eye and thought what an arsehole he was. She didn't like creepy strangers trying to flirt with her. It felt like a grotesquely intimate intrusion.

'I bet you've got a lot of boyfriends.'

She could happily have hit him then but the lift reached the ground floor and the doors opened. She stepped back to let him go first but Si misunderstood and, thinking she was flirting back, insisted that she go first.

'Is it a boyfriend who's picking you up?' he said, catching up with her at the door.

'It's my brother,' she said firmly.

Despite her hearty protestations Si insisted on waiting with her outside the gates until Liam turned up in his Triumph Herald. 'What an unusual car,' he said, as Maureen walked away.

II

Peeler

Liam's Triumph Herald had a soft top, and a back end so rusted that it looked as if it might snap off in a brisk wind. It had been bought as camouflage during his days as a dealer because no one would suspect the driver of being anything but a mug. As Maureen brought the cigarette to her mouth, the wind blew live ash into her hair and she heard the tiny crackle of hairs burning, smelt a whiff of sulphur.

'Who was that?' asked Liam.

'The old lady's son,' shouted Maureen, above the noisy engine. 'What a creep. Has Una been in touch with you?'

'Not in the half-hour since ye last asked me, no,' Liam shouted back. 'Don't worry, she'll be late. First babies are often late.'

Liam spotted the red light up ahead and cursed it. He slowed the car, trying not to reach it before it changed back, but the lights didn't budge and the engine petered to a coughing stop. He whipped off his shades and looked accusingly at Maureen.

'Fuck all to do with me,' she said.

'Well, you're sitting there,' he muttered, and began the long ritual of the choke.

The lights changed and impatient cars behind them began to hoot. Eventually the Triumph spluttered to life, taking off just as the lights changed again, trapping the other cars behind it. Liam grinned as they honked. Maureen wished that she'd had the chance to speak to Ella alone. She looked pretty shocked.

Liam coughed next to her and she looked at him. He might not tell her when the child was born. He didn't know what the birth meant to her: he didn't know what she was planning for Michael. The only people who knew were Doyle, because she'd told him, and Sheila, because she'd guessed. Liam might decide not to tell her because it would upset her. She hoped she could read it in his face if he was lying. They were gathering speed on the broad road to Dennistoun and he smiled to her and raised himself up in the seat a little, enjoying the warm wind chewing his hair. Maureen smiled back. She'd know if he was lying. She felt sure she would.

Siobhain McCloud opened the door to Liam's familiar knock. She had sunglasses on, exactly the same model of Ray-Bans as Liam. She didn't wait to see who it was or even welcome them but walked away wordlessly down the dark hall and back to her beloved outsized television.

'Hiya,' called Liam, stepping into the hall. 'I've brought Mauri with me.'

Siobhain didn't reply. Liam shut the door behind Maureen, nodding for her to go into the living room ahead of him.

Siobhain was sitting on the beige settee watching a Gaelic film about North Uist. She seemed to have taken to wearing her shades indoors a lot because the TV brightness was set so high that both Maureen and Liam had to put on their sunglasses to make sense of the picture. The programme showed a group photograph of islanders from the sixties, a line-up of thick-legged girls in miniskirts with indistinct knees and innocent grins. She turned over suddenly to *Montel*. A woman in a flowery dress was crying and Montel took her hand.

'What's happening?' asked Liam, sitting down next to her on the settee.

'She's crying,' said Siobhain, 'and Montel is holding her hand.'

Maureen sat down in the armchair. Siobhain's house was depressing. The settee was beige, the walls were beige, the carpet was beige, everything inoffensive and inexpensive. The only ornamentation in the living room was a small watercolour of irises and a big oil painting of her younger brother, done from a small snapshot photograph, a little boy standing on a hillside many years ago, squinting into the camera.

As part of a university project, Liam had made a film of Siobhain. She talked to the camera about her people and the Highlands, showing irrelevant pictures cut out of ladies' magazines. She told the story of her childhood with the travellers, how her brother drowned in a burn and her mother left the land and came to the city to die. It was a peculiar film. It should just have been annoying but it was strangely touching, fat Siobhain barking in her Highland accent at the camera, her stilted delivery seeming affected and mistimed. Liam had written an end-of-term paper on his film, a vague and pretentious piece about the rare beauty of reality. He failed and was having to do a resit exam over the summer.

Maureen would never have thought of them as friends, much less close friends, but since the film Liam had been over at Siobhain's all the time, watching television, showing her films and asking her what she thought.

Siobhain had been very fat when Maureen met her but it didn't disguise how beautiful she was. Her nose was a straight arrow, her plump mouth a tidy rosebud and her cheekbones high and proud. Her black hair had started to grey prematurely but in most lights the silver strands looked like a glossy sheen. Angus Farrell had almost broken her. As a senior psychologist at the Northern Psychiatric Hospital he had had unlimited access to the ward where Siobhain was being treated for depression. Farrell had tethered the women with rope, around the ankles, around the wrists. Of the other two victims Maureen knew about for sure, Iona McKinnon had hung herself and Yvonne Urquhart had had a stroke that left her severely brain-damaged.

It might have been the shock of seeing herself on film, or just that she had pals, but Siobhain had changed dramatically in the last six months. She went on a crazy diet of steak and citrus fruit, which caused her to exude a sharp, rotting smell. It also made her fart soundlessly every fifteen seconds although she steadfastly denied it every time Leslie challenged her. She had lost half her bodyweight. Because the weight loss had been so rapid her skin was just catching up with her, contracting around the new shapes and forms. She had had a chicken neck for a month but it had settled back now to show a strong jaw and slim neck. She still moved as if she was obese: swinging her legs around each other clumsily, holding her arms out stiffly to the sides. When she sat down she cleared space for her phantom belly, sitting with her legs wide open as if she still had forty-inch thighs.

She needed new clothes and trawled the charity shops with Maureen and Leslie, choosing a peculiar mixture of old lady flowery dresses, a big yellow anorak, tennis shoes and bright jerseys in blues and oranges. It was the first time she had ever chosen her own adult clothes. She dressed like no one else they had met. Today she was sporting white tennis shoes with red soles, a red skirt and a green shirt with button-down breast pockets.

Maureen could tell she was enjoying her new self and the

shades were part of that. She had taken to brushing her hair and making sure her collars weren't tucked in.

'Siobhain,' said Liam, handing her the newspaper, 'we want you to look at this.'

Siobhain moved her face in the direction of the newspaper. It took them a minute to realize that under her shades she was keeping her eyes on the crying woman and Montel.

'Siobhain, read it,' said Liam impatiently, cracking the paper with a flick of his finger. 'This shit's on all the time.'

Maureen had never seen anyone swear in front of Siobhain without getting pulled up about it. She looked at Liam curiously. He was sitting forward, watching Siobhain as she looked at the paper, his hands clasped between his knees.

Siobhain finished reading and looked up at Liam, her face blank, her mouth hanging open.

'He can't hurt you,' said Liam quickly, taking his own specs off. 'He can't get anywhere near you. We won't let him.' He looked to Maureen for confirmation and she nodded.

'He's still in prison,' said Maureen, shedding her cheap glasses. 'They're just trying the case.'

Siobhain raised a hand to her face and took her own glasses off, dropping them on to the settee, her hand hanging limp on her lap. 'Will they let him go?' she said quietly.

'No,' said Liam quickly.

Siobhain looked at him suspiciously. They didn't really know what would happen. As far as they knew Angus Farrell was just as likely to be sent to a chip shop for life, without the possibility of vinegar. 'I'm not stupid, Liam,' she said softly.

'We don't know what'll happen,' said Maureen, 'but we

do know that the trial'll go on for a while and he'll be in all the papers and we wanted to warn you about it.'

'He's in court,' Siobhain said.

'That's right,' said Liam, leaning into her. 'But he can't get to ye.'

Siobhain dismissed him with a look and spoke to Maureen. 'He's in court in Glasgow?'

'Yeah.'

Siobhain looked at the picture in the paper and slowly lifted her face to Maureen, tipping her chin and taking a deep breath. 'Will he go to prison for what he did to me?'

Maureen and Liam looked at each other.

'I don't think so,' said Maureen. 'The paper says it's just the murders he's been done for.'

'Will they ever try him for the other things?'

Liam shook his head. 'We don't know.'

Maureen knew the police had tried to be kind when they questioned Siobhain. She wouldn't survive a court case. Maureen sat forward a little. 'Siobhain,' she said, reasoning that an outright lie was the kindest course of action, 'he's being tried for murder and the police don't think he'll get off. He's just being tried for the murder.'

They fell silent and watched Montel on the giant television. It was the only expensive thing in Siobhain's house: everything else had been provided by Social Services when she came out of hospital. Douglas had given Siobhain money too, a fat roll of cash that Elsbeth didn't know anything about.

Montel was trying to coax the woman to speak through her tears by telling her something about his military experience. The woman had been accused of insurance fraud and was facing twenty years in jail.

'She is going down,' said Siobhain, and dropped the paper to the floor.

*

Out in the street, two gangs of tired ten-year-olds were fighting about a football. A mum hung out of a window, calling someone in for bed and telling them to learn to fucking behave, for fucksake. Liam tugged the hood up on the car and slapped open a rusted hinge. 'She's terrified,' he muttered, glancing up at the window.

'She seems okay to me,' said Maureen. 'I've seen her terrified. She freezes and cries and throws up.'

'Maureen,' he said, authoritatively, as if he was the only person who had ever met Siobhain, 'you don't know what she's feeling.'

'Well, you don't know either. All you've got to go on is what she says.'

He snorted and walked around the car to tackle the roof on the passenger side. 'I think I know Siobhain,' he said prissily.

'Aye, better than she does?'

Liam didn't answer but pulled up the hood of the car, blocking the sun from her face. Maureen sat in the shadow, waiting patiently as he clipped the hood to the windscreen. She saw him turn and look up to Siobhain's window, hoping for a final glimpse. She wouldn't be standing there, Maureen knew she wouldn't, not while Montel was on. He climbed in next to her and shut his door, pulling out the choke. 'Liam, do you fancy Siobhain?'

He turned stiffly to face her, a pale pink blush spreading over his neck and face. 'No,' he said, his eyes open wide, his bottom lip twitching.

'Has Una had her baby yet?'

Liam looked confused and the blush receded. 'No. What's that to do with anything?'

Maureen smiled to herself. 'Never mind,' she said. She'd definitely know if he was lying. 'Ye know, that sort

89

of poetic sorrow can be very seductive. If you like Siobhain at least make sure you fall for her, not just her tragic past.'

'Maureen, I don't even know what you're talking about,' said Liam, and pulled out very fast into the street.

As she climbed the last weary flight of stairs Maureen felt certain she could hear Jim Maliano watching her through the spy-hole in his door. It was a horrible habit of his. She turned around and stared at the door, looking straight into the spy-hole, mouthing 'Fuck off.' She had said it ten times when she heard him creeping, tippy-toed, along the carpeted hall, a hand brushing the papered wall as he steadied himself. Inside her own door the answer-machine blinked at her. She went into the kitchen, unscrewed the lid from the whisky bottle and drank. It tasted like a longed-for deep breath. She was going to get dead drunk tonight. The answer-machine had a message from Hugh McAskill, asking her to call him at home, and one from Kilty checking in to say hello. The last was the usual forlorn weekly message from Winnie.

When Winnie was drinking she was a shameless phone pest. Since Maureen had cut contact with her, Winnie could phone six, sometimes seven times in a day. Her personal best was a round and magnificent fifteen. Each time she rang she'd be at a different stage of drunkenness and sounded like a completely different person. Her moods ranged from heart-wrenching sadness to apocalyptic anger, and every call was aimed at getting Maureen to phone her back. Maureen had cut off nearly a year ago, when it had become clear that the family no longer believed that Michael had abused her. Winnie had gone to AA and got sober in the intervening period and now phoned once a week, every Friday at five o'clock when Liam would have told her that Maureen was still at work, and repeated the same three sentences: 'I love you, I miss you, I want you to contact me.' Maureen appreciated the kindness of phoning when she would be out. She found herself wondering about sober Winnie, fantasizing about talking to her, the two of them reminiscing about the good times. Liam was closer to Winnie now that he had softened and she was sober. He said she was deeply sorry for all the grief she'd caused but really didn't understand the extent of it. Winnie was the funniest person Maureen'd ever met. She found herself imagining an idealized mother in place of Winnie and it became hard to remember what was true and what was fantasy. Liam told her that Winnie was almost prepared to consider the possibility that Michael had abused Maureen, and knew at least that it wasn't a deliberate, malicious fabrication.

A sudden unfamiliar, officious-sounding knock at the door made her jump. She looked out of the spy-hole, expecting to see Aggie Grey, the woman with ££s to spare. It was a man, dressed formally in slacks and a short-sleeved shirt, holding a brown envelope. He was slim with dyed blond hair and a badly sunburned face. The brown skin was peeling off his chin and neck, leaving patches of brilliant pink. His forearms were going as well and, as he waited for her to answer the door, he pulled a tin of Vaseline out of his pocket and rubbed it on his forearm. The skin came away beneath his fingers, rolling into greasy, grey little cigars. He made a disgusted face and brushed it on to the floor, picking at the bits stuck in the hairs. Maureen frowned at the door, wondering why Aggie Grey would send someone who looked like a courier. Suddenly it hit her: the illegal fags. It might be a warrant to search the house.

Maureen ran on tiptoe back into the kitchen and pushed

the sleeves of cigarettes into the bottom of a cupboard, shoving empty poly-bags in front of them. The front door banged again. Panting, she stood up, shut the cupboard door and looked at it. The man chapped again, faster this time, more impatient. She picked up a chair carefully, trying not to make a noise, and sat it in front of the cupboard door, stepping back to look at it, hoping it looked natural. She couldn't tell. She couldn't remember what natural looked like. He knocked again.

'Coming,' she shouted, trying to sound casual. She could say the fags were for her own consumption, that she'd been abroad recently and had bought them. Calmer, she brushed her hair from her face, stepped out to the hall and opened the door. 'Can I help you?' she said, remembering that she didn't know where the fags were from. If she said she'd been to Greece and they were from France he'd know she'd lied.

'Miss Maureen O'Donnell?' he said suspiciously.

'Yes.' Maureen stepped out on to the landing and pulled the door closed behind her, realizing, too late, how shifty it made her look.

'You took your time,' he said, giving her a sidelong glance.

She looked straight at him 'It's my time to take,' she said stiffly, and wondered what it meant.

The man looked puzzled for a moment. 'I'm here to deliver this,' he said, handing her the envelope.

Maureen took it. It wasn't sealed at the back so it came open easily and she took out a small sheet of paper. It had her address on it but it didn't seem to be a warrant. 'What is this?' she said.

'It's a witness citation.'

She read the letter. She was invited to appear for the prosecution at HMA – v.–Farrell. The start date was only a week away. Maureen couldn't bear the thought of seeing

Angus again. She imagined him standing up in the dock, shouting across the court to her, something about Michael that only the two of them would understand, something calculated to fuck her up for months afterwards. She shook her head, trying to hand it back, but the man held up his hands. He said she couldn't give it back now that she had it. When she asked why he smirked at her. '*Because it's a citation*,' he said.

He was laughing at her and she had no idea why. 'What is a citation?' she asked.

'Don't ye know?'

'Don't you?'

'It means that ye have to come to court on the day it says.' He jerked his head at the sheet, 'Just turn up and wait and you'll get called.'

'What if I don't want to?'

'Ye *have* to,' said the red man. 'You'll go to prison if ye don't.'

Maureen's heart sank. 'Prison?'

'Aye,' he said confidently. 'They'll do it as well – they sent a woman last week.'

'For not wanting to go? What if you're scared?'

'Still send ye,' he said, as if he didn't approve either.

They stood in the chilly close, Maureen imagining herself in black and white, raising birds and fashioning chivs out of spoons, the peeling man wondering if he was cut out for this job or should go back to filing at the DSS. She looked at his forearm. 'Ye shouldn't use Vaseline,' she said, pointing at the pink patch. 'Use aftersun. It'll cool the skin down.'

'What's wrong with Vaseline?'

'Too heavy, your skin can't breathe.'

The man looked at his raw arm. 'Is that right? What about calamine?'

93

'Aye, calamine's good but messy on your clothes. After-sun's better.'

'Aye, cheers, anyway,' he said, and walked away downstairs.

He stopped on the first landing. 'By the way, Joe McEwan says he'll see ye there.'

Maureen shut the door and dropped the letter to the floor, taking the whisky bottle back into the living room, thinking of all the different sides to Angus. Angus the kind therapist who had made her think for the first time since hospital that she might have a life and a future. Angus as Douglas used to talk about him, the competitive edge, the small defeats and gains between them. The aftermath of Angus, dead Douglas in the living room, his blood everywhere and Martin Donegan on the floor of his little cupboard hidey-hole, his blood black and silky beneath her feet. And then the epiphany: Angus turning up on the ferry to Millport, coming for Siobhain, coming to kill her to tidy up the details of his rapes in the Northern Psychiatric Hospital. She didn't want to see him because of what he had said to her in the room, about Michael, about the dreams. But if she didn't turn up they'd send her to prison and Una's baby would have no protection from Michael.

She sat on the window-sill, drinking from the bottle, felt the warm sun on her face, a gentle breeze licking her hair. She had been deferring the decision about Michael and now the possibility of going to prison made it more urgent. She had to make up her mind and do it within the next week. It was all coming to an end. She knew now that deferring was just a game. These undecided days had been the most content and precious she could remember. She remembered sitting in the garden of the Northern Psychiatric Hospital with Pauline, pressing the flat of their palms together as they passed a lit cigarette from one to another, Pauline's hands larger than Maureen's but stick-thin. Her skin was see-through.

Maureen turned her face to the sun, letting golden glory tears roll down her face. She wasn't going to abandon the child to fate, whatever happened, whatever Sheila said.

12

Twice Rice

Her head was aching at the back, a dull hangover pain reminding her that there were good things in life, like drink and more drink. While washing her face, she found a painful inch-long bruise under her chin and a parallel bruise on her forehead, just above her eyebrows. She was trying to remember the night before and work out where on earth the bruises could possibly have come from when the postie's tired feet tramped up the stairs. She heard him stop, flick through some letters, and watched one slip through and drop on to the mat. Maureen picked it up and opened it.

It was a cheap brown envelope containing a small printed sheet telling her when and where to turn up for the small-claims case. It was due to be heard the following Friday at two thirty in the afternoon. Ella McGee's name wasn't even on the letter. Maureen tutted. She knew she'd filled in the bloody form properly. If she met creepy Si McGee again he'd think she was suing him, implying a relationship between them, suggesting the necessity of contact. She decided to go to the hospital that afternoon and tell Ella when the case was, then have nothing more to do with either of them.

She looked around the tiny hall. She wanted to get out of the flat. She was pulling the front door open before she had finished her first fag of the day. A small white envelope that had been sitting against the door flopped onto the toe of her trainer. She picked it up. There was no address on it.

It was sealed at the back, the paper warped in a wide rim around the seal, as if it had been wetted with a brush or a cloth. She shut the door and stood in the hall looking at it. She ripped it open.

Inside was a laser-printed image in smudgy black and white on photocopy paper. It was a picture of a child of about eight, standing in a hallway. The girl's eyes had been blanked out with a thick black line. She was crying, mouth open, lips and cheeks wet with tears, crying and looking up at the person taking the photograph of her. She was naked and cupping her little fanny protectively, her arms taut, her chest hunched nervously. Maureen shuddered and dropped the picture to the floor, stepping back to get away from it. The picture landed face up and the eyeless child was in her hallway, crying up at her.

Maureen looked into the envelope again but it was empty and it occurred to her that DNA could be taken from saliva. She crouched down and turned the picture over but there was nothing written on the back. The child was almost the same age she had been when she was abused. Angus Farrell would know that. It had been hand-delivered but she knew it had come from him: he was the only person who sent her threatening letters. Angus probably knew a whole network of freaks and weirdos in the city, people he would have met through his work, through his patients and through his own personal interests, any one of whom could have sent it. He was trying to upset her and he was succeeding.

She looked down at the picture again. The child's pain seemed so immanent, the threat to her so urgent, that Maureen felt a rush in her stomach and flush on her cheeks. She wanted to do something, run into the street and punch someone or something, take action and save the wee girl but the picture could be decades old. And all she could tell the police if she phoned them was that she had been sent a cheap photocopy of a picture of a girl who seemed upset. She crouched down by the picture and put her fingertip on the child's hand.

Weeping, she picked up the picture by its edge and put it in the hall cupboard, facing the wall. She shut the door, resting her head on the frame, and decided to get out of the house.

As she pulled the front door open, her eye caught the wicker laundry basket sitting under the basin in the bathroom at the far end of the hall. Suddenly irritated by the innocuous item, she left the front door open, walked down the hall, emptied the basket on to the bathroom floor and carried it down the stairs. She threw it out of the back door, into the midden.

She bought a can of Coke in Mr Padda's and put her shades on, sitting on the low wall outside her door between the jagged metal stumps, remnants of railings sawn off in the war. She smoked a cigarette and drank, watching for the van. She would go and see Ella McGee this afternoon, tell her about the date of the small-claims case and then wash her hands of it. Since she couldn't talk about it in front of Si McGee she decided to dress up smartly and sneak in before the visiting hours started. She wasn't going to think about the photograph or talk about last night's citation until she'd spoken to Hugh McAskill. He'd tell her what it meant and what she should do about it.

Leslie arrived and, to Maureen's astonishment, was upset about Cammy. They had spent the previous evening trying to settle who owned what in the flat but he kept crying and Leslie had had to restrain herself from comforting him in case he took it the wrong way. Maureen suspected that Cammy knew exactly what he was doing. Leslie chucking him out meant he'd have to go back and stay with his mum, pay digs money out of his giro and at least pretend to try to get a job.

The market was bustling with the Saturday crowd. They were different from the weekday punters, less purposeful and more likely to browse, but the takings could be good. Some of the stalls in their tunnel were only used on Saturdays. Punters wandered around in groups of two or three, silting up the market's arteries. Foreign tourists came to the market on Saturdays because the tour guides wanted to fit in the Barras weekend market on the same day. It was a healthier crowd than during the week, when the underfed and under-privileged gathered together to trade reusable rubbish. They were unpacking the van and setting up the stall when Leslie started peering above Maureen's eyes.

'Mauri, you've got a wee mark there.' She tried to rub off the tender bruise on Maureen's forehead.

'Stop it,' said Maureen, slapping her hand away. 'It's a bruise.'

'What is it?' asked Leslie.

'I dunno,' said Maureen, and tipped up her chin. 'Look. There's another under here.'

'How did ye do that?'

'I dunno. I must have done it when I was asleep.'

'D'ye put your head in a vice when you're sleeping?'

Maureen smiled and rubbed her forehead. 'Aye, mibbi.'

Engaging with a person who wasn't Cammy for thirty seconds had taken it out of Leslie. She looked down the tunnel to the bright lane. 'Cammy bruised his big toenail at football. It's still black. He did it months ago, as well.'

It was half eight in the morning and Maureen was already furious with everyone. She was angry with Leslie for not listening, angry with whoever had delivered the picture, angry at the thought of seeing Angus again and with that fucking laundry basket for taking up so much fucking space for so long. She thought of it sitting out in the dusty back court and hoped it would rain.

Leslie was red-eyed but standing firm. Maureen listened to her talk about Cammy, trying to care. She was angry, she could feel it gnawing at the pit of her stomach. She tried breathing in deeply to dilute it, trying to bring her mind back to Cammy and the disputed ownership of an Orb album.

The market died off in the early afternoon. Leslie went to get the lunch and came back with bacon and egg rolls.

'Getting sick of rolls every day,' said Maureen, throwing hers, half eaten, to Elsie Tanner.

'Yeah,' said Leslie, licking runny yolk from the back of her hand, looking at her roll as if Maureen had taken the good out of it.

'I got a letter this morning,' Maureen said reticently. 'Hand-delivered. I'm sure it's from Farrell.'

'How could he deliver it by hand?' asked Leslie. 'Isn't he still in hospital?'

'Aye, but I figure he probably knows someone. Gave them my address.'

'What was the picture of?'

'A wee girl, naked and crying.'

'Fuck, Mauri, that's creepy.'

'It's supposed to be,' said Maureen, scratching her head.

Maureen and Leslie took turns going for walks up and down the lane. After one walk Leslie came back looking shifty and carrying a Marks & Spencer food-hall bag. When she set it down the bag's contents slid to the side, the top gaped open and Maureen saw two portions of chicken tikka and a double portion of rice. Leslie pushed the bag into her hold-all and sat down on her stool.

Maureen lit a cigarette as she walked down the lane to

the river. The market ended at a disused iron bridge over the river. Greenery sprouted from between red riveted girders like the hairs on an old man's ears. On a sofa in the shade of the bridge sat two drunk men with sun-baked faces, looking out at the rusting underbelly. One man watched her pass, smiling genially. His pal was either asleep or dead, slumped sideways at an improbable angle over the arm of the sofa.

She went into the Sutherland Vaults, a dingy pub painted black throughout. The Saturday drinkers were there, propped along the bar, looking as sober as the settee men. Around a blind corner a sad old song was being played on a fiddle, accompanied by the exhausted heartbeat of a bodhran.

She used the pay-phone and called Hugh McAskill at work. He said hello and that he would meet her for a curry the next night. He talked as if they'd already made the arrangement and were finalizing details. They had never so much as been for coffee together before. When she agreed to meet him at Charing Cross at seven thirty he said, 'Yes,' and hung up on her. She stood for a moment, wondering if it had been Hugh she'd spoken to. It had sounded like him.

She hadn't intended to do it, but the bar was there and she was pissed off and worried so she ordered a triple whisky, without a mixer, and drank it down like medicine. When she left the glass on the bar and stepped out into the road the day was warmer, the sunshine less corrosive and the colours of the cars against the deep green of the river were vibrant and thrilling.

The market was all but deserted by half one. It was too hot and everyone was staying in their gardens or hanging about the park. Maureen suggested that they shut up early but Leslie didn't want to. They argued about it apathetically for half an hour and Leslie was proved right when one of the regulars came jogging down the aisle breathlessly at two o'clock and bought a whole box of Regal and a packet of tobacco. 'For the weans,' he said, and wheezed a laugh.

Leslie had nothing to do but go home and cry so she agreed to drive Maureen to her flat, wait for her to change into some fresh clothes and take her to the Albert. Maureen wanted her to wait outside and give her a lift home again afterwards but Leslie thought she was pushing it. 'I'm not just being lazy,' said Maureen, 'but her creepy son tried to drive me home yesterday and I want to leave with someone.'

'Well, okay,' said Leslie, adding quickly, 'but I'm not going to see her. I don't even know her.'

'I don't want ye to come up and see her,' said Maureen, 'just run me about the town for an hour or so.'

'What else am I doing?'

Maureen had dressed in smart office clothes – a clean white shirt and black skirt – hoping to sneak in to see Ella before visiting time and Si's arrival. She walked quickly down the corridor, keeping her head down and slipping past the big metal lunch trolley, inconspicuous in her nice clothes. The triple whisky she had had at lunchtime had worn off a long time ago and she was aching for another. It occurred to her that three small whiskies made her feel the way everyone else did normally. If she could keep a bottle in her bag and top herself up she'd probably feel all right most of the time.

Maureen opened the door to Ella's room a little, checking before she entered. It was empty but the sound of running water came from a tiny closet room at the far side of the bed. She flinched at the sound of a flush, worried she might have walked in on Ella doing the toilet, and fell back to the doorway.

A stick appeared at the door first, followed by a shuffling

Ella, bent heavily, swinging a leg in full plaster behind her. A female nurse with short auburn hair walked behind her, one hand on Ella's waist as she flattened her paper nightie down at the back. Ella looked up at Maureen and staggered to the side in surprise. The nurse caught her and helped her over to the bed. Ella's eyes were healing a little, the red breaking up into spots of orange, like poached blood on white linen.

'Who are you?' the nurse asked Maureen sharply as she turned to help Ella on to the bed, her sagging little bottom visible between the sides of the gaping paper robe.

Maureen didn't know what to say.

'Are you here to visit Mrs McGee?' said the nurse. 'Visiting doesn't start for another half-hour. You'll need to wait downstairs.'

Ella was sitting on the blankets. The nurse struggled to lift her up with one hand and push the sheets back. Maureen stepped forward and pulled the covers out of the way. The nurse looked at her, disapproving, as if she'd tried to curry favour. 'You'll still have to wait downstairs,' she said, lifting Ella's plastered leg on to the bed. Ella groaned under her breath and shut her eyes. Maureen felt disproportionately guilty.

'Come back,' said Ella awkwardly, and Maureen realized why she hadn't spoken the day before. Her top set of dentures was broken, snapped in half between the two front teeth.

Maureen shook herself. It was ridiculous to feel so guilty. She hadn't started a food fight in the middle of an operation, she was just interrupting the nurse's toileting round. 'The date came through for the small-claims case,' she said, clumsily, pressing the letter into Ella's hand. 'It's next Friday.'

Ella hunched over suddenly and grimaced, letting out a

low, desperate yowl of regret, crumpling the letter in her bony fist. The nurse bent down suddenly, trying to look her in the eye, thinking she was having an attack of some kind. Ella pushed the woman away, shaking her head over and over, and Maureen knew she shouldn't have brought the letter here, not while Ella was in hospital and so afraid already. It would hardly kill her to be kind. She crouched down in front of Ella, chucking her chin to make her stop shaking her head. 'D'ye need nighties?' she asked.

Ella's eyes moistened and she nodded. 'I need ...' she started to cry '... a comb.'

Maureen petted her hand a couple of times, stood up and left. She heard the nurse asking Ella if Maureen was her daughter. She took a back door out to the street so that she wouldn't pass Leslie on her way to the shops.

The department store was thick with Saturday shoppers, wandering around in family units, holding up lamps and running their hands over carpets and curtains while restless children ran in the aisles and played with information leaflets about zero-interest credit. It was cool in the windowless store: it might have been winter outside.

Maureen took the escalator up a level and found the nighties next to the sportswear. Given her financial state she should have gone for the cheap nylon mix but she thought of loveless Ella sitting on the bed without a comb and chose two brushed-cotton full-length nightdresses with pansies printed on them, one in pink, one in blue. Ignoring the nagging worry about money, she picked up a comb, a bar of soap in a fancy box, a matching tub of talc and a lavender washbag from the same set. They had a small makeup display and she chose a blister-packed eyeliner pencil for Ella to draw her eyebrows on with. She tried not to look when the assistant tallied it up, and paid for it with a card.

The nurse smiled at her as she came up the corridor for the second time. 'Your brother's already here,' she said, and smiled wider when she saw the expensive department-store bag.

Si was sitting exactly where he had been the day before, at the foot of the bed, watching Ella lying still, as if he was guarding her, waiting for her to try something so he could jump up and stop her. He turned and greeted Maureen with a glance that took in skirt and blouse. She saw a smile flicker in his eyes. Si had either left before the post arrived this morning or hadn't realized that she was the Maureen O'Donnell named on the small claims letter. He thought she had dressed up to please him. He turned back to Ella, who was looking at her feet again.

'Hi again,' said Maureen, keeping it breezy, 'I got ye some nighties. And a wee washbag.' She sat down next to Ella on the bed, facing Si, and pulled out the soap, comb and talc. 'Nice to have nice smells,' she said, smiling at him, presenting no threat.

Ella reached into the bag and pulled out the Cellophane bag with one of the nighties in it. Slowly she peeled open the glued-down strip at the back and worked her hand into the bag, feeling the soft material.

Maureen nodded and smiled patronizingly. 'D'ye like that, Ella?'

Ella nodded.

'Will we get ye out of that paper thing now?'

Ella nodded again, slowly. They both looked at Si. He stood up reluctantly, pushing the chair away noisily with the backs of his knees and left the room, purposefully leaving the door an inch ajar. Maureen stepped forward and shut the door properly. 'Can ye sit up, pet?' said Maureen, loud enough for Si to hear.

Ella managed to push herself forward from the pillows and Maureen undid the string ties at the back of her gown. Beneath her gold chain, her bruised back was emerald-green tinged with blue, like badly spoiled meat. 'What the fuck's going on here?' she whispered.

Ella let her broken teeth fall into her hand. Her cheeks collapsed and she looked up at Maureen, crying, as afraid as the child with no eyes in Maureen's hall cupboard. 'Get me the fuff out of here,' she whimpered, cursing through flaccid lips.

Maureen crackled the Cellophane noisily. 'Here ye are. This'll be nicer for ye. That's nice and soft, isn't it?' she said loudly, and lowered her voice. 'What happened to you?'

'Please, God, get me out of here.'

Maureen faced her. 'Ella, listen to me: you'll be safe in here, there's nurses all over the place. What happened to you?'

'I fell.'

'Did ye fuck.'

'I fell. Don't tell anyone.'

Maureen lowered the neck of the nightdress over the old woman's head. 'If ye fell over why are ye worried I'll tell anyone?'

'I fell.'

Maureen had to take the drip-bag off the metal hook and thread it through the arm of the nightie carefully, guiding Ella's hand and arm after it. 'Ella,' she said, slipping the second arm in, 'are you dropping the small-claims case, then?'

Ella looked at the door. 'He doesn't even know about that yet.' Her face contorted in a panicked sob. 'He'll fucking kill me.'

A knock at the door stopped them dead. 'Won't be a moment,' called Maureen, in a stupid singsong voice. She pulled the sheet up, too embarrassed to smooth the nightie under Ella's bare backside, and sat on the bed.

The women composed themselves, Ella carefully slipping her broken teeth back in, fitting the snapped edges together and catching her breath. 'Please,' she whispered, watching the door, 'get me out of here.'

'Look, you're safe in here,' said Maureen. 'There's nothing—'

The door opened and Si came back in. 'Ooh,' he said, looking at the nightie pooled around his mother's waist, 'that's a nice one.'

The nurse with the auburn hair was chatting to a porter in the corridor but she broke off when she saw Maureen lingering there, waiting to catch her.

'Do you know what happened to her?' said Maureen, playing the concerned daughter. 'She won't talk about it. The nurse last night said she'd fallen over but it's both sides of her face.'

The nurse folded her arms. 'Don't you know?'

'I know she didn't fall.' Maureen folded her arms too.

'Didn't your brother tell you?'

Maureen looked at the floor. 'My brother and I don't talk, I'm afraid.'

The nurse nodded. 'I see, I see. Your mum was mugged, in her house.'

Maureen was sceptical. 'Shouldn't the police be told, then?'

The nurse didn't like her. 'The police have been up twice for a statement,' she said coldly. 'She couldn't tell them much. Luckily your brother was here to hold her hand.'

13
Let them

Angus was back in his room. The door was shut, the spy-hole open, meaning they could look in at him at any time. He listened for footfalls outside, for air moving in the corridor. Being perpetually on show required a condition of alertness, so much so that he had stopped swallowing his medication on alternate days. They gave everyone in here medication, to make them slow and malleable. Slo-mo pills to make the population manageable. He wanted to have been off everything before the case came up. He had things to do.

He lay on his bed, turned to the wall so that his face was hidden, and thought about her. Cheap clothes, hair tidied. If his friend did as he had promised Maureen would start to get the envelopes soon. He tried to imagine her looking at the pictures, the shock, the dismay, disgust even, perhaps being excited by it. Probably not. He rolled on to his back, tucking his hands behind his head, crossing his feet. There was a crack on his ceiling, a ragged pencil line coming from a corner. Cheap clothes, hair tidied, opening an envelope, and still a week to go before the court case. He knew what she was up to, knew what she was thinking. He could play her, make sure she said what he wanted her to say in the witness box. She was getting him out of here.

And after the trial, when he got out, the police would clamour to protect Maureen O'Donnell. They would form a cordon around her, a cushion to keep him away from her, to stop her being one of his girls. Angus looked at the cracked grey ceiling and allowed himself a wry smile. Let them.

14

Hello, Stranger

It was sweltering in the van. Leslie hadn't been able to find a shaded spot to park in and the black plastic seat burnt the back of Maureen's legs as she sat down. They opened both the windows and Leslie drove fast through the town, trying to whip up a breeze in the cab. Maureen told her that Ella might not have fallen over and about the nasty edge to Si.

'He's got a posh accent like mine,' said Maureen. Leslie smiled. 'Your accent's not that posh.'

'Yeah, but I don't talk like Home Gran, do I? I think he hit her.'

'Why?'

Maureen had promised not to tell anyone about the small claims. 'She kept asking me to get her out of the hospital. She's really scared of him. He's creepy, like, puts a sexual slant on everything, and he's angry . . .'

Leslie didn't look convinced or even interested, but then she was going home to a Saturday night of crying Cammy and fuss.

They were both covered in a sheen of sweat by the time they got to Garnethill. The road was lined on both sides with parked cars and Leslie had to stop in the street to drop her.

'Shouldn't you tell the police about the picture?'

'Nah,' said Maureen. 'They couldn't trace her and I don't want them up at my house.'

'The girl might be from Glasgow. It might be important.'

'Didn't ye see that Wonderland Club case on the news? Sixty men and each of them had handed over ten thousand pictures of kids for membership.'

'Well, it's up to you,' said Leslie, looking up at Maureen's window. 'Will you be all right up there?'

'Yeah,' said Maureen. 'I think Angus just wants to frighten me.' She took the bags out of the back of the van, leaving behind some fags for Leslie's traumatic weekend. She called through the van to her, 'I've left sixty fags here for ye, Leslie. Good luck tonight.'

'Cheers.'

She shut the back doors and Leslie drove off down the hill.

The moment Maureen looked up she knew something was wrong. Her close door was jammed open, lying flat against the wall. No one staying there ever did that. It wasn't a safe area and they had to keep the door shut all the time so that people thought they had a buzzer entry system. Someone who didn't belong there was inside.

Maureen looked at the floor inside the close. Sometimes when he washed the stairs Jim Maliano left the door open to dry them, but the floor was dry today and dusty. She stepped into the close, stopped at the foot of the stairs and listened, the sweat on her face and arms suddenly chill. The noise of TV game shows and the high, excited voices of sports commentators whistled under the neighbours' doors. She couldn't hear anyone in the close but felt the still air moving a few floors up, heard the gentle scuff of material brushing against material. Quietly, she walked up to the first landing and stopped. Someone was up there. An alarming trickle of sweat escaped from her hairline, startling her as it ran down her cheek. She raised her hand, patting her face audibly, and the presence above her shifted at the noise.

She considered going down again and slipping out the back. She listened. They weren't all the way upstairs, they weren't outside her door. The close had eight flats in it, they could be visiting anyone. She heard sudden footsteps, someone falling from foot to foot, coming towards her quickly, just round the corner.

He was watching his feet as he walked and his dark hair appeared before the rest of him. He looked up at her. 'Hiya,' he said simply.

Maureen dropped the bag and a deep, joyous laugh gurgled up from her belly, an intoxicating blend of relief and delight. 'Vik Patak, you gorgeous bastard. How the fuck are you?'

It was tea-time. Beyond the drawn red velvet curtains Saturday traffic passed noisily a few blocks down, leaving the city centre to catch its breath before the evening began. A soft light seeped in through the heavy curtains, the blue sky casting a pink and yellow sheen on the ceiling. Somewhere in Garnethill, beyond the bedroom window, a bird was hollering. Maureen stretched out, arching her back off the bed and grinning to herself. Vik caught a curl of Maureen's dark hair on his toe and tugged it playfully. She looked at him, still smiling. 'Ye okay?' he said.

'Oh, aye.' Wondering at skin so soft, Maureen placed her fingertips on his bare hip, the skin slick to the bone. She traced the tight dip of powder skin before the small swell of his belly. She didn't even want a drink. 'I'm glad you came to see me,' she said.

Vik rolled to face her, resting his head on her thighs. 'Shan told me about that Farrell guy's trial coming up. I came to see if you're all right.'

'I'm fine,' she said, resenting the intrusion of reality into the handsome moment. 'Has Shan been called as a witness?'

'No, but he'll be there.'

Vik's cousin, Shan Ryan, had been a nurse in the Rainbow Clinic. He knew about Angus, had put the pieces together himself. He and Douglas had been swithering about what to do when Douglas was murdered. She didn't want to think about that just now. 'It's nice to see ye again, Vik.'

'You could have phoned me,' he said reproachfully.

'I could have, I wanted to, but I didn't think it would be fair.'

'Why not?'

She was a shit girlfriend, she knew she was, but she didn't know how to say it without sounding as though she was prompting a denial or looking for reassurance. 'Dunno, just, I'm a bit distracted. 'S not very fair on you.'

'You didn't seem very distracted a minute ago. You were concentrating pretty hard every time I looked at ye.'

They smiled lazily at each other.

'It's amazing, isn't it?' said Maureen softly. 'There's a point when you'd sell your soul for a come and then two seconds afterwards you can't really remember what happened, but the world isn't half as bad as it seemed before and the light's different and everyone means well.'

'God's own medicine,' said Vik.

She looked at him. 'I like it that you don't make things into a drama.'

Vik knew what she really meant, that she didn't want a scene or heartfelt declarations. 'I do, sometimes.'

They looked at each other. The last time they had met like this it was winter, they had been boyfriend and girl-friend, going out, meeting his friends. She hadn't liked it. Thinking back honestly, she wasn't used to making all the compromises normal dating required. Because Douglas had been married she could tell him to fuck off when he annoyed her, and he'd still come back. She could refuse to see him when she didn't feel like it and still maintain the moral high ground. She could indulge herself because mistresses have few duties. She wondered if Sheila was right, if it was just petulance and immaturity on her part that made a relationship seem impossible. Being brutal with herself, she thought it probably was. 'Vik, I'm still not up for the whole, full-on relationship.'

He placed his hand on her stomach, softly pressing the flat tips of his fingers into the skin, one after the other, as if he was playing her. 'It's all right,' he said. 'I've just had one of those.'

'Oh.' It hadn't occurred to her that he might have been off with someone else.

'Other women do find me attractive, ye know.'

'I know.' She nodded over and over. 'I know.'

'Tell me you haven't been out with other guys.'

She shrugged nonchalantly, said, 'Oh, yeah, yeah,' and gave herself away. She hadn't been out with anyone, hadn't fancied anyone or thought of anyone but him.

When she looked up he was smiling and pleased. 'I like that,' he said.

'Fuck off.'

But he was still smiling. 'If ye haven't been out on the ran-dan with loads of hunky men what have ye been doing? Have ye been going to art galleries?'

She smiled back at him 'Naw, God, I haven't done that in a while.'

'But you love looking at art.'

'I know, I should—'

'Ye should make time.'

'I should,' she said.

'My wee cousin takes me to exhibitions all the time and

I kept expecting to see you there. She's training to be a curator.'

'How do ye train to be a curator?'

'Master's course in Belfast. She gets in everywhere free. You should do that.'

'I've got a job,' she said, and smiled ruefully, imagining herself in a big suit, with a CV and prospects.

'What's your job?'

'I sell drugs to schoolchildren.'

Vik looked at her, half believing, until she reached across the bed and picked up her cigarettes, shaking them at him. 'Down at Paddy's,' she said, and he smiled.

They sat up, Vik shuffling around on the bed so they were sitting next to each other, bare hip to bare hip, looking out of the three-inch space between the red velvet curtains. 'If you could look at any painting in the world,' he said, 'what would it be and where is it?'

'Good one.' Maureen nodded, savouring the challenge. 'The *Demoiselles d'Avignon*, in New York, or Matisse's *Arab Coffeehouse* in the Hermitage.'

'Why the *Coffeehouse* one?'

'I dunno, because it's so still. If you could see anyone play, who, where and when?'

'Obviously Elvis in Vegas, early seventies.'

'Not the Las or the Birthday Party?'

'Nah, I like hearing about their gigs but I wouldn't want to have been there.'

She put the ashtray on the bed and reached over to light his cigarette.

'That's my lighter,' he said, holding her hand and looking at it.

'Yeah, you left it here that last time.'

'You kept it.'

'Yeah.' She felt embarrassed. 'It's a good lighter.'

'No, it's not, it's crap. The flint chimney's too wide. I thought I'd lost it.'

She dropped it into his hand, ashamed of how much store she'd set on it. 'Well,' she said briskly, 'you've got it back now.'

He smiled, lowering his head to look her in the face. 'Maureen, did you do something romantic?'

She pulled her chin away. 'What?' she said, sounding huffy. 'Found your lighter?'

Vik took a draw on his cigarette, gazing out of the window. 'You like me,' he muttered at the curtains. 'You like me, ya sneaky wee bird.'

They sat smoking and smiling at the window, listening to children calling to each other in the street, the summer birds shouting and cars speeding past up the steep hill. She looked at his shoulder, a perfect sphere with dimples where the tendons attached the muscle to the bone. Two long dark hairs stuck out to the side like symbolic epaulettes. He had been sunbathing with his shirt off, and the skin on his chest was darker than usual, glistening. Vik looked at her. 'Are you going out tonight?'

'No,' she said, and immediately regretted it. Vik was in a band and had a large group of friends, none of whom she had anything to say to, none of whom had anything to say to her. She hated being a sidekick and sitting with the other girlfriends.

'Well,' said Vik, as Maureen calculated the relative excusing values of sudden sickness and a family trauma, 'how d'you fancy a picnic?'

'What kind of picnic?' she said stiffly.

'You and me up the hills. Nice food, bit of a smoke?'

'Just us?' she said hopefully.

'Yeah.'

'Your band aren't playing Hampden tonight, then?'

He stubbed out his fag in the ashtray. 'Not tonight, no.'

The Campsie Brae is a steep ridge overlooking the city from the south side. It was as close to the country as Maureen had been for a long time. They skinned up and smoked on the way over, keeping the windows up on Vik's Mini so that the car functioned as a giant bong. By the time they arrived they were giggly. Cars, large and small, old and new, were stopped along the dark country road, seeming abandoned until the headlights hit steamed-up rear windscreens and picked out shadows inside. Vik drove out on to the brae, moving away from an epileptic Honda Accord and over to the far side of the ridge. Below them lay the city, a carpet of yellow and red lights under a black sky. In the foreground were the high towers and small windows of Castlemilk housing scheme. As Vik stopped the car and pulled on the handbrake, the headlights picked out the nose of a shopping trolley thrown beyond the ridge. He tutted. 'This isn't the country, this is the city with nae hooses.'

Maureen grinned and handed Vik his bag of chips and gravy. 'This is as close to the real country as I like to get,' she said.

'Why?'

'It's scary out there. There's no lights and the shops are rubbish.'

They laughed loud and long because they were spliffed, they'd just had sex three times, and they were together.

She sat up in the bed, watching him settle into sleep. It was too hot even for a sheet and his elbows were tucked into his sides, his hands modestly hiding his nipples, his cock lolling to the side when he shifted his legs. She said a soft good-night to the child in the cupboard, feeling safe because Vik was here. As she looked at him she remembered all the transient boyfriends who had bridged the lonely gap between hard nights and harsh mornings. Still asleep, Vik's hand fumbled anxiously to find hers and hold it. Tenderness on the hinterland of intimacy.

15
Nightie

As Maureen woke up her first thought was of Ella, lying in the bed in the Albert with the sheet over her mouth and her red, vacant eyes. She sat up slowly, trying not to wake Vik. Yellow splinters of morning sun prickled around the heavy curtain and the air felt warm and sticky. She slid out of bed and went to the loo. Si'd be there again today, staring at Ella, frightening her, bullying his seventy-year-old mother. Maureen wanted to go and visit again, just to show him that Ella had a pal, someone who'd cross the town to see if she was okay. Back in the kitchen she made two cups of coffee and realized that she didn't know what Vik took in his. She made an approximation of all the coffee variations: a bit of powdered milk and one big sugar, leaving it unstirred so that he could drink the first half of the cup if he didn't take it.

Vik was still asleep, snoring gently, his face loose, his big hands clasped together on his stomach. She put the cups down on the side table and climbed back on to the bed, stroking his bristled cheek with her fingertips. 'Wake up, Vik,' she whispered softly. 'Your mum's here and she's absolutely furious.'

Vik was awake and sitting bolt upright within three seconds.

The day seemed especially bright as Vik drove her across town to the Albert. The white light breezed lazily, deflecting into the shadows, melting the sharp edges of the buildings. Maureen felt normal, sitting in the nice car with her handsome boyfriend and her formal clothes on again. She imagined being seen from the outside by some mystery viewer. She'd look happy, at peace, loved and cosseted, like a real person with a life and a future.

The smell of smoke and gravy lingered inside the Mini. They wound the windows down and sang along to Aretha's 'Natural Woman'. The song was miles out of both their ranges and they squeaked and growled, stopping and catching the tune whenever they could. The roads were quiet and Vik parked outside the hospital, switched Aretha off and turned to look at her. 'Are you sure about the records?' he said, nodding to the stacks in the back seat. Maureen had given him her record collection. Her record-player was broken and she wanted to get the dusty, pointless piles out of the house.

'Aye,' she said.

'I'll give them back to ye later, if ye like.'

'I don't think I'm going to want them.'

'They're not all shit.'

They smiled at each other.

'I'm sorry,' he said, and paused. 'I'm sorry things are the way they are with you. Ye seem happier.'

Maureen didn't want to remember any of that when she was with him. 'Mibbi I am. Will ye come and see me again?'

'Well, Shan and I are coming to the trial next week.'

'But will ye come and see me afterwards, just yourself?'

Vik raised a salacious eyebrow. 'Listen,' he said, 'after the welcome I got last night, an Ebola quarantine wouldn't keep me away.'

Through the open doorway to Ward G Maureen saw a young man in a suit in the centre of the ward hammering out a plodding rendition of 'Nearer My God To Thee' on an electronic keyboard. She remembered the holy rollers coming round her ward at the Northern on Sundays; and a particular Sunday when Angie, the tiny woman in the bed next to her, emptied a bottle of Lucozade into a box of Bibles.

Maureen tried to remember how she had been with Si McGee. He would have received the small claims letter and she didn't know what she could say about it. She could pretend it hadn't happened, hope Ella had owned up during a warm chat with her son, but it didn't seem very likely. It was just a mix-up and she was the cheery mug from the market. Getting into character, she speeded up her walk and made her way to the nurses' station. There was no one there. A hot cup of tea sat on the wooden desk, burning a damp ring-stain into the surface. The door to Ella's room was firmly shut. Maureen took a deep breath, remembering who she was meant to be, knocked briskly and opened it. Ella's bed was empty, the blankets neatly folded on the end. The windows were open to air the room. Maureen turned to find the nurse standing behind her. 'Has she gone?'

Disconcerted, the nurse took Maureen by the elbow, holding her quite tightly, guiding her firmly towards the station. Thinking she was in trouble for passing herself off as Ella's daughter, Maureen tried to act surprised and confused. Si must have found out and corrected the nurses. But they could hardly arrest her for that. She hadn't said she was the daughter, she just hadn't contradicted the nurse.

The nurse sat Maureen down and asked whether she would like a cup of tea, pointing at the steaming cup to illustrate the tricky concept. Maureen refused it nervously. Behind the nurse, standing upright between a filing cabinet and the wall, was a polythene bag and sitting on the top was the blue nightie Maureen had bought for Ella. 'Wait a minute,' said Maureen, 'where is she?'

The nurse sat down heavily on the chair. 'I am so sorry,' she said, taking Maureen's hand. Her hands were damp and smelt of Dettol. 'We didn't have a number for you and your brother couldn't give us one. I'm afraid your mother died yesterday.'

'She's dead?'

'I'm afraid so. I'm sorry.'

The door opened behind them and the sullen beardy nurse took two steps into the room. 'Oh,' he said, startled and staring at their clasped hands. 'Sorry.' He backed into the corridor and shut the door.

'She was all right yesterday,' breathed Maureen.

'Are you sure you wouldn't like a cup of tea?'

'What happened?'

'She slipped away yesterday.'

Maureen tore her hand from the nurse's. 'What the fuck are you talking about? She was all right yesterday.'

'Her heart ...' the nurse looked confused '... failed. It can happen in older people.'

'What – they just stop living?' said Maureen angrily. 'That's it? Is that what you're saying?'

'Maybe you should speak to the doctor,' the nurse said, and moved to stand up.

Maureen grabbed her by the wrist, holding it tight. 'When did this happen?'

The nurse looked alarmed. 'In the afternoon.'

'What time?'

'After four, before teas at five. Please let go of me.'

Maureen released her wrist. 'Was he here?' she said quietly.

The nurse was bewildered. 'Who?'

'*Was he here?*'

The nurse clasped her hands on her lap and looked at them. 'Yes,' she said quietly. 'He was with her when it happened, with his wife.'

'His wife?' Maureen hadn't thought of Si as married. 'Are you doing a post-mortem?'

'Why?' said the nurse, looking up sharply.

'Could he have smothered her?' said Maureen. 'Could he have poisoned her?'

'Look, I'm not in a position to say,' said the nurse carefully, realizing she had stumbled into the middle of a bad family feud.

'How do I get a post-mortem done on her?'

'Maybe you should speak to the doctor about your mother. He'll be back on in an hour.'

'You listen to me,' said Maureen, leaning across the desk, pointing in the nurse's face. 'I'm going to phone the police and if I find out that her body has been released to him I'll hold you personally responsible.' She turned and opened the door.

'It's nothing to do with me,' said the nurse anxiously. 'It's not even my department. Don't ye want to see her?' Maureen was suddenly calm. 'Yeah. Yeah, I do.'

She had to wait in a converted cupboard, sipping sweet milky tea that someone had forced into her hand. The department-store poly-bag sat against her ankle. Si had left everything she had bought for Ella. She was in the bowels of the hospital, deep in the earth, three floors below the lobby. The artificial lighting was bright and, despite the insistent heating, the walls still smarted damp and cold. Maureen was only wearing a vest and jungle shorts and her arms were covered in goosebumps. They would never have let her see Ella's body if they didn't think she was her daughter. Ella's real daughter couldn't have come to see her at all. She sat forward, bending over her knees, wishing she could smoke. Si'd had his wife with him. Maybe he was married to the foreign woman Ella had mentioned when they were filling in the form. She tried to remember whether he had a wedding ring on his finger but couldn't.

A small black man with tidy features stuck his head around the door. He wore a white coat with bulging pockets and wire-framed glasses. 'Hello there. Would you like to come through and see Ella now?' His voice was low, and Maureen appreciated the thought that had gone into reading the toe-tag before he came through.

He led Maureen across a hallway, unlocked a small door and took her through a narrow corridor to the Chapel of Rest. Designed to offend no one's religious sensibilities, the chapel had none of the symbols that would have made sense of it. There were no crosses in the room, no doves, no crescents, just a red and white stained-glass lamp, a narrow shelf with a bunch of silk flowers on it and a trolley, prettied up with a sheet.

The sheet was folded down under Ella's chin, tucked in tight as if to hold her in place. The plaster cast had been cut off her leg. Her eyebrows were still missing, her hair brushed back flat against her head. She looked like a venerable old gentleman. Her arms were by her sides, the gold necklace was missing, presumably in Si's pocket. Her teeth were in her mouth and Maureen could see where her lip curled up that the break had been stuck together with clear glue. The soft light made her look restful.

Ella's own daughter hadn't come to see her. Maureen didn't imagine Ella had been a particularly good mother, but no one had mentioned Si's father. Ella had stayed and done all the work, just like Winnie. Maureen thought of Winnie lying there, with everything unsaid between them, nothing resolved. Winnie had stayed and brought them up.

Maureen wanted to reach out and pick Ella up, wrap her arms around the pushy old woman and stroke her hair, pet away all the grief and sorrow. Lying in the simple room on a cold table, Ella looked like a monument to the forgotten constancy of women.

'Here ye are,' said the wee man, handing her a crumpled tissue.

'Thanks,' said Maureen, wiping away selfish tears.

The little man stuck his hands into his pockets and rocked on his feet, thinking about it, choosing his words carefully. 'We did a post-mortem. We have to, if people die in hospital. She died of a heart-attack.'

'Oh,' she said, and sniffed. 'You're very nice to tell me that.'

'Aye,' said the man firmly. 'I am very nice.'

Maureen looked at him and snorted a laugh, blowing her nose on her face by accident. 'Oh, God, I'm sorry,' she said, and holding the inadequate single hankie up to her face. 'That's disgusting.'

The man dug in his pockets for more tissues. 'I work in a morgue, hen,' he said kindly. 'It takes more than snotters to get me sick.'

Maureen cleaned her face and the man stayed with her while she looked at Ella again. 'Is he taking her home?'

'I don't think so,' said the man. 'She's just going straight to the crematorium.'

Si had made his confirmation, he knew what he was doing. He was leaving Ella here among the dead, with no one to say the rosary for her, no friends or family to hold a wake and fend the devil from her soul until the blessing of the mass. Maureen didn't suppose that Ella had been especially devout – the truly ardent are rarely secretive about it – but in death the old traditions are more than religious observances. The wake is a measure of attachment, when friends and family can prove themselves by reciting tedious prayers for love. And after the prayers the sum of a life and a character, the stories they generate, can be told over and over. Taking the body home meant that even in death someone would claim you for their own. Ella McGee might never have been here at all. Maureen tried to think her way through a decade of the rosary but she couldn't even remember who Mary was blessed among. She blinked back a second wave of tears. 'Can I put some makeup on her?' she said.

The man looked at her for a moment. 'It's nothing daft, is it?'

'I want to draw her eyebrows in, she always had eyebrows.'

'Sure. Just make sure ye don't push her about too much. Want me to leave ye alone?'

She shook her head. 'I'd rather ye stayed.'

She used the comb from the poly-bag and backcombed the front of Ella's yellowed fringe into a little halo, smoothing it with the comb. She took out the unused eyeliner pencil and pulled off the packaging. It was black, not dark brown like Ella always wore, but she did her best and drew the arched eyebrows on her forehead. Because she was leaning over the body, the far-away eyebrow was a little higher than the other, making Ella look faintly indignant. Maureen thought suddenly that the morgue man would think this was a daft thing to do to a corpse, that she was making the body look ridiculous.

'She did do that,' she said, pointing to Ella's forehead as she stood back. 'I'm not just drawing all over her . . .'

She stepped close to Ella again, reaching out to correct the eyebrow, but realized that she would be smearing dead skin. It wasn't disgust so much as not knowing how a dead person's skin would react. If she pressed too hard it might just fall off. She was standing on tiptoe, looking at the body indecisively, and her eye fell on Ella's right hand. It had a deep cut on it where the bandage had been, right through the skin; she could actually see a glint of silver through the hole. It was open like a wordless mouth. 'Where did that come from?'

The man stood up and looked at the hand. 'Aye,' he said, 'that was funny. She had that when she came in. It was about a week before she died. She told the nurses she cut herself in the kitchen. We thought she did it herself, it looked kind of deliberate.'

'Why would she do it herself?' said Maureen.

He looked at Ella's face uncertainly. 'Well,' he said, 'how could ye do that by accident?' He held up his hand and used the other to mime a stab motion. He had to hold his splayed hand away from himself, his thumb pointing at his feet. 'It's awkward, isn't it?'

'Could someone else have done it to her?' said Maureen, holding her splayed hand up in front of her face as if protecting herself.

'Aye, but why wouldn't she say?' The man reached round to his back pocket and held out a battered tin hip flask, watching her face to see if it was all right. She smiled hopefully and he unscrewed the lid, letting out the sweet smell of good whisky into the disinfected room. He gave her the first slug and she took a drink, giving back the flask.

'Are you sure it couldn't have happened when they were resuscitating her?'

The man shook his head. 'They didn't give her resus,' he said quietly. 'She was down in her notes as "Not For Resuscitation".'

'Really?'

'Yeah.' He looked at her slyly. 'I thought you'd know that.'

'Why would I?'

"Cause it says on the notes that the doctor discussed it

with the family.' He looked at her, knowing that she wasn't family and had no business being there.

Maureen shrugged at him and he gave a little shrug back. They sat down on the bench and the man took a tiny nip of whisky and exhaled appreciatively, raising the flask to the corpse in front of them.

'Poor Ella,' said Maureen, feeling awkward.

'Aye,' he said, handing the flask to her.

Maureen swallowed. 'She did do her eyebrows like that, honest.'

'Aye, well.' He took the flask back from her and upended it, swallowing three mouthfuls and exhaling appreciatively. 'I think she looks lovely.'

16

Hugh

The hot night had a frantic atmosphere: too many people out, too much effort made, like a teenage party that would end in tears. A drunk couple walked past, huddled together, eating from the same bag of chips, leaving a vapour trail of hot vinegar. Maureen leaned against a shuttered shop front and watched two women on the other side of the street laughing and pulling each other around by their handbags. She didn't know why Hugh had insisted on meeting her but she was nervous. She'd had a bit of a drink in the house before she came out to steady herself. He'd be coming down the hill, coming from his work at Stewart Street police station.

She lit a cigarette as she waited, thinking about the wee girl in the photograph and Ella McGee. She felt a familiar anaesthetizing despair at a world full of unchecked bullies, like Michael and the crying girl's photographer and creepy Si. The thought of Si made Maureen feel angry again. Maybe she'd go to the small claims case instead of Ella – she'd signed the papers, after all. If he started any of his shit with Maureen she'd be ready for him. Mentally rehearsing punching him in the face, over and over like a stuck computer game, she felt a rush of adrenaline and the muscles on her back tighten. The punched face began to toggle between Si and Michael, getting faster and faster. She realized that Hugh's arrival was imminent and she had to calm down. She took a deep drag on her cigarette and leaned forward, thinking of Vik driving the car and how normal and happy they must have looked.

Hugh McAskill was walking down the hill towards her. He waved when he saw her and she walked towards him, glad she had her shades to hide behind, taking deep breaths to make the anger subside. She greeted him with a coy elbow nudge.

'How are ye?' he said, frowning uncomfortably, as if she had tricked him into coming.

'Aye,' she said, hoping it wasn't going to be a heavy night, 'fine. Nice night. How are ye yourself?'

'Fine.' Hugh glanced around, nodding her into step with him. 'Let's get some grub.'

They took the arcing pedestrian bridge over the motorway and went in search of a great Glasgow curry.

Hugh suggested the Indian Trip restaurant: he said he'd been a number of times with his wife and the food was good. He still wasn't letting on about the purpose of the meeting but Maureen had a feeling she wasn't going to like it. 'It's always busy,' said Hugh, filling the ponderous conversational space. 'We'll be lucky to get a table.'

But she didn't want to eat: she just wanted to hear what he had to say and go somewhere and get pissed alone.

The area they were walking through was too near to the town to be residential. Not yet the coveted West End, it was a transient area of cheap hotels peopled by disappointed businessmen and twenty-four-hour shops. Great sweeping Georgian terraces were deserted or chopped up into mean little offices. One block away was Kelvingrove Park, midnight home to homosexual encounter groups and muggers. Si McGee's business was around here. Maureen imagined the ghost of Home Gran across the road somewhere, mopping up in a gym or hoovering at reception. Maybe that's where she'd got the inspiration to wear tracksuits all the time.

When they got to the restaurant Hugh asked the waiter for a table upstairs. It was a strangely shaped room, an angular rhomboid with dark walls and windows on two sides looking down the length of Sauchiehall Street. Yellow and red car lights traced the line of the long road. A soft breeze whispered through the open window, whipped up by passing lorries and buses.

They ordered and the waiter jotted in his notebook as he backed away from them. Maureen and Hugh both felt uneasy at the intimate surroundings: it felt like the start of a reluctant love affair between desperately unhappy people. Hugh kept his eyes on the road, sitting back in the shadows, out of view of the street. The food came quickly. Maureen looked out of the window as the sun set low over the road and ate a mouthful of bindi bhaji. The aromatic flavour and slow-heat aftertaste were lost on her. She didn't want to eat.

'How's the bindi?' asked Hugh, gnawing his way through tandoori chicken, getting the red food colouring over his mouth and chin.

She sipped her lager to clear her mouth. 'Nice. A man came to my door the other night,' she said, 'and gave me a citation.'

'For Farrell's trial?'

'I don't want to go but he said I have to.'

Hugh picked up his shandy. 'He's right,' he said, sipping and swallowing. 'You do have to.'

The restaurant was busy, and around them tables of men and women chatted and laughed together, oblivious to the crying girl in Maureen's cupboard.

'Are they going to ask me about the letters?'

'No,' said Hugh. 'The letters aren't relevant any more.'

He chewed between the parallel bones on a wing. A small

yellow lump of fat, tinged red at the edge, fell on to the table. Maureen frowned. The whole point of Angus Farrell sending the letters to her had been to help prove his insanity. 'I thought he'd use them to prove he's insane?'

'No,' said Hugh certainly. 'They had a hearing six months ago and found him insane but he's better now. The drugs have worn off.'

Maureen didn't understand. She was sure that was why Angus had sent the letters. 'Is he saying he's guilty, then?' she asked.

Hugh put down the pared bone, cleaned his chin with his napkin and leaned across to her. 'No.' He didn't seem to want to add anything to it.

Maureen wondered why he had asked her here and wished he'd get on with it. She abandoned her dinner and took out a cigarette under the table so that Hugh wouldn't see the duty-free packet. She used Vik's disposable lighter and inhaled deeply. 'The citation guy, he said I'd go to jail if I don't turn up.'

'He's right,' said Hugh.

'That's not very fair,' she said. 'You can't jail people for being frightened.'

Hugh held up his hand. 'Wait a minute,' he said slowly, 'it's not the police who do that. Anyway, if no one had to give evidence no one would ever go to jail. There'd be a lot more frightened people around.'

Maureen drew on her fag and pushed strands of bindi around her plate, glancing up at Hugh, who had gone back to eating his chicken.

'This is nice,' he said. 'D'you want to try a bit?'

'What if I go but refuse to answer certain questions?'

'They'll put you in jail to consider your position,' said Hugh, looking up at her through his red eyebrows, warning her not to disappear.

'Is there nothing I can do about it?'

Hugh picked a lump of clear gristle out of his mouth and laid it on the side of his plate. 'Just go and tell the truth, Maureen. That's the smart thing to do.'

Maureen laughed bitterly. 'The smart thing?'

'Maureen, the legal system has been coercing reluctant witnesses for over a thousand years. You're not going to think up anything they haven't come across before.'

Maureen drew on her cigarette again and reminded herself that none of it had happened yet. It was all in the future. She kicked him gently under the table. 'How are you, anyway? Why weren't you at the survivors' meeting on Thursday?'

'Work. How was it?'

'Aw, ye fairly missed yourself.' She flicked her ash on to the floor. 'Colin was very sad, Alex was very angry, and I was very confused.'

Hugh smiled sadly. 'That sounds ... uplifting. Sheila told me you went back to her house for a cup of tea.' He was building up to ask her about Michael.

'So, how's your head this week?' she asked, heading him off at the pass.

'Fine. D'you not want to talk about it with me, Maureen?'

She thought of Vik lying on her bed, his burnished skin, and the sheet slipping off the dip on his hip. 'Not just now, no.'

Hugh looked out of the window. The eggshell skin beneath his eyes flushed blue to match his watery eyes. 'Well, what do you want to talk about?' He sounded annoyed, as if she was cutting him out, as if she'd invited him here on false pretences. A table behind them was getting out of hand, overexcited and noisy.

Maureen looked out of the window with Hugh, trying

to make it the two of them together again. 'Where's the gym around here?'

'There's no gym around here,' he snapped.

She blinked long and hard. 'I'm entitled not to talk about this.'

'I know, I know,' he nodded, 'I'm just tired, I'm worried.'

'Sheila shouldn't have repeated what I said to her, you know.'

'And I shouldn't be here with you,' said Hugh, under his breath, watching the road in case he was seen. 'I shouldn't be here with a witness in an upcoming trial but I'm worried. Don't do anything to your dad, Maureen. You've got to keep your nose clean.' He looked up at her. 'Please, don't do anything. I can contact the Social Work for you. I'll pick your dad up, me and the guys'll give him a kicking in the back of a van and warn him, but please, don't do anything.'

The image of Hugh kicking Michael in the back of a van pleased her. Hugh, holding the crescent moon aloft, lifting his leg sadly but justly, and a withered, vanquished Michael on the floor at his feet. 'Why do I have to keep my nose clean?'

'Look, Joe McEwan thinks Farrell's getting off because of you. He fucking hates you, he's hell-bent on getting you for something.'

She sat back. 'Joe thinks he'll get off?'

'There is a chance. Because of the acid and other stuff. There isn't that much evidence, really. We'll be lucky to get a conviction on Douglas Brady. It really depends on Martin Donegan's case being proved successfully.'

'Fuck,' said Maureen simply.

Hugh furrowed his eyebrows. 'Fuck's an understatement.'

'And I'm getting the blame?'

'I'm afraid so.'

The colour had drained from Hugh's face and she noticed

134

for the first time that the whites of his eyes looked dry and yellow. 'Are you well, Hugh?'

Leaning his elbow on the table, Hugh rubbed his face. 'No,' he said quietly, 'I'm not. I'm tired and this heat makes me feel sick.'

'I think you should go home and get some rest,' she said, signalling to the waiter for the bill, hoping they'd never be this intimate again.

Outside the night was humid and rank. Dark currents flowed down the road as night swirled into the city. A drunk man was staggering across the road towards them, shouting at the sky, shaking his fist at ghosts. A crowd passed him and a heavily made-up woman bent double, bawling at the man that he was fucked in the head, her voice cracking, her boyfriend dragging her away by the arm.

'The city's crazy when it's hot,' said Hugh, pulling on his jacket. 'Some poor bastard's gonnae get it tonight.'

He said he'd walk her home to Garnethill but she wanted to get away from him and said she'd planned to visit Kilty who lived in the opposite direction. She wanted to tell Kilty about Vik and have a girlie squeal and feel normal. Hugh insisted she get a taxi but she didn't have the money and knew he'd try to give it to her if she said so. She hailed a cab and climbed in, waving to Hugh, trying to look cheery and untroubled as the taxi drove away, calling out of the open window that she'd see him on Thursday. The cab drove a block and turned the corner. 'Can ye let me out here, driver?'

Watching her resentfully in the rear-view mirror, the driver went further down the road than he needed to, adding twenty pence to the meter before pulling over.

Maureen took off her jacket, tied it around her waist and walked. The ragged blue remnant of the day lingered on the horizon. Following the tree-lined avenue that led through the centre of the park, she passed a small clearing set around a high statue of a forgotten military hero being brave on a horse. Three young men stood talking to each other in the shadows, smoking. They watched her pass, angry eyes sliding to the side, watching her because she was watching them. Slow cars glided up and down the avenue and guilty-looking men walked quickly by, staring at the pavement in front of them.

Joe McEwan would never let her go. If she did anything to Michael, Joe would make sure that she paid for it. She didn't want to spend the next ten years in jail, she didn't want to sit in an ugly cell, smoking wee fags and being told what to do, least of all for Michael. She took a deep breath and looked up. She hadn't done anything yet, not yet. She took a right and headed for Kilty's house at the Botanic Gardens.

When she had first come back from London, Kilty lived in Maureen's sitting room. In all that time Maureen had never fathomed her, never identified a consistent pattern of behaviour, could never anticipate her. When they first met, Maureen thought Kilty had no chip on her shoulder and found it incredibly refreshing. As they grew closer Maureen realized that Kilty's chips were of a different shape and size, invisible to her because they weren't familiar, but they were there. Kitty had a horror of marrying well and living near the country. She was a mesmerizingly odd woman, tiny and slim with features that should have made her ugly – buggy eyes and thin hair – but she looked exotic and beautiful.

The morning Kilty's parents arrived, unannounced, to visit them in Garnethill they were unable to hide their shock and disappointment. It was a Sunday morning and Maureen was wearing the dressing-gown Kilty had given her. It was an antique, a rotting apricot silk thing with a scary stain on the hem and a rip on the arm that Kilty insisted had happened during a tangoing incident in Rio. Maureen went to get dressed and when she came back Mrs Goldfarb asked her what the stains on the living-room floorboards were. Maureen said that it was a spill of balsamic vinegar from a salad she had been serving to friends. Mr Goldfarb remarked that it must have been a very big salad: the vinegar had spilled everywhere.

Her parents had bought Kilty a flat as an inducement to get her out of the poky house in the bad area. Kilty refused to go house-hunting with them. They chose a flat near to the children's home where she was working and had to blackmail her into coming to look at it. She had made Maureen come with her.

Maureen gushed about the flat, but it wasn't hard. Despite being decorated by a lilac-lover it had definite possibilities. It was in a well-preserved Victorian tenement and overlooked the large glass dome of the Botanic Gardens, illuminated at night like a giant luminous mushroom. The windows were floor to ceiling and the rooms large and plain. Kilty accepted her parents' gift, and Maureen and Liam helped her paint every bit of the flat white over one long weekend. Kilty lifted the carpets and lino from the floors, varnished the bare boards and filled it with sturdy utility furniture.

Maureen looked up at the living-room window. It was dark but she thought she could make out the flickering blue light from a television. She crossed the road, climbed the stairs to the door and pressed the buzzer. Kilty's voice crackled over the intercom. She yipped when she heard it was Maureen and released the door. As Maureen climbed the steep stairs she saw Kilty hanging out of the storm doors to her flat, dressed in gigantic stripy pyjama bottoms and a *Charlie's Angels* T-shirt.

'Hiya,' called Kilty, as Maureen wearily climbed the stairs. 'There's a scare-u-mentary on about sharks and I've got a bottle of gin.'

Maureen broke into a sprint.

17

Birth

Una's fingernails were pressing hard, digging into the drum of Alistair's thumb, piercing the skin. 'Bastard,' said Una. 'You shitty, shitty bastard.'

'Breathe,' he said.

The midwife smirked to herself as she checked the monitors. 'I expect they told you to expect this in the classes.' She smiled at Alistair across Una's belly. 'I hated my hubby when I was in labour. Doesn't seem fair when you're in all that pain.'

Una's contraction ebbed away and she gasped for a deep breath. She stared up at the midwife, holding Alistair's hand just as tightly as she had been when the contraction was coming. 'He left me,' said Una loudly, concentrating hard to speak as another contraction hit, 'for my neighbour. When I was three months pregnant.' She lost her breath to the contraction and turned red, her face contorting. She was holding Alistair's hand so hard that her fingernails buckled against his skin. He began to bleed.

It was half four in the morning and the maternity unit was quiet. Across the corridor, sitting in the waiting room, Winnie O'Donnell dabbed her eyes and prayed to a distant god. Dear God, she prayed, please, God, if there is a God, don't let it be a girl. She took out the Alcoholics Anonymous card and reread the serenity prayer. She'd have to pray for acceptance if it was a girl, but it might not come to that. Please, God, thy will be done, not a girl, thy will be done.

Finding no comfort, she unclasped her hands and looked up. Behind the long window, dawn was breaking over Glasgow and Winnie's reflection was fading. She could see her outline, the white hanky to her face, and the doorway next to her leading into the bright corridor. Asleep in the seat next to her, George was drooling on to his chin, his big work-swollen hands clasped in his lap, his legs sprawled untidily in front of him. Una was across and two doors down, giving birth to Winnie's first grandchild. Winnie hung her head again. Please, God, don't let it be a girl.

She smelt him before she saw him. Michael was standing there, reeking of cheap lager and stale fags, holding on to the doorframe to steady himself. He looked at Winnie's fading reflection in the window, paused, then swung himself into a seat across the room. His forehead and nose were badly sunburnt and he was sweating. 'You're late,' said Winnie. 'He called you hours ago.'

'Aye,' he said. 'I'm here.' He was slurring heavily and seemed very drunk. Winnie envied him. He reached for his fag packet and took one out.

'Ye can't smoke in here,' said Winnie, but he ignored her and took his lighter from the other pocket. '*Ye can't smoke in here.*' She stood up, stepped towards him and smacked the fag from his mouth. Michael looked startled, as though he had forgotten she was there. '*You can't smoke in a hospital,*' she said, backing into her own chair.

'Hospital?' Michael seemed confused and looked to her for confirmation.

'Una,' said Winnie ferociously.

'Una?'

'She's having her baby.'

'Oh,' he nodded, 'Una. That's right. Una.'

George woke up, rubbing his face and blinking hard. 'Yes?' he said automatically.

Michael nodded at him and growled. George looked around the room and smiled, remembering where he was. 'Oh, yes,' he said, patting Winnie's knee excitedly, and settled back for another nap.

Michael spotted the fag on the floor. He leaned forward, picked it up and slipped it back into the packet for later.

Winnie looked at him. He was drunk and confused with a bitter distance in his eyes. His belly hung forlornly over his belt, his scarlet sunburnt head was freckled with liver spots and tenuous tufts of hair. He saw her watching him and snarled as he tried to cross his legs. He was too stiff and couldn't lift his leg high enough, his knees banged off each other. He tried again, swinging his foot on the diagonal, but couldn't reach his knee. He was wearing nylon trousers, white socks and dirty trainers, all personal dislikes of Winnie's. She had loved his jaw, she had loved his hair, his dear, dark hair. When they met, Michael was going to write like Hemingway, tell tales of derring-do. He could command the attention of any party with his stories, flatten anyone with a punch and move like no other guy at the dancing. And now he was an unemployable abusive drunk whom no one liked and she, the doll on his arm, was six months sober with thirty years of apologies pending. As Winnie looked at him the years concertinaed and she wondered how they had got from there to here, if there was some sign she should have picked up on, if she should have known. But everybody drank in those days, she told herself, everybody drank.

They heard a scuffle in the corridor and Alistair was at the door, his face smeared with blood and tears, cradling his bleeding thumb as if it was the baby. 'Beautiful,' he said, and covered his face to cry.

*

Una held the baby close to her chest and Winnie tried to smile. Please, God, if there is a God, not a girl.

'It's a girl,' said Una, exhausted and cheated.

'Oh,' said Winnie, grinning as her eyes welled. 'Lucky.'

They looked at each other, Una angry, Winnie sorry. Winnie reached out for the child but Una pointedly handed the little bundle to Michael, who had staggered in at her back, elbowing in front of George. They could all smell the drink off him. He reached out for the newborn, hands trembling. Concerned, the midwife stood at Michael's back, ready to catch the baby if he fell. Michael cradled her in one arm and poked a nicotine-stained finger at a nose that had been used for forty breaths. The baby sneezed twice.

'Have ye decided on a name?' asked Winnie, letting the insult go.

Una bristled, straightening the sheets. 'I'm going to call her Maureen,' she said. 'I like the name.'

Alistair frowned at her. 'You can't do that,' he said. 'There's already a Maureen in the family.'

'Not any more there isn't,' said Una firmly.

Michael blinked slowly and looked at the baby. 'Hello, Maureen,' he said.

18
Fight Night

They sat on their canvas seats at the stall and stared at each other, passing a monosyllabic morning. Maureen guessed from the paucity of chat that Leslie had repledged her troth to Cammy the Wanker over the weekend. She didn't want to tell Leslie about Si McGee or Ella's death. She wanted to keep it to herself and let it fester.

It was Monday, Liam's night for getting paid. Traditionally, Leslie came home with Maureen, and after they'd paid pecuniary homage to Liam, they sat and drank together and fantasized about what they'd do with all the money if it was extra, if Leslie didn't have rent and her mum to sub, and Maureen didn't have debts. Maureen would pretend to hanker after foreign destinations, spending a week in the Hermitage in St Petersburg, hanging out in Berlin and going to the Käthe Kollwitz museum. Leslie would pretend to want a big bike or a car. They sounded grander than a house full of whisky and new shoes, more unobtainable, as if they had big plans, foiled by circumstances. In truth, neither of them wanted the big stuff, they both wanted peace and to keep working at the market and having a laugh together until the tunnel damp crept under their skin and gave them arthritis. They wanted to keep this time going for ever but they both knew, each for her own reasons, that it couldn't last.

Leslie was working her way round to not coming over tonight, Maureen could feel it, and she wanted her to stay away. She couldn't listen to another shoddy rationale for Cammy turning out to be a good guy after all. Besides, she had plans.

'God, my head's getting really bad,' said Leslie, rubbing her forehead and frowning in a manner that demanded sympathy.

Leslie was a terrible liar: she could say the words but her face just looked angry, as if she was furious at the indignity of having to stoop to subterfuge. 'Maybe you should stay in tonight,' said Maureen, hoping to cut short the angry fiasco.

'No,' said Leslie, dropping her fag and squashing it out with a twist of her shoe. 'I said I'll come to see Liam and I'll come.'

Maureen knew she should reciprocate, act angry herself so they could have a fight and then make peace tomorrow when Leslie'd had her way, but she didn't have the emotional reserves. 'You never said you'd come to see Liam,' she said calmly.

'He'll be expecting me,' said Leslie stiffly.

'Well, whatever. Do what ye want.' Maureen stood up and went to the loo.

When she got back Leslie was in reconciliatory mood. 'I'll come,' she said, as though Maureen had insisted.

Maureen took 'a deep breath. 'Leslie, I can read everything that's going on, now stop it.'

She saw a glint of recognition behind Leslie's eyes and then the curtain came down. 'I don't fucking know what you're talking about,' she said, and stormed off with the key to the toilet.

Maureen sat chewing her nails and watching the traffic in the tunnel. She shouldn't have to put up with this crap. If Leslie wasn't so ashamed of taking Cammy back she wouldn't be angry but it was hardly Maureen's fault.

'Are yees having a fight?' asked Peter, calling over the

heads of some customers. Maureen rolled her eyes. 'She's some kid, eh?' smiled Peter.

'Aye,' muttered Maureen. 'Some kid right enough.'

Ten minutes later Leslie came back with a diffident, hurt attitude. 'Maybe I should just leave it tonight, if you're going to be in this mood,' she said.

It rankled, but Maureen agreed.

'Are ye fighting with her now, Leslie?' shouted Peter. 'Ye like the fights, don't ye?'

Leslie shot Maureen a disgusted look. 'Ye had to fucking tell him, didn't ye?'

Kilty was walking up the hill as they drew up to the pavement. She'd come straight from work, was wearing clamdiggers, a vest and big mad trainers with red lights in the heels, which flashed when she walked. She saw them driving up and waved, trotted up to the van window and hung in. 'All right, Leslie? You shot of that nippy prick Cammy yet?'

Leslie's lips withered and she stared straight ahead. 'Cammy's fine, thanks,' she said sarcastically.

Kilty slapped her arm. 'Come on, chuck him and we'll all go out on the pull. Did Mauri tell you about her lumber the other night?'

Leslie looked at Maureen as if she'd been unfaithful.

'Vik.' Maureen was unable to sustain misery in Kilty's company. 'Are ye sure ye won't come up?'

'No,' said Leslie, double huffy because she felt usurped by Kilty.

'Ah, come on.' Kilty tried to drag her through the open window by her arm, putting a foot flat on the door by way of leverage.

Leslie almost smiled. 'No, I'm not feeling well and I should go home.'

'You pull,' said Maureen to Kilty, 'and I'll push.'

Maureen tucked her hands under Leslie's legs and Kilty tugged at her arm. Leslie's face erupted into a wonky, reluctant grin. 'Fuck off, no, stop.'

Maureen climbed out of the van and tumbled round to Kilty's side.

'Chuck him, chuck him, chuck him,' chanted Kilty, banging her fists on an imaginary table. 'Look how miserable you are.' She pressed her fingers on Leslie's cheek and flicked her face away. 'Get on with your life, lovely woman. Ye're coming to the wedding?'

Leslie shook her face free of Kilty's hand and let the van roll down the hill to the lights.

'She is coming?'

'Aye,' said Maureen. 'We're all coming.'

Kilty's brother was getting married in two days' time. Predictably it was to be a huge affair, a thirty-grand extravaganza, with a reception in Cameron House, a castle hotel on the banks of Loch Lomond. The venue presupposed a car. Kilty didn't know her brother's friends and had insisted on bringing Liam, Leslie and Maureen. Maureen knew that part of the reason Kilty liked being seen with them was because they inspired shock and disappointment when introduced.

Maureen and Kilty sat at the kitchen table, sipping coffee while they counted out the coins and notes from the week into freezer bags of fifty quid. Maureen wanted a whisky but knew Kilty would object. She didn't approve of Maureen's drinking and had sat her down the previous spring and suggested she get help for it. Having worked in a detox unit in London for a while, Kitty was a bit over cautious. Given a choice between giving up drinking or disguising it in front of Kilty, Maureen opted for the latter.

As they counted, Maureen told her the story of Ella and the small claims case, about the hospital and Ella crouched on the cross-bar and the way Si was with her. As she told the story she felt the familiar heat in her belly and the tension in her neck. She liked it.

'So,' said Kilty, sweeping a pile of pound coins into a plastic bag, 'what makes you think the son did it?'

''Cause she was so scared of him, she said, "Get me out." He was really creepy and she said she'd had a fall and he told the police she'd been mugged. And then suddenly she's dead.'

Kilty looked unconvinced. 'Is it any of your business?'

'No,' said Maureen, trying to remember why she suspected Si, 'but it's weird, isn't it? She wouldn't speak when her son was there and he watched her all the time. Like, on Saturday, he really didn't want me to be left alone with her and even when I was changing her into a nightie he left the door open a bit.'

'Kinky,' said Kilty, tapping a sheaf of fivers into a tidy bundle.

'The guy in the morgue said she'd died of a heart-attack.'

'But you don't think she did.'

'I don't know,' said Maureen. 'If she did, it was because she was terrified.'

'Could the son have bribed them to say that she died of a heart-attack?'

'Nah,' said Maureen, wondering if Kilty was getting her to talk herself out of it. 'It'd cost a right few bob to get them to change the cause of death on a certificate, wouldn't it? He'd need to bribe doctors and everything. He didn't look that well heeled to me.'

'What if he just bribed the guy in the morgue to say it to you? D'you think he'd know you'd come back to visit and ask about it?'

'Yeah.' Maureen thought of the poly-bag with the nighties and the soap in it. 'He knew I'd be back.'

"Cause if the police think she was mugged and died of her injuries they'll be looking for a murderer. Do you think it could get a bit heavy?'

Maureen hesitated. She didn't know. 'Well,' she said sourly, 'are ye not going to come with me, then?'

Kilty sat up and looked at her. 'Keep your fucking hair on,' she shouted, breaking into a grin. 'Drama, drama, drama.'

'How could we find out the cause of death?'

'Dunno,' muttered Kilty. 'Ask her doctors?'

'I don't know the doctors.'

They went back to the count, filling Liam's bags with notes because he had other people to collect from. Maureen took most of the smash for herself, because it was going in the cupboard and she didn't need to carry it anywhere. There were six bags each for Maureen and Leslie.

At seven o'clock exactly Liam knocked at the door and Kilty went to let him in. 'All right, Kilty?' he said, coming down the hall with a fag in his hand. 'How are ye?'

He looked pissed off and tired, and Maureen guessed he was nervous about his resit the next day. He had three people to visit before he came to her and they weren't always as co-operative as she was. 'You all right, Liam?' she asked.

'That fucking wee arse up in Springburn wasn't in.'

'He's done that before.'

'Well, he won't be doing it again. I'm not supplying him any more.'

'All set for your exam tomorrow?'

Liam flushed and looked nauseous. 'Don't even talk about it. Have you seen this one?'

He handed her a Sunday newspaper from the day before. On page five it carried a double-page story detailing Maureen's breakdown and her stay in hospital. It had a whole lot of rubbish about how she'd met Douglas when she was still in there and had fallen madly in love with him. In the accompanying photograph, taken after a bad fight during a family dinner, Maureen was arm in arm with their oldest sister, Marie. Marie was beaming and pretty, wearing a beautifully cut scarlet dress. Next to her, Maureen looked sulky and rude. It was taken during the good times for Marie, before she and her husband had become Lloyds Names and gone bankrupt, before her husband left her and went off to farm wheat in the Ukraine. 'This is unmitigated crap,' she said. 'Why's Marie in this picture? She should sue them.'

'Look.' Liam leaned over her shoulder, pointing to an italicized paragraph at the bottom of the article. Marie had sold her story to the paper.

'How fucking dare she?' breathed Maureen. 'She wasn't even there, we haven't spoken to each other for fucking years.'

'I know. She's a shit.'

Maureen was staggered. 'She wouldn't even know I'd gone out with anyone called Douglas if he hadn't been killed.'

'I know.'

'Let's see,' said Kilty, and took the paper from Maureen.

Maureen looked at Liam furiously, demanding some sort of response, but Liam just shrugged. 'They offer a lot of money, Mauri, and she's bankrupt, ye know. Winnie's furious with her.'

'That's rich,' said Maureen. 'She gave them that picture of me in Millport.'

'Yeah,' grinned Kilty. 'I like you in that picture.'

'But,' said Liam, 'Winnie was blackout at the time and doesn't remember doing it.'

'Thank fuck it's a Tory rag. At least no one in Paddy's will have seen it.'

'I wouldn't worry about it,' said Kilty. 'It's funny seeing you in the paper.' She leaned across and poked Liam in the tummy. 'And you're still driving us up to the wedding?'

Liam sat down at the kitchen table. 'Aye, yeah.' He held the cigarette between his teeth, sliding the freezer bags across the table and dropping them into his bag. 'Haven't ye got any other hillbilly pals ye can frighten your family with?'

'No,' said Kilty seriously. 'You're the roughest people I know.'

Liam rubbed smoke out of his eye. 'Do you get out at all?'

'I don't want to know *real* rough people,' said Kilty, going back to read the paper, 'just slightly rough ones like you.'

Liam smiled at Maureen. 'Isn't that a nice thing to say?'

'She's got the patter right down,' said Maureen, draining her coffee cup.

'Is it two o'clock we're picking you up at?' asked Liam.

'Yep,' said Kilty. 'Outside my house.'

Liam looked around the table curiously. 'Mauri, don't you always get pissed on Monday nights? Why are you two drinking coffee?'

'We're going out,' said Kilty.

'Yeah,' said Maureen, 'we're going out.'

19
Safe Home

The Glasgow underground system has two concentric tracks, one running clockwise, the other anticlockwise. The trains are painted orange, hence the nickname the Clockwork Orange. Through a peculiarity of design, the Bridge Street underground station sucks down air from ground level, and half-way up the short flight of stairs is a windy vortex. Kilty and Maureen left the cold platform, battled through the buffeting Arctic wind and walked out into a calm sunny Gorbals evening, just south of the river.

The monolithic high flats stood grey and black across a dusty lawn of wasteground. Not a single car was parked outside. Eighteen storeys up, three empty window sockets had black smoke smeared above the lintels. The same bossy blue signs that had pitted the front of Sheila's block were here too, ordering residents to do this, stop that and get your bloody hand out of there.

Number fifty-four had a security door and they couldn't get in. Kilty pressed the buzzer for the concierge but got no answer. They were standing about for a couple of minutes, trying to think of something to do, when a small man behind them pressed his key to a pad and the door buzzed open. They stood back, thinking it would be rude just to push in after him but the man held the door open for them.

'We could be desperate robbers, ye know,' said Kilty, once they were safely inside.

'Aye, ye look like right villains.' He smiled and walked away to a stairwell.

The lobby was in good nick, no graffiti, no burn marks anywhere, and the lifts appeared to be working. The floor was covered in large black rubberized tiles that would have been trendy in a loft. A janitor sat behind a glass wall in a small room to the side, watching television under a sign that read 'Concierge'. Maureen found the lift that stopped at the even-numbered floors and pressed the button. The doors opened and they stepped into a smog of piss and detergent. Maureen used the hem of her T-shirt to press the button for Ella's floor.

'God, fuck,' said Kilty, choking and covering her mouth. 'Why? Why piss everywhere?'

Maureen held her nose and tried not to breathe in. The lift stopped and they staggered out on to the landing. On either side of the lift shaft, flights of stairs led up and down, the reinforced glass on the outside wall filling the stairwell with a pissy yellow light. Maureen and Kilty looked up and down the corridor at the rows of grey doors. The place was deserted. Buzzing strip-lights flickered at the far end. A sudden brutal clang behind their heads made them jump. The noise continued, falling away from them. The bag of rubbish finished its journey down the chute and Kilty grinned at her. 'I'm not tense,' she said, opening her eyes manic-wide.

Maureen found Ella's flat three down from the lift. The door frame was covered in a sheet of raw plyboard, nailed into place. It looked so final, as if everything about Ella was being blocked up because she was dead.

'Did someone kick the door in?' asked Kilty.

'I dunno,' said Maureen. 'They wouldn't do that because she's dead, would they?'

'No, doors still lock after you're dead. It looks as if the

door's been kicked in. Can't have been her son who attacked her then. She'd've let him in, surely.'

'He didn't look the sort to kick a door in anyway. Let's ask the neighbours. You ask up there,' Maureen pointed to the next door and swivelled on her heels, 'and I'll ask down here.'

Kilty walked away, trying to effect a Robert Mitchum swagger but looking as if she'd pissed herself and sprained both ankles. Maureen knocked on a nearby door. No one answered but she could hear a television inside. She banged again. Still no answer. Kilty wasn't having any more luck. They moved across the corridor and tried the doors opposite Ella's but still couldn't get an answer.

'No one's in,' said Kilty.

The noise of a lock cracking open made them turn to the end of the corridor. An old woman stepped out into the silence. She locked her door carefully, picked up the plastic bag at her feet and walked towards them, looking past them, pretending they weren't there. Her footsteps echoed around the corridor. She was wearing a bandage around her calf under thick support tights. As she approached Maureen and Kilty, the old woman's path veered steeply to the opposite wall and she kept her eyes down.

'Excuse me?' said Maureen, stepping towards her.

The woman looked skittish and twitched to a stop, glancing at Maureen's shoes.

'I've been up seeing Ella McGee at the hospital,' said Maureen, hoping to attract her attention with the promise of gossip.

The woman looked up at her. 'She okay?'

'She died, I'm afraid,' said Maureen. 'What happened to her door?'

The woman seemed startled and glanced at the wooden slab. 'It got broke,' she said.

'Did someone break in?'

The woman looked uneasy and dropped her voice. 'From the inside,' she said. 'It was all smashed out the way.'

'Gee-so,' said Kilty.

Apparently offended by the use of a bowdlerism, the woman stumbled back a step and stared at them dumbly.

'Do ye know her son? Si McGee?' asked Maureen.

The old woman shook her head and looked at Kilty.

'Sorry,' muttered Kilty, and Maureen stepped back against the wall to let the nervous woman pass.

She scuttled off down the corridor, pressed the button for the lift, looked back at them again and hobbled off down the stairs.

'Look at that granny go,' muttered Kilty. 'I don't think anyone here'll talk to us.'

'I think you're right,' said Maureen.

They heard the whine of the lift approaching and went over to it. The doors opened on a bare knee, a naked thigh, a smoking cigarette. A very drunk man was loitering in the lift, propped up against the side, smoking casually. He was naked, his tired little belly sagging in perfect semicircles, like Gothic drapery. He raised his cigarette, opening his mouth wide, as if he was going to bite an apple, and let his lips slowly alight on the filter. 'What are you doing?' said Kilty indignantly, jamming the doors open with her foot.

'Eh?'

'What are ye doing in there? There might be children getting in that lift.'

The man's gaze slid around the floor then bounced over to Kilty. He shut his eyes and pointed at her with his smoking hand. 'You don't even live here,' he drawled, his lips sliding freestyle across his teeth.

'Children might get into this lift and you're naked. And you've got half a hard-on.'

The man felt his stomach. He clearly didn't know he was naked until Kilty told him. From his mild discomfort Maureen guessed that things like this happened to him quite often. 'No one takes the lift,' he said.

'*You* shouldn't take the lift and then maybe someone else could.'

Maureen stepped in front of Kilty. 'Hey, did you hear about the lady on this floor who was attacked?'

He shook his head, and kept his eyes shut. 'Ella the Flash. Are you the polis?'

'No.'

'Well, tell her hello from me.'

'Does she know ye?'

'Everb'dy around here knows me.' He opened an eye but the other one seemed to be stuck shut. 'I'm famous.'

'What for?' asked Kilty, and Maureen looked at her incredulously as the door slid shut.

It was ten o'clock and still as bright as noon. Traffic lights ordered ghostly legions around the empty roads.

'What does Ella the Flash mean?' said Kilty.

'Dunno,' said Maureen.

As they walked across the deserted car park Kilty flapped her T-shirt to disperse the memory of the smell from the lift. She was completely unperturbed by the naked man. As a social worker she saw things Maureen couldn't conceive of. She was never shocked at horror stories of deprivation and seemed to know all the names of the big men in the city.

'Have you ever heard of Si McGee?'

Kilty shrugged. 'I know the name.'

'How much force would it take to smash a door from the inside?'

'The other doors looked pretty sturdy. I don't think Benny

Lynch Court would be the most sensible place for the council to make big savings on front doors.'

'Why could he possibly be that angry with her?' Maureen mused.

'Maybe it was bringing the small claims case.'

'Naw,' said Maureen. 'Whatever went on in there happened on Thursday night and he couldn't have received the letter about the small claims until Saturday morning at the earliest.'

'He got the letter for the small claims on Saturday morning and then, suddenly and out of the blue, she died?'

'Yeah,' nodded Maureen. 'Suspicious, isn't it?'

'It is a bit,' said Kilty, biting her lip.

They walked to the mouth of the underground and bought their tickets. Kilty stopped at the turnstile. 'Look, is this any of your business, Mauri? Are you sure you're not just worried about Una's baby and looking for a morbid distraction?'

'She asked me to get her out, Kilty, she asked me and I said she'd be fine.' Maureen flushed, shoved her ticket into the slot and pushed through the turnstile.

Kilty got halfway down the stairs and turned, the wild wind flattening her thin hair hard against her head, making her look like dead Ella. 'I've definitely heard that name somewhere,' she said, as if that would console Maureen.

It didn't make her feel any better. The platform was empty. Through the dark tunnels on either side they could hear a rumbling. The train clattered into the station and they got into a deserted carriage, sitting next to each other. As the train took off Maureen leaned across to Kilty. 'How could ye get into a lift and not even notice you're naked?' she shouted over the noise.

'He'd be blacked out,' she said and left it.

It struck Maureen that her drinking was taking over her

life. Whatever course she took in her life there would be no dignity in it. She could only see two options: ugly cells or a life of perpetual streaking. Kilty read the concern on her face. 'You don't black out a lot, do ye?'

'No.'

Kilty smiled. 'You answered that awful quick. Are you sure?'

'What is a blackout?'

'That's when you can't remember hours of what happened last night. They get worse if your drinking escalates. It can go on for days.'

Maureen smiled for her. The drinking was getting worse: she could dress it up as a crisis, she could call it Michael, but she knew deep down that it would have happened anyway, that she was like Winnie.

Kilty leaned over and tapped her leg. 'Blacking out for days is pretty extreme, Mauri, it means your brain's shrivelling. I don't think you'll get that bad.'

Maureen nodded.

'You should cut down, though,' she said, once again displaying her inability to understand the siren call of drink. 'I've said that to you before.'

Maureen looked at kind Kilty's pretty wee face and would have sold her to the devil for a double there and then.

She stayed on the train to Kilty's stop, passing Garnethill, knowing if she got off she'd run upstairs and take a drink. Kilty talked about her brother's wedding most of the way home, how she couldn't stand his friends and knew the feeling was mutual. They thought she was a loser freak for working in a children's home. Maureen asked her what sort of work they did.

'Sell things, buy things,' said Kilty. 'Like you and Leslie but from offices.'

She looked and saw that Maureen was only half listening.

Her responses were shallow and a beat too late. Una's baby was due soon. She must be worried sick.

It was dark outside Hillhead underground. The big sky was as yellow as a wolf's eye. Kilty tried to convince her to come up for a cup of tea but Maureen said she needed a walk and had to get up early for work the next day. They kissed and Maureen thanked her for coming to Benny Lynch Court with her. Their parting felt strange and formal, like a Judas kiss.

Maureen planted her hands in her pockets and walked down the street. The students were away and the area was quiet in the lull before closing time. It was still warm. She wanted a drink: her mouth wanted a fresh drink, her gut wanted a searing drink, her fingers wanted to cradle a precious glass, her heavy heart wanted succour. The watchful yellow sky hung close and she heard a high breeze rustle the dark trees in Kelvingrove Park. She wouldn't drink, wouldn't stop at a bar and order a triple. She'd just go straight home. But she had whisky at home in the cupboard. She slowed down.

She was approaching the Indian Trip, thinking about the lager she'd had with her dinner there, she could almost taste the cool sweet tinge of it, when she realized that she was close to the business address Ella had given for Si. Becci Street or something. She cut down a narrow street of tall grey tenements.

The road opened out into a dark, run-down square with failing trees in a bald central island. To her left stood an old church with anti-fascist slogans painted in five-foot letters. It looked like a cross between a Masonic hall and a synagogue, with four outsized columns and a fussy rotunda looming on the roof. The doors were painted pale blue. The Church of Scotland seemed to have bought a job lot of the paint from somewhere and all their doors were the same colour, regardless of a building's style or period.

She looked at the road signs on the corner. It was the junction between Coleworth and Becci Street. Thinking it was a dark area for a health club, she followed the line of the square round towards the park. Past the church, she came to a Georgian yellow sandstone block of grand windows and imposing doorways with broad sets of stairs leading up to them. The corner flat of the block had a broken window, boarded over with wood stamped 'Hurry Brothers, Emergency Glaziers'. The other windows in the flat were covered in inappropriate burgundy plastic. A brass plaque on the wall announced it as the Park Circus Health Club. It didn't look like a health club. Maureen was looking at it, puzzling, when the door opened and a man came out, walking down the stairs with his hands in the pockets of his anorak. He didn't have a sports bag with him and he wasn't wearing sweats. He caught her eye and glared at her, as if she'd done something awful, turned on his heel and hurried away down the street.

Maureen walked across the square and sat down on a set of stairs opposite, facing the health club, wondering about it. She lit a cigarette and watched as night fell.

One and a half cigarettes later her mouth tasted foul. She chewed her tongue to force out some saliva and was swilling it around her mouth as a black cab pulled up across the road. The light flicked on as the door opened and a woman stepped out, pulling a shoulder-bag after her. She trotted up the steps and Maureen recognized her, somehow, from the straightness of her back and the hair pulled carefully into a tidy chignon. Glaswegian women tend to dress wishfully, in clothes they'd like to suit – in short skirts because they want long legs, in vest tops because they want thin arms – but the woman on the steps was dressed beautifully, in clothes that fitted her and suited her shape, like a French

159

woman. She turned on the top step, saw the red tip of Maureen's cigarette flare against the dark and looked across at her carefully, keeping her head down before opening the door and slipping inside. Maureen watched the door and wondered if she was the foreign woman Ella had mentioned, the one she had fought with her son about, and the wife who was at the hospital with Si when poor old Ella died.

A car drew up at the bottom of the steps and a man climbed out of his car, locked it, jogged up the steps to the door and pressed the buzzer. The door opened and Maureen saw into the lobby, a shot of thick blue carpet, pea-green wallpaper, a yucca plant against the wall, and the man disappeared inside. Maureen smiled at her own naivety: it had taken her twenty-five minutes and two cigarettes to realize it was a brothel. She stood up, grinning, dropped her cigarette and ground it into the pavement, thinking of all the fucking miserable lives in Glasgow. Poor women on their backs to ugly men for shit money, and nothing in her life seemed that bad. Fuck it. She'd go home and have a drink.

Across the square the door opened again and a bodybuilder in a suit came out. His neck was thick, his arms stuck out to the side like stabilizers on a bike; his thick thighs rubbed against one another, gathering the material in his trousers at his crotch as he walked across the square to her. He stopped fifteen feet away, stood in the road and raised his eyebrows at her. He seemed to be panting. 'What ye doing?' he said aggressively. His voice was high to be coming from such a manly body.

Maureen pointed up to the front door behind her. 'Waiting for my pal,' she said.

He saw that she wasn't angry or obviously up to something, and dropped his hostile stance. 'Ye locked out?' he said softly.

'Naw, I don't live here. I just came to see someone but she's not in. Did ye come over to see if ye could help?' she said, and smiled. They both knew why he had come over.

'Huh, aye,' he said, looking back at the health-club door. 'Sometimes we get women waiting, you know, outside.'

'What are they waiting for?'

He looked away. 'For their man. To catch him.'

'Is it expensive?'

'They're not always bothered about the money.'

She had the feeling he was reluctant to go back in. 'Is that what happened to the window?' She pointed to the Hurry Brothers board.

'Aye.' He gave a small smile.

They stared at the ground for a bit, listening to the wind hissing through the dead trees.

'I'm gonnae go anyway,' said Maureen, dropping her foot to the next step. 'I think my pal's out for the night.'

'Mibbi she got lucky,' he said, as if that'd never happened to him.

'Mibbi,' said Maureen.

She tipped her chin goodbye and walked off down the street. She was almost at the corner when he spoke. 'Safe home,' he said gently.

She was walking up the hill to her house, feeling low about the drink and Michael and everything, when she saw a grey Saab with silver trim idling in the street outside her house. It wasn't parked, just stopped in the street, and the driver was looking up at the building. She walked close to the buildings, keeping in the shadows, and stopped outside Mr Padda's, hiding in the dark doorway as she looked into the car. Si McGee was gazing at her house, his mouth open a little, making his weak chin look even weaker than it was. He was smoking a small cigar, driving around and checking out her house the day after his mum died. He must have seen her address on the small claims form. Maureen stood still and waited for him to drive away, watching the red tail-lights until they turned the corner.

20

Pissed

Maureen awoke to the insistent sound of someone banging loudly on her door, over and over. She covered her head with the thin sheet, as if that would make them go away. They continued to bang, stopping for short rests and starting again, rhythmically, like a nervous tic. Maureen got up and went to the door, pulling on a T-shirt.

He was wearing a suit, his shirt a little crumpled. Behind him stood a photographer, ready and waiting with a large camera trained on the door. Maureen recognized the journalist. He had come to the Apollo Theatre when she worked there, just after Douglas's murder, and refused to leave. She was tempted to pull open the door and tell the men to piss off but she realized, just in time, that the incessant banging technique was designed to make her do exactly that. She made a coffee to the accompaniment of the journalist's knuckles getting shredded on the badly planed door.

After forty minutes it became clear that the man was not using his bare hand to knock. The banging stopped and started again, a few minutes between bursts but never less consistent or loud. Maureen pulled the phone into the kitchen, shut the door and phoned Leslie to tell her she was trapped.

'Just come when ye can,' Leslie whispered back. 'I'll set up the stall without ye. Listen, gonnae bring my money?'

'I will, I will.'

After an hour the journalist gave up and by the time he

and the photographer had left the close Maureen had gone through fury and indignation, annoyance and numb surprise to something like awe at the man's persistence.

She was sitting on the settee, sipping a coffee and pulling on her trainers when an image of Michael came into her mind. He was sliding behind her, just out of her line of vision, and he was close. She drew on her cigarette to make him go away but he was still there, just behind her ear. She ignored him, taking deep breaths and looking out over the city. He was still there. She had three strategies for dealing with flashbacks: Angus had told her to change the ending. She reached down to the side of her chair and pulled up a shotgun, firing blind over her shoulder. It used to work sometimes but he was still there. He was smiling at her: he wasn't afraid at all. The skin on the back of her neck warmed with fright. The other two strategies were to wash it away with alcohol or live through it. She walked into the kitchen and looked at the bottle. Michael was still at her ear. She had made a deal with herself in the past few months: she could drink as much as she wanted at night and during the day as long as she didn't drink in the morning. The day started at eleven thirty and it was only ten forty-five. Forty-five minutes off target. Fuck it. She lifted the bottle and swallowed a mouthful, the cheap whisky burning her gums and teeth, stinging her throat on the way down, making Michael dissolve. She lit a fag with a soggy hand and carried the bottle back into the living room. Fuck it.

As the whisky did an inside job of warming, her, she drew on her fag. The coffee in her hand tasted particularly sweet and dry. She felt good. She felt better than good, she felt great, and she sat back and wondered why she had worked so hard for so long to resist a morning drink.

With the benefit of a drink inside her she considered trying to stay off the whisky for a while at some point in the future, just to prove to herself that she could. Perhaps she'd try brandy: it seemed medicinal and easier to justify than rum. She couldn't think of drinking vodka because Winnie used to drink vodka. If she started drinking vodka she'd definitely have a drink problem. It was five past twelve. She had meant to phone Liam and wish him good luck in his exam. She called his house and found him home. 'How did the exam go?'

'Dunno. I stayed till ten minutes before the end, so that's a good sign. You sound a bit strange.'

'I am strange,' she said, feeling giggly because of the whisky. 'Sorry.'

'Look, come over here and we'll talk about it.'

'I can't. I've got to go to work, I've got Leslie's wages.'

'Will ye come over tonight, then?'

'Aye. Have you ever heard of a guy called Si McGee?'

'Nut. Promise ye'll come over tonight?'

When she opened the door a white envelope dropped into her hall. It was the same size as the other one and the paper was warped at the back. She hesitated before opening it. It was another picture, of a small boy, eyes uncovered this time, taken from the waist up. He was lying down, the picture taken from above him, naked and laughing, oblivious to the meaning of the leather-studded shackles on his wrists with the chain between them. Maureen put it back into the envelope and sat it in the hall cupboard on the floor. She was going to tell the fucking police about this and get the bastard who was leaving these things at her door.

She was locking the flat when she heard a noise across the close. She turned and looked at Jim Maliano's door. He was watching her through the spy-hole. She stomped across the close and banged on his door. He waited for a moment

165

before opening it, pretending he'd been elsewhere in the house. 'Oh, hi, Maureen.'

'Stop fucking watching me,' she said, pointing at him. 'You fucking weirdo freak.'

Jim mugged at her, his face a guilty give-away. 'I don't know—'

'Are you leaving weird shit on my doorstep?'

Jim looked insulted. 'Am I leaving what?' he said, having misheard and thought she'd accused him of defecating.

'Are you leaving fucking envelopes on my doorstep?'

'No,' he said, looking bemused.

Maureen walked away down the stairs.

'You're a rotten neighbour,' called Jim, leaning over the banister to half shout, half whisper at her, 'The police were never in this close once before you moved here.'

Maureen stopped at the bottom of the stairs and looked up at him. 'Stop fucking watching me, ya weird wee bastard.'

Outside, the dreary sun was doing its thing and office workers in heavy shirts and skirts ambled along the road, reluctant to go back inside after their chores were done.

Leslie was pleased to see the carrier-bag full of money and pushed it under the stall where she could keep an eye on it. She looked at Maureen with big insecure eyes and wanted to know all about the night before with Kilty and whether they had had a good time. Maureen didn't tell her about the trip to Benny Lynch Court. She said they had had a good laugh but it would have been better if Leslie had been there and left it at that.

'I'm stuck, Mauri,' said Leslie quietly. 'He's like shite on my shoe, I just can't get rid of him.'

'What can I say?' asked Maureen, feeling cocky. 'Every fucking time ye say stuff like this you're pissed off with me later for hearing it.'

'I want shot of him. I want nights with you and Kilty. I hate going home.' Leslie hung her head. 'I'm thinking about asking for a transfer.'

'You can't move out of Drumchapel, that's your bit. All your family are there.'

'But I can't keep living there if this goes on. He can see my veranda from his mum's house.'

'The Drum's your bit. Fuck him.' Maureen punched her arm. 'Look, give him his stuff, change the locks and come and stay with me for a couple of weeks.'

Leslie thought about it for a moment. 'You sure you wouldn't mind?'

'Naw,' she lied. 'And if I do your head in,' she said, hoping she would, 'Kilty'll put you up for a bit. And if she does your head in Liam'll take ye in. Everything'll be great.'

Leslie sat up straight for the first time in ages. 'I'm going to do it,' she said.

'Brilliant,' said Maureen, punching the air and laughing.

'I'll tell ye what's really scary.' Leslie gestured to her to come close. They leaned in until their faces were inches apart, Maureen excited, expecting a big, juicy, derisory secret about Cammy. 'It's half twelve in the morning,' said Leslie gravely, 'and, hen, you're fucking pissed.'

They sat on their little stools, staring at one another's feet and smoking. Maureen had sobered up during the day and her stomach was clawing for a drink. She stayed on her stool, afraid to go outside in case she ended up in the pub.

It was getting late and they were thinking about shutting when, looking over Leslie's shoulder, Maureen thought she saw a familiar face out in the lane. She had never seen him in the sunlight before, and because he was unusually thin, she thought she might have been mistaken. He was looking at cards on Gordon-Go-A-Bike's stall, leaning over the table with his hands crammed into the pockets of his dirty jeans. Gordon looked down at him, said something short. Paulsa looked up at Gordon and smiled slowly, giving him a one-word answer. Gordon didn't look pleased. Still smiling, Paulsa wandered away from the table, looking happily around the lane and turning his face up to meet the sun. He squinted into the dark tunnel and stepped in.

Paulsa was a user. The last time Maureen had met him he was jaundiced yellow and down on his luck. Having bought a job lot of bad acid he had lost all his money and was desperately looking for friends to bail him out. When Liam needed an alibi for Douglas's death Paulsa came forward and admitted that he had been with Liam that afternoon, at Tonsa's house. Paulsa tiptoed everywhere, as if afraid that making proper contact with the ground might mitigate his delighted, drug-induced stupor. He passed Ella's empty stall, still smiling, and looked over at Lenny's TVs. He tiptoed sideways, cupping his groin to get past Elsie Tanner's friendly nose, and turned and looked at Maureen. They stared into one another's eyes for longer than a passing glance. Shoulders up around his ears, Paulsa turned back to the tunnel mouth, as if hoping hard would make him invisible, and tiptoed away.

Maureen loped after him, grabbing his elbow. Paulsa had his eyes shut and was cringing so much that he could have held a half-pint in each of the deep dips on his collarbone. 'Paulsa,' she said, 'how are ye?'

Paulsa opened one eye. 'Hi.'

'Where were ye going?'

Paulsa looked around dumbly. 'Too cold in here,' he said.

'Are you avoiding me, Paulsa?'

Paulsa exhaled a pale imitation of a laugh. 'God. No. God, why?'

She let go of his elbow and he rubbed at it as if she'd

been holding it tight. 'You're keen not to see me,' she said. 'Have ye seen Tonsa recently?'

He shook his head, shuffling almost imperceptibly around to the door. 'Naw, not Tonsa, definitely havenae seen her.' Near to tears, Paulsa looked to the back of the tunnel. 'Is Tonsa here?'

'Naw, Paulsa,' said Maureen kindly. 'I'm just asking after mutual friends.'

'Oh.' It took Paulsa a moment to sift through the information, determine that there was no threat to him in it and wheeze a laugh. He looked longingly out to the lane and freedom. They stared at each other for another minute.

'Paulsa, have you heard anything about this case that's coining up?'

Paulsa looked afraid again and shook his head. 'Nut.'

'Aren't ye going to ask me which case I'm talking about?'

Paulsa shook his head again.

'Is Liam in trouble, Paulsa?'

Paulsa tried to get past her by ramming himself into the space between her and the wall. He stayed there, pushing slightly, his head hanging over her shoulder. She stepped away and Paulsa fled past her, tiptoeing with long strides down the lane, leaping balletically to avoid bodies and stalls.

'What was that about?' asked Leslie, when Maureen came back.

'I don't know.' She sat down, leaning forward so that only Leslie could hear her. 'That's the guy I bought the acid off, the stuff I gave to Angus. I think he'd read about the case in the paper and was frightened that I'd finger him or something.'

Leslie took a long draw on her cigarette. 'Didn't look like a big reader to me, to be honest.'

21

In a Jiffy

Hesitant, spluttering rush-hour traffic left a gritty blue haze over the road. Maureen had sobered up during the day, leaving her with a dull ache to the back of her head and a terrible sense of hopelessness. She had meant to go for a drink on the way home but Leslie insisted on dropping her at the door. She was so grateful to Maureen for letting her move in and said a run up the road was the least she could do. Maureen felt she was being handled, the way the family used to handle Winnie, the way Una made sure they only ever ate in unlicensed cafés, the way drink brought by visitors was confiscated by the children at the front door, the way George made sure she wasn't left alone before they went out. After Leslie moved in tonight Maureen would be hiding in the bathroom, drinking from secret stashes like Winnie used to. She opened the passenger door. 'Listen, I'm going out in a minute,' she said. 'I might not be in when ye get there, but you've got the spare keys, haven't ye?'

Leslie seemed disappointed. 'You'll be back later though, won't ye?'

'Oh, aye, yeah. I'll be back later.'

'Where are ye going?'

'See Liam,' she said, and climbed out.

The corner of a yellow Jiffy bag peeked out from the side of her door as she climbed the stairs. She stood and looked at it. It had been placed there by someone who knew she was out at work. If Jim Maliano was delivering for Angus he wouldn't have left another package so soon after she had accused him: he wasn't sharp enough for a double bluff. And when she thought about it without a drink in her she realized that Jim didn't know Angus. It had been the drink talking. She opened the front door and nudged the envelope into the hall with the tip of her toe, afraid to touch it, and shut the door behind her. In the bedroom she changed her T-shirt and walked past the yellow package to the bathroom, watching it as though it might bite her ankles. She splashed water on her face, dried it, and turned back to the hall.

Trying not to touch the Jiffy bag more than necessary, she pulled at the lip. It came open easily and she exhaled when she saw the strip of black plastic. It was a video cassette. She took it out, sat it on top of the envelope and looked at it, chewing her cheek hard and frowning. Maureen didn't have a video machine any more. She wasn't going to watch it. She could guess what was on it anyway. She leaned forward, picked up the envelope by the edges and lifted it, video and all, on to the worktop in the kitchen. She picked up her purse, keys and fags and walked out, slamming the door shut behind her.

She knew that using the phone was an excuse, that there were pay-phones outside the pub she could have used. She bought herself a second triple and balanced it on a scarred balsawood shelf. 'I can't come tonight, Liam, something's come up. Can I come over tomorrow?'

Liam sounded furious. 'I can't just sit about here all night waiting for you, Maureen. I haven't had my dinner because I was waiting for you.'

'Liam,' she laughed, lighter again because of the drink, 'for fucksake, it's only half past seven.'

'I was hungry,' he snapped.

'Well, can't ye get yourself a bit of bread or something?'

'Why don't you come over later?'

'I can't. Leslie's moving into mine to shake off Cammy and she's coming over tonight.' She heard Liam tutting. The pips went on the phone and the last sixpence tumbled away on the digital display, 'That's my money gone. I'll talk to ye tomorrow.'

'Mauri, I need to—'

And the phone cut out.

22

Burbs

His driveway formed a break in a continuous stone wall leading up the hill and disappeared around a corner. The houses on the road were detached and solid, Victorian maybe. Si's house was on the summit of a short, steep drive. It had two large windows on either side of the front door and three above. The garden was tidy but not loved. It had the look of a professional gardener about it, a neatly striped lawn, bordered by a single row of pink roses. An intermittent sprinkler spat a circle of water on to the green. The grey Saab was parked in the drive.

Maureen wondered what the fuck she was doing there, loitering behind the gatepost, trying to scare him back. She was waiting but didn't know what for. She had an urge to go and chap the door and ask Si if be was happy now his mother was dead. She was there looking for a fight. The light changed behind the glass panels on the front door, it swung open, and Si stepped out, pulling on a leather jacket. He was holding his car keys. He unlocked the Saab with a remote beeper and climbed in, reversed and turned down the narrow drive, flicking on the right indicator. Maureen stood back against the gatepost, keeping as flush to the wall as she could. Si drove down to the road, paused, then pulled right. She stayed still for a while, waiting to see if he'd spotted her and would come back.

The back garden was as tidy as the front. The layout was the same: plain grass and thin borders, a dutiful effort by someone who didn't care. There were no children's toys or odd bits of garden furniture left sitting out. Through the kitchen window she saw that the place was clean: a single cup sat in the sink, waiting to be washed, the circular pine table was empty apart from a couple of unopened letters and a folded newspaper. The furthest window looked into a utility room with a washing-machine and tumble dryer. On a wooden pulley hanging from the ceiling was a series of black Y-fronts and three shirts. There were no women's clothes in the room. Either Si and his wife were separated or the woman at the hospital had been someone else altogether. She stood there, licking whisky fur off her teeth, and wondered why Si had bought a family mansion when he obviously lived alone.

'Excuse me, please.' A firm hand grabbed her elbow, swung her arm behind her back and fitted the handcuffs on to her wrists tightly.

'What the hell are you doing?' said Maureen, turning to face two overweight uniformed police officers.

'Actually, miss,' said the burly woman holding on to her, 'we might ask you that.'

Maureen realized that she was drunk. She wanted to get away from the police officers and go and drink more. Protesting her innocence from the back of the car, she told them that her name was Lizzie McCafferty. Affecting her poshest accent, she told them that she had booked a viewing of the house but the owners weren't in when she got there. Because she was a bit pissed, she half believed it herself and got genuinely annoyed when the officers didn't. Officer Fatman frowned hard. 'The owner saw you standing at the gate for ten minutes, and called us before he left the house. Why were you standing there for so long? Why not just go straight up to the house?'

Maureen tutted. 'I wasn't there for ten minutes. I just wasn't sure of the address.'

'There was no for-sale sign outside the house,' said the woman officer, turning from the wheel. 'Didn't that make you wonder?'

Maureen rolled her eyes. 'It was supposed to be a private sale.'

The female officer looked at Maureen's crumpled T-shirt, her baggy shorts with sagging pockets full of fags and money and tissues, at her outsized skate trainers and smiled. 'Were you going to buy the house with cash, miss?' she said snidely.

Maureen looked her in the eye. 'I was viewing it for my dad. He's coming back from the Emirates next week. He's retiring to Scotland and I'm supposed to find some places for him to look at when he gets here.' Maureen congratulated herself: the Emirates, nice touch.

The female officer thought about it, wavering in her conviction that Maureen was a master burglar. She looked out of the window at the house and back at Maureen. She was going to let her go. 'Which other properties have you—'

'Maureen O'Donnell.' It was Fatman. He was smiling and shaking a finger at her, 'Garnethill.' His smile blossomed into a toothy grin. 'Douglas Brady.'

They had called ahead to Stewart Street to see if Joe McEwan was interested. Maureen didn't understand what had been said in reply because it was coded but the officer started the engine and headed towards the town. The fat man turned to look at her as his colleague drove.

'What are you staring at?' said Maureen, sweating with annoyance.

He looked her up and down. 'I saw you in the paper, in Millport. D'ye like Millport?'

Maureen shrugged.

'I like it there,' he said, turning back into his seat. 'Pretty.'

Joe McEwan must have been having a quiet night because he had the time to come and see her arrive at the station. He was standing at the top of the stairs as they came into the lobby, smiling slightly, dressed in a pair of beige trousers and a dark blue silk shirt. He raised his hand in a bitter little wave as the person on the desk took Maureen's details. She didn't wave back. 'Am I being charged with something?' she asked the desk sergeant.

'No,' he said, apparently surprised that anyone in front of him had the wherewithal to ask such a technical question. 'We just want to talk to you.'

'Nice,' said Maureen, drumming her fingers on the desk and glaring at Joe as she raised her voice. 'I always have a nice time when I come here.'

The desk sergeant wasn't listening to her: he was filling in a form and writing something on a clipboard. She took out a cigarette and lit it, breathing in the smoke like a dying asthmatic on an inhaler.

Joe was smiling and smoking a cigarette. He wasn't asking her questions, just smiling and smoking, smoking and smiling. He opened his mouth to speak once but glanced at the tape-recorder and stopped, going back to his cigarette for another puff. Sitting next to him, Hugh McAskill was doing a great job of covering up their friendship. He blinked at her a couple of times, telling her to calm down. She knew he was right but the sight of Joe McEwan enjoying himself so much grated on her. She was sobering up and it was making her agitated. She wanted a drink. 'Have you got a sunbed?' she said.

Joe smiled at her reproachfully, in a way that suggested it

would take more than that to get a rise out of him.

'I'm just asking because you're always brown.' He didn't answer and she could tell he wasn't afraid of her. 'You'll ruin your skin if you keep it up, ye know, and then the smoking too. Bad for you.'

Joe blinked and cut her off, took a deep breath and moved forward over the table. 'Si McGee's house. What were you doing there?'

The hairs on her neck stirred. Not 'Simon' but 'Si'. Way too familiar.

'Nothing. Do you know him?'

Joe nodded and smiled, creeping her out.

'How do you know him?'

Joe shrugged, a little uncomfortable. 'That's not your business.'

'Does he live near you or something?'

Joe blinked, brushing the question away. He licked his top lip slowly and moved his right hand across the table, watching his index finger unfurl from his fist. He tapped it once on the table top. 'Ella McGee works at Paddy's. You work at Paddy's.' He looked up at her and clocked her genuine surprise that he had such a handle on her movements. She glanced at Hugh but remembered that she'd never told him where she worked. Joe was trying to disconcert her. And then she realized: Joe didn't know Ella was dead. He looked at the table top and tapped his finger again. 'Si McGee, brother of Margaret Frampton who, one year ago, made an assault allegation against your brother, Liam O'Donnell.' He saw that she didn't know who he was talking about. 'Tonsa,' he said.

Maureen frowned and leaned forward. 'Tonsa?'

Joe nodded, disappointed that she was so confused. 'Tonsa Frampton.'

'Tonsa is the sister of the guy who owns that house?' It

dawned on Maureen that it was Tonsa she had seen standing on the steps of the Park Circus Health Club; Tonsa, and not a foreign wife at all. Tonsa had been a crack courier when Maureen had last heard of her. Just when it mattered most, during the worst part of the investigation into Douglas's death, Tonsa had told Joe McEwan that Liam had beaten her up. She looked like a well-groomed lady, wore Burberry overcoats and dressed carefully, but her eyes were frighteningly dead, watery and open just a touch too little, focused on nothing.

'Why else would you go up there?' said Joe, bringing her back to the small room.

She ran through the dad-from-the-Emirates story, but couldn't think of a variation that would work in this context. 'I was looking for Si McGee,' she said.

Joe smiled smugly and sat back. 'Care to tell us why?'

Maureen sighed. 'His mum died.'

Now it was Joe's turn to be surprised. 'Ella the Flash is dead?'

Maureen nodded. 'The hospital couldn't get hold of him. I didn't want him going up there to visit and finding out. I wanted to tell him myself.'

'What happened to her?'

'She was in hospital.' Maureen exhaled deeply and found that the tears came easily. 'She just slipped away apparently.'

Hugh leaned forward and she could tell he was shocked too. 'Why did you lie to the officers who came to pick you up?'

'I don't trust the police to be discreet,' she said. 'I just wanted to tell him myself.'

Joe sat back heavily and blinked several times. 'Does he know yet?' he said.

'Dunno,' said Maureen.

'Bloody hell.' He took a draw on his cigarette and stubbed it out. 'Ella the Flash.'

'Why was she called that?' asked Maureen.

'Is she not called that at Paddy's?' asked Hugh.

'Naw,' Maureen said, 'not that I'd know. We call her Home Gran because she wears those tracksuits and all the gold.'

Joe smiled sadly. 'Yeah.' He cleared his throat, stopped smiling and restored the distance. 'She was too old to wear those. She was called the Flash because she always dressed well, even though she worked the streets. Wore hats and good coats and things. Had a bit of dignity about her.'

'Did you know Ella long?' asked Maureen, enjoying the kindly atmosphere.

Joe and Hugh looked at each other and Maureen saw how long they had known each other, how they had grown up together on the police force. She suddenly appreciated how decent Hugh had been to her and how easily he could have blocked her out.

'She was my first collar,' said Joe.

'And mine,' said Hugh.

'Did she get arrested a lot?'

'No,' said Hugh. 'We were together.'

Hugh and Joe seemed sorrowful somehow, sad for who they had been or who they had become.

'Si's running a brothel in Kelvingrove,' Maureen blurted.

Joe shook his head. 'No, Tonsa's involved in that but it's nothing to do with him. He's an estate agent.'

'You know there's a brothel there?'

Joe sucked his teeth. 'The city licenses a number of saunas,' he said, and added defensively, 'Well, it's better than them standing around on street corners.'

'Is Si McGee married?'

'No, I don't think so,' said Joe suspiciously. 'Why? D'ye fancy him?'

'No,' tutted Maureen, indignant at the thought. It had been Tonsa at the hospital when Ella died: the nurses had probably just assumed she was Si's wife. Maureen thought of poor cold Ella lying on the metal trolley and felt tearful again. 'She was a kind sort of person, wasn't she?' she said, overcome by drunken sentimentality and starting to cry. 'I mean, she was a good person. A mum and that.' She wiped her nose on the back of her hand.

'Maureen,' said Joe, 'are you drunk?'

23
Red Teeth

Angus Farrell sat on the end of his bed, undoing his shirt buttons and stripping to his vest, going slowly through his ablutions, maintaining the momentum, aware always of the possibility of being watched and having his behaviour reported back. He stood by the small sink and squeezed the toothpaste. He opened his mouth and began to brush, shutting his eyes, finding privacy in the moment.

Maureen O'Donnell opening the door to her flat, finding the pictures, wearing cheap clothes and a little makeup, smoking maybe. Not on the doorstep, she wouldn't smoke on the way out of the house. She'd smoke after she saw the pictures, though. Sit in another room and smoke a cigarette, feeling upset. Angus opened his eyes to find his bearings and spat into the basin. It was pink: his gums were bleeding. He smiled and shut his eyes again, brushing hard on the other side. She would sit in the living room, smoking a cigarette, trying not to look at the pictures. She'd put the pictures back in the envelope, cry over them, maybe. When she got the video she wouldn't want to watch it, she'd resist, but he knew she would watch it eventually. She wasn't one for avoidance, even if it was defensive. He spat again. Blood. He could get scurvy in here, the diet was so bad.

He ran the tap, cupping his hand under the bitter chill of the water and rinsing his mouth. He cleaned the bowl, drying it with his towel, hung the towel over the back of his plastic chair and took off his trousers, folding them neatly and putting them on the table for the morning.

He lay in bed with his two blankets over him, hands behind his head, and watched the bulb, waiting for lights out. Maureen O'Donnell smoking a cigarette, her lips sucking gently on the filter, her cheeks drawing in, a lick of smoke trying to escape from her nostril. The video clicking into the machine, the picture lighting up the screen, and Maureen not wanting to watch it but unable to stop because it was a film of her old chum. She would know it was from him. She'd be terrified when she appeared in court, knowing that she didn't have the measure of him, not by half. It was a pleasing image and Angus had his friend to thank for that.

Lying in his tidy single bed, Angus Farrell looked up at the sickly light from the bare bulb and smiled again, his teeth smeared pink with blood.

The car slowed as it approached the red light. It was dark now and a blanket of clouds covered the fat white moon. Maureen had sobered up and the chill sweat had dried on her back, leaving her feeling dirty and spent. Joe was worried because she was drunk and wouldn't let her leave without an escort. It was only when Liam walked in through the lobby doors that she realized Joe had been counting on her calling him. He made some snide remarks about junkies and Tonsa and let them go, calling to Maureen that he'd see her next week, if not before. Liam waved at him, smiling superciliously as if Joe was his slightly confused granny.

Maureen could ask Mark Doyle about Tonsa. She'd seen them having a drink together in Brixton the year before and was sure that he'd know what Tonsa was into now. She just wasn't sure he would tell her. The car engine spluttered and stopped. Liam sighed and pulled out the choke, revving the engine until it started again. He raised a placating hand to the driver behind him and took off. 'What was that Tonsa crack about?'

'Joe McEwan thought I was up at the guy's house because he's Tonsa's brother.'

Liam turned to look at her. 'Tonsa's got a brother?'

'Yeah, a dead creepy one. I think he runs a brothel. He's a bit of a gangster.'

Liam pulled up outside her house and parked nimbly on the corner. 'He doesn't sound like a gangster if he saw you outside his house and called the police.'

'He might not have known it was me, though.' She lowered her voice. 'Joe mentioned the assault again.'

'I told you it was crap.'

'I know, I know,' she said, too insistently.

'Mauri, Tonsa's made allegations left, right and centre. Remember her mental boyfriend got slashed and she went to the papers with it? She said it was the UDA.'

'Listen, we've got a wedding tomorrow.'

'Advertising herself all over the town. What wedding?'

'Kilty's brother's wedding.'

'Auch, shit. I forgot all about that. Kilty's family would have loved all this, wouldn't they?'

Leslie was sitting in the dark, her legs tucked into the sleeping-bag and a cigarette burning in the saucer next to her. She was hugging her knees and rocking slightly when they opened the door, tear tracks streaked down her face. Around her in the living room were bin-bags of clothes and tapes and shoes. She was in for the long haul.

Maureen carried all the bedding she could find through to the front room, spread the duvets over the floor and brought in a big pot of tea and cups, slipping some whisky into her own. They sat up through the dawn, smoking fags and drinking tea, talking about Cammy and telling Liam about Si McGee and poor dead Ella and the door caved in from the inside. Maureen told them about the hand-delivered letters and the pictures, and Liam and Leslie looked at them and agreed that they were probably from Angus. Liam offered to watch the video in his house and tell her what was on it.

Insistent birds were chorusing and the sky was smeared pink and blue like Cinderella's dress as they nodded off. It had been such an eventful night that it didn't occur to Maureen to ask Liam why he had wanted to see her so much and Liam hadn't had the heart to tell her.

expensive perfumes, sweet and lingering, like the alien scent of certainty. Everyone was loud and excited.

A few people greeted Kilty as she approached, smiling to hide their ambivalence. They called her 'Kay' and apologized for not having seen her since she got back. They glanced behind her, assessing Maureen, Liam and Leslie, deigning them unworthy of interest. A kilted man shaped like a cube ran towards Kilty and gave her an unwelcome hug, leaving his arm around her shoulder while she introduced him as Tugsy. 'Brilliant to meet you all,' he said, trying hard to smile at the alarmingly scruffy threesome, then backed off. 'Andy's inside.'

Kilty went into the church. Afraid of being left alone with a load of happy strangers, Maureen, Liam and Leslie traipsed after her.

Andrew Goldfarb was a handsome man. He looked like Kilty but with darker hair and less buggy eyes. She had told them that he was a skinny, specky kid at school but had beefed himself up with an obsessive gym regime, muscle drinks and contact lenses, a process she referred to as 'exorcizing the Jew'. He was dressed in full Highland regalia with kilt and ruffled shirt, black jacket with tails, a sporran trimmed with silver and an ornamental skean-dhu. Traditional lace-up shoes made his feet look girlish and dainty below heavy calves.

'Kay,' said her mother sternly, glancing disapprovingly at her friends, 'go outside and watch for Henrietta.' They stood on the gravel path and lit cigarettes to keep the midges away, feeling uncomfortable and excluded from the throng. The sun began to burn their faces and they moved into the shade of a large tree next to a path made from ancient gravestones. 'Why do they all call you Kay?' asked Leslie.

'My Polish grandmother chose Kilty. Dad only agreed because he thought she was dying. She was always dying.

When I was ten she finally did pop her clogs and they changed it to Kay.'

'I like Kilty better,' said Maureen.

'So do I,' said Kilty, puffing inexpertly on her cigarette, 'but it's immigrant so Mum doesn't. They're happy to socialize in the Polish Club but don't want anyone to know Dad's a Jew.'

'That's a pity,' said Liam, ''cause Poles love the Jews, don't they?'

A cloud of midges moved round from the far side of the tree and chased them back into the sunshine. By the time the ushers came out to round up the guests they were cowering in the church door, hiding from gangs of increasingly narky flies. Kilty waited outside so that she could warn them when the bride arrived.

It was cold inside the chapel. The organist played long, senseless notes and people whispered greetings to latecomers filtering in through the aisles. There was a small commotion at the back of the church and they saw Kilty scuttle up to the front pew just as the organist belted out a chord that commanded attention. A hush fell over the congregation and the participants in the ceremony began their strange, stiff dance.

Maureen watched Kilty up at the front. Her face was set in a harsh reserve and her prominent eyes looked tired and worried. She seemed plain and slightly pretentious. The clasp that had looked so pretty when they picked her up now hung from her thin hair like Gene Kelly off a lamppost. She seemed to shrink when she was with her family, as if her spirit was wilting.

After the ceremony the newly expanded Goldfarb family gathered outside for the photographs and Kilty stood at the edge, just outside the tight little group. Maureen realized as she watched that Kilty was the runt of the litter too, and thought suddenly of Una. She looked at Liam, laughing at a joke Leslie had made. He'd have told her if the baby had been born. She knew he would. First babies were often late.

Kilty sat silently, looking out over the road, as they drove back down the loch to the reception. Liam asked her if she was all right and she said, yeah, yeah, she was fine, give her a fag, for Christsake.

The hotel was a small country house on the banks, close to a marina and a water-ski centre. Much extended at the back, the building was essentially a small modern conference centre with a nice front. Inside, the decor was of the shortbread school: dark tartan wallpaper and *faux* country trimmings. A giant stag's head hung over the ornamental fireplace. It took one and a half hours of watching other people have a nice time before they could go in and sit down. They were bored to the verge of violence by the time the prawn cocktail arrived.

Their dinner companions were three single men and a slim, plain young woman who laughed at everything the men said, as if she was afraid they would attack her and was trying to fend them off. During the meal the men didn't acknowledge any of the strangers across the table and didn't seem to know Kilty at all. They had been at school with Henrietta and hadn't seen each other since.

Eventually Kilty picked up, sitting upright and unclenching her jaw. She joined in the conversation a little and whispered to Maureen that the day was almost halfway through. It wasn't really, but Maureen said, yeah, it would be over soon enough. She was enjoying being out of Glasgow, away from the complications, playing the wedding game of drinking as much complimentary wine as quickly as possible and making it look casual. As the meal wore on the strange schoolfriends talked loudly, insulting each other and laughing insincerely, jostling for status.

'You're the world's biggest prick,' said one and the other man laughed.

'Well, pal,' he said, pointing with his fork, 'you're the world's smallest prick.'

They laughed, joined in descant by the nervous woman. It was getting depressing. Quite suddenly, Liam joined in the laughter, slapping the table with inappropriate vigour, and pointing at the vying men. 'I think you're both pricks,' he shouted.

The other side of the table refused to talk to them after that and began to whisper among themselves. Maureen watched as the laughing woman, now sulking in unison with her compatriots, ate. She gathered tiny morsels on to her fork and raised it to her open mouth, moving her head forward, pulling the fork away slowly, distastefully scratching the food off with her front teeth.

Individual strawberry cheesecakes arrived. They took two spoonfuls to eat and then the plates were whipped away and replaced with coffee. Various people gave bad speeches and a small army of waiters and waitresses came in and cleared a dance floor in front of the top table. A band clambered on to a stage at the side and set up. The doors at the far end of the hall opened and those invited to the reception only filtered in drinking second-best champagne. The first dance went without a hitch and Kilty began to relax.

'Nearly over now,' said Maureen, drawling slightly.

'I think the soonest we could go home would be in about an hour,' whispered Kilty.

Leslie came back from the toilet looking pale. Holding her fag between her teeth, she stood behind Kilty and adjusted the green flower in her hair.

'All right there, Leslie?' said Maureen, feeling warm and not a little pissed.

'Aye,' said Leslie. 'My stomach's killing me. I think I should lay off the drink for a while.'

'Is it a bug?' asked Maureen.

Dunno,' said Leslie.

Kilty smiled at her watch. 'Let's get some air.'

It was cold outside, the air thick with the smell of cut grass and water. The setting sun was low behind the hills, casting a deep shadow over the loch basin. Kilty veered right, coming off the path, and walked down to the trees, sitting down on a grassy ridge, reckless of her dress now that the ordeal was over. Leslie, Liam and Maureen settled by her, lighting cigarettes to keep the midges at bay. Behind them the brilliant white lights from the hotel blazed into the night, spilling on to the black water. Houses and hotels were reflected around the dark perimeter of the loch. Maureen held up her cigarette in a toast to Kilty. 'Well done, wee hen,' she said.

'Yeah, ye got through it,' said Leslie.

'Here's to ye,' said Liam.

Kilty dropped her chin to her knee. 'I hate it.'

'It's done now,' said Maureen. 'You'll never have to attend a sibling's wedding again.'

'I know,' said Kilty. 'By the time this marriage breaks down I'll be old enough to say fuck it.'

'Ye should say fuck it anyway,' said Leslie, master of the art of impoliteness. 'I don't understand why you're so keen to humour them.'

Kilty tried to explain the need for approval to Leslie, who simply didn't understand. Maureen smiled, thinking about her own family. Kilty's family weren't able to have open discussions and honest expressions of emotion. The O'Donnells could do nothing else. She looked at Liam. 'Hey,' she said quietly, letting Kilty and Leslie continue their conversation, 'how's Una?'

Liam looked as if she'd slapped him. Frightened and offended, his mouth hung open and his eyes slid to the grass behind her. She felt suddenly cold, as if something small and hopeful had died inside her. He tried to speak but she stopped him with a hand on his arm.

'You can't just do whatever the fuck you feel like,' insisted Kilty, behind him. 'You have to have some regard for these people. They brought you up and stayed in and spent their money feeding you and dressing you and were nice when they were tired and stuff like that. There's an obligation to do the right thing by them.'

Leslie sighed theatrically. 'But you shouldn't have to betray yourself to spare their feelings.'

'Boy or girl?' muttered Maureen.

'They're good people,' said Kilty. 'They're just different from me.'

'Girl,' said Liam.

They sat and smoked and fought on the bank for a while, until the chill wind coming off the loch began to eat into them. Maureen looked out at the water, somehow knowing this was the last time she would see Loch Lomond, or the last time she'd see it like this anyway, without blood on her hands, with the precious conviction intact that she'd never really done anything irreversibly bad in her life. She looked up at the summit of the hills and saw herself falling, tumbling, hurtling down towards the deep, cold water. She felt like running back into the reception and shagging someone in the toilets.

'Shall we go and get our coats?' asked Kilty.

Maureen shook her head as they stood up, wanted to say no, wanting to stay. Liam rubbed her back too roughly before she was standing up properly and almost pushed her over. 'Don't worry,' he muttered.

Maureen wanted to be sarcastic and make light of it and

say, thanks, yeah, that helps a lot, but her mouth wasn't working.

Kilty thought they should go in and do one last tour of the reception to make it look as if they'd been there all the time. They went over to their table and sat down, drinking what was left of the wine. Liam guzzled spring water and watched Maureen nervously. On the dance floor three kilted men stood in a row, baring their arses to unwilling witnesses. One young buck's mother got up, slapped him on the back of the head and dragged him away. The others whooped and hollered with delight, baring their arses again. Maureen surreptitiously trawled the table for bits of leftover drinks, downing anything she could find. Kitty turned to her. 'We're getting the fuck out of here.' She grinned. 'You look very pale. Have you got a bug like Leslie?'

'Tired,' said Maureen, and stopped dead. Si McGee was across the hall, wearing a white dinner jacket with satin lapels and a red handkerchief in the breast pocket, smoking a slim cigar. He was standing in a group of men, nodding at Mr Goldfarb, as thick white smoke oozed lazily from his mouth and crawled up his face. Maureen caught Leslie's sleeve. 'McGee,' she said. 'McGee's over there.'

'Where?' said Leslie, looking around.

'The one with no chin,' said Maureen, panicked. 'Kilty, who's that man in the white dinner jacket?'

Kilty looked across to her father. 'He's a guy from the Polish Club.'

'*That is Si McGee*,' insisted Maureen.

Kilty looked at him again. 'From Benny Lynch Court? No, that guy was at St Aloysius with the rest of them.'

'Yeah, he was a scholarship boy,' said Maureen.

'No,' said Kilty, absolutely certain. 'He's got a string of estate agencies around Lanarkshire. He's quite well off.'

'Introduce me,' said Maureen, pushing Kilty in front of her.

'Look, Mauri, don't say anything rude,' Kilty primed her, as they made their way across the dance floor. 'You really don't know anything about the guy except that his mother died. Will you behave yourself?'

'Yeah, I will,' said Maureen, nudging Kilty on with her shoulder.

Si McGee was not pleased to see her. He tried to smile as Kilty introduced them, holding out his hand as if he'd never met her before.

'I'm sorry about your mother,' said Maureen, as his eyes took in her tight dress.

'Yes,' he said, his accent even more clipped than it had been in the hospital. 'Thank you.'

The businessmen looked at him curiously. 'Is your mother ill?' said one.

Si looked at his shoes, forcing a smile again when he looked up.

'Mrs McGee died,' said Maureen, making herself look gauche and thoughtless.

'Oh, I'm sorry, Si,' said Mr Goldfarb, rubbing McGee's arm and looking reproachfully at Maureen. 'So sorry. Was it sudden?'

'Yes,' said McGee, taking Maureen by the arm and leading her away from the group, 'quite sudden.'

He was tall actually, standing next to her, holding her arm tightly. She had thought him smaller. She lifted her shoulder awkwardly, trying to wriggle her arm free, but he held on. She stopped walking, keeping her body rigid, and his grip was so strong that her feet skated along the polished dance floor. Kitty caught up with them.

'Get your fuckin' hands off me,' shouted Maureen, attracting the attention of the arse-baring men on the dance floor and subsequently the entire wedding party.

'I thought you were falling,' said Si, just as loudly. 'You seem very drunk.'

'I saw you at my house,' bawled Maureen. 'You were at my house.'

Kilty took Maureen's other arm, and Si let go graciously, wiping his hand on his trouser leg.

'What did Ella do that was so bad?' hissed Maureen, just as her feet slid away from under her. She landed hard on one knee, blushing and cringing. An appalled hush fell over the hall. One of the arse-baring men giggled loudly. Si shook his head pityingly, and looked back to his friends for support. People around the dance floor whispered among themselves.

'Why did you drag me over here?' said Maureen, unsteadily pulling herself upright. 'Are you going to beat *me* up now?'

Si McGee stepped back, surprised. 'I thought you might want to come to my mother's funeral,' he said.

Maureen stared at him and he stared back, his eyes wide and calm behind the glasses, mouth hanging open, meaning no harm. Distracted by a tiny movement, she looked at his neck. The roll of fat on his chin was quivering, giving away a hidden tension inside. 'Where's the funeral?' she asked.

'Ten thirty on Monday, St Stephen's in Partick.'

'I'll see you there,' said Maureen defiantly, taking Kilty's arm and walking away.

'Mauri,' said Kilty, when they were safely ensconced in the car, 'I'm not saying I didn't enjoy it, but you were really out of order there.'

'What did she say?' asked Leslie.

'She asked the guy if he was going to beat her up, apropos of nothing, when he was trying to invite her to the funeral.'

'His neck was shaking,' said Maureen.

Worried, Liam glanced at her in the rear-view mirror. 'It was,' she drawled sullenly. 'His neck was shaking.'

It was only eleven o'clock when Liam dropped them off at Garnethill. Too tired to speak, they climbed the stairs slowly and went about getting ready for bed. Maureen put on the television to fill the irksome silence. The door banged and Leslie, passing and unthinking, opened it. A woman with a square face and a crew-cut stuck a tiny tape-recorder in her face. 'Maureen O'Donnell?'

'Eh, no,' said Leslie. 'She doesn't live here any more.'

The woman sighed heavily.

'I'm Aggie Grey. *If* you see her,' she said, loudly enough for Maureen to hear, 'will you tell her my paper'll pay a lot of money for her story?'

'I won't see her,' said Leslie.

'Just, if you do.'

'I won't.'

Grey turned to go.

'Haven't you got anything better to do with your time?' said Leslie.

The woman turned on the stairs. 'What do you mean?'

'Is this your life, harassing innocent bystanders?'

Grey stumbled back a step, and caught herself on the banister. 'It's part of my job,' she said.

Jim Maliano's door flew open, slapping against the hall wall, and he half leaped into the close, 'Get the hell out of here,' he said. 'There are people in this close who know the police, who can report you for this.'

'I just chapped the door, for Godsake,' said Grey nervously.

'She's going, Jim,' said Leslie.

'Is Maureen in there?' he said, peering behind her, trying to see into the flat.

196

'Go back in, Jim, she's just leaving.'

Jim looked from one to the other, backed off into his hall and shut the door.

Aggie Grey looked at Leslie. 'Is she in there now?' she said.

Leslie scowled and blushed a little. 'Piss off,' she said, and shut the door.

Aggie Grey held the letterbox open, calling through it to Maureen, saying she'd pay a lot of money for her story. Maureen and Leslie carried on as normal, going about their business and getting ready for bed as Aggie bawled through to them. At one point Maureen was coming back from the bathroom when, five feet from the front door, she heard Aggie Grey exhale, burring her lips. 'Oooh, fuck it,' she muttered.

Maureen stopped in the hall.

'What am I fucking doing?' Grey was speaking so quietly she couldn't think anyone would hear her. 'How the fuck did I end up here, hassling nutters for fucksake?'

The letterbox slapped shut and Maureen heard Aggie Grey stand up slowly from the step. She stepped over to the door and watched her through the spy-hole. Grey straightened her legs, muttering curses to herself as she held her sore knees. She picked up a polythene bag and walked heavily away down the stairs.

25
I Spy

Maureen couldn't move. Hinged at the jaw, her head flipped back like a Fabergé egg, opening her tender insides to the elements. It was a sharp rod dropped straight through her, skewering her and passing through her vagina, causing a howling pain in her lower abdomen. She felt the hot wetness on her thighs and woke up with a start, thinking she'd peed the bed. She hadn't. The sheets were wrapped around her legs and she had managed to turn all the way round in the bed.

Maureen lit a cigarette and looked out of the window on a perfect summer's day. Another baby girl had been born to the O'Donnells. The thought made her feel sick. She didn't want to talk about the baby, she didn't want to talk about anything ever again, and Leslie would be sitting staring at her all day. As she pulled on her shorts she found the number from Mark Doyle in the pocket. She looked at it for a while, losing herself in the numbers.

The town was busy, everyone moving fast, like cold-blooded lizards overheated by the sun. She stopped at a large chemist's for some painkillers, walked through the jets of warm air into the cool shop and cosmecutical stands. When she had had a lot of money Maureen had come here a lot, buying overpriced vanishing cream and miracle conditioners. She loved them, loved the promise of change, of not being herself any more after a mere three months of consistent application. The pharmacy was at the back of the shop. It was just after eight in the morning and willowy junkies were already there, handing in used needles and getting doses of methadone. A slow-blinking man with filthy black hair drawled to his pal, 'Come on, Jonny, man, it's sunny.'

Jonny-man was not relaxed. The chemist pursed her lips tight and refused to look at him as she placed the small plastic cup on the counter. The thick blue-green liquid inside was as dark and inviting as the loch the night before. The agitated man lifted it and drank, rolling his tongue around the inside, lapping up the last few drops. He put it down on the counter again, watching it ruefully, wishing it full again. He turned and walked away.

The chemist pinched a smile at Maureen and knocked the used cup into a bin with a wooden spatula. 'May I help you?'

'Painkillers,' said Maureen. 'Nothing dissolvable.'

She walked back up the hill to the house, chewing on a bitter paracetamol, reflecting on the injustice of Una having a girl. Una would use the baby to prove she didn't believe Maureen had been abused. She'd encourage contact, bring Michael over to the house, maybe even leave the baby alone with him. Maureen had often wondered how the horror of her own abuse could have occurred under the noses of neighbours and friends, teachers and doctors, priests and the gang of interchangeable nuns who taught them catechism. She felt sure someone must have seen something, a change, a withdrawal. Some adult somewhere must have seen some small clue and they ignored it, did nothing, sent her home to Michael. She could see the clues now and she wasn't going to ignore them. Angus's trial started on Monday. If she fucked up and got sent to jail, she wouldn't be able to do anything to protect the baby. If she was going to do anything about it she had four days left.

Back at the flat Leslie was still feeling ill and had made an appointment with the doctor for the afternoon. She was fretting about Cammy and so agitated that she didn't notice how tired Maureen was. 'God,' whined Leslie, 'everyone knows he's been living with me and now I've realized that he's such a prick. Everyone must have known, you knew didn't ye?'

'Yeah.'

'It's so humiliating.'

Maureen was thinking about Michael and Una and Winnie together, another child fed to Michael to appease him, another girl spending her life getting over him. Leslie was pausing, waiting for her to respond to something she'd said.

'Oh, well,' said Maureen.

Satisfied, Leslie launched off again. 'I feel like I've made an arse of myself. D'you think I've made an arse of myself?'

'Oh, for fucksake, Leslie,' snapped Maureen, 'being humiliated doesn't mean you've done anything special, it just means you got out of bed. Life's humiliating.'

Leslie stopped still. 'What's the matter? Are you embarrassed about last night?'

'No,' said Maureen, furiously. 'That guy's running a fucking brothel and I should be embarrassed?'

'You were pissed, Mauri. You fell over on the dance floor.'

'I don't give a shit. It probably made Kilty's night anyway.' She felt it in her stomach. An overwhelming swell of sorrow raced up her throat and she burst into tears.

Leslie sat her down in the living room and brought her a coffee.

'Let's go and see this woman I know,' she said sweetly. 'She's called Joan and she works with prostitutes. She'll tell us if she's ever heard of McGee. We'll go and see Joan, okay?'

'Who the fuck is she anyway?' said Maureen, drying her eyes petulantly. 'I'm sorry, it's just that guy – what he did to his mother – it's awful.'

'Think rationally, Mauri, why would a small claims case matter enough for him to kill her? It's only seven hundred pounds – that jacket he had on must have cost a few quid. He's obviously not short of cash.'

'It might not be about the money. Maybe I'll ask him when I see him – the case is tomorrow.'

'You're not going?'

'Yeah, I'm going. I want to show my face for Ella, just to piss him off. Show him I'm not frightened.' But she was hoping that Si would mind very much, she was hoping for a fight. She sipped her coffee and thought about Ella. 'Kilty said the mortician might have been bribed to lie to me about the cause of death.'

Leslie was losing patience. 'Why would anyone bother doing that?'

'Because,' explained Maureen, trying to be coherent when she wanted to smash the cup off the wall, 'if Ella died of her injuries after being battered, the police would be looking for the person who beat her up. They'd get done for murder. If she died from her wounds I could tell the police about her fight with Si and then they could deal with it all.'

'So if you think it was a spontaneous heart-attack you'll leave it?'

'Yeah.'

'Can't we get a copy of her official death certificate from the hospital? They think you're her daughter, don't they? Why don't you just ask the police?'

'Because they think I'm a mental case.'

Paddy's was busy but not at their end of the tunnel. News of Ella's death had reached the market and several people came up to offer their condolences to Maureen, as if she was Ella's family. She saw the women whispering about her, talking to each other, telling each other that, despite slumming it here, she was a good sort after all and had been kind to that Ella. Everyone asked her when the funeral was but she didn't expect a big turnout. The service was on a working day and Ella hadn't been popular. Maureen couldn't even go herself; the court case started that day.

The heat from outside trickled down the tunnel on a breeze, warming the damp, making the tunnel feel clammy. Maureen was too miserable to take turns going for walks outside and Leslie couldn't sit still. Every shadow in the doorway was Cammy coming in to make a scene. They swapped seats so that Leslie could watch the door but that just made her more jumpy. She kept going for walks, coming back, sitting down, getting freaked out and going away again. Maureen's sympathy was threadbare. By the time Leslie left for her doctor's appointment Maureen was glad to see the back of her.

She was keeping an eye on the wheelie bin and watching Peter's stall while he went to get lunch when she saw Mark Doyle coming down the tunnel towards her, wearing his overcoat on the hottest day of the decade. He kept his head down as he walked towards her. She smiled up at him. 'You've not phoned me,' he said abruptly.

'I haven't done anything yet,' she said.

He nodded, nervous and tired, wrapping his arms around his middle as though his stomach ached. 'I thought ye'd decided not to phone.' His voice was so quiet she could hardly hear him.

'I've had a lot on,' she said. She nodded him on to Leslie's stool but he shook his head.

'Ye don't seem busy,' he said, looking down the quiet tunnel.

She smiled. 'You don't read the papers, do you?' Doyle frowned quizzically, not understanding the connection.

'I looked at your number this morning,' she said. 'I was thinking about phoning ye. It's just ... I think I should make my mind up first.'

Doyle sagged at this, glancing out towards the bright door. 'Hen,' he said, suddenly, 'you don't know about this ... kind of thing. You'll get done.'

'Ye won't change my mind, Mark,' she said firmly, 'not once I've decided.'

'Ye want to go tae jail?'

She stared at her feet. 'There's a baby, it's not just about me.' She looked up at him. The edges of his mouth had turned down, the muscles on his jawbone twitching as he ground his teeth.

Doyle dropped his voice. 'I can help ye. I can tell ye ... stuff. Where to go, how to get away. Ye'll get done otherwise. Phone me, whatever ye decide.'

He made her nod before he turned and walked away, passing Leslie unnoticed at the mouth of the tunnel. Maureen shivered in her seat. He'd help her get away. At a stroke Mark Doyle had robbed her of her best reason for not doing it.

'I've got a bug,' said Leslie. 'Doctor gave me antibiotics.'

Maureen watched Doyle squinting against the sun, deciding which way to go. He disappeared down the lane.

'It's boiling out there,' said Leslie, crouching into her seat. 'An old woman fainted in the lane and had to be carried into the café so she didn't get sunburnt while she waited for the ambulance.'

'Did you see that guy pass you on the way in?'

'What guy?'

'The tall guy with the overcoat on.'

'What guy?'

Back at the flat Leslie boiled some pasta, stirred in a bit of pesto and dropped cheese on it. Maureen listened to her speculate about what Cammy would be doing right now. The pasta was bland and rubbery and the cheese tasted rancid. Maureen moved it around her plate a bit and emptied some of it back into the pot when Leslie went to the toilet. She couldn't stop thinking about Michael and the baby. A rage was growing inside her belly, a white-hot fury snowballing in her chest, taking from her to feed itself. The thought of spending a night listening to Leslie ramble about Cammy made her head ache.

'What'll we do tonight, then?' said Leslie cheerfully, sitting down at the table.

'I've got my meeting,' said Maureen.

'Oh, it's Thursday, isn't it?' said Leslie, disappointed.

'Never mind. You get a video and fall asleep watching it, I'll be back late.' Leslie looked at her curiously. 'Sheila said she wants a chat,' added Maureen. She'd have to tell her about the baby soon, otherwise Leslie would think she hated her for moving in, but the truth and what she could safely tell anyone were getting confused in her mind. When she thought about killing Michael she couldn't remember if she needed to or wanted to, if she would be doing something useful or indulging herself like Angus.

Leslie was sorry to see her go out but she settled back on the settee with a cup of tea to watch some crap telly. As Maureen stood in the hall and looked at the back of her head she knew Leslie'd phone Cammy within the hour. 'Why don't you phone Kilty and get her to come over?' she suggested.

'Yeah,' said Leslie, without turning round. 'I might well do that.'

Maureen opened the door and stepped out into the cool

close, knowing she should have stayed with her sad pal.

In Sauchiehall Street a drunken crowd of sensibly dressed women were waiting at the taxi rank, howling a gentle ballad. She passed a team of teenage boys, hanging about in a pedestrian precinct, kicking a bin. When the rain and the darkness returned, all the office workers and teenagers would look back on this time, some from jail cells, some from maternity units, and wonder what they'd been thinking of. Maureen crossed the river, passed the Sheriff Court and Ella McGee's high-rise. She knew it was a rough area, not one for walking through alone, but she almost hoped that someone would jump out at her, attack her, so she could vent her fury. She walked on into the south side, walking until the soles of her feet hurt.

It was a good area, full of architectural finds, large cars and delicatessens. The houses had burglar alarms outside, flashing red or blue high on the walls. As she turned the corner and approached the house, she knew that Una was inside because her pride and joy, her green Rover, was parked in the street under the shade of an old tree. It was a company car, a symbol of her success, and the leather seats and walnut dash reassured her that she was making it.

Una's house was the bottom floor in a squat three-storey tenement. The large three-bedroom flat had two reception rooms and a big kitchen which led into a sliver of private garden, most of it concreted over. The reception rooms were at the front and, as she approached, Maureen saw that the lights were on in the living room.

In the street in front of the flat was a small fenced-in island garden. It was thirty feet across and a hundred yards long, with signs on the gates reserving use of the garden for key-holders and residents. A driver had crashed into the fence and the replacement chicken wire hadn't been soldered yet. Maureen pulled out the overlap, climbed through, and sat on a bench directly opposite Una's front room. She watched and waited.

In the course of an hour and a half no one came into the room but as the light began to fade she noticed movement through the open door in the hallway. She waited until she could be sure of what she was seeing, worked out the geography of the house, and slipped out of the garden, following the lane round to the back of the flat.

Una would have done up the garden for the baby coming: she was too organized and controlling to let a major consideration like that slip by, but when Maureen got there and peered through the thin hedge, she discovered that nothing had changed. The concrete was still there, three white plastic garden chairs were still sitting out, uncleaned after the grimy winter. Maureen was so self-involved she'd forgotten about Una's troubles, hadn't really considered how hard Alistair's affair with the upstairs neighbour must have hit her sister.

Crouching down, keeping her head below the hedge, she looked into the brightly lit kitchen. The windows were barred with Venetian blinds and she had to concentrate hard to see, screwing up her eyes and disciplining herself to stare at one slit of light despite movement in others.

Una had changed her hair. It was a relationship break-up hairdo, a radical change, chosen in a state of upset. She'd cut it short, above her ears, and had streaked it different hues of blonde. She was sitting at the table with her back to the window, her hands busy in front of her. Alistair came and went from the room, bringing things, taking a nappy bag away. He kept his eyes down, only looking at Una's chest, smiling when she wasn't talking to him. Una must be holding the baby, feeding it. The television news flickered blue and grey on the worktop. Una was usually meticulous about the house but dirty plates and baby bottles were stacked on the counter, and the table was strewn with wipes and a blanket.

Una tugged at her jumper and lifted a bleary-eyed baby to her shoulder. Maureen couldn't see its face, the blind was in the way, just a tiny red mouth and chubby jowls. The mouth opened and a slick of white sick dripped down Una's shoulder. It took her a moment to feel the wetness of it. She looked at the baby, as if demanding an explanation, and sat it in a plastic carry-chair, folding the handle back. Then she turned and spoke to what Maureen had assumed was the top of a grey soft toy before leaving the room.

The man stood up unsteadily, looking at the baby, and turned to the window, his face red, sweat stains on his collar, and Maureen knew him immediately. It was Michael.

26

Hope

He was eating a slice of toast when he opened the door and looked out at her. He didn't speak. He took in the vomit splatters on her T-shirt, her dirty, cut knees and the hedge leaves in her hair. She tried to look up at him but only got as far as his chin when she started to cry and raised a hand to hide her face. Liam dropped his toast on, the floor and reached out, took her by the wrist like a lost child and pulled her into the house. It took over an hour to suture the tears.

'Calmer?' asked Liam.

She wiped her face, feeling like an idiot.

'Come on.' He took her into the kitchen, sat her on a chair at the table and poured some milk into a pan. As he took the Ovaltine out of the doorless cupboard he caught her eye and smiled at her. She breathed in, shuddering at the unaccustomed depth. 'Are you making that for me because I'm a pathetic fucking idiot?' she said.

'Yeah.'

He set two cups on the worktop, spooning sugar and malty powder into them. Liam had been forced to stop refurbishing the kitchen because of his resit exam, but he'd already ripped the doors off all the cupboards and pulled up the filthy lino. It was quiet in the house and there was comfort in watching Liam, sure and steady, performing a chore. Maureen prayed that he wouldn't be mentioned in the court case. She wiped her nose on her hand. 'It's nice in here.'

Liam looked at her sceptically as he poured the warm milk into the powder.

'I mean it's nicer. Cleaner. It's clean.'

Liam put the cup down in front of her. 'Drink that,' he said. 'It'll calm ye down.'

'How?' She sniffed. 'Is it drugged?'

Liam grinned as he sat down. 'Yeah,' he said, and made a joke of forgetting which mug had the drugs in it and reaching anxiously for her cup. When she wrapped her hands around the warm mug the gentle heat seeped into her chilled fingertips. She sipped it and the creamy drink slid down her throat, warming her tired, tight belly. 'Have ye watched that video yet?' she asked.

'Oh, God, no, not yet,' said Liam. 'I'm building up to it. Are ye going to tell me what happened to you tonight, or will I guess?'

'Guess.'

'Una?'

Maureen nodded.

'Michael?'

She nodded again, seeing Michael's face again in her mind's eye. Her stomach tightened and she had to rub her eyes hard to make the image go away.

'Mauri, he's not going to abuse a newborn baby. The baby isn't you, remember? Alistair's there, Una's there, and they've got a nanny coming in during the day. Una won't leave the baby with Michael. I don't even know if he's going to be there that much.'

She looked up at him, appreciating the kind lies, knowing he meant well.

'I went over there,' she said quietly. 'I saw Michael through the window. Una left the baby alone with him.'

Liam sighed. 'Mauri, why did you go there?'

'I just wanted to know. I want to know where he is. I want

209

to know what he's doing and what he looks like ...'

'You're just upsetting yourself.'

'I want to know, I need to know things ...'

'Honestly, spying on him through a window. Ye couldn't know everything that goes on, you'll just worry yourself.'

Maureen sat back and looked out of the window at the dark garden. 'I'd like to know everything,' she said wistfully. 'Everything I've ever wondered about. D'ye ever think that?' She tried to smile at him but Liam looked worried. 'I'd like to know everything about everyone. No mysteries left. No secrets.'

Liam sipped his drink and looked at her, licking the frothy moustache from his top lip. 'He's not a well man, Mauri. By the time the wean's up a bit he'll probably be dead.'

'How can she see him?' said Maureen, getting angry. 'How can she have him in her house? He's nothing to us. He was never even there.'

Liam pulled a cigarette out of his packet and lit up. 'I think Una and Marie remember him differently than we do. All he ever was to us was trouble. I think they remember him before he got really bad. You know? Happier times.'

'Well, I don't remember any of them.'

'But I think that's what they're chasing, those happier times. He's very sick.'

'What's wrong with him?' asked Maureen, hoping for a virulent cancer.

Liam watched her drink her Ovaltine. 'Winnie thinks it's a brain tumour,' he said solemnly.

Winnie never suspected anyone of having a slight cold or being overtired. For Winnie every symptom spoke a massive, dramatic, terminal malfunction. Maureen spluttered the milky drink over the table and they started laughing, looking around the room, enjoying the release.

Suddenly she remembered Michael alone with the baby. Her face became hot and she began to cry again. She caught her breath. 'Just the mild headaches, then?' she said, wiping Ovaltine off her chin.

Liam snorted and leaned over in his chair, balancing on two legs as he picked up the kitchen roll from the worktop. He pulled three sheets off the roll and mopped up the milky mess in front of Maureen. 'I think', he said, 'it's a bit more than that. He shakes a lot and his legs are a bit unsteady. He can't really be left alone.'

'What do the doctors say?'

'He won't go. They'll tell him to stop drinking and smoking. Keeps insisting there's nothing wrong with him. I think he'll be dead by Christmas.'

'They said that about the war.'

Chan, Liam's Chinese student lodger, tiptoed down the passageway into the dark kitchen. He nodded politely to them, bending from the waist and smiling. 'Hello,' he said, pretending not to notice Maureen's swollen eyes and red nose.

'Hi, Chan,' said Maureen.

'Yeah,' said Liam, gruffly.

Sensing the extent of his intrusion, Chan grabbed a family-sized packet of crisps from his open food cupboard and left as quickly as he had come in.

'He's paying rent here, Liam, ye shouldn't be so rude to him.'

'I fucking hate having strangers in here. Why can't they fuck off home for summer?' He stood up and picked up his cup. 'Let's go outside.'

They sat on the cold stairs leading up to the garden. Neighbourhood cats yowled at each other, creeping through the undergrowth.

'Una's very bitter,' said Liam sadly. 'I swear she's spending time with him because it upsets everyone.'

'What the fuck is she bitter about? She wanted a kid, she's got one, she's got a good job and a nice house. Marriages split up but she's not exactly on her uppers, is she?'

'Yeah, well.' Liam sighed and scratched his neck. 'Una had hopes, I think.'

'More fool her,' muttered Maureen, watching the moonlight creep about the garden.

'I don't know if it is foolish,' said Liam. 'I think it's kind of hopeful. Coming out of Winnie and George's house and dreaming of a good life. It was one of the things I liked most about her. She's as sour as a leech now.'

'Yeah?'

'Aye. Sees badness everywhere. It's a shame. Bitterness is a terrible thing. Sucks the good out of everything. What would you hope for? If you could have anything.'

Maureen smiled at the thought of herself having a future but Liam was earnest. 'Dunno,' she said, looking out into the dark garden. 'Maybe I'd go back to college. I'd be a curator and be surrounded by beautiful things. I'd be content, I suppose. Stop worrying all the time.'

He tutted derisively, as if she'd never known a moment's grief. 'What are *you* worried about?'

'What've ye got?' she said, chewing an imaginary match.

'Just you bide your time, wee hen,' said Liam softly. 'Don't worry about Michael. You'll see, one day soon, everything'll come up, Maureen.'

Maureen smiled and nodded, but she knew she would be watching Michael night after night just to know where he was in the city.

27
Skank

The sheriff court was a huge building facing the river with modernist columns in grey granite and windows set well back, giving it a solemn, unwelcoming air. Maureen had been fresh and clean when she left the market but during the short walk across the bridge the hot sun made her legs damp and her skirt ride up, the thin inner lining gathering around her waist. She kept expecting McGee's hand on her shoulder as she came off the bridge and followed the path to the imposing front steps. The doorway was four storeys high, a smoked-glass window leading into a vast lobby and the hollow heart of the courts. Inside the door, security staff were gathered around a high-arched metal detector. Two large signs, one on each wall, ordered people to leave their knives, swords and guns outside. Maureen walked through the metal detector without setting it off and approached a reception desk. 'I'm looking for the small-claims court,' she said, and noticed that her voice sounded shaky.

The man behind the counter nodded her to a spiral staircase in the centre of the lobby. 'Court three,' he said. 'Up to the top.'

Her knees were trembling as she climbed the stairs but she thought of Ella lying on the cold metal trolley in the makeshift chapel and took hold of the handrail firmly, pulling herself up. The door to the court was locked and the claimants had to wait on soft chairs in the corridor, facing each other, watching for their adversaries to come and sit next to them. An old man across from Maureen, dressed in his best cheap suit, scraped the sweat from his palms with the edge of an underground ticket. A woman next to him was twitching and being comforted by her tarty daughter in a pink plastic skirt and white vest top. Everyone had their papers with them, held in folders or envelopes, some with crumpled letters from the court, folded to fit into a pocket. Maureen sat down and watched the stairs. At exactly two thirty a small man in a blue uniform unlocked the door from the inside, pinning it open into the corridor.

The court was partitioned off into concentric circles by low wooden walls. In the centre of the room stood a large, highly polished table with wigged and gowned lawyers sitting around it, speaking quietly to one another and looking through papers. The lawyers' strange outfits made them look like the perpetrators of a bizarre practical joke. Below the judge's bench, sitting alone, was a young woman with silver-rimmed glasses and a dark, sleek bob showing beneath her white wig. Surrounding the table was a low wooden partition wall with areas for hemming in the public, the jury and, furthest away and higher than everyone else, the judge's big fancy chair.

The man in the blue uniform told the public to sit down in the two rows of benches near the door. Maureen tried to get in first in case Si turned up and she had to sit near him, but everyone wanted to sit there. She had to settle for a seat next to the aisle. When they were all sitting down the bobbed woman lawyer explained that she was the clerk of the court. As their cases were called, she said, they were to stand up and come through the little partition gate to the big table and wait to be asked about the details.

'Only answer questions from the Sheriff and only speak through the Sheriff. Do not speak to each other while the Sheriff is dealing with your case, is that clear?'

They nodded dumbly, and the blue man went off through a side door. The tarty girl giggled about something and her mother huffed in dismay. Maureen was watching them when, out of the corner of her eye, she saw a tall, slim woman slip in from the corridor and sit three benches back. She was wearing a smart grey trouser suit with a pale slate scarf. She settled her expensive leather handbag on her knee, her gaze focused on air. It was Tonsa. She didn't look around, didn't try to find anyone among the crowd, but Maureen knew that Tonsa was there to warn her.

The usher came back out of the side door, told them all to stand up and the Sheriff came in. He walked along the back row and sat down. The usher told them all they could sit down now, and they did.

Maureen looked around at the public benches. Everyone was frightened and apprehensive, not knowing what was going to happen next or what was expected of them. The Sheriff called the first case and they relaxed back into their chairs as they realized it wasn't them. Two of the lawyers in the central pen stood up and told the Sheriff that they were representing the respective parties to the case. They all muttered to each other and the Sheriff read for a bit and told them to come back later. The bobbed clerk read through her papers and gave them a date. After a short read the Sheriff called another case. The nervous mother with the tarty daughter leaped to her feet and turned this way and that, looking terrified. The usher beckoned her through the little partition and she stood at the table with the lawyers and waited expectantly while the Sheriff read through the notes. The woman was shaking. Even the skin on her back seemed to be trembling under her nylon blouse. Behind Maureen the woman's tarty daughter giggled unhelpfully and told the man next to her to look, look at the state of her. When the Sheriff finally asked her a question the nervous woman looked as if she might go into spasm. The Sheriff asked if the other party was represented. One of the lawyers said he was there on behalf of someone or other. The Sheriff told them to come back later and the clerk gave them a date.

This long and tedious process continued. Maureen was getting increasingly anxious. Tonsa wasn't looking at her: she was staring blindly ahead, not fidgeting like the other members of the public, sitting still like a snake laying a trap. Maureen looked her over. Her face was blank. She blinked, making Maureen jump and turn back to the court, afraid she had been spotted.

As she watched it became obvious that the Sheriff hadn't read any of the papers and was so disinterested that all he could do was put the cases off for two weeks. Another set of disappointed people came back to their seats in the public benches, and she felt a gentle tap on her shoulder. Kilty was standing behind her, nudging along the bench to sit down. 'Hiya,' said Maureen, unreasonably excited in the circumstances.

'I skived off my work,' whispered Kilty.

'I'm glad,' said Maureen, happily looking around now that her pal was with her.

Ella's case was called. Maureen looked at Tonsa, expecting her to stand up and go to the table. Tonsa didn't move. The case was called again and Maureen stood up, trembling, and made her way through the partition to the table, embarrassed because Tonsa was watching her. One of the lawyers sidled up next to her with an impressive bundle of papers and leaned on the table with his fingertips, turning the knuckles white. The Sheriff looked up at Maureen over his glasses and through force of habit she smiled at him. He did not smile back. He went back to reading the papers. 'Are you representing Mr Simon McGee?' he asked eventually.

The lawyer next to her nodded. 'Yes, Your Honour.'

the grass next to Kilty. 'You were great in there,' he said to Maureen. It was Si McGee's lawyer.

'But I got chucked out.'

'I know,' he said, grinning as he took out a packet of cigarettes, 'but you fundamentally undermined his authority. It was a bit of a shambles after you left.'

He offered them a cigarette each and Kilty took one, even though she was sharing with Maureen. He was the same age as them with fat red lips and a single dark eyebrow that dipped to a widow's peak in the middle of his nose, setting his face in a perpetual frown. He would be amazing-looking when he got older and filled out, when his lips lost some of their lustre and his eyebrow bushed up and turned grey.

'Kilty Goldfarb.' Kilty held out her tiny hand, and as he took it Maureen understood why he had approached them.

'Josh Menzies.'

Josh and Kilty grinned at each other, got embarrassed by what they were both thinking, and looked away sharply. Maureen couldn't handle the tension of sitting on the grass waiting for Tonsa to attack her for a minute longer. 'It's an interesting building, the Sheriff Court,' she said.

'Yes,' Josh nodded, 'it is interesting.'

Kilty and Josh smoked in silence.

'Maybe you could show us around it,' said Maureen.

'Yes!' Josh exclaimed. 'I could show you around the building. There's a café, we could have a coffee together.'

'Oh. My. God,' said Kilty, as if he was offering unlimited access to Jesus, Tom Jones and the Crown Jewels. 'That would be brilliant.'

Josh and Kilty simultaneously threw away their barely touched cigarettes and got up, brushing themselves down and grinning widely at the river. Maureen hadn't finished her cigarette but felt it would be churlish to insist. She already felt superfluous as they walked back to the Sheriff Court and up the steps. Josh and Kilty weren't talking to each other but they were smiling coyly, weaving back and forth towards each other as they walked up to the door.

Josh took them on a dull tour of the building, which consisted mostly of him pointing at different doors and saying that there was a court in there. Throughout the tour Kilty simpered and Josh basked. When their interest in one another got too blatant or they got stuck looking into one another's eyes, Maureen asked a question. Josh was a lawyer and he came from Edinburgh. His dad was a bus driver and his mum ran a newsagent's. He lived in Glasgow now, in the West End.

'Just like me!' squealed Kilty.

'So, do you know Si McGee, then?' said Maureen, keen to change the subject before Kilty had a public orgasm.

'No,' said Josh. 'We just get the papers for small claims, we don't get briefed.'

'His sister was in there, did you see her?'

No, was she? I don't know either of them.'

He took them to the cafeteria. It was a large room, running the full length of one side of the building. Only the lawyers and court staff were allowed to use it. Suits and gowns and uniforms clustered around tables, keeping with their own kind. Because it was late on a Friday afternoon the café had run out of sandwiches. There were only crisps and biscuits left. They ordered three tasteless coffees in orange plastic cups. Josh insisted on paying for them, winking flashily as he took out a twenty and waved it at Kilty, who giggled.

They were sitting down at a long table, sipping coffee, when Maureen became aware of someone standing just behind her at the limit of her line of vision, like Michael.

The person was looking at her and, sure it was Tonsa, Maureen spun round to catch her. Benny Gardner was staring at her.

Benny Gardner had been Liam and Maureen's mutual best friend at school. As stamp collectors find each other at church fêtes, as paedophiles meet at bus stops, the children of alcoholic families know the signals and find their own. Benny had been expelled from school for being pissed in class and setting fire to a toilet. At the tail end of his drinking, Benny was blacking out so much that his stories started to sound like other people's dreams. One day he woke up in an Alcoholics Anonymous meeting and miraculously, against all bets, got sober, went to university and did a law degree.

He had changed in the year since she had seen him. He was dressed in a conservative suit, a white shirt and a dark tie. He was balder and had two long parallel white scars on his jawline below his ear. His shoes were highly polished. He looked at her helplessly, opened his limp hands towards her, pleading.

'Hey, Benny,' said Josh, 'come here.'

Benny approached the table, circling Maureen as if he was afraid of her. Josh tried to start some showy banter with him, teasing him about his team, but Benny didn't respond. He was looking at Maureen. 'Can I speak to you?' said Benny quietly, his teeth clenched tight.

'I've got nothing to say to you,' said Maureen, looking at her coffee.

Maureen and Liam didn't see Benny any more, not since Angus Farrell blackmailed him, threatening his golden future, using him to inveigle his way into Maureen's house and plant evidence. Liam beat up Benny so badly he spent two weeks in hospital. They lied to each other now and said they didn't miss Benny, didn't wonder what he was up to or think about him. There was some suggestion that Winnie had met him at AA but Maureen was afraid to ask Liam about it.

'I need to talk,' said Benny. 'It's about Monday.'

Maureen looked at him. Benny had grown up. He had dips in his cheeks, under his eyes, Al Pacino pouches that made him look old. The last time she had seen Benny was after Liam beat him up: he had been lying in a bed at the Albert, his eyes purple and swollen like tennis balls, his wrist broken and his jaw wired together. She'd poked him in the eye and walked away. Had it been any other time, even a couple of days ago, she'd have snubbed him but now everything was coming to an end and Benny felt like part of a happier past. He knew Angus, had fucked her over for him before, and as far as she knew he was probably the source of the video and the pictures, but she wanted to talk to him. She wondered if Liam would see it that way. He probably missed Benny just as much as she did but he'd never admit it. She stood up slowly, and followed him to a nearby empty table, clutching her coffee and sitting down opposite him, waiting for him to speak.

'How have ye been?' he asked.

'Okay.'

Benny looked around the table top. 'I heard about Farrell's case coming up on Monday, I saw you in the papers.'

'You've got scars.' She gestured to his jaw and he raised his hand, touched the ridges of skin on his face.

'Aye,' he said sadly. 'Long-term reminder of the fact that I'm a skank.' He tried to smile at her but she wasn't having it. He put his hands on the table, sitting one on top of the other. 'Mauri, I'm so sorry. I know ye can never forgive me.' He looked up to see how he was doing but she glared back and he dropped his eyes to his hands again. 'I can't defend what I did. I didn't think Farrell was that smart, I didn't think he'd get away with what he did. He threatened to make my record public if I didn't help him. I'm sorry I hurt you.'

'You didn't hurt me, Benny, ye put me in terrible danger, ye discussed aspects of my psychiatric history with a man so he wouldn't spoil your chances of a good job. Do you know why he killed Douglas?'

Benny looked at her. 'I thought they fell out.'

'Angus was raping catatonic patients in a psychiatric unit and Douglas found out. He killed him to cover up. That's what you were participating in, that's who you were helping.'

Benny cringed, rubbing hard at his eyes, digging his fingers deep into the sockets.

'And you claim to be sober and leading a good life?' she said.

'I don't claim that,' he said, sitting up to face her, looking like the Benny she used to know. 'I just claim to be doing my best. At that time I didn't know what the consequences of my actions were. I lied to myself about what I was doing and why I was doing it. I thought ye'd be okay, I was lying to myself. I don't have an excuse but I'm sorry and I'm trying not to lie to myself now.'

He sat back and dropped his head, showing her his crown as he rubbed his hand over the cropped hair. It wasn't a very satisfying explanation but it was honest and he wasn't pretending not to be responsible. She heard his hand rasp across his head and wondered if he was still in the same flat in Maryhill, how his sister was and whether he'd seen Winnie, what films he was into just now and why he was in court today. But he'd fucked her over for Angus before. He could have run up the road to her house in his lunch-hour, dropped the video and been back here without anyone noticing.

'What videos are ye watching these days?' she said, watching his face carefully.

'Oh, man,' his face lit up, eager and enthusiastic, 'Takeshi Kitano. Have ye seen anything by him?'

She shook her head.

'You should. *Violent Cop*, it's fucking brilliant. And *Hana Bi*. Get it out.'

There was nothing in his face or manner to suggest that he knew what she was hinting at so she tried again. 'You enjoy watching videos, don't you?' she said solemnly.

Benny looked at her dumbly.

'And looking at photographs.'

His face twitched and he sat back, staring at her, baffled. 'Wha'?'

She leaned in, watching him carefully. 'Do I like to look at photographs, do you think?'

Benny laughed, puzzled. 'Are you trying to find out if I'm a mason or something?'

Maureen realized that she sounded like a Cold War cliché. She snorted, trying not to catch his eye or guffaw at the preposterousness of it all.

'How's the big man these days?' he said.

It was an old joke. Liam was half a foot shorter than Benny. She didn't like him sounding so familiar. 'Liam's studying,' she said formally, claiming ownership.

'I heard he got into uni.'

'He's making films.'

'I see Winnie sometimes. She tells me you two aren't speaking.'

'Well, she's lying out of her arse. *I'm* not speaking. She won't stop speaking.'

They looked each other in the eye but it was too much too soon and they looked away to opposite sides of the room.

'See this Monday?' said Benny.

'Aye.'

'This has to be in confidence. I heard this from someone in his lawyer's office. If it gets out they'll know it's come from me. Promise ye won't repeat it?'

She didn't trust him. 'I won't repeat it,' she said, uncertain that she was telling the truth.

'He's pleading automatism. D'you know what that is?'

'Sounds like a sci-fi disease from the thirties,' she said, imagining a giant tin robot doing Angus's bidding.

Benny smiled. 'It kind of is.' He glanced cautiously up at her. 'Automatism means he didn't have the mental intent to do it. He's bringing evidence that he was given drugs without his consent or knowledge and that the drugs made him do it.'

Maureen was startled. 'But that's crap,' she said. She had fed him the acid long after he had killed Douglas and a good few days after he had killed Martin.

'They don't have much physical evidence against him for Douglas. They'd probably need to bring evidence of the rapes to get a conviction for killing him. I don't know who drugged him. I think it was you but—' Benny looked at her for a prompt but she didn't give him one. 'They're going to make a big thing about you having a copy of Douglas's marriage certificate in your house as well, try to build on it, say you were jealous and stuff like that. Be careful what you say. You could find yourself on an assault charge.'

Maureen had stopped listening. She was sitting upright, staring across the room, smiling to herself. She could get Ella McGee's death certificate from the registrar's office, just as she had got a copy of Douglas's marriage certificate. She noticed that Benny was watching her.

'They can't force me into giving evidence against myself, can they?'

'Yeah,' said Benny. 'Of course they can.'

'Can't I plead the Fifth Amendment?'

Benny smiled. 'That's American law, not Scots,' he said.

She blushed. She was so out of her depth. 'Sorry.'

'Don't be.'

'They'll think I'm a fucking idiot if I come out with something like that, won't they?'

'Naw. They'll think you're a well-disguised pensioner. People used to plead the Fifth all the time during Jimmy Cagney's heyday.'

'Will they convict me of attacking him?'

'No,' said Benny slowly. 'Listen, this is a case against *him*. If they were going to bring a case against you for drugging him that would be a separate case.'

'Can they suggest things like this when I haven't had a case against me?'

'All the prosecution need to do is prove it enough to raise a reasonable doubt in the jury's mind about his guilt. Did you give him the drugs?'

She looked at him sceptically. 'Yeah, Gardner, I really trust you now.'

He rasped his hand over his head. 'I think they'll lead evidence that you got it off Liam.'

Maureen's eyes filled up. 'I think that too,' she said, swallowing hard. 'And I have to answer the questions or I'll go to jail.'

'To consider your position.'

'To consider my position.' She looked up at him, their faces two inches apart, as if they were going to kiss. She could smell his breath – tea and chocolate with a hint of smoke. Slowly they pulled away from one another.

'Don't tell anyone I told you that,' he said.

'I don't remember anyone telling me that. How's Winnie doing?' she asked softly.

'She's in and out, to be honest.'

'Drinking?'

'Sometimes I think she'll make it, though. Eventually. She keeps coming back. She says she's going to be a granny.'

'She is a granny,' said Maureen.

'Right?' said Benny. He didn't know what questions to ask. 'Um,' he said, 'is it a heavy one?'

'It's a girl,' she said, saving him the bother of working it out. 'Una's healthy and so's she.'

'Thanks. I'll pretend I don't know when I meet Winnie.'

Maureen smiled at her cup, pleased in some way that Winnie was still drinking sometimes. If she met her mother again, at least she'd recognize her.

'Your dad coming back to Glasgow's been hard on her,' he said. 'I think she's had to face a whole load of stuff she wasn't ready to look at.'

'Like what?' said Maureen, resentful that Benny knew more about what was going on with her mother than she did.

'Her part in everything. The stuff she's responsible for.' He sat back. 'I shouldn't be discussing this with you, it's not my place to tell you what she's feeling.'

'But you are.'

'I am,' Benny nodded, 'because I'm evil.'

As they walked back across the bridge to Paddy's, Maureen felt Benny's business card in her pocket and rubbed a finger across the embossed lettering. She wished she trusted him, wished that they could go back to evenings in Benny's house, watching videos and eating sweeties together. He'd worked for Angus before. In fact, there was no one in the city she could trust less than Benny right now, but he was funny and that always scrambled her instincts.

'Josh asked me out tonight and I said Sunday afternoon,' said Kilty, 'I didn't want to seem too eager.'

'Good for you.'

'I really fucking fancy him,' said Kilty ardently.

'I'd never have guessed,' said Maureen.

28

Death Cert

Martha Street is a dead end. The steep hill leads to a pedestrianized area outside a students' union building, with large concrete bins of flowers and benches for the students to sit on while they eat their lunch, take disco drugs and end the night with a kebab. The road ended at a dowdy building coated in jagged grey Artex. It was the Public Register Office and the wedding suite. Leslie parked the bike outside and they climbed the steps to the door. Inside, the walls were panelled in fake walnut, so yellow and solid that it looked like the car ceiling of a homeless smoker. Through a second door they came to a wooden desk, barring public entry into the office proper. A tired, distressed-looking young man was waiting on a wooden chair just inside the door, his elbows on his knees, his head hanging limp between his hands.

There were three women in the office. Two elderly women sat across a desk from one another, eating supermarket sandwiches, taking the smallest mouthfuls and chewing them slowly. The third woman was sitting at a desk on her own. She was very overweight and wore a skirt and vest top, showing off arms as big as fleshy wings. When she saw Leslie and Maureen at the desk she glared accusingly at the two elderly women before standing up slowly and coming over to the desk. 'Who's first?' she said loudly.

Maureen and Leslie looked at the man in the chair and,

sensing something, he stood to wobbly attention. 'I'm here to register a birth,' he said, waving a yellow card and a bit of paper.

Maureen and Leslie took seats and waited for the man to finish his business. They looked around the room at the public information posters pinned to the far wall, listening to breathless cars negotiating the steep hill.

'Are ye sure we can get it here?' muttered Leslie.

'Nut,' said Maureen. 'It was just a thought. We might need to go through to Edinburgh.'

'Will it have the cause of death on it?'

'God, I dunno, I'm just guessing. I've never seen a death certificate.'

'Me neither.'

It took ages for the woman to do the registration. She kept glancing at her colleagues resentfully and telling Maureen and Leslie that she wouldn't be long. Eventually, the man stood up straight, put something in his pocket and sloped out of the office. The portly woman looked behind her, stared at the others eating their sandwiches. They didn't look back. When she finally turned to face Maureen and Leslie, she was puce and couldn't bring herself to speak.

'Um,' said Maureen nervously, 'I wonder if you could help us. We're trying to get a look at the death certificate of a woman who died a week ago in the Albert.'

The woman nodded repeatedly, as if she was mentally nutting them. 'I need details,' she said.

'What sort of details?' asked Maureen, looking behind the woman to see if her colleagues had noticed the state of her. The pair sat facing each other, one taking minute nibbles, the other dabbing her mouth elaborately with a paper napkin.

'Date of death, name and age.'

'I haven't got her age but I know the name and place and a date, would that do?'

The woman made her write it all down before telling them to wait and storming off to the back office. As soon as she was out of the room one of the elderly women started to laugh and the other reached across the desk and slapped her hand playfully.

They were on the benches outside the students' union, smoking cigarettes and calming down.

Maureen sighed. 'Ella, ya wee shite,' she said, hanging her head and taking another draw. She unfolded the certificate again and looked at it. 'A fucking heart-attack. Protecting him to the last.'

29

Candies

The office area behind the bus station was a quiet, reserved grid of imposing Victorian office buildings. Even the high summer sun couldn't penetrate the tall streets and most of the area was in shadow. At night poorly dressed women stood on the street corners under the gilt company clocks, waiting for men to come and choose them, before taking them up the delivery alleys, making money to score with.

It was after office hours on a Friday night and Leslie had arranged to meet her pal Joan in a pub across the road from her office. Apart from needing an introduction, Maureen wanted to talk to the woman alone but Leslie and Kilty had insisted that they come with her. They gave her a lot of daft excuses – they had nothing else to do, it would be nice to spend time together – but she knew that they thought she was wrong about everything and unfit to be out on her own.

The Attaché pub would have been busy during the week, full of office workers delaying the return home. Dirt encrusted at the edge of the wooden floor and sticky beer-barrel tables testified to busy spells. It was deserted now because it was a sunny Friday evening and none of the regulars felt obliged to linger in the town.

Leslie's pal was already twenty-five minutes late and they had finished their lovely long, strong drinks. Maureen wanted to order another round but knew Kilty and Leslie would try to stop her.

'If,' said Kilty, swirling the ice around the bottom of her

weight but either didn't know or was making a feature of it: her skirt was very short and her top tight, displaying rolling thighs and an undulating stomach. She had a hard face, badly pockmarked skin and a crooked nose that looked as if it had been broken. The tallest woman was skinny and swaying slightly, drooping forward from the shoulders, her hands hanging redundantly in front of her. They didn't look happy and they didn't look like sex workers. They looked like people so lowly and picked on that they had splintered off from the underclass and formed a social stratum all of their own.

The women eyed them suspiciously as they approached, keeping their faces to the road, watching them from the corners of their eyes.

'Hello,' said Kilty, 'we're not the police. I'm a social worker and these two sell fags in Paddy's. Can we ask you about something?'

None of the women spoke. They shuffled, the smallest sliding away to the far side of the tallest.

Kilty tried again. 'Can we ask ye questions about something?' she said.

The smallest woman looked away. A car coming down the hill slowed as it approached them, the driver lowered the window on the passenger side electronically and looked out at them from the safe shadow. He saw how many of them there were and speeded up, passing fast and turning the corner.

'We'll give ye a tenner every fifteen minutes ye talk to us,' said Kilty, 'in a public place, no touching.'

The tall, swaying woman turned at the mention of money and the chubby hard woman stepped towards them. 'Pay up front?' she said, and folded her arms. 'In a public place?'

'We can talk to ye here, if ye like.'

'Naw,' drawled the tall woman. 'Get them away. Punters willnae stop.'

Kilty nodded and they backed away.

'Can we speak to both of you as well when we get back?' asked Maureen.

'If we're here,' said the tall woman, and stared up the street again.

Kilty led the way and Maureen, Leslie and their new companion followed her. They could tell the woman was wary of them, wondering if they were going to jump her, steal her money maybe. She tottered gracelessly in her high heels, walking with a pronounced limp as though her right hip hurt. Maureen moved round to Leslie's side so they weren't flanking her and saw the woman glance at her gratefully.

'My name's Maureen.'

'Candy.'

Maureen was about to comment that it was an unusual name but managed to stop before she made a complete arse of herself. 'Nice and sunny, eh?' said Maureen, trying to keep the ball rolling. 'Must be shit standing out here when it's cold.'

'It's shit all the time,' said Candy, with deep conviction.

They walked along in silence for a hundred yards until they came to the pub they had been drinking in earlier. Kilty dipped through the narrow door. Maureen and Leslie stepped back to let Candy through first. Candy stopped, crossed her arms and shook her head. 'Won't serve us in here.'

'But you're with us,' said Leslie. 'We're gonnae buy drink.'

'They won't even let us buy fags or a half-bottle in there. They won't even let us do a pee. I'm not going in.'

'That's fucking outrageous,' said Leslie.

But Candy wanted cash, not allies. 'Are ye gonnae give

me my tenner or what?' She pretended to look at a watch even though she didn't have one on. 'That's five minutes already.'

Maureen took a loose tenner out of her pocket and handed it over just as Kilty came back out of the pub looking bewildered.

'Candy says she can't go in there,' said Maureen.

'Why?'

Leslie explained to her as Candy led them round a corner behind a glass and marble office building with a walled car park behind it. She sat down on the low wall, rubbing at a bulging vein on the back of her shin. 'Ye've got eight minutes left.'

Maureen settled next to her. 'Well, I'll get to the point then. Have you heard of the Park Circus Health Club?'

Candy nodded.

'What do ye know about it?'

'It's a house up by the park. They've got a lot of rooms, maybe ten. They've got a dungeon for hitting them.' She nearly smiled. 'That's it.'

'Who owns it?'

Candy looked at her bruised knees. 'Dunno,' she said. She didn't sound convincing but Maureen could hardly blame her.

'Do you know anyone who works there?'

'Nut.' Candy was looking around them, at Leslie's thick hair and good skin, at Kilty's silly trainers with the lights in the heels.

'Anyone who's ever worked there?'

'Nut.'

'Doesn't everyone know everyone else?'

Candy looked at her, annoyed. She had suddenly seen herself in relation to the other women there and she couldn't stand it. It was unbearable, the power differential between them. 'We're not in a union,' she said, pulling back her lips and baring her gums, shaking her head in Maureen's face. 'We don't have Christmas fucking parties.'

If it came to a fight Candy could probably take them all on and walk away without making her limp any worse. Maureen held up a hand in surrender. 'Sorry,' she said.

'Aye, ye fucking should be sorry.' Candy stood up, shouting, and her voice bounced off the near walls in the lane. 'Ye fucking should be.'

'I didn't mean to insult ye,' said Maureen, standing up to meet her.

'Fuck ye!' shouted Candy. 'Ya fucking cunts, the lot of ye!'

She turned to all of them, shouting unreasonably, calling them names and trying to frighten them. She reached out to push Kilty, the smallest, and Maureen and Leslie went for her instinctively, standing next to Kilty before the hand reached her.

'Too far,' breathed Leslie, holding up one finger.

Candy backed down.

'Come on, I'll walk ye back.' Maureen said it as if nothing had happened but they were both breathing heavily. Candy looked wildly from one to the other and tripped after Maureen making her way out of the alley and into the bright street. 'Thanks for talking to us, Candy, that was good of ye.'

Candy said nothing but limped along angrily. Maureen slipped her another tenner and Candy tore it from her hand. Maureen liked it that she was angry, that she didn't just accept her place. It was no place for anyone, so shunned she couldn't even go into a pub for a piss.

A car slowed next to them, the man leaning across the passenger seat. He was handsome, with short brown hair

238

and a fine jaw, small eyes and nice teeth. 'Show us your cunt,' he said.

'Fuck off,' said Maureen.

'Forty,' said Candy.

'Not you,' said the man, 'her,' and he pointed at Maureen.

'You can fuck right off, son,' said Maureen venomously.

'She's not working,' said Candy. 'Thirty.'

The man looked at them and assessed the situation. He glanced down the road to the gangly woman standing on the street corner and slid back reluctantly into the driver's seat. 'Twenty-five,' he said.

Candy broke away and got into the car, slamming the door shut behind her. Maureen watched the car pass and, through the back window, saw Candy and the man ignoring each other, a canyon of space between them, already behaving like an unhappy couple. The car turned up a side-street and disappeared out of sight.

Back on the corner the smallest woman was missing. Her gangly pal was bleary-eyed and trying to make sense of a cigarette.

'Are ye all right to walk?' asked Maureen, and she followed her along the road. Suddenly, a fast car full of young men screeched past, crossing the grid, bravely defying the give-way sign. The windows were down and they hung out screaming 'Cunt,' and 'Bitch,' and 'Slit,' at the women, whooping and laughing uproariously as they passed. Maureen had a sense that in a few years' time one of the boys in the car would be back here, harassing the women, raising a hammer to someone's head in a dark alley. And no one in the car would connect the two incidents because it was just a bit of fun.

'God,' said Maureen, 'it's fucking horrible here.'

'Tell me about it,' said the woman sagely.

'I'm Maureen, by the way.'

'I'm Candy,' said Candy II, and Maureen smiled.

Candy II was less fraught than Candy I, principally because she was so off her tits she could hardly remember where she was. She sat on the wall, blotchy legs drifting out in front of her, her head sagging into her chest, and Maureen thought they should get the questions over and done with. 'Do you know the Park Circus Health Club?'

Candy II pressed her lips tightly together and held out her hand. Kilty put a tenner into it. Candy II clenched her fist and retracted her hand, closing her eyes and nodding. 'No,' she said. 'I've never heard of it.'

'Have you ever heard of Si McGee?'

'Oh, aye, yeah.' Maureen was afraid to believe her.

'Where do you know him from?'

'Gorbals. His ma lives in Benny Lynch Court. I was at primary school.' She looked up and seemed startled, as though she wasn't where she had supposed she was.

'Have ye heard of him being in this business?'

'No,' Candy II was certain, 'he went to St Aloysius. He's a businessman.' She smiled slowly. 'He used to sit next to me in assembly. D'ye know his sister?'

'Tonsa?' said Maureen.

'Aye. She's mental.'

And then a strange thing happened. The inside of a Kinder-egg, an orange and white plastic capsule, dropped from nowhere and rolled on the ground. It was wet and glistening. The sun trickled down the lane, lighting up the egg and shining through it. Inside, a little rectangle of something settled against the side. They all stared at it, apart from Candy II.

'You've dropped your ...' Kilty trailed off, not knowing what to call it, and Candy looked to where Leslie's reluctant finger was pointing.

'Oh, aye.' She fell forward from the waist like a rag doll,

picked up the wet thing and wiped it clean on her leg. She opened her knees, lifted her bum off the wall, pulled the crotch of her pants aside and fitted the thing back into her vagina. She sat down again and looked at them expectantly.

'I can't think of anything else to ask ye,' said Maureen.

'Excuse me for that,' said Candy II, knowing she had breached the formal rules of etiquette.

Maureen had to ask: 'You're not using that as birth control, are ye?'

Candy II laughed a high happy laugh, wrinkling her nose and squeezing her eyes tight. She looked like she'd be a good laugh if she was at herself. She held her hands up. 'No pockets,' she said, looking down at her bra. 'They'd steal this if it was their size.'

'Why would they steal from ye?' asked Kilty, smiling. 'They must have money to come to ye in the first place.'

'Oh, they love ye till they shoot it. Then they fucking hate ye, like ye made them come looking for ye. They want tae hurt ye, a lot of them.'

'Why is that?'

'Shamed,' said Candy II nodding sadly. 'They're all ashamed.' She stood up abruptly and Maureen took an extra tenner out of her pocket and handed it to her. 'Ye haven't asked me why I do it,' said Candy, suddenly coherent.

'Do what?' asked Maureen.

'*This*,' she said, pointing at the ground. 'That's what everyone wants to know. How did we get started, why we do it.'

Maureen shrugged. 'I'm not bothered about that, Candy, everyone's got their reasons.'

'I do it for my weans,' said Candy II, talking to the far wall, her eyes wetting, her mouth drooping at the corners, 'because I love them. I never wanted this. I want them to have all the things I never had.'

The line sounded heavy and hollow, like the words from an old song. Maureen and Leslie looked at the ground, embarrassed. Kilty watched Candy, enjoying the performance.

'I love my weans.' She looked at the two tenners in her hand and wept.

'That's nice,' said Maureen. 'I heard a lot of cars there, I think you might be missing trade.'

Candy II made a sad clown face. 'I really love them,' she whispered, and followed Maureen out of the lane.

'Thanks for talking to us, Candy, that was nice of ye,' said Maureen, when they were back in the bright street.

'Why did ye want to know about Si McGee?' asked Candy, no longer sad at all.

'Uch, his mum died and I was just wondering about her.'

Candy II had stopped walking. 'Ella the Flash is dead?'

'Aye, she died on Saturday. I went up to the hospital to visit her and she was dead.'

'Aw, that's a sin.' Candy II's whole body had changed. She stood upright, and crossed her arms, head dipped to the side like a woman passing on local news in a supermarket. 'She was a gamey old dame. She was a pro an' all.'

'Aye, I know,' said Maureen. 'She'd retired. She'd been working at Paddy's selling tapes, that's how I knew her. I saw her laid out in the hospital and she hadn't her eyebrows on—'

Candy smiled. 'They big mad eyebrows she used to draw on her head?'

'Aye. Anyway, I drew them for her and brushed her hair up a bit.'

'Aw, that's nice. That was from the flicks, the eyebrows. From Greta Garbo or someone.' Candy started walking again. 'She never took no shit from no one, Ella. Always dressed nice. Got him an education. He lives in Bearsden now. Good on her, eh?'

'Aye, good on her,' said Maureen, suddenly choked. Her eyes began to prickle. Maureen wouldn't have credited her with the wherewithal but Candy II saw she was upset and rubbed her back briskly.

''S about all ye can ask, innit?' said Candy II.

The smallest woman was back at the corner, tugging her skirt down and looking pissed off. Maureen was slightly annoyed to see her there. No one knew anything about Si McGee and she didn't want to lose another twenty quid.

'Go wi' her,' said Candy II to the woman. 'She'll give ye money for talking. And she'll not ask why ye do it either.'

Candy II stepped away and over to the kerb, watching the occasional cars pass, looking in at the drivers. The small woman followed Maureen round the corner. 'Is your name Candy?' asked Maureen.

'Naw, Alison.'

She was younger than the other women and clearly hoping to cash in on it. Her bunches looked grotesque and she had drawn rosy cheeks on her face.

'I'm Maureen.' She held out her hand and Alison pulled a face.

'You don't want to touch my hand,' she said apologetically, wiping her palm hard on her skirt.

Alison was terrifyingly young, hardly sixteen, and her body had the unformed look of someone still developing. Her wee breasts were smashed into a tight orange bra, pushing them up to make them look like something. Maureen pointed back to the corner. 'How many kids has she got?'

Alison looked back at Candy II and frowned. 'She hasn't got kids.'

They walked on.

'Alison,' said Maureen carefully, 'I know ye probably get asked this all the time, but how old are you?'

'Is that what you're paying to ask me?' said Alison curtly, turning the corner into the alley.

'No.'

'Well, fuck off, then.'

They settled on the wall. Alison took a cigarette from Leslie and a tenner from Kilty.

'We want to know if you've ever heard of a guy called Si McGee,' said Maureen.

Alison thought about it, repeating the name under her breath. 'Naw. Don't think so.'

'What about the Park Circus Health Club?'

'Oh, aye, I know that, yeah. Up by the park?'

Maureen nodded.

'I knew a lassie worked up there,' said Alison, 'but she's chucked it now. Don't know where she is.'

'Why did she leave?'

'She got Jesus,' said Alison, waving her hand dismissively, as if she herself had something altogether better. 'Heard she was doing voluntary work up at the Wayfarers' Club.'

'Is that the soup kitchen by the river?'

'Aye,' she said, making fists and grimacing. '"Breed and jam, breed and jam."' She saw that they didn't understand and added quietly, 'That's what they say in the queue.'

'Your pal who worked there,' said Maureen. 'What's her name?'

Alison took a draw on her fag. 'Candy.'

30

Charlie Adams

The man pressed the buzzer and waited on the dark stairs. He saw a glint of light from the spy-hole and smiled at it automatically, as if for a photograph. The door opened and Kevin welcomed him in. The man had been here many times, so often that now he almost got hard at the sight of green wallpaper or a blue carpet. He smiled to Cindy behind the desk but she looked away, knowing what he was here for. Kevin was standing at the top of the stairs to the basement, wearing the same cheap evening suit he always wore.

'All right, Kev? said the man, handing over his three hundred quid in fresh twenties.

'No bad,' said Kevin, holding the banister, bulky and ungainly on the shallow steps. 'How are ye yoursel'?'

'No bad, no bad.'

The décor stopped at the bottom of the steps. The basement walls were a glossy grey, the floor bare concrete, adding a frisson of solemnity. Kevin led the man along the long corridor to a room at the end. 'Oh,' said the man nervously, 'I've not been in this room before.'

Kevin smiled as he took out his keys and looked through them. A lot of the punters liked to make small-talk before they went in, to chat and make it all seem normal.

'Aye,' he said. 'It's a nice room. Soundproof.'

The man was tense but attempted a tight smile. 'Good,' he said, and wiped his damp lips. 'Good.'

Kevin swung open the door. She was skinny as fuck, dressed in cheap knickers and a bra with a see-through dress pulled over it, sitting on a double bed with a nylon flowery cover. She looked surly. The man looked in at her. 'Hello. Speak English?'

She didn't answer. The man walked into the centre of the room, nodding and pulling off his belt. He called out as Kevin shut the door, 'It's okay, isn't it?'

Kevin glanced back at the sulking Polish bitch on the bed. 'Anything,' he said, knowing she couldn't understand. 'Anything at all.'

In the six months since they had started the business, Si McGee had never seen his sister so worried. She was flicking the ash from a pink cocktail fag with a gold tip over and over into the bin, kept going over the same details and wouldn't go home even though she had nothing to do here. For Margaret, emotional behaviour of any kind constituted a full-blown panic attack.

'I'm telling ye,' she said. 'I'm telling ye, she was there and she was noising up the Sheriff. We don't need this. We don't need this now. Charlie'll go fucking spastic. He'll make his move if there's a squeak of trouble.'

'There won't be trouble,' said Si. 'Calm down. There won't be trouble.'

Margaret squashed out the cigarette against the side of the metal waste-bin and took out her handbag, clipping it open and lifting out the black and gold fag packet.

'Why did you put it out if you're going to light another one?' he said, trying to get her off the subject.

Margaret flicked back the gold paper and selected a green cigarette this time. 'The bit near the filters gives ye cancer.' She lit up and began flicking it into the bin interminably. 'You don't know the Adams family like I do. You've never met them. Nothing stops business. A bit of trouble and they'll wipe us.'

'They'll move on us soon anyway,' Si pointed out. 'You said so yourself. As soon as we're up and running, they'll wait for us to move on them, and if we don't they'll move on us.'

'It's the worst time for this shit to fucking happen, I'm telling ye.' She was frightened, and Si knew from his management course at university that now was the time to take charge, show leadership. 'Look.' He lifted her bag off his desk and handed it to her. 'Put that on the floor.' On the desk between them was a copy of a newspaper, open at a picture of Maureen. 'We've got her picture,' he said. 'We both know what she looks like. We took care of Ella and we can sort her out too. It's a problem, I grant you, but it's a fixable problem. Tell me it's a fixable problem.'

Margaret glared at him resentfully.

'Tell me it's a fixable problem,' he repeated slowly, trying not to smile.

She didn't smile back at him, but that didn't mean she didn't get it. Margaret rarely smiled. She swallowed and puffed her cigarette.

'It's a fixable problem,' she said obediently. 'But I cannae fix it. And you cannae. The court case'll finger us both.'

'We'll just have to delegate, then,' he said patiently. 'What about Kevin?'

Margaret tutted under her breath. 'Fuck off. He's fucking useless. Charlie Adams'll go fucking mad if anything happens here. He'll say he was coming in tae get his dough back and wipe us out, take the whole fucking thing over.'

'You think I don't want rid of her too? She shouted at me *in front of my schoolfriends*.' He blushed at the memory. The kind regard of the St Al's old boys was all he had left now the estate agent's business was closing up and Maureen

O'Donnell had tried to humiliate him, to take even that away from him. He took a deep breath. 'We'll take care of it. Stop worrying.'

Margaret stubbed her cigarette, sending a cloud of orange flecks into the bin. 'Will we ever be big enough to fuck Charlie Adams over?'

'Maybe,' Si said, lifting the edges of the file and slapping it shut. 'Soon. And the minute we're big enough to pay him off and clean our own money, he'll try and fuck us.'

'Just keep *him* sweet,' she said, nodding to the fire exit.
'I will.'
'Charlie sets a lot of store by him.'
'I will,' Si repeated. 'I will.'

He had to stop and catch his breath. He wasn't young any more. The combination of everything, the woman, the warm room and the flecks of blood, it was too much. He swung his legs over the side of the bed, put his feet flat on the floor, and hung over his knees, breathing in deeply. Behind him he heard her panting and moaning. 'D'ye like that, do ye?' he said, wiping the sweat from his face with an open hand. 'Yeah? You fucking like it, don't ye?'

'I'm love you,' she said.

He thought he had misheard her, thought the heat and the exertion were making him imagine words but she said it again. 'I'm love you.'

He laughed, disbelievingly, and looked up at her. She was tied to the wall, her hands together above her head, her feet chained to the bedposts. Her naked back and buttocks were swollen with red welts from his belt and bloody scratches where the buckle had cut her. 'You love me, do ye?'

She twisted on her shackles, bending her head over her shoulder so she could see him out of the corner of her eye. Her eyes were dark and open wide, looking around at such a sharp angle that she resembled a frightened cow. 'I live your home?' she said.

'You'll leave my home?'

'I live you? You out me, I live you?'

He understood what she meant. 'You wantae come and live with me?' he said, climbing on to the bed.

'I live you,' she said, turning back to face the wall.

He took hold of her ankles and yanked her legs further apart on the bed. 'You wantae live wi' me? Is that it?' He stood up behind her, resting his chin on her skinny shoulder, running a fingernail across her ripped back. 'What makes ye think I'd have a cheap cunt like you in ma fucking house?'

Kevin was at the door. 'Mr G?' he said softly, nodding to Si. 'Spot of bother. Complaint from a punter.'

Si beckoned him to come in. 'What sort of complaint?'

'One of them's speaking English, asking him to get her out of here.'

Margaret picked up her handbag and pulled out her Swiss Army knife. 'Show me,' she said.

Kevin led her down the corridor to the far room, fumbling to find the key. Kevin didn't like being alone with Margaret and she knew it. He had seen too much of her to think she was harmless.

'Are ye a bit nervous, Kevin?'

He pressed his lips together and pushed open the door. The woman was still on the wall, slumped and hanging from her wrists, her legs buckled beneath her, bent at the knees, the tops of her feet flat on the pillow. Margaret ordered Kevin to bring her down off there and he held the woman up by the waist as he undid the straps, trying not to hold her so close that he got blood on his suit. He put the woman down on the bed, not roughly but not gently either. Her exhausted arms rose of their own accord, settling by her ears, folding over the top of her head. She had been punched on the nose and it looked fat and broken. Her eyes were swelling up. She tried to look up and see who was there.

'Awake?' said Margaret softly.

The battered woman nodded.

Margaret pointed to the door. 'Get out?' she said.

The woman looked around, tried to work out who was there and what was going on. She tried to sit up but couldn't bring her arms to her sides. She cringed and lay back on the bed, folding her arms over her head again, letting the fingers of one hand flop over her eyes.

Margaret leaned forward and took the hand in her own. She yanked it away, making the woman cry out. 'Out?' she said loudly. Kevin saw a glint of silver and a sudden spill of blood coming from the back of the woman's hand. 'Ye want out?' Margaret held the tip of the knife in the open wound, twisting, letting the weight of the penknife press down into the open flesh. The woman was crying like a child, and coughing, her skinny back arching off the bed. Margaret lifted her hand and, just before she brought it down on the woman's sore face, Kevin saw an expression on it. Her eyes were open a little wider than usual. He didn't know what it meant. He'd never seen any expression on her face at all. For the first three months here he'd wondered whether she had Parkinson's.

As he was locking the door he asked her about using the knife. 'Why's it always on the hands?'

'We don't need their hands.'

At exactly eight o'clock they heard a single, soft rap at the fire door. Si McGee checked the grey CCTV monitor on top of the filing cabinet and saw who it was. He flicked off the fire alarm and stepped across the room, pressing the bar down and opening the door.

Mark Doyle swung the bag in front of him, sitting it on the desk as Si shut the door behind him. He sat down, clicking his knuckles before zipping open the bag and taking out a wedge of laundered twenties. 'Is it all here?' Si said, his greedy little eyes lighting up.

'Ye say that every time,' said Doyle. 'D'ye think Charlie Adams is ripping ye off?'

'Not at all,' said Si, staring into the bag. He knew a single remark out of place would be reported back to Charlie Adams. Doyle was his eyes and ears, the sole protector of Adams' investment. 'I don't mean that at all.'

Doyle's glance fell to the table and the open newspaper. 'What's this?' he said, tapping the picture of Maureen O'Donnell with a finger.

Bewildered, Si looked up. 'Oh, her.' He saw Doyle looking at it intently. 'Do you know her?'

'She works in Paddy's,' Doyle said, his face impassive. 'I've bought fags from her.'

Margaret slithered over to the desk and picked up the paper. 'She's trouble. We need someone to sort it out. D'you know anyone?'

Doyle scratched at a raw patch on his cheek and Tonsa looked away. 'It'll cost ye,' he said.

'Much?'

'Ten.'

Si frowned at the bag. 'Ten's a lot.' But he knew he had thirty thousand in clean notes in the bag and was due the same again in a month's time.

'Ten's what it takes to get it done right,' Doyle said. He picked up the paper and looked at the picture of Maureen's close.

Si knew how important Doyle was to Adams. One word

from Doyle and they'd be gone. He would be the best person to deal with O'Donnell. It was just a question of convincing Margaret.

Doyle shut the paper and put it down on the desk. 'Forget it.'

He was at the fire exit, his hand pressing down on the bar, when Margaret spoke. 'Wait.'

A mile away, standing in a dark lane, Mark Doyle folded the newspaper and tucked it under the lid of a dustbin. She was his only remaining link with Pauline and no fucker was going to touch her.

31
Stopping

It was Friday night, they had two bottles of spirits and fifteen hundred cigarettes but they were still miserable. Kilty was sad for the Candys. Leslie had started a course of antibiotics and couldn't drink, which made her fractious. Maureen had to decide what to do about Michael within the next two days and last night outside Una's had made her think that all she could do was give up. The three women sat next to each other on the settee watching the Friday night comedy shows on television, instinctively letting off sickly smiles in time to the laughter tracks. It was an airless night and sweat trickled down their necks and foreheads. They kept having to stand up and peel their T-shirts from their backs. On the screen some pals had a group hug and the adverts came on.

'The Life of the Candys,' said Kilty. 'What must it be like?'

'Ye know,' said Leslie, sipping her cranberry juice, 'a huge number of them have been abused as children.'

'Really?' said Maureen.

'Yeah,' said Leslie. 'Massive correlation. Same as rent-boys.'

'Why do men do it?' said Kilty. 'How could anyone get horny enough to touch Candy I?'

'It's not about being horny,' said Leslie. 'If it was about uncontrollable male sexuality the men would all be ado-

253

lescent boys. They're men in their twenties and thirties and most of them are married anyway.'

'Are they married?' said Kilty, most surprised.

'Yeah, a good proportion.'

Kilty sank into the sofa. 'God, that's really creepy.'

'Those poor women,' said Leslie. 'It's sexual oppression, it's straightforward. Same the world over.'

Maureen shrugged. 'I don't think so. I mean, it's a shit job and ye'd hate to do it yourself, but miners get paid danger money and work in horrible conditions that damage their bodies. They do it because there's a local custom of thinking that's an acceptable way to make a living and all those conditions apply to prostitutes.'

'They're not prostitutes, Maureen,' said Leslie. 'They're prostituted women.'

Maureen tutted at her and wished Leslie'd have a drink.

'Oof,' said Kilty, forcing fake cheer. 'That's depressing, isn't it?'

Maureen could tell by Kilty's resolutely upbeat tone that she was here to gee her along. The introductory music to the next programme started and they settled back, watching and laughing. The second half of the programme came on and they watched a beautiful couple in a perfect house get on, fall out and make up.

'He's gay, that guy,' said Kilty absently, pressing out her cigarette and folding it over itself in the ashtray.

Leslie sat forward before the final tag line. 'Cammy's asking me for deposit money to get his own flat,' she said suddenly.

Kilty looked horrified. 'Hen,' she said sternly, 'he's a fucking chancer. Stay away from that guy.'

'I'm gonnae, I'm gonnae,' said Leslie, so emphatically that neither of them believed her. 'I'm just trying to talk about all the things I've been keeping to myself.'

'Will we go and find the missing Candy tomorrow?' said Maureen. 'We could go and ask at the Wayfarers' Club, see if they know who she is.'

Leslie and Kilty stared at the television for a minute. Kilty coughed and sat forward. 'D'ye think they'll know who you're talking about, though?'

'Yeah,' said Maureen. 'If she was God-bothering she'll probably have told everyone what Jesus saved her from.'

It was a dark night and their line-up on the settee was perfectly reflected in the window: three women squashed together on a sofa, holding drinks, with ashtrays, fags and lighters balanced where they could be. Leslie looked at the reflection, watching her pals staring at the flickering television. 'What do you suppose other young women do with their Friday nights?' she said.

They all looked at each other.

'Well,' said Kilty, 'I suppose they go out dancing or something.'

Maureen said nothing and raised her eyebrows.

'Should we go dancing?' said Leslie.

'Fuck off,' Maureen replied.

Outside the window, in the sprawling city beyond, every person under thirty simultaneously wondered what everyone else of their age was doing and whether they were having a better time.

They settled back to watch the next show and Maureen noticed, out of the corner of her eye, Kilty and Leslie nodding to each other, making wordless plans.

'Mauri?' said Leslie, when the ads came back on. 'Kilty and I have been talking.'

'Good for you,' said Maureen, pretending to be mesmerized by the terms of a new credit card.

'And we want to talk to you about something . . .'

She stared at the television, hoping she could stall them by simply not answering.

'Mauri,' said Leslie, 'you're drinking way too much. We both think you should have a look at your drinking pattern.'

Bitches. Fucking bitches. Of all the things they might have said to her, Maureen felt that this was the lowest subject they could have brought up. The drink was the only fucking thing that was standing between her and howling, self-harming madness. She thought of Winnie's defensive fury when anyone challenged her drinking and stopped herself saying what she thought.

"Kay.'

'Why were you steaming at half twelve in the morning the other day?' asked Leslie.

'I got up late,' Maureen said, and tried to smile.

Kilty patted her leg like a patronizing shit. 'Will you look at your drinking?'

Maureen wanted to shout at them that, fuck it, they drank too, and she'd seen both of them match her drink for drink, but she hadn't ever seen Kilty do that and Leslie hadn't managed it for a long time.

'Will you cut down?' asked Kilty.

'This is a bad time,' she spluttered, 'with the trial and the baby and now Ella dying. I just don't think this is the time to do it.'

'It is a bad time,' Kilty acknowledged, and Leslie hummed in agreement.

'I can't even think about it right now.' Maureen sat back. 'I'll think about it after I've sorted out this Ella thing.'

'Mauri,' said Kilty softly, 'leave it. The woman died of a heart-attack. Her kids are horrible and they probably worried her to death but there's nothing you can do about it.'

'He killed her,' said Maureen, 'and she asked me to get

her out.' They'd obviously talked about this at some length, behind her back, on the phone, and neither of them had even fucking mentioned it to her.

'Mauri,' said Kilty. 'It's a distraction. You know it is.'

'Neither of us is asking you to stop drinking right now—'

'You have to want to stop,' interrupted Leslie.

'Yeah,' said Kilty. 'Ye have to want to.'

The suggestion that Maureen should stop drinking altogether made her feel sick. She might have humoured them and considered cutting down but stopping altogether sounded like dying. 'I'm not that bad,' she said weakly.

'No, Mauri,' said Leslie. 'You *are* that bad.'

They sat in silence for a minute, Kilty and Leslie feeling uncomfortable and unkind while Maureen fumed.

Kilty leaned forward. 'Can you even—'

'Could you stop for ever?' shouted Maureen at Leslie. 'You're just being sanctimonious because you're on fucking antibiotics.'

Leslie held up her hand, telling Maureen to back off. They sat back and watched some television, waiting for the ads, each planning what they were going to say when the break came. The little square appeared at the corner of the screen, warning them that it was coming. They sat through the first ad, each waiting for the others to start first, and Maureen stood up. 'I'm going for a piss, if that's all right with both of you,' she said.

Leslie stood up to meet her, pointing in her face. 'You've just been for a fucking piss,' she shouted.

A sharp banging on the door made them all jump. Maureen thought it might be the SAS branch of AA and Leslie thought it might be Cammy.

'Did you order pizza?' said Kilty to no one in particular.

The banging started again and didn't sound friendly.

'I don't think that's a pizza,' whispered Leslie.

They got up and tiptoed out to the hall, taking turns to look out through the spy-hole.

Maureen looked last. Two familiar policemen from Stewart Street station were standing in the sharp white halogen light of the close. Inness was a snide unsophisticated toady with a gay biker moustache. His young companion, Something McMummb, was a skinny, shy guy who spoke so quietly that, although Maureen had met him many times, she'd never managed to catch his name. Inness sneered at Something so smugly that he looked nervous. Trying to keep Leslie and Kilty out of it, Maureen opened the door just a little, as if she had a crowd of nosy puppies behind it.

'Hello, Miss O'Donnell,' said Inness.

Back in the living room an ice cube cracked loudly in a glass of whisky.

'Tell me what this is about,' she said, 'or I'm closing the door.'

The policemen looked at each other and hid smiles. 'We're here to get an assurance from you that you'll be in court on Wednesday morning.'

'I thought it was Monday.'

'It's changed to Wednesday now,' said Inness.

'I'll be there,' she said, and went to shut the door, but Inness had stuck his foot in the way and pressed it open again.

'You sure?'

Maureen rolled her eyes. 'I'll be there, okay?'

'Have you changed your mind?' asked Inness. 'The guy who served the citation said you weren't going to cooperate.'

'Yeah, I decided to stop being frightened when I found out I'd be going to jail if I didn't.'

Inness smirked at Something again and Leslie yanked

the door open. 'Are you two having an affair?' she said. 'Why d'ye keep looking at each other?'

'Yeah,' said Kilty, still angry from the argument. 'Have ye got no fucking manners at all?'

Inness pointed at her. 'Don't you swear at me or I'll have you for breach.'

'Yeah?' said Kilty. 'Well, fuck you.'

Suddenly, Something McMummb reached into the hall to grab her by the arm but she skipped backwards and Leslie stood in front of her. '*Stop it*,' said Leslie.

McMummb didn't like her tone. 'We could take any one of you in,' he muttered angrily.

'For what?' demanded Kilty.

'Breach of the peace.'

'Breach of the peace?' shouted Kilty. 'We're standing in our own hallway taking shit from you bastards—'

Leslie put an arm over Kilty and pushed her back into the hall. 'Thank you for coming this evening,' she said calmly. 'Miss O'Donnell will be at court on Wednesday morning.'

But the policemen were not to be placated. They had come to take someone in and spend the rest of their shift sitting in an office drinking tea and filling in forms.

'You,' said Inness, reaching into the hall to grab Kilty.

A sudden loud crack rent the air and Jim Maliano was standing in the close, his chest puffed out like an improbable super-hero. He was wearing a blue shirt tucked tightly into his pink slacks. '*Enough*,' he declared, tapping a small notebook with a specially sharpened pencil and pointing at the policemen individually. 'The both of you have been up here before, causing trouble at this house. I have already been on the phone to your station. That's four times altogether I've done that and they assured me that the matter will be dealt with *forthwith*.'

The policemen were smirking again but not as confidently now. They backed away from Maureen's door and turned on Jim Maliano. 'And what is your name, sir?'

'My name,' said Jim, pink and tremulous, 'is James Maliano. My cousin is Detective Inspector Nicolas Farquharson of the Midlothian Police and he will be advising me how best to pursue my complaint against the lot of you at Stewart Street.'

No longer confident that Jim could be bullied, they looked at each other. Something shrugged and hesitated before dropping an uncertain foot to the first step. Inness dipped his head, reluctant to give in, but his companion nodded him away.

'You,' said Inness, pointing at Maureen, 'be there.'

He backed down the first two steps and Kilty stuck her head out of the door. 'Bye-ya,' she said, in a girlish falsetto.

The policemen glared at them.

'See ye later,' sang Kilty. 'Take care now.'

Jim Maliano was glaring at Maureen, and she wondered how she could possibly have suspected the officious little twit of being in league with Angus. 'I have warned you,' said Jim, 'about the noise level in this close.'

'Sorry, Jim,' she said, backing into her hall. 'Sorry about all of it.'

Back in the living room they settled uneasily into their respective places on the settee but it didn't seem as cosy now, as if the visit had burst the boundaries of their evening, letting the big scary world seep into the house.

'Would they have jailed ye?' asked Leslie quietly.

'Yeah,' said Maureen, holding her cold fingertips to her burning eyes.

'For not turning up?' asked Kilty.

'For thinking about not turning up,' said Maureen, taking a long drink.

260

Kilty and Leslie watched her. 'What d'ye think'll happen in the trial?' asked Leslie.

'Joe McEwan thinks he'll get off,' said Maureen, drinking again.

'And then what?' said Kilty quietly.

'He'll come for me.'

Leslie sat down on the settee, staring out of the window and thinking. As if she was going to hit Maureen's legs, she reached out quickly, snatched up the bottle of cheap, own-brand whisky and filled Maureen's glass. 'Bad timing,' she muttered.

Kilty smiled and sat down too, glad it was over. 'Yeah,' she said. 'Bad timing.'

Maureen drank again, enjoying it while she could. She decided not to tell them that Hugh had promised that her house would be full of policemen when Angus came. She'd tell them after the drink was done. As she drank she realized that delaying the trial meant she had an extra two days to do something about Michael, two more days to get herself together enough to face him. Being allowed to drink and a two-day stay of execution made the night feel quite luxurious.

'Why will he get out?' said Leslie.

'He's saying that I gave him drugs, and the drugs made him do the murders.'

'Did ye give him drugs?' asked Kilty.

Maureen and Leslie looked at each other.

'She did,' said Leslie.

'I gave him a load of bad acid but it was *after* the murders.'

'We went to Millport on Cumbrae and he followed us on the ferry,' said Leslie. 'Because we had Siobhain with us and he wanted to kill her to shut her up. Mauri fed him the acid and tied him to a bed.'

'Where were you?' Kilty asked her.

Leslie looked at her hands. 'I shat it,' she said. 'I encouraged her to do it and then I shat it and left her to do it alone.'

'You stayed with Siobhain,' said Maureen. 'Someone had to stay with her.'

'I shat it.'

'Where did you get the acid?' asked Kilty.

'I got it from a wee guy who knows Liam,' said Maureen, 'but they're going to say I got it from Liam and tell everyone he's a drug-dealer. The uni might even chuck him out.'

'You don't know that,' Kilty reassured her.

'Naw, I don't, but they've raided him and they've got that evidence to bring so it makes it easier to get the audience to believe I did it—'

'The jury, Mauri,' corrected Leslie.

'Yeah, the jury. Them.'

They settled back, watching adverts, and Maureen thought of poor dead Ella lying on her cold metal bed, leaving nothing in the world but Si and Tonsa.

The Friday night porno started on television. Two women rubbed about on each other, one looking nauseous, the other in an advanced state of sexual excitement for no discernible reason. Maureen stood up and turned it off. 'Look,' she said, 'I know you don't believe me about McGee but will you humour me over it for a wee bit?'

Kilty and Leslie looked at each other again and Maureen wondered just how close they were.

'For how long?' asked Kilty.

Maureen shrugged. The court case was this week and she'd have to decide about Michael before she ended up in jail. 'A week,' she said, randomly.

Kilty and Leslie looked at each other. 'A week,' agreed Leslie.

They sat with Maureen for a while to show her they were

sorry for talking about her drinking. Eventually Kilty stood up and picked up her bag. 'We going to look for Candy III at the Wayfarers' Club tomorrow then?'

'Yeah,' said Maureen. 'Can we talk to your dad about Si McGee?'

Kilty smiled uncomfortably. 'I dunno. He's not very keen on you at the minute.'

Kilty promised to meet them the next evening and left, shutting the door quietly behind her. Leslie waited until Kilty's last footfall had finished echoing around the close. 'Mauri,' she said, 'why are you so afraid of Angus Farrell?'

'Nothing.'

Leslie, not known for affectionate gestures, reached out and touched her arm. 'You've been freaked by him since Millport. What happened there? I know ye didn't just feed him the acid, I know something else happened.'

Maureen sighed into her chest. She wanted to speak, wanted to say it out loud, but it stuck in her throat and swelled. 'You know the dreams?' she said. 'About the fingernail and the blood?'

'Yeah,' said Leslie, filling in the hesitation.

'He said ...' she swallowed hard against the lump in her throat, ' ... Angus said Michael raped me.'

Leslie sat back against the sofa and together they looked out at the black sky. 'He said this in Millport, right?'

'Yeah.'

'After you'd given him the acid? After you'd tied him up?'

'Yeah. But he was my therapist, he was astute, he knew things.'

'Mauri, that's a lot of shite. He said it to hurt ye, to frighten ye. If ye'd been raped at that age ye wouldn't get a wee nick inside the wall of your fanny. It would be split all the way up.'

'But he said—'

'Mauri, I think Angus Farrell probably said a lot of things to a lot of people.'

Maureen looked into the deep swirling amber in her glass. 'I feel as if I'm losing it again,' she said, in the quietest voice.

Leslie was afraid she was right.

Without meaning to, they slept on the floor in the living room. It was the breeziest room in the house with the biggest windows and everywhere else was unbearably hot. When they woke up it was eight o'clock and they were already late for the market. Outside the window a pitiless sun glared over the city and they both wished it would rain.

The market was busy and the Saturday crowd of buyers were waiting impatiently for them. They served the backlog and settled on their wee stools, glad to be in the cold tunnel.

'There was guys here looking for the two of you earlier,' said Peter.

'There was a gang of men when we got here,' said Leslie.

'Two guys looking for you.' Peter pointed at Maureen. 'One of them had a suit on and the other one had a camera. Guy in a Celtic shirt was asking for you, Leslie.'

After little discussion Maureen and Leslie decided to pack up for the day. They told Peter to spread the word that they wouldn't be back for a week or so.

32

Authentiky

Leslie didn't want to go to the country but she had promised to humour Maureen for a week and, anyway, she had nowhere else to go. Maureen lit two cigarettes and handed her one as she rattled the old van down the slip-road from the motorway and stopped at the roundabout.

Lanarkshire is fine countryside. Lush old trees hung over the road or sat softly on the rolling hills. Past the concrete sprawl of Motherwell, residents had paid enough to relish the luxury of privacy and there were few houses near the road. Behind hedges and trees, the hills were scattered with new bungalows and solid old houses built when the area was farming land, before its proximity to Glasgow made it commutable. The road was narrow and busy at weekends. The only set of traffic lights in the area caused tail-backs of up to half a mile on Sundays, when the car-boot sale was open. As the van passed a field with opaque Nissen huts cloaked in rippling Cellophane, Maureen spotted a sign-post. 'There,' she said. 'Dreyloan.' She checked the address in the phone book on her lap. 'That's it. Left up here.'

Leslie turned the van over the old stone bridge. Far below they heard the sound of cool water splashing through a rocky crevasse.

Dreyloan village was picturesque and litter-free. The cars parked in driveways were new and expensive. Even the Saturday visitors from the city looked healthier than average and certainly better dressed. Their shoogly van attracted interested glances as they parked by the green. Leslie pulled on the handbrake and turned off the engine, pocketing the keys. She waited for Maureen to get out so she could shut the passenger door from the inside but Maureen didn't move. 'Will we get out?' said Leslie.

Maureen was smiling straight ahead, her head tipped to the side. In front of the windscreen, on the edge of the village, a small office in a pretty pink cottage had a large to-let sign nailed above the door. It was McGee and McGerty, estate agents.

'That doesn't mean anything, really,' said Leslie, worried by how pleased Maureen seemed. 'There could be a lot of other explanations.'

'Aye,' said Maureen. 'Could be.'

The village green was a long bumpy stretch of grass. In the centre, at the intersection of two diagonal paths, stood a solemn monument to the war dead from the village. Around the perimeter of the green, villagers and visitors were catered to by a cake shop, a camping-equipment store, a curry-house and an olde authentiky coach-house pub, doing three-course meals for a fiver. Around and about, visiting families climbed out of cars after long drives in hot weather, a couple of men in obscenely clinging Day-glo outfits stood next to fancy racing bikes drinking from water bottles and panting, wiping sweat from their necks. Maureen and Leslie headed straight for the estate agents.

The cottage was a squat single storey, with deep windows and a step down to the entrance. McGee and McGerty had one window of the cottage; the other was occupied separately by a small post-office-cum-newsagent. The window display only showed six houses for sale but they were laid out tastefully on grey card, without prices. They were cottages, a barn conversion and a manse, photo-graphed in perfect sunshine and with bare, expensive graphics laying out the details. Maureen looked at them and it occurred to her that she could sell her house, take the money and just piss off.

'Posh,' said Leslie.

Inside the front door the two businesses had built their own entrances, diagonal doors facing the main entrance like a moral choice. Maureen pushed the door, setting off a tinkling bell, and stepped into a small room with plush carpeting and a single desk. The man behind the desk, elderly, in a pink and baby-blue Pringle sweater and grey flannels, was on the phone. He looked as if he had been pulled off a golf course and made to sit there. He clearly wanted the person at the other end of the line to think he found them hilarious. With sorrow-sodden eyes he laughed and nodded, texturing his laughter with high and low intonation, rocking back and forth in his chair. Maureen and Leslie sat down across the desk from him. He mouthed at them that he'd just be a minute and laughed some more before hanging up and looking sadly at them. 'What can I do ye for?'

'We're interested in the lease for this place,' said Maureen.

He smiled insincerely and looked at them. 'Can I ask what you do?'

'We're web designers,' said Leslie.

He frowned at his papers. 'Really?'

'Yeah,' said Maureen.

The man didn't know what else to ask them because he didn't know anything about web design, which was just as well because they didn't know anything about it either.

'Are you handling the lease?' said Maureen.

'Yeah.' He pulled open a drawer of his desk and lifted out a summarized schedule on stapled sheets.

'What's the walk-through like here?' said Leslie, making Maureen flinch. Even she knew that web designers didn't care about trade from idle passers-by. The estate agent, however, didn't seem to be aware of this.

'Well,' he said, sitting back, pressing his fingertips together, making a church of his hands, 'it's good for the area because of the post office next door and the pub across the way. Also, because there's damn all to do in the village, lots of people walk around the square.' He pushed the schedule across the table as if he couldn't be bothered talking any more. 'It's a big village for the overall area and people come here to shop. There's a Spar around the back of the kirk.'

'Nice,' said Leslie.

'So, is this room all that's included in the lease?' asked Maureen.

'No, no, there's this room and a back office and upstairs as well.'

He stood up to show them round but Maureen waved him back into his chair. 'We're looking at a lot of places,' she said. 'You said the walk-through's good, so why are you leaving?'

'No, no,' he said. ''S nothing to do with this place. The business is winding up.'

'Going bankrupt?'

'No,' he said defensively, 'just dissolving. The senior partner's retiring.'

'And the junior partner?'

The man broke eye contact.

'He's not . . . as experienced.'

Maureen smiled. 'It's McGerty who's got the money then?'

The man looked up at them. 'Who are you?'

The olde authentiky pub had a lot of young bar staff decked out in black uniforms with fussy white pinnies over them, serving the tables. Maureen ordered a pint and Leslie asked for a cheese and ham toastie and a bag of smoky-bacon crisps. She asked Maureen to have something while the tweeny waitress stood there and smiled at them. 'I'm all right,' said Maureen, lighting a cigarette.

'What are ye going to have for lunch, then?' said Leslie.

'I'm not hungry,' insisted Maureen. 'I'll have something later.'

'Have something now.'

Maureen looked at the waitress. 'That's all for now, thanks,' she said, and waited until the girl had written everything down in longhand and gone away. 'How's the stomach now?'

'Wee bit better,' Leslie said, wrinkling her nose. She looked out of the window at the McGee and McGerty office. 'It doesn't mean anything.'

'McGee's business is going down the tubes and it doesn't mean anything?'

'Well, lots of people change what they do for a living. It doesn't mean the automatical next step is moving in to whoremastering.'

Maureen smiled knowingly. 'Do you think Si McGee is the sort of man who could happily take a drop in his income and social status?'

'How do you mean?'

'You were right,' she said. 'It's not about the money at all. McGee's not interested in money. It's about status, proving he's as good as the other good old bhoys. It means everything to him.'

33
Video

Maureen was feeling confident and ready for anything. She knocked on the glass panel and stepped back. A shadow moved in the kitchen corridor and Liam opened the door. He didn't have a top on and had been sitting in the garden.

Liam's house was the one good thing that had come out of his foray into the underworld. It was a three-storey townhouse in the middle of the West End, with high ceilings, magnificent windows and a stretch of garden at the back. In times gone by the West End had been a tatty, cheap area to live. Students clustered together in damp old houses with boilers held together with sticky tape and glue. Men left drink-ruined marriages and came to live in bedsits here, trying to revive their glory days. It was a better area now. The housing boom meant that bomb-sites and inches of spare ground were being developed into cramped flats for short, thin people with no possessions. Deserted shops and boarded-up garages had been taken over by sandwich bars and international coffee-shop chains. The bookshops had shut, replaced by designer clothing outlets.

When he was dealing, Liam had left the downstairs of the house dirty and unaltered to discourage his sometimes desperate clients from trying to rob him. Since enrolling as a student he had become obsessed with renovating it. He used all his spare time to strip the flock wallpaper, bare the scored plaster and woodwork, filling the rooms up with a lot of chairs he bought in auctions. His obsession with chairs was getting to be too much: the place was beginning to look like a Quaker meeting house. He had left the garden and kitchen until last and had just started making inroads on them. Maureen had never known him to have any interest in gardening, much less skill at it, but the long dry stretch of mud had sudden thin grass growing on it. Just outside the kitchen window a small herb bed had been planted with cuttings and sticks with pictures on them, proclaiming the potential. A seemingly ready-made shrubbery was flourishing at the far end.

They were sitting in the first-floor sitting room, above the noise of the traffic. The floor-length windows clipped the top of the roofs opposite but mostly they were filled with blue sky, textured with occasional puffs of white cloud, like living paintings. It was a blue room, kept plain and empty apart from the Corbusier lounger, the cracked leather chesterfield and the telly and video.

Liam handed her a mug of tea and pointed at the Jiffy bag on the floor. 'It might be completely innocuous,' he said.

'I know.'

'It's probably a promo for Disneyland or something.'

'Probably.' Maureen didn't move to put the video into the machine but sat looking at the envelope, sipping her tea.

'But you don't think it is?'

'No.' She sipped again. 'He's the only person who sends me anonymous mail.'

'It's not from the hospital, though, is it?'

'No. It was hand-delivered. He must know people on the outside.'

'Okay,' said Liam, slapping the back of the sofa. 'I'll watch it.'

She was on strict orders to wait downstairs but found herself hovering in the hall, smoking a fag and trying to hear anything from upstairs. It would last about an hour, she guessed, from the big reels, or maybe even just half an hour. She could hear the floorboards creak as Liam walked to the video, the click of the tape being sucked into the machine. He walked back to the sofa and pressed 'play' on the remote. She listened. There was no sound for about five seconds then suddenly Liam scarpered out of the room and leaned over the banister. She looked up at him, turning a little circle on the stairs to see his face properly. His mouth was open and he seemed to be swaying. 'Liam?'

He fell back heavily against the wall. Maureen put down her tea and ran up the stairs to find him hunkered on the floor.

'What is it?' she said, rubbing his back.

Liam coughed hard. Maureen fed her cigarette to him, holding it against his lips and Liam inhaled a full centimetre. 'Pauline Doyle,' he said, exhaling thick smoke as he spoke. 'On a bed.'

'Pauline alive?'

Liam hung his head. 'On a bed.'

She had never thought of herself as more hardened than Liam but she could watch it and he couldn't. He was sitting downstairs in the front room, chain-smoking and sipping medicinal bourbon while Maureen watched Pauline on a Bed.

It was a small room with girlie curtains in flowery peach and a single bed. The bedstead was green velour. There were two people in the shot. Outside the window cars and lorries sped past on a distant dual carriageway. It was home-made, the date and time were stamped in the corner of the screen, four months after Maureen's discharge from hospital. Pauline had been in the hospital recently, that much was clear, because she was over six stone. It didn't look like a rape. To anyone who didn't know Pauline, it was a normal, grubby home-made porn tape. Pauline sat on the single bed wearing a dirty red nylon bra and pants with scratchy lace trim, looking at the man's face apprehensively, trying to catch his eye, glancing occasionally at the video camera. A casual viewer, chugging along to the action, wouldn't notice the similarities between the skinny bird on the bed and the guy doing her, wouldn't notice that behind the apprehension she was asking him, please, not to hurt her.

Pauline's father touched her here and there, pointing her at the camera, showing it her flower and her wee tits, touching her in a way that communicated disrespect tinged with disgust. He did things just because he could do them, slapped her leg really hard with a belt buckle, showing how compliant she was. Pauline, unmoved by indignities she had experienced many times before, watched his face, looking for signals that it was all about to get much worse.

The father was talking to the camera but there was no sound on the tape. He seemed to be asking for encouragement, pausing with a knee on the bed and nodding at the viewer, turning Pauline over as if this was what had been requested, checking back for reassurance. He got his spindly old cock out and fucked her up the arse, flashing a smile at the camera. He didn't even have a full hard-on. Pauline was on all fours, her bony wee bum two-thirds to the camera, shuddering when his pelvis banged against her, absently watching the cars pass on the dual carriageway.

Maureen was on her third cigarette in twenty minutes. She was sitting forwards, her hands holding her face, tears spilling from her eyes as if they were trying to wash grit away. The father finished, pulled out and, while he was standing there, pointing at her, the shot zoomed in on

Pauline's bum. The father lifted her by the hips and moved her a few inches across the bed like a dog being shown, so the camera could get a better shot of her genitals. Pauline didn't struggle, didn't even bend in the middle. This had happened before. Her hole was as dilated as a fifty-pence piece. The screen went blank.

Maureen didn't know much about video cameras but assumed the zoom wouldn't be remote. There had been another man in the room watching all of this, a man working the camera. Pauline's other brother was there and the father had been talking to him, nodding to him, asking him things. Maureen sniffed hard and wiped the hot tears from her face. Mark Doyle had grown up with these people. No wonder his skin was trying to rot away.

She stayed in the room for a while, watching the sunlight flicker on the varnished floor, the fervent blue sky over the rooftops opposite. She hadn't stayed in touch with Pauline after she got out of hospital and this was what had happened. Maureen should have had Pauline to stay in her flat, sleep on her floor, take her bed, even – she would have given her the bed if she'd known. But she had known, Pauline had told her: her father and brother had been raping her anally for years. She just hadn't bothered to imagine it. Pauline had refused to tell the police because she was afraid it would have killed her mother. Maureen knew now that she was right.

Liam called from downstairs. 'Is it finished?'

It took her a while to find her voice and when she did it was weak and cracked. 'Aye. Finish.'

He climbed the stairs slowly and paused before he opened the door. 'Is it off?' he said, staring at her face.

'Yeah.' She pointed to the blank television screen. 'It's off.'

Liam sat down sideways on the Corbusier lounger,

bending over his knees, looking small. 'It's not from Farrell then, is it?'

Maureen rubbed her nose with the back of her hand. 'Aye,' she said finally, 'it is.'

'But how could he know about Pauline?'

She was in shock, she knew that, and it was taking her a while to answer. 'He worked at the Northern for eight years. Pauline was in there for ages before I went. Farrell's a predator. He'd've read through case notes, found her in there, probably.' She flicked her cigarette into the ashtray. 'If he was asking about me he'd have heard she was my pal.'

Liam was trying not to look at the television, as if the image were still up there. 'Why would they make a video like that, condemning themselves?'

Maureen shook her head. 'They didn't just make that video for themselves. They made it for other people to see. There's networks of these people, ye know. They swap videos of things they do. There was a paedophile gang, UK-wide, got done last month for swapping films of themselves on the Net. It's a status thing among them. Farrell probably got to know that network. Any vicious pervert in Glasgow could have sent that.'

Liam leaned over, took a cigarette from her packet and lit it. He pointed to the video machine. 'Will we take it to the police?' he said.

'For what?' The final image came to Maureen's mind again and she bent over her knees, wishing she could be sick. 'Both of the people in it are dead.'

'The dad's dead?'

She nodded.

'How do you know that?' he said.

'Know her brother.'

'Not *the* brother?'

275

'No.' She shook her head, 'the other brother. His dad and the other brother are dead, he told me.'

'Poor guy,' he said, and it occurred to Maureen that Liam and Mark Doyle probably had a lot in common. 'What's he like?'

Maureen didn't know how to describe Doyle. She stopped for a minute and thought about him, growing up with that, maybe not knowing the details but aware of the atmosphere, the implications. 'He's ... I dunno what he's like. He's covered in sores and he walks about as if he's dead already. Can a zoom on a video work remotely?'

'Yeah, if there's a button on a lead.'

'What about without a lead?'

'Nut,' said Liam.

'It zoomed in at the end,' she said. 'The other brother was in the room.'

'But why would Farrell get it sent to you now?'

She sat back and took a deep breath. 'He must have heard I'm giving evidence, he wants me to lose it again.'

They sat for a while, Maureen looking out at the perfect sky, Liam bent double, picking at a loose strip of plastic on his trainers. 'Ye know what's really disturbing about that video?' he said eventually. 'It looks like other pornography, but I know Pauline didn't want to be there and I know that's her dad and I know she killed herself because of it.'

'So?'

'Makes ye think about other porn, doesn't it?'

Maureen sniffed hard. 'Not just a bit of saucy fun when it's your hole, is it?'

34
Argot

Three men were sitting on the pavement outside and smiled up at them as they walked past. The Wayfarers' Club was a soup kitchen serving out of the cavernous, Gothic arches under the Central Station bridge. The entrance was a grey metal door built at the far end of a glorious blond tricept. Uplighters filled the dome and the structure quivered and hummed as a train passed overhead.

Maureen rang the bell and stepped back. They were dressed for the Polish Club, in conservative skirts, makeup and jackets, all of which felt ludicrously inappropriate down by the river.

'God,' said Kilty looking up, 'it's beautiful. Why doesn't someone do something with this space?'

'Well, they are doing something with the space,' said Leslie, ringing the bell again.

'But there must be more suitable spaces for a soup kitchen than a Gothic cathedral.'

The giant steel door scratched open a little and a stocky wee man in glasses looked out, assessing their clothes. 'Aye?' he said quickly.

'Hello,' said Kilty. 'I wonder if you could help us. We're looking for someone who used to work here, her name's Candy?'

He thought about it. 'Nut,' he said, and started to shut the door.

'That might not be her name,' said Maureen, stepping

forward and putting her foot in the door. 'She worked here and she was very religious.'

'She's not working here now.' The man's voice was a nasal squeal. 'We're short-handed and I've got twenty loaves to butter.'

'Why don't we give ye a hand?' said Maureen, and realized immediately that she should have kept that bargaining tool as a last resort.

The man was about to open the door but stopped. 'Are you the police?'

'Naw, we're just looking for our pal.'

'If she's your pal how come ye don't know her name?'

Kilty stepped forward. 'She was a prostitute and she got out of it. We want her to come and talk to someone we know, see if she can help them get out of it as well.'

He looked quite interested and glanced at Leslie's long, bare legs. 'Are yous all prostitutes?'

'No,' said Leslie.

'No,' said Maureen. 'We're just trying to help someone.'

The man's eyes slid back to the hall behind him and all the work he had to do. He opened the door. 'Come in, well.'

The hall was gigantic, a vast rectangle. At the top of the room stood a small rostrum, above which hung a shakily hand-painted sign inexplicably declaring, 'Wayfarer's – Are Go.' Along each of the windowless walls leaned high stacks of chairs and folding tables. A blond man with his sad past written in the droop of his shoulders stopped setting up the serving table at the top of the hall and stood, staring, as if he had never seen women before.

'Hiya,' said Kilty, raising her hand.

The man raised a hand, bewildered, and turned back to what he was doing, suddenly self-conscious.

'Yous can set up the chairs and the tables along the way.' The nasal man gestured sideways with his hand.

'D'ye want an aisle down the middle?' asked Maureen.

'Aye. Just fill the hall half-way.'

'And after this you'll talk to us?'

'Aye.'

He scuttled away down the length of the room, disappearing through the door at the side of the rostrum. Kilty dropped her handbag by the wall and they set about laying out the chairs and the tables in rows. Above them a train rumbled out of the station, gathering speed, filling the hall with a hissing groan. Maureen nodded to the handwritten sign. 'D'ye think that's supposed to read "Wayfarers Are Go!"?' she asked when the train had passed.

'Or "Wayfarers' Argot"?' muttered Kilty. She nodded at the kitchen door. 'That guy's taking the piss. He doesn't know who we're talking about.'

'Yeah,' said Maureen, swinging two plastic chairs from the stack to the floor.

Kilty picked up some chairs and carried them over to the blond man. He was setting up the sturdy serving tables at the top of the hall, grabbing handfuls of plastic spoons out of a cardboard box and laying them on the table, spreading them wide to avoid a crush of bodies when the hungry men came to grab them. Maureen could tell from the tension in the man's neck and shoulders that he felt Kilty's approach.

'Hiya,' said Kilty.

The acoustics of the hall were such that every word was audible. It must have been deafening when it was full. The man winced and looked up, greyer than before.

'I'm looking for a pal of mine that used to work here,' said Kilty.

He nodded, holding his breath.

'Her name was Candy at one time but she might have changed it. She'd been a prostitute down at Anderson but she got Jesus and chucked it.'

'Maddie?'

'Was that her name?'

Struck by sudden stage-fright the man blushed. He attempted a casual shrug but the muscles in his shoulders clenched tight, making him look as if he was doing a tiny Michael Jackson dance move.

'Ye don't happen to know her second name, do ye?'

He trembled a headshake. 'She goes to the Holy Cross now,' he whispered.

'Where's that? Coatbridge?'

'Springburn.'

Kilty stood a little nearer to him, spreading out the cutlery carefully, keeping outside his space. 'You don't meet a lot of women, do ye?'

'Naw.' He tried to laugh but it sounded like a death rattle.

'How's that? Are ye just out of poky or something?'

He nodded and blushed some more. Maureen knew Kilty had a nice manner but she'd never seen her use it before. If she had tried to flirt with the man he would have died. It was a great skill, to make people feel comfortable without seeming vulnerable herself.

'Why are ye working here?' asked Kilty. 'Is it a parole condition?'

He reached into the spoons box. 'I want to do some good,' he whispered.

'I'm sure you will,' Kilty said, and backed off before the man exploded with discomfort.

Kilty helped Maureen and Leslie finish setting up the tables. When they looked up the blond man had disappeared into the kitchen. They approached the door by the rostrum and opened it. A smog of moist heat hit them. Four industrial cooking pots of red soup were bubbling on the stove and the stocky man and the blond guy were spreading margarine and cheap jam on rectangular slices of stodgy plain loaf, laying them out on stacked baking trays.

'We're away,' called Maureen. 'That's the chairs and tables laid out.'

The blond man kept his head down, afraid to look up. 'Ye said ye'd help us with the bread,' said the other sneakily.

'Yeah,' said Maureen sarcastically. 'Thank you for all you've done. Thanks.'

'We're working for a good cause here, ye know,' said the man.

'That's not a mandate to take the piss.'

She let the door fall shut and they walked out, picking up their bags and jackets on the way. The crowd of hungry men outside had doubled. The kitchen wouldn't be open for another hour.

The Polish Club was to the Wayfarers' as brandy is to gravel. Overlooking Kelvingrove Park, the front door of the terraced house was fifteen feet high and broad enough to allow two wheelchairs to enter side by side. Kilty's dad had lent her his swipe card and she fitted it into the lock and pulled it down. The door released with a soft buzz and Kilty pushed it open. They could hear the hum of happy, drunken chatter wafting through a nearby doorway and Maureen prayed that Si McGee wasn't in.

The entrance hall was high with a dark wood staircase and rich green carpet. A white marble fireplace to the left was so clear and flawless that it looked like crystallized milk. Maureen touched it, pressing the dip of her palm into the cool curved edge. Sitting in the hearth below was a glass globe vase, full of ripe, stinking tiger-lilies, their stamens brimming clear and sticky.

They suddenly felt terribly cheap. Maureen pulled her skirt down and Leslie straightened her shirt. Kilty gestured to them to follow her as she nipped through a small open doorway, into the dining room. A grand piano stood under the windows, surrounded by empty tables laid out with good green linen and silver. Along the walls hung pictures of luminaries in military uniforms, interspersed with paintings of civilians, one of which was a woman.

To their left was the bar. It was a small part of the room but the well-to-do men and women were smashed into that corner of the room as if it was a fire drill. Middle-aged and pissed, they were talking too loudly and laughing. On the edge of the crowd a happy-drunk old woman in an evening dress was reeling on her feet, holding on to a reluctant man for ballast.

'Come on,' said Kilty, skirting past the throng at the bar and going through a glass-panelled door.

The smoking gallery was a huge room, with walls clad in dark wood. It had a glass ceiling framed by dark timbers, like the underside of a viewing boat. Behind the glass the evening sky was turning neon pink.

At the far end of the room, under a torn Polish flag, sat Mr Goldfarb in a large brown leather armchair. He was alone in the room, smoking a big cigar and reading through the business section of the thick Saturday papers. Smoke from his cigar floated sideways lazily, a small blue cloud over his right shoulder. 'Hi,' said Kilty as she approached.

'Hi, Kay,' said Mr Goldfarb, and stood to give her a peck on the cheek. Not quite sure how to greet Maureen and Leslie, he raised his hand and waved as if they were a mile away. 'Hello, girls,' he said genially, and offered them seats around him. 'Can I get you a drink or anything?'

'No, Dad, we're fine.'

'By rights I shouldn't offer you a drink,' he said to Maureen.

'Sorry about that,' she said, pretending to care.

He smiled patronizingly. 'Well, what's a Glasgow wedding without a fight?'

Kilty sat on a stool at her dad's feet. Maureen and Leslie pulled up small chairs and sat next to her. Their chairs were lower than Mr Goldfarb's and they settled in front of him like children waiting to be told a story.

'Sure I can't tempt you with a coffee or something?' he said uncertainly.

'Yeah.'

Without his bombastic wife Mr Goldfarb seemed smaller, less certain of everything. Kilty was kinder to him when they were alone, touching his hand and smiling at the sight of him. 'Dad,' she said, rocking on her chair towards him, 'Dad, can we ask you about someone?'

He took a puff on his cigar and held his breath. A ribbon of smoke wormed from the side of his mouth. He exhaled. 'Simon McGee?' he said.

Kitty nodded.

'Kay, Mr McGee was in the year below me at school. I can't imagine what you think he's been up to.'

Kilty hummed. 'What's his business?'

'He's an estate agent. He has a number of offices in Lanarkshire.' He looked at her curiously and flattened the newspaper on his lap. 'What have you heard about him?'

Kilty cleared her throat. 'That he runs a brothel.'

Mr Goldfarb laughed at that, rolling the tip of his cigar in the ashtray, stray strands of smoke escaping from his nostrils as he breathed out. Now that Maureen thought about it, it did sound like a schoolyard taunt. 'I don't think Mr McGee is a madam.' He looked at Kilty reproachfully. 'Really. Where did you hear that?'

'From his mother.'

'The lady who died recently?'

'Yeah.'

'Well, she was quite a character by all accounts. A real East End character.'

'She wasn't from the East End,' said Maureen. 'She was from the Gorbals. So's McGee.'

Mr Goldfarb nodded and smiled, as if they had been in agreement all along.

'Is Si McGee's dad Polish?' asked Maureen.

Mr Goldfarb cocked his head. 'I don't know.'

'Why's Si in the Polish Club, then? Ella wasn't Polish.'

'I'm not sure what his connection is to Poland but there must be one. He even attends services at the Polish chapel.'

Kilty shifted in her chair.

Maureen wanted to go; it was obvious that McGee and Mr Goldfarb were close and there was no way he was going to incriminate his pal. Even if he knew something he would probably avoid saying it to them. 'Well,' she said, 'thanks for talking to us anyway.'

'Why are you trying to find out about him?'

'Maureen was friends with his mum,' said Kilty, 'and she helped her fill in a form for a small-claims action against McGee for unpaid wages—'

'His mother was working for him?'

Kilty looked at Maureen.

'Yeah,' said Maureen. She was about to censor the story, but realized that she needn't. 'Ella said she worked for him, cleaning at the brothel, but he hadn't paid her because they had a fall-out about a girl. She was a fit old lady, she could spin on a pin, and then suddenly, just after bringing the case against him, she fell over in her house, smashed her face up and had to go to hospital. She told me she'd fallen and he told the police she was mugged. Her bruises weren't consistent with a fall.' She could see Mr Goldfarb getting annoyed and Kilty and Leslie looking away, disowning the story, but she didn't give a shit. Mr Goldfarb's life seemed

284

to consist of private-club niceties and big cigars. Even though he was Kilty's dad, Maureen found herself disliking him, as if he was the one who had picked on Ella. She wasn't even keeping her voice down. 'Me and Kilty,' she continued, and saw him make a mental note of both the grammatical error and the immigrant name, 'we went up to her house in Benny Lynch Court and the neighbours wouldn't talk about her.'

'There could be a lot of reasons for that. Isn't it a bad neighbourhood?'

'Anyway,' Maureen said weakly, 'Ella was recovering and then I miss a day's visiting and she's dead, of a heart-attack, and no one can tell me why a fit old lady would pop off during visiting times in a hospital when her son's there.'

Mr Goldfarb sat back in his chair and tried to smile.

'Did you know his business is going down the tubes?'

'No, no. McGerty's retiring. That's why they're dissolving.'

'Isn't it more usual for the other partner to take over when someone retires?'

'Only if they have the money to buy them out. It's not always the way.' He waited for her to say something else he could disagree with. 'Basically,' he said, 'there's no evidence of anything, then?'

Leslie and Kilty agreed with him but rather than say that they looked at their hands or at the floor. Mr Goldfarb chose the glass ceiling, a peach colour now that the sun was setting. He looked at Kilty. 'Why would you bother with all of this?' It sounded like an argument they'd had a hundred times before.

'Because it's not fair,' said Kilty firmly, and pressed her lips together.

Mr Goldfarb rustled his paper, his expensive cigar dozing off in the ashtray. It was time to leave. Maureen stood up.

'Well, thanks for the offer of a drink, anyway,' she said.

'I'll tell you something about Si McGee,' he said, patting his paper with a flat hand, crumpling the pages. 'He's a good man and gives a lot of money to charities.' He shook a reproachful finger at the three girls. 'More money than you'll ever earn.' He seemed to think that them earning a low wage was an affront. 'He has pumped money into Eastern Europe, into a scheme to give students, girls like you three, the chance to study in this country. Young people with a future can come over here and extend their education to better themselves, make something of themselves. And he never talks about it, doesn't want it widely known. He gives generously and does so as a modest man should. I don't want any of you blabbing about this.'

The three of them were still.

'How do you know that, Dad?'

Mr Goldfarb was oblivious to the implications of what he had said. 'Because he needed a letter of recommendation to the Polish government by a National before he could set up offices there.'

Kilty's eyes bulged. 'You used your dual nationality and wrote the letter?' she said quietly.

Mr Goldfarb nodded, and Leslie and Maureen looked at each other. McGee was importing women from Poland. Mr Goldfarb picked up his cigar and relit it with a slim gold lighter. He looked at Kilty from behind a flaming stub.

'Dad,' said Kilty, standing up and handing him the rest of the paper, 'you should read more than the business section.'

35
Happy-Jesus-Good-Guy

It was a warm, still morning. Leslie wasn't well again and didn't feel up to driving the van. The bus pushed through the stagnant yellow air and headed up Springburn hill. Splatters of milky Sunday-morning vomit punctuated the pavement and greedy pigeons picked out the best lumps. It was approaching lunchtime and people were stirring, coming to the shopping centre for hangover cures of Irn Bru and fresh rolls, to the newsagent's for Sunday papers and cigarettes.

Springburn Cross was an ugly place without scale; high flats jostled with higher flats on the hill, all looking down to the low-level shopping centre and the railway station. Across the valley, ringing the summit of a little hill, a circle of white prefabs with pale blue roofs watched the valley like a defensive encampment.

As they stepped off the bus, Maureen and Leslie saw an angry woman across the road pushing a baby stroller, the child inside wearing pyjamas. The woman was old before her time, baggy-eyed with thin brown hair hanging loose about her shoulders. She had a pale blue home-made tattoo, a Charles Manson cross between her eyebrows. 'D'ye think she did that herself?' murmured Maureen.

'Ye'd think she'd have the wit to grow a fringe if she didn't,' said Leslie.

Without meaning to they had slept the night in the front room again, keeping Kilty with them, afraid to let her go home alone. They tried reassuring her, saying that her father clearly didn't understand what he had done, that they didn't even know for sure whether McGee was trafficking women. She was silent most of the night, watching Maureen and Leslie talk, glancing occasionally at the television but mostly just sitting on the floor, looking out of the window and smoking their duty-frees. She didn't want to join Maureen in a very big drink and was still quiet when she left this morning to get ready for her now reluctant date with Josh.

Maureen had fallen asleep feeling slightly high: if she was right about McGee and everyone else was wrong, maybe she was right about what to do about Michael. Maybe Doyle would make it all right and she'd walk away from it unscathed. This morning she was feeling secretly excited, hoping they'd find evidence against Si. She was betting her soul on whatever Maddie said.

Maureen and Leslie followed the road past the shopping centre and around to the side of the station. The hill was steep and they were both damp by the time they stopped outside the Holy Cross community hall, across the road from a disused, blackened kirk. The complex of rooms centred on a gravel square with a concrete slab path running around it. Two plain women waited outside on the steps, one in a navy blue summer dress with short sleeves, the other in a white blouse and peach skirt. As Maureen and Leslie approached, the women turned and their faces fell a little: Maureen smelt of stale drink, and they both looked tired and crumpled.

'Hello,' said Maureen, ignoring the implied snub, taking an outstretched hand and shaking it. I'm Maureen.'

Leslie took the other hand. 'Hiya,' she said, and pumped the hand. 'We're looking for Maddie?'

'Inside,' said the summer dress.

The small room was unadorned and empty, apart from a

couple of microphones on a raised stage and about twenty chairs set out in rows in front of it. An elderly black woman sat alone one row back from the front, dressed in an overcoat and matching hat with her handbag on her knee. A spindly young man was tuning up his electric guitar at the side of the stage and another man was standing in front of three adoring women, chatting and nodding, blinking slowly and holding photocopied sheets of paper. He saw them and broke away from the group, coming over with his hand outstretched, his eyes contracting in a practised smile that hid everything beneath. 'Hi,' he said, closing his eyes like a smug cat as he shook their hands. 'I'm Jack Gibb. I'm the pastor. I lead the services around here, not that that makes me anything – anyone.' He had a Sheffield accent. It had escaped neither Maureen's nor Leslie's attention that, despite thinning brown hair on top, Jack Gibb had a scrawny wee ponytail. Alone, neither would have objected ferociously to it but in their collective consciousness a ponytail on a man was the greatest fashion crime of all.

'We're looking for a girl called Maddie who comes here,' said Leslie stiffly, trying not to look at Maureen.

'Has she spoken to you?' said Jack Gibb, pastor and nobody. 'About the church?'

'Oh,' said Maureen, 'no, not really, it was a separate thing.'

Jack wasn't pleased but he nodded none the less. He pointed them to a small underweight woman sitting on the stage listening enraptured to the guitarist tuning up, swaying back and forth. 'She may not want to talk just now, the service is about to start.'

Maddie had short brown hair, cut in a functional style, and was dressed with great reserve: a long-sleeved nylon blouse with a modest vest underneath, an A-line black skirt that came below the knee and moccasins with flesh-coloured soles. She looked like a foreigner who had been misinformed about the dress code.

She looked up as they approached her, hopeful at first. She had large brown eyes with slashed wrinkles under them like tidemarks. In her ears she wore small gold hoops, sitting loosely in long drooping holes used to far heavier earrings.

The guitarist stopped tuning up and watched Maureen and Leslie approach. Maddie stood up as if she was in trouble. Maureen introduced herself and asked if they could have a word. Maddie bristled, making it clear that people had been having words with her for a long time and it was never to tell her she had been voted Queen of the May. She shuffled to the side, moving away from the guitarist. 'What's it about?' Her voice was low and quiet.

'A lassie called Alison told us about you,' said Maureen. 'She wears bunches?'

'We're not the police,' said Leslie.

'Who are ye, well?'

'It's a long story. Look, can we talk to you?'

Maddie wasn't sure.

'I know you're not doing that now,' said Maureen, 'but we're trying to find out about something and you're the only person who might know about it.'

'What is it?'

'It's about a lady called Ella the Flash. She worked the Gorbals for years and years.'

It was as unthreatening a story as Maureen could think of and Maddie nodded. 'How d'you know Ella?' she asked.

'We work in Paddy's, her stall's near us.'

Maddie nodded again. Behind her the service was starting. The expected deluge of sinners and converts hadn't come and the seven members took their places, only three in the audience, most of them on stage. No one seemed to have spoken to the black woman.

'If ye stay for the service we could talk afterwards?' Maddie smiled. Leslie and Maureen agreed reluctantly and followed her into the front row of seats.

Jack Gibb led the singing from the photocopied sheets, accompanied by the inappropriate electric guitar. Although there were plenty to go round, Maddie offered to share her hymn sheet with Leslie and Maureen and leaned in so that they couldn't avoid singing along. It was a poor rendition of whatever the song was. The black woman behind them sang with gusto but the Scots, unused to singing without libation, muttered and stumbled along to the tune. Jack Gibb shut his eyes and sang loudly but not well. The song petered out and they all put down their sheets as Gibb raised a hand on either side of his head, swayed from side to side, and started telling them in a strange, strangled voice that Jesus was a good guy.

The Jesus-is-a-good-guy stuff went on for some time and Maureen, not quite recovered from the night before, dearly wanted to sit down. She was feeling distinctly faint when Maddie broke away from her side and clambered up on the stage, a glassy look in her eye, and took the microphone from Jack. She gave a speech in the same strangled voice as Jack, rocking back and forth, egged on by the rest of them shouting intermittent encouragement. Maddie's speech went on for a good five minutes and Jack had to ask her to give someone else a chance but the gist of it was that Maddie used to be unhappy and selfish but now she wasn't and it was great. Thank you, Jesus. She didn't mention a life of sin or shame or guilt but Maureen supposed that those were Catholic conventions anyway. Some other people said they had been wee shites as well, but that they weren't any more, and then they all prayed that hundreds of people would come to their service. Amen. Another song, badly mauled, ended the service and Maureen was never so glad to be a heathen as when the doors opened at the back of the room and let in the air. How anyone could do this every Sunday morning was beyond her.

Maddie was making the refreshments and they had to wait around while everyone sipped tea and ate chewy scones someone had made, chatting about how great the service had been and how nice the scones were. The middle-aged black woman left as soon as the service was over, leaving a grand total of seven worshippers and two people who wanted to talk to Maddie.

'Why do you put so many chairs out?' asked Maureen, to be sociable.

'Faith,' said Jack, and they all smiled as if they were in on the secret.

'You should try it,' said a woman with rolls of fat where her neck should have been. 'It works wonders.'

They all smiled again. Maureen tried to eat a scone to kill the time but couldn't work through the parched starch. Squeaky bicarbonate clung to the back of her teeth.

Finally Maddie was ready to leave and waved off her holy pals with a promise to meet them at a prayer meeting later in the week. The neckless woman made a great show of hugging her warmly and told her to live in Jesus in the meantime.

'I thought she lived in Springburn,' muttered Leslie as they crossed the gravel to the street, and it seemed like the funniest crack in history because everything else was so alien and dreary. Hands on her belly, Maureen bent back and guffawed at a clear blue sky. Maddie spun round and glared at her distrustfully.

Maddie never really got back into pliable Jesus-loving mode again. She didn't want to take them to her house and there wasn't a café open so they bought cans of juice and stood in the freezer-centre car park next to three bell-shaped bottle banks. It was coming up to midday and the tar was soft beneath their feet. Shimmering heat rose from the ground, melting the high-rise flats and wetting Maddie's vest. They lit cigarettes and offered one to Maddie. She took it guiltily and enjoyed it.

'Can't afford these any more,' she said, and giggled, a little excited. 'No harm in a wee treat.'

Leslie stood back, rolling her cold can on her forehead, and let Maureen do the talking.

'Maddie,' said Maureen, wishing they were somewhere more private, 'I respect your new life and what you're doing for yourself—'

'Aye, get on with it,' said Maddie. Her skin was hard and tough: she looked less as if she was ageing than desiccating.

'We knew Ella,' said Maureen. 'She's dead now—'

'Ella's dead?'

'Aye.'

Maddie took a sip of her fizzy orange and a trickle of sweat rolled down the side of her face, dripping from her sharp chin. She must have been boiling in her vest. 'D'ye know her son, then?' she said.

'That's what I want to talk to you about.' Maureen decided not to mince her words. 'I think Ella tried to warn me about him, tell me what he was up to, about the health club at Kelvingrove, but she died before she told me straight and I think he killed her.'

Maddie nodded.

'I liked Ella,' said Maureen.

'That's 'cause ye didn't know her.' Maddie took a long drink and finished her can. 'She was an evil cow. God forgive me, but she was. Cruel.'

'How was she cruel?'

Maddie put the can down on the tarmac. She shut her eyes and Maureen could see her lips moving in prayer. Her

293

hair was wet around the nape of her neck. She let her finish and Maddie looked up again.

'Are there Polish women in there?' asked Maureen.

Maddie coughed, agitated and angry.

'Look, Leslie and I both used to work at the Scottish Women's Shelters,' said Maureen quickly. 'We're concerned about that place. No one knows that Si McGee's involved in it, apart from folk like you, folk who've been there—'

'I don't know nothing about him,' said Maddie, her voice high, her eyes wide.

'Maddie,' Maureen said, 'I sat outside and watched that place and someone came out and told me to move on. That's not normal, even for a sauna. Ella told me that he was involved there—'

'She told ye?'

'She got me to submit a small-claims form to the Sheriff Court with the health club as his place of work.'

Maddie snorted and looked away to the high flats, then back at Maureen, her mouth open, tongue moving, glistening as she thought of things to say but stopped herself. She opened her eyes wider. 'Did ye send the forms in?' she said.

'Yeah, but Ella died just before the case came up.'

Maddie snorted again: ''S a bit suspect, innit?'

'Look, Mauri,' said Leslie suddenly, 'I'm fucking dying here. Can we go and get a cup of tea at least?'

Maddie turned away, her blouse stuck to her back, articulating a knobbled spine and razor-sharp shoulder-blades. 'Come to mine,' she said, and led them up the hill to the high flats.

A crowd of young neds were hanging about in the shadow of the tall block. Dressed in tracksuit bottoms and vests, they lay around on the bald grass lethargically, cursing each other and smoking rollies made to look like spliffs. They called to Maddie, shouting that Jesus loved her and so had everyone else in Springburn. One boy ran over and tried to pull up her skirt. Maddie skipped out of his way, muttered at him to fuck off and pulled open the door into the lobby.

It was cool in the lift and they pulled at their damp clothes, getting air to their suffocating skin. The flat was a small studio, a bathroom off the hall on the way in, a living room with a sofa-bed in it and a galley kitchen off to the side.

The front room looked out on to another set of high flats and the sharp sunlight glinted off the windows across the way, glaring into Maddie's flat like a searchlight. The window was open, letting fresh cool air filter in. There was no television in the room, just a lone shelf on the wall with a few books sitting on it: a Bible, a prayer book and a couple of Scott Pecks. Maddie called from the kitchen over the noise of the gurgling kettle, 'D'yees want tea?'

'Please,' said Leslie.

She brought in a tray with three mugs, a fourth with milk in it and a stack of paper sugar sachets on the side. 'I haven't stolen them,' said Maddie, indicating the sugar. 'I only take them when I've bought a tea in a shop. I've paid for them.'

Maureen smiled at her concern and Maddie grinned back, the yellow light softening her face. They sat down, Maddie and Leslie on the sofa and Maureen on the floor in front of them, sipping their tea and enjoying the breeze. Maureen lit up and offered the packet around. Maddie took a pie tin down from the window-ledge so that they could use it as an ashtray.

'What can ye tell me about the health club?' said Maureen finally.

Reluctantly Maddie shrugged her shoulders. 'I was there for a year and a bit. Then they chucked us all out. How's Alison with the bunches?'

'She's okay,' said Maureen.

'I tried talking to her,' said Maddie, 'but what can I say?' She gestured around her bare room. 'Ye sleep better?'

'Are there Polish women in the club?'

'I don't know where they're from. They're foreign. They only know a few words in English.' Maddie looked at her cigarette. 'They're not always there. They move them on.'

'Are the women brought into this country by Si McGee?'

'Dunn,' said Maddie unsteadily, her faint voice fading. 'They move them to a different city every couple of weeks so the punters don't get to know them. They chuck the Glasgow girls out when they're coming, don't want us there at the same time. I think they come from Newcastle. I don't know where they go.'

'Why don't they want the punters to get to know them?'

Maddie looked out of the window, a haunted, guilty shadow in her eyes. ''Cause they'll try to help them,' she said.

'Help them how? Get them out of prostitution?'

Maddie looked from Maureen to Leslie. 'Ye don't know anything about this, do ye?'

Not knowing how they'd given themselves away, they couldn't bullshit their way out of it. Maureen shook her head. 'Actually, no. All we know is that he's got an employment agency in Poland, that Ella got beaten up and died after she'd submitted the small claim and you used to work there.'

Maddie drew on her cigarette, sucking her thin cheeks into her mouth. She looked as if she'd just been tickled. 'That's it?'

''Fraid so.'

'No,' said Leslie defensively. 'Everyone knows that young women from Eastern Europe are being tricked into coming here, thinking they're waitresses and au pairs and being forced into prostitution.'

But Maddie sneered. 'Isn't that terrible?' she said. 'Would ye think it was terrible if they came over thinking they were gonnae be working girls and just weren't given any of the money they earned? Would ye be here if that was it?' She waited patiently for an answer.

'I don't know if we would, no,' said Maureen finally.

'But what if these dirty bitches had their passports taken away and got battered if they tried to leave? What if they were told they'd to pay off a massive loan before they could keep any money? What if they'd to do stuff they didn't wantae?' Maddie looked out of the window and they could see she was really angry now, and hiding it behind a big empty smile and a cigarette. 'See?' she said, flicking her cigarette into the ashtray. 'People like you only want to save people like you. Yees don't want to save us, just women like you, women who'd need to be tricked into it.' She took a draw and narrowed her eyes, looking at Leslie. ''Cause you think you'd never do that. You think that's beneath ye, like your dignity cannae be took away.' She stopped and tried to calm herself, taking deep breaths, moving her mouth as if she was counting.

'We just don't know anything about it,' said Maureen softly. 'We don't mean—'

'What if the women were doing it to keep their kids and they didn't get paid? It's all right if it's for weans, isn't it? Ye think ye know how low pros are until ye are one. No one cares. Down at Anderson we were getting raped and battered. No one cares.'

'Don't the police care?'

'Oh, the police do care,' she said quickly. The Glasgow police are decent enough, they try and help ye out of it and tell ye where to get a cup of tea and medical attention and stuff, they're all right. It's people. It's the public. They'll walk past ye getting your face kicked in, they laugh at ye and hit ye for nothing. There's been one pro murdered every year in Glasgow city centre for the past nine years and they never get anyone for it. Murdered in the street, in the open some of them, and no one seen nothing. And d'ye know what sickens me about it? It's not the same guy, it's different guys. I have to pray not to get angry about that all the time.'

Maureen touched her arm. 'Sometimes it's good to be angry.'

Maddie frowned and blushed. 'It's bad. I have an anger in me.' She stopped, trying to word it. 'It's like a fire that'll eat me, eat my being, know what I mean?'

Maureen and Maddie were leaning close in to each other. Leslie muttered an excuse and went to the bathroom, shutting the door after her.

'I do know what ye mean,' said Maureen.

'I've been angry and feart since I was wee,' said Maddie, hopelessly. 'Cannae shake it off.'

Maureen saw Maddie blink and when she opened her eyes again she had gone back to another time, to an angry, fearful time when she was small. She pulled her legs up under her on the sofa-bed, clutching her knees defensively, keeping them together. Maureen thought suddenly of the picture of the child in her cupboard. 'Your dad?' she whispered.

Maddie looked up, appalled and afraid at what she had said. She pressed her lips tight together and shook her head but her hollow eyes contradicted her. Maureen touched her hand to her chest. 'My dad too.'

Maddie took it in, lips pursed, not looking at Maureen, wanting her to talk about something else.

'Tell me about Si McGee,' said Maureen.

'Anger is not accepting things as they are,' said Maddie.

'That's what Jack says. When we accept life as it is, we're no longer angry.'

'I think that's shite,' said Maureen. 'We should try to change things. Anger's a good thing. It can make ye challenge things that aren't fair. It's not comfortable and it's not even nice to see in other people but it's there for a reason. D'ye think he should be allowed to take women from Poland or wherever and make money from their wee bodies and for it to happen next door to houses with children in them and bars and curry-houses and no one says anything?'

Maddie didn't like that. She drew on her cigarette, inhaling the anger, sucking it all down. 'He'll get what's coming to him,' she said.

'On Judgement Day?'

Maddie inhaled heavily again. '"Judge not lest ye be judged,"' she said. 'I know something about being judged by other people.'

'What about the next woman he brings over? Should she not judge him?'

Maddie ground her teeth.

'See, justice in the hereafter's all very well,' said Maureen, 'when all ye need to do is contain your anger. If you're being raped and battered every night in the week it's a bit more complicated.'

'"Judge not lest ye be judged,"' said Maddie weakly.

Maureen couldn't remember if it was from scripture or just the words of a hymn but she gave it a pop anyway. '"Whatsoever you do to the least of my brothers, that you do unto me,"' she said.

Maddie flushed. 'I try to be kind,' she said quietly. 'I'm talking to you, amn't I?'

With a flush and the crack of a door, Leslie came back from the toilet. Maureen was glad to see her, glad to have the intensity between them broken. 'Why don't the

Glasgow girls tell on McGee?' asked Maureen.

'Well,' Maddie smiled softly and Maureen could feel her slipping back into her happy-Jesus-good-guy frame of mind, 'how does the devil appear to us?'

'How d'ye mean?' said Maureen, bending forward to the ashtray and breaking eye-contact.

Maddie tapped Maureen on the top of the head and made her look up. 'When the devil comes, when temptation comes, how does it seem?'

'I dunno,' said Maureen. She was glad it was so bright in the room. She could at least hide her distaste for the holy chat behind a heavy squint.

'Well, it doesn't come as a threat, does it?' Maddie opened her eyes, trying to look scary.

'No,' said Maureen reluctantly.

'No, the devil comes as a friend,' Maddie said. 'He doesn't come with knives in his eyes.' Maureen wondered if she were quoting a revelatory pamphlet. 'He comes as a friend and promises us what we want. The selfish things, the fearful things.'

'Right,' said Maureen. 'So Si McGee's friendly to them, promises them good money and they keep quiet about it?'

'Money and threats. The guys who put up the money are from London. They're mental. Ye wouldn't cross them if ye could help it. Anyway, we never got to know the women. They kept them downstairs and they couldn't speak English.'

Maureen nodded. 'Listen, Maddie, I go to a group on Thursdays. It's a survivors' group, for people who were abused.'

Maddie had frozen on the sofa-bed, clutching her legs, her back rigid, staring from Maureen to Leslie as if they were attacking her.

'Would ye like me to tell ye where it is?'

300

Maddie's headshake was so tiny it looked like a tremor.

'Okay. Well, thanks for the tea,' said Maureen, feeling as if she had violated her, 'and for giving us your time.' She wanted to hug her, or say something that would make it okay, something to finish off the conversation and reassure herself that Maddie would be all right left alone. She reached out to touch her hand but Maddie recoiled.

'Should we just go?' Leslie asked her.

Maddie nodded once, watching their shoes as they walked out to the hall and shut the door behind them.

36
Equal

They were alone at the bus stop. The sun shone in through the thick, warped perspex roof, refracting and fracturing in the shelter. They had bought more cans of juice and sat on the bench, sipping and watching for the bus.

'So, he's bringing them in and keeping their passports,' said Maureen.

'It's not just him, though,' said Leslie, sipping her Vimto. 'He might have the agency but there must be others involved if they're moving them around the country.'

They sat for a minute, trying to catch their breath in the heat.

'Does it really change everything for you if they know what they're coming over for?' asked Leslie.

'It does. It shouldn't, but it does. What about you?'

'D'ye want to drop it, then?'

'Fuck, no,' said Maureen quickly. 'It shouldn't make a difference.'

'Just 'cause they've consented to be prostitutes doesn't mean that they haven't got any rights, does it?'

'No.'

'And anyway,' said Leslie, 'how free is anyone to consent to that?'

'I don't know, Leslie, if it's a choice between juggling asbestos for thruppence a year or doing that and making money, ye can see why people would take that option. We shouldn't try to impose what we want on them.'

The bus appeared on the horizon and they stood up, peering through the scratched perspex until the number on the front came into focus. It was theirs.

'Maybe your problem,' said Leslie, reaching over and patting Maureen on the stomach, 'is that you've a Jesus-shaped hole inside ye.'

'How would you know?' smiled Maureen. 'You've never seen my hole.'

They caught a bus into town and Leslie insisted they go for breakfast at the Equal because the fry-ups were great, weren't they? Really, though, weren't they? Maureen smiled back and wondered what she was up to.

The Equal café was a fifties throw-back with black Formica tables flecked with gold, a red and chrome coffee-maker and airbrushed pictures of ice-cream dishes on the wall. It was used by flush art students and office workers and was always quiet on a Sunday. It was down the hill from Maureen's house and she had come here with Douglas for breakfast sometimes, when he got the chance to stay over. The food was cheap and the fry-ups magnificent, but the service was compromised by the sullen old waitress's perpetually sore leg and short-term memory loss. She rarely brought a complete order to the table. Decades of small orders had started to blend and merge in her mind so that lasagne could transform into a toastie or a Coke into a coffee cake in the ten-foot amble between the table and the kitchen hatch.

Maureen and Leslie sat at a table by the window. West Sauchiehall Street was full of pubs and casinos, and the now deserted road was littered with take-away chip wrappers and bottles from the night before. Outside, worshipful Sunday shoppers passed in ones or twos, making their way down to the malls, heading east towards the resurrecting midday sun, squinting at the blinding brightness of it. The waitress shuffled over to them. Her brand-new orthopaedic shoes had crêpe soles on them that shrieked against the lino. 'What d'yees want?'

Maureen was pleased to see that the waitress's foot had healed. She had been wearing slippers with the toes cut out for months, apparently to get the air around some sort of fungal infection. Leslie ordered a fry-up, Maureen asked for a coffee, and the waitress screeched away from them over to the kitchen.

'What do you think about it, then?' said Leslie. 'Is Mr Goldfarb an evil flesh-trader?'

'I don't know,' said Maureen, lighting a cigarette she didn't want. 'I can't see him as an unwitting partner in anything but he wouldn't have told us if he'd known. What I don't get, though, is why Poland? And why would McGee go to the trouble of getting Mr Goldfarb to sort this out for him? The agency would be a traceable connection between McGee and those women. He's so careful, why would he take that chance?'

Leslie stared out of the window. 'To be honest, Mauri, I thought you were off your head there. I didn't think there was anything in it at all.'

Maureen sat back in her chair and smirked. 'Is that you being honest? Ye hardly kept it a secret, did ye?'

'Didn't I?'

'Leslie, you told me you didn't believe me.'

'Did I?' She looked surprised. 'I don't remember.' She took a cigarette and lit it slowly. 'I've been worried.'

'About me?'

'About you.'

Maureen was irritated. 'As is your close friend, Kilty?' she said sharply.

Leslie looked resigned and sat back, smoking and looking at her, chewing her tongue. 'What do you weigh?'

'Are you weighing me in for a fight?'

'Mauri, if you could make eight stone with your shoes on I'd be surprised.'

Maureen glanced at her and shifted her gaze to the window. The weight was always the give-away. She couldn't hide it because it came off her face first. When things got bad she couldn't eat, couldn't bring herself to swallow properly, and she started smoking more and more so that her tongue got burned and she couldn't taste anything anyway. When she was first admitted to hospital she had been under seven stone. Leslie was watching her across the table and she felt suddenly aware of her body, profoundly conscious of the bones of her bum rubbing against the seat, of the deep dip between her sharp hips and the baggy waistband on her shorts. 'I'm doing fine,' she said. 'Don't worry.'

'We are worried,' said Leslie softly. 'I mean, okay, this was never going to be the time of your life, with the trial and the baby due and everything—'

'The baby's born.' She was surprised she'd said it. She didn't even know she'd taken it in yet. She blinked hard at the table and breathed in deeply.

Leslie hesitated. 'Born?'

'A girl.'

During the twenty-minute taxi ride up to Drumchapel the driver tried to engage them in chat about the weather. Yes, they agreed, it was hot, very hot, most unusual for Glasgow. The driver told them authoritatively that it was because of global warming, like the floods all over England. The world was going to end soon, nothing surer.

Leslie wasn't keen to go upstairs but they needed to get the crash helmets. When she unlocked the front door the stale air hit them and Maureen saw how much Cammy had wormed his way into Leslie's life. In the front room all the furniture had been moved around, as if he had been desperate to make his mark. The bedroom had been painted by a non-professional, the line between the white ceiling and the blue wall had been badly negotiated and the window-frame had solid drips of gloss on it. Through the kitchen window she could see that Leslie's beloved veranda had been cleaned up and the carpet of dead plants cleared away. Even the stained deck-chairs had been washed so that the white stripes were no longer an off-yellow.

Leslie came out of the bedroom with her leather trousers and jacket on, holding two crash helmets.

'He's done a lot of work in here, hasn't he?' said Maureen.

Leslie frowned. 'He actually suggested I pay him for it because he wasn't working.'

Maureen thought back on all the conversations they had ever had about the importance of wages for housework and looked at Leslie's big, miserable face. 'What an arsehole,' she said.

The motorbike was chained securely in the backyard of Leslie's close. Maureen watched the children playing on the dusty hillocks while Leslie undid the padlock. A group of small girls were watching them and messing about. Not one was over ten but they were dressed like mini pop stars, in tiny crop tops and leggings, their girlie tummies sticking roundly out in front of them. At the side of the group, two wee girls with wild dusty hair pushed a smaller girl towards Maureen and Leslie. The big girls were sniggering nervously, the shovee resisting with flailing arms and a shy grin. They stopped pushing her and huddled together, giggling and hatching a plan and Maureen saw a fifty-pence piece exchange hands. The small girl pocketed it and set her shoulders square for the bike, stomping towards them as if she was annoyed.

'We've got a visitor,' said Maureen, smiling.

The child reached them and Leslie smiled up at her. 'Hello, Kylie-May. How's your—'

'Your Cammy's been going with Ian McIntyre's wee sister and he loves her and they're having a baby and he's chucked you.'

She turned and bolted back to the girls who had sent her, running past them, gathering them in her wake. The crowd of girls ran away over the hill, squealing with panic and laughing hysterically. They ducked into an open close mouth, glancing back at Leslie.

Leslie didn't say anything for a while, didn't move or twitch. She stood still, open-mouthed, holding the chain and the padlock, her eyes watching the space where the children had been until finally her chin dropped to her chest. 'No.'

Back upstairs, Maureen poured them both a glass of vodka in the kitchen, drinking hers and filling it again before she took them through to the living room. Leslie was sitting on the settee, crying quietly with her face in her hands. 'Drink this,' said Maureen, handing her the vodka.

Leslie pushed away the glass.

'Doesn't mean it's true,' said Maureen, 'just 'cause a wee girl out the back said it.'

'It is true,' said Leslie, rubbing her red face. 'I fucking knew something was going on. He stayed out a couple of nights without phoning and he's never at his mum's when I phone so I knew he wasn't staying there. I fucking knew.' She threw herself across the settee and grabbed the phone, pulling it towards her as she sat up.

'Don't phone him, Leslie,' said Maureen, as she dialled. 'Wait till ye calm down a bit.'

Leslie shot her a filthy look and carried on dialling. 'Mum?' she said, gesturing to Maureen to sit down next to her. 'Aye. Yeah. Listen, that Katie McIntyre, is she pregnant?' She glanced at Maureen. 'How far gone?' She looked at Maureen again. 'Four months? Aye, yeah, I will, yeah. Goodbye.'

Maureen could hear Isa's distant voice still wittering through the receiver as Leslie hung up.

Leslie stood up and lurched into the kitchen. The sudden sound of crockery smashing was accompanied by screams and curses. Maureen knew she should go in and calm her down but she thought Leslie probably didn't want calmed down and, anyway, Maureen was afraid of getting hurt. Having run out of crockery, Leslie swerved out of the kitchen and ran into the bathroom. Maureen could see her back as she ripped a new toilet-roll holder from the wall and turned her attention to a matching towel rail, pulling off a big lump of plaster. She sat down heavily on the edge of the bath, sobbing and holding her face, her fingers digging into her scalp. Maureen went over and put her arms around her but Leslie shook her off. 'Don't fucking cuddle me,' she spluttered. 'I'm too fucking angry to get touched by fucking anyone.' And she went back to sobbing.

They had been back in the house for an hour, Leslie sobbing and periodically getting up to break things, Maureen sipping vodka and trying not to become alarmed. She went into the kitchen and cleared up all the broken plates. She had been giving Leslie a Barbie crockery set, piece by piece, for years, and it was all shattered on the floor among the plain plates and glasses. Leslie had opened the cupboards and swept everything out of them, even the pots. She stormed back in and found Maureen cleaning. She stamped on an almost intact serving bowl, smashing it to small bits.

Maureen could see Leslie was either calming down or tiring herself out. They had smoked a cigarette while sitting in the same room and Leslie stood up. 'We should go,' she said.

'Leslie, are you all right to drive?'

'I need to drive.'

'No, ye don't. We could get a cab.'

'I'm fine,' said Leslie, picking her helmet off the floor. 'We need the bike. How else are we going to watch Michael?'

Maureen phoned Kilty from her house. Kilty had spent the day searching the Net for information about students coming from Poland to brothels in Britain. She had cancelled Josh at the last minute and arranged a rematch for Tuesday night but was afraid he wouldn't turn up because she couldn't think of a decent excuse and he'd probably just think she was a head-do. She didn't really care. Did Maureen know that a lot of these women thought they were coming over to work as waitresses and chambermaids?

'I don't think that matters,' said Maureen. 'What else did ye turn up?'

Kilty said that the gangs who recruited them didn't always keep the women. Sometimes they sold them to another gang and the women had to work for nothing to pay off the debt. It took years sometimes and the going rate was fifteen thousand pounds. If the police caught the women they treated it as a local matter and just deported them back to their country of origin. Deporting the women meant there was no witness against the gangs and no case. 'And guess what? Remember ye couldn't work out why McGee is so attached to Poland? I'll tell ye: trafficking isn't an offence in Poland.'

'Fucking bastard.'

They had to kill a couple of hours before meeting Kilty. Leslie used the time to mope and smoke, looking wistfully out of windows and periodically locking herself in the toilet to cry. Maureen saw her glaring at the phone a couple of times, as if it was a direct line to Cammy.

37
Calm Down, Leslie

They were sitting side by side like the three wise monkeys, watching the door and not knowing what to do. They had been there for a while and the cold stone step was numbing Maureen's bum. Across the square the Park Circus Health Club was busy. Punters arrived and left. They were middle-aged men, out for their Sunday-night fuck. Mostly they were alone but a couple of twosomes arrived, smiling hard as they jogged up to the door. A fat man with thin legs arrived in a car and paused on the top step before pressing the bell, wringing his hands with his elbows bowed to the sides.

'What's he doing?' asked Kilty.

'Taking his wedding ring off,' said Maureen.

Leslie sighed heavily.

'You all right, Leslie?' said Kilty.

'No,' she said.

Kilty took Leslie's hand, squeezing it hard and holding on to it. Maureen could see it made Leslie uncomfortable but she didn't want to yank her hand away so she left it, glancing at it a couple of times, wishing Kilty would get off her. Eventually she had to offer her a fag to make her let go.

They watched the man press the bell. The door opened and they saw the body-builder inside, leaning against the wall, smiling and greeting the man with an outstretched hand.

'My stupid fucking father,' whispered Kilty.

'He didn't know, Kilty,' said Maureen. 'He wouldn't have told us if he knew.'

'Yeah.' Leslie rubbed her back. 'He didn't know.'

'Piss off,' said Kilty gently, knowing they were trying to be kind. 'All it takes is a glance at the fucking newspapers. These poor women think they're coming here to study—'

'I think they know what they're coming here for,' said Maureen.

Kilty seemed disappointed. 'Why do you think that?'

'That's what Candy III said, really. She said they get their passports taken away and made to work for nothing.'

Maureen could tell that Kilty had a problem with it. 'But why would Ella fall out with her son about that, then?'

'Ella was a pro herself,' said Maureen. 'We might have trouble seeing how wrong that is but Ella wouldn't.'

It was dark now and the grassy hills in the park had turned a velvet blue. The rusting iron gates leading into the park hung idly from their struts. Maureen thought of Ella's bitter son Si, furious at what his mother did for money, never thinking what she was giving up for him, never wondering at the resourcefulness it took to do that. Candy II wasn't bitter, and look at her life. She thought of bitter Una, sitting in her big house with a healthy baby and a brand-new car at her door. And she thought of herself and her past, of all the golden moments that had passed unappreciated because she was bitter too. The one thing they had in common was their victimhood, and that mantle was a negation of all the wonder in life, a licence to brutalize without compunction. She wondered if she was using it to kill Michael, if it seemed inevitable simply because she wanted to do it so much. Back across the road, the light in the doorway flickered, and as Maureen looked up she imagined a school assembly line-up, with Si McGee and dead-eyed Tonsa sitting on a parquet floor next to Candy II, gleefully spitting mucus-covered Kinder eggs over the floor towards a row of angry teachers.

Across the square the door opened and shut. The body-builder looked straight at them as he walked down the steps, and ran a slow, graceless jog over to them, swinging his overworked arms. He stopped in front of them and looked along the line as if he was memorizing their faces. Maureen nodded at him and went back to staring at the door. 'What are you girls doing out here, then?' he said, sounding jolly and friendly.

Maureen jerked a thumb at the house behind her. 'Locked out,' she said.

He laughed, thinking it was a joke, and stopped when he saw that she wasn't joining in. 'Come on,' he said, reaching forward and cupping his hand under Leslie's elbow, lifting her, 'time to go home.'

Skinny as she was, Leslie turned on him. '*Get your fucking hand off me,*' she spat, wringing her arm free and stepping back. She had her finger in his face, a stiff, angry finger, and she was shouting. 'Do you own this street, do ye, eh?' She didn't give him time to answer. 'Do ye own this fuck street and everyone in it, do ye? Your fucking street, is it?' She was close to hitting him, they could all tell. He backed off. 'Calm down.' He looked at Maureen for support.

'You fucker. You fucking fucker.' Leslie was screaming at the top of her voice. Lights flicked on in front rooms around the quiet square. 'You're running a fucking brothel over there. D'ye batter them if they won't work for ye? Do ye?'

The body-builder had been nice for long enough. He pressed his lips together. 'Calm down,' he said, telling her this time. He reached for her roughly, grabbing her arm, holding her tight. Kilty, seated three feet away, launched herself, landing mouth first on his wrist, biting him as hard as she could. Yelping, he let go of Leslie who seemed to have grown two feet taller than any of the rest of them.

Her mouth was a thin, furious line, her voice low and hard. 'The man's not born that can raise his hand to me,' she said, and punched him on the side of the neck. They hardly saw her hand go out, just retract, heard the sound of skin slapping hard against skin and the body-builder went down like a bag of bricks.

'What the fuck . . .' said Maureen.

'I'm afraid I've lost my temper,' said Leslie, with super-natural calm. 'Perhaps we should leave.'

They were buzzing with nervous excitement as they queued to get into the all-night café.

'I enjoyed that,' said Leslie, standing tall and proud, her eyes open a little too wide. 'Can't we just go back to Maureen's?'

'No,' snapped Kilty disapprovingly. 'I think we should stay out until you've calmed down.'

'Dunno why you're so snotty about it,' said Leslie aggressively. 'You bit him.'

'I was defending you,' said Kilty. 'Anyway, there's no food in hers. I haven't eaten since yesterday.' She poked Maureen hard in the ribs. 'And you look like Bobby Sands.'

'Give it a rest,' said Maureen, and nodded at Leslie. 'She's already had a go at me today.'

It was a strange café, furnished with old school desks and a curvy bit of a church pew. Two avocado-coloured baths took up valuable floor space and had plants growing in them for no good reason. It was kept busy with the waves of homebound pub-goers, clubbers and lost loners who just couldn't sleep. Kilty ordered a whole lot of things from cups of cocoa to eggs Benedict and they dutifully handed their menus back to the exhausted waitress.

'What was all that stuff?' asked Leslie.

'Calming food,' said Kilty, getting a pink Powder Puff Girls notebook out of her handbag and flipping it open. 'We need to calm down and think about what we're going to do about this.'

'I don't want to calm down,' said Leslie. 'I enjoyed that.'

Kilty took out a pen, clicked it open and wrote an elaborate '1' in the tiny margin. 'We need to think. What are our goals here?'

'What d'ye mean?' Leslie asked.

'What are we going to try to achieve? It's better if we work that out before we come up with a plan.' Then she explained, 'Social work post-grad, course 101.'

They saw the logic.

'I want to bring that bastard McGee down,' said Maureen.

'I want to help the women in there,' said Leslie reproachfully, and Maureen realized that she should have said that too.

'Right.' Kilty wrote slowly, in a jagged but precise hand. Then she looked up. 'I want to make my dad wake up,' she said, waited for them to nod and jotted it down as the hot chocolate arrived.

Maureen ate her Flake with showy gusto, spooning warm cream into her mouth and swallowing it as if she was enjoying it. Leslie was taking her out on the bike to look for Michael after this and the last thing she wanted was heavy food but she ate to reassure the others. All three looked at the notepad and the three points, nodding and thinking about it as they drank milky chocolate.

'If,' said Kilty ponderously, 'trafficking isn't an offence in Poland, and McGee's name isn't on anything here—'

'We don't know that,' interrupted Leslie. 'What about Ella's court case?'

'That's not evidence, that's an allegation,' said Kilty succinctly. 'And if he's fly enough to traffic from Poland because it's one of the few countries that isn't a signatory to any convention, you can bet your arse he'll have kept his name off the sauna licence.'

Leslie stirred her chocolate, coaxing the settled cocoa powder from the bottom.

'If his name isn't on anything,' continued Kilty, 'what can we do? We can't go to the police. They'll tell us to piss off.'

They all thought about it, each trying to think of alternatives to going to the police.

'We could blow him up,' said Leslie stupidly.

'Yeah.' Kilty looked at her askance. 'I think you should get back with Cammy before ye kill someone. Leaving your commando tendencies aside, goal two is get the women out.'

They couldn't think of anything for that either and were feeling discouraged as the food arrived at the table. Kilty got the waitress just to put it all in the middle and they tried to share it but everyone wanted the eggs and it turned into an unsightly scramble.

'God,' said Leslie, 'that was gorgeous.'

'Taste the Croque Monsieur,' said Kilty, pointing her to a golden toastie. 'They make it with butter.'

'The problem with helping the women,' said Maureen, 'is what do we do? Do we get them out and send them home?'

'Yeah,' said Kilty. 'Otherwise we'd need somewhere safe for them to hide from Immigration and the bastards who brought them over here. We don't have those kinds of resources.'

Leslie sat back. 'I'll go in with a gun and get them out, if that's what it takes.'

'Look, you can't use being angry with your boyfriend to

shoot up a licensed premises,' said Kilty, as if she'd been involved in a tremendous amount of paramilitary activity. 'You might remember the good times half-way through and then where will ye be?'

'Standing in a brothel with a gun and a whole lot of foreign women?' said Leslie, as if she'd really thought about it.

'How would ye get the women to leave with ye? What would you say to them?'

'That I'd come to rescue them and if they came with me they'd be safe—'

'In Polish? Or Latvian?'

'Oh.' Leslie looked deflated.

'And what about afterwards? What if they want to carry on working? Would you take them to your house?'

'They can't stay with me, even if they're not working,' said Leslie firmly. It seemed a strange line for a mad bomber to stand firm on. 'I'm gonnae . . . I need my space,' she said, and looked shifty.

Maureen leaned across the table. 'What about upsetting your dad? Couldn't you just tell him?'

'Nope,' said Kilty. 'He'd just do what he always does and say I was mad. Anyway, getting one lot of women out probably won't even cost Si that much money.'

'See,' said Maureen, 'I don't think he really cares about the money.'

'Why?'

'Well, think about it. He's a poor scholarship boy at a Catholic school, his mum's a prostitute and the other boys probably know that, his sister's a psycho. He doesn't want money. The money is a side issue. He wants respectability.'

Leslie shook her head. 'How can this even be happening in this day and age? It's un-fucking-believable.'

'Yeah,' said Kilty. 'They count on that, like the child

prostitution racket. I read today that lone child immigrants seeking asylum routinely go missing in the UK. The cops think they're being prostituted and used to make pornography by organized gangs but they can't find them. Who'd believe that?'

'No one,' said Maureen.

'No one,' said Leslie miserably. 'And even if they did they'd roll their fucking eyes and do nothing.'

Sitting on the back of the bike, holding on to Leslie's waist, Maureen shut her eyes and wished herself anywhere else. She felt sick and dizzy, and suddenly aware of her bare legs and arms and the danger of the night traffic. If they crashed and skidded on the tarmac she'd be skinned alive. The possibility still seemed more inviting than their destination. Leslie had agreed to help her watch Michael but had no idea what Maureen was planning. She pulled up at a junction, flicking the bike into neutral and kicking down the stand. Her voice was muffled through the helmet. 'Ye're hurting me,' she said, working her fingers into Maureen's clenched fists, making her relax her grip.

'Sorry.'

'Just loosen it a bit.'

The front of the house was dark again and Una's Rover was parked outside the front door. They stood behind the strip of communal garden in the street for twenty minutes, watching the lights in the hall through the open living-room door, but saw no movement. 'Let's go round the back,' whispered Leslie.

'Wait here a bit.' Maureen was afraid she'd be sick again and shame herself in front of Leslie who'd just KO'd a brick shit-house.

Leslie elbowed her hard. 'There's nothing going on here.'

Maureen pushed her elbow down. 'Wait a bit, though.'

Leslie, still bristling with adrenaline, pushed her arm. 'What's the point in us standing here—'

The close door opened and Una stepped out into the street, followed by a small, bald man. Maureen froze, holding on to the chicken-wire fence. Una had gained a lot of weight since they had last seen her, and her haircut was worse from the front than the back. It stuck up at the top and hung over her ears. She was wearing purple leggings and a giant pink T-shirt. She raised her hand and pointed at the car. The lights flashed and beeped and she walked round to the driver's seat. Michael was shuffling and looked as if something demeaning had just happened to him. As he reached forward to open the door Leslie grabbed Maureen's arm and pulled her away to the bike parked on the corner. She had to lift Maureen's leg to get her on the bike and slammed the helmet on her, banging the top of her head so hard it rang and buzzed. They took off, following the Rover at a distance.

Maureen shut her eyes, leaning her head on Leslie's shoulder, trying to take herself back to Vik. They were crossing the river at Jamaica Street when the anger in her belly stirred awake, swirling around her gut, mustering allies among the hormones. She sat up. They were on the Maryhill Road, heading up to where she knew he stayed. They passed Benny's house and she tried to see if his lights were on, but they were doing forty and whizzed under the railway bridge marking the boundary with Ruchill.

Three cars in front, Una took a left, disappearing off the road. Leslie followed her round the corner and suddenly came to the Rover, parked at the back of a shop. Leslie passed by just as Una opened her door, flicking on the internal light. Michael had on a white T-shirt with a Nike tick across the front, the soft material articulating his drooping belly and rounded back. Maureen wanted to lean across and grab him from the bike, forgetting who he was, thinking he was McGee or Angus or someone else. She wanted to grab him and drag him along behind her, skin him alive on the pot-holed road.

Leslie turned the block and rejoined the main road, following it back to the town. At a set of lights she wrestled with Maureen's clenched hands again, loosening them, digging at them with her nails unnecessarily.

Back in Garnethill, Maureen cracked the lid off a brand-new half-bottle of whisky and drank it. Leslie said she only had another couple of days on the antibiotics and watched her enviously, sipping a cup of tea. They hadn't bothered to put the lights on in the living room and the dark orange sky filled the window.

'Maureen,' she said, 'ye have to remember that the baby isn't you. It could be different this time. I mean, he's a hundred and ten years old and Una doesn't trust him to get a taxi home on his own. I don't think she'll be leaving him alone with the baby.'

'I've seen her leave him with the baby,' said Maureen. 'I've seen her do it.'

'Can't you be patient?' said Leslie quietly.

'Why would I be patient?'

'He's not going to live long, Mauri, he was having trouble walking.'

Leslie nodded off on the settee and Maureen tiptoed into her bedroom. She sat on the end of her bed, drinking from the bottle as she looked out over the city to the blackened Ruchill Tower, drinking and thinking about skinning Michael.

38

Tonsa

'You didn't even know her,' said Leslie watching Elsie Tanner sniff at a stained lamp-post.

'I knew her as well as you did,' said Lenny, defensively, tugging at the itchy collar of his dark jacket. It was chafing his neck red raw.

'But my pal did know her.' Leslie pointed at Maureen. Behind her sunglasses Maureen's eyes were burning. A yearning for sleep made her blink every two seconds, dragging her eyelashes back and forth across the lenses of her shades like a boa on a burlesque stage. She had woken up with a familiar inch-long bruise under her chin, a parallel bruise on her forehead between her eyebrows and she could not work out where on earth they had come from.

'You've got something on your head,' said Lenny helpfully, leaning in to see better.

Maureen raised her hand and touched it self-consciously. 'I know, it's a bruise and I don't know where it's come from. I've got another under my chin again as well.'

'Pull your fringe down,' said Leslie, flattening hairs over it so that it looked like a big horizontal bruise with hairs stuck to it.

Despite being hung-over and bedraggled, Maureen, Leslie and Lenny were one of the more glamorous parties at the small funeral. The family had yet to arrive but a couple of other groups had gathered by the door to the church. Three elderly men with withered, pinched faces stood in front of it, smoking fags held in cupped hands and laughing at each other's jokes. Two casually dressed young women sat on the church steps, offering their already brown faces up to the sun. Maureen guessed that they had come in lieu of someone else.

They were in Partick, down by the river at a small Catholic church. The building across from the chapel had been knocked down, leaving a stretch of wasteland, currently being used as a makeshift car park. Behind the church, on the banks of the slow river Kelvin, stood an old sandstone mill recently converted into flats.

The small church was unassuming; an arched wooden door was set at the gable end, flanked by small flying buttresses and two long windows of brightly coloured glass. To the side of the door, a ragged lump of granite with a large brass shield attached stood on a concrete plinth. Etched with the Madonna crowned with stars and a stiff heraldic spreadeagle, it was a thank-you gift from the Polish servicemen and -women who had attended mass there during the war.

The arched chapel doors opened. A young priest with sandy hair the same colour as his skin greeted everyone, inviting them inside on the condition that they were part of the McGee party. The old men finished their fags and the young women stood up. Maureen, Leslie and Lenny walked towards the door, Lenny shouting back to Elsie Tanner to stay, Elsie, stay. Elsie sat down suddenly and started licking her fanny. As the priest walked away down the aisle to the vestry, every single person present climbed into the back row, knowing they hadn't been central to Ella's life.

The altar was a plain wooden rectangle with matching panelling at the back. A cloth-covered trestle sat in the aisle, waiting to receive the coffin. The priest came down the aisle and whispered orders for them all to move up to the front. The old men shuffled out to the aisle and everyone else pretended they were going to move but as soon as the priest left they settled back where they belonged, leaving the old men standing ostentatiously at the front. Lenny closed his eyes and began to pray, clasping the flat of his palms together and sticking his elbows out to the sides, as fervent as a child saint.

They heard cars drawing up outside, doors slamming, someone giving orders, and Ella the Flash made her last big entrance. Following behind a glossy white coffin came Si McGee. Tonsa was hanging heavily on the arm of a man with a slash scar running from his ear to his nose. She was dressed in a beautiful black woollen suit with gold Chanel buttons and a veiled pillbox hat. Maureen turned to watch her and saw that although her body was grieving her face was blank, her eyes staring steadily at the floor in front of her. Her boyfriend had been in the papers a few years ago, complaining that the police hadn't even tried to catch his slasher. He had aged dramatically in the interim, his hair turning from brown to white, his skin from white to grey.

The priest performed his incantations while the congregation stood, sat and stood again, singing reluctantly through barely opened mouths without accompaniment. Maureen looked back once or twice and saw Elsie Tanner standing in the sunshine, wagging her tail and looking into the dark church, anticipating Lenny.

As the sad service drew to a close, professional pallbearers came forward, picked up Ella's gorgeous coffin and carried it to the waiting hearse. The priest, Si, Tonsa and her scarred man followed the coffin out into the bright day. Tonsa got straight into a car, leaving the priest and Si waiting by the door to thank the sorry turnout for coming.

Maureen wanted to look at him now: she wasn't afraid

of him any more, wanted him to know she was smart and knew what was going on. In front of her in the queue, Lenny shook Si's hand warmly. 'She was ... a lovely lady,' he said, voicing the one thing about Ella that everyone knew wasn't true.

Si pulled away his hand before Lenny had finished shaking it. He turned to Maureen, trying to smile through his distaste. 'Yes,' he said, even though she hadn't said anything. 'Thank you for coming.'

'Warsaw,' said Maureen.

He widened his smile. 'Sorry?'

'Gotcha,' said Maureen, and moved on into the sun.

Leslie caught up with her on the pavement. 'His neck *was* shaking,' she whispered.

They were four steps from the church when the door of the black car in front of them opened, blocking their path. Tonsa stepped out and unfurled her long, slim self. She looked down her nose at Maureen and nodded, as if she had spoken to her.

'Hello,' said Maureen. Tonsa didn't answer. 'I'm sorry about your mum. I worked near her in Paddy's.' She gestured to Leslie. 'We both did, actually.'

Tonsa cocked her head and narrowed her lips. 'What ye doing here?'

Uncertainly, Maureen thumbed back to the chapel doors. 'Um, your brother,' she said. 'He invited us.'

Tonsa seemed to be staring at Maureen's hands and her mouth hung open, a wetness glistening behind the mesh veil. Unnerved, Maureen clasped her hands behind her back. 'I think I met you years ago,' she said. 'At the Barras.'

Tonsa looked at her face.

'With my brother, Liam?'

Tonsa lurched forward, like a drunk falling and catching themselves. 'Your brother,' she said loudly, dead-eyed as ever. 'He battered me.' She threw out a loosely cupped hand, as if she was going to punch Maureen in the stomach. Maureen looked at it. A ragged red scar ran from the wrist to the base of her thumb. 'Cut me,' said Tonsa. 'My hand don't work right now.'

'Why on earth would he do that?' Maureen asked.

'Screwed him over a deal.' Tonsa looked at her hand, as if seeing it for the first time, and unsteadily traced the length of the scar. 'He was teaching me a lesson.'

'Yeah?' Maureen retorted. 'If he did that, why did ye drop the charges?'

Tonsa's hand fell to her side. 'He said he'd do the other hand.'

Maureen pretended not to believe her. 'I think you know a friend of mine as well,' she said.

'Who's that?'

'Mark Doyle? I saw ye having a drink together in Brixton once.'

For the first time ever in their long, if distant, acquaintance, Tonsa's eyes displayed an expression. She nearly smiled. 'Cheerio,' she said flatly, and climbed gracelessly back into the Jag on all fours.

39
Rake

When they rang the bell there was no answer, but they could hear a radio coming from round the back, the tinny sound of quacking voices rattling down the tall alley between the houses. Maureen and Leslie followed it to the garden, and pushed open the rotting wooden gate. As they turned the corner they saw Liam sitting on a kitchen chair, wearing nothing but a pair of shorts, his back, chest and thighs sunburnt pink, as if they had been slapped. He was smiling, with his feet up on another chair, watching Siobhain at the far end of the garden. She was pottering around the shrubbery in a giant straw hat and sleeveless sundress with cherries on it, shouting remonstrances back at him about keeping it nice and putting the work in. Liam nodded and smiled, calling yeah, yeah, sure thing. Siobhain had a small wicker basket of old gardening tools and was poking at something in the bare soil, pulling out stringy plants. It was such an unexpected and self-sufficient scene that both Maureen and Leslie hesitated for a second in the damp shadows.

'Hello?' said Maureen, as if she had never been there before.

Liam and Siobhain stiffened guiltily as they looked up and saw them.

'How long have you been there?' said Liam.

'Oh, right?' smiled Leslie. 'Nothing to hide, then?'

Siobhain grinned, and Leslie stepped into the sunny

garden and walked over to her, punching her arm playfully. Siobhain shrugged innocently, as if it had been a game, as if she hadn't been involved in a deception.

Liam and Maureen were standing still, staring at each other. Liam raised his hand and brushed the hair off his face. 'Give us a hand with the tea, Mauri,' he said, and jogged down the steps to the kitchen.

Maureen followed him, watched by Siobhain and Leslie, who were no longer laughing, knowing that something was amiss. It was dark in the kitchen. Liam pulled cups from the open cupboard on to the worktop.

'Are you blushing,' said Maureen flatly, 'or sunburnt?'

'A bit of both,' he said, and turned to face her.

Maureen was furious. 'I specifically asked you about Siobhain,' she hissed, 'and you lied to me.'

'I don't have to tell you everything,' he said quietly.

'This isn't *everything*,' she shouted. 'Liam, this is Siobhain. She's had a shit time and a miserable fucking life and the last thing she needs is some melancholy rake trying to save her from herself with beef injections.'

'Excuse me,' he said, genuinely insulted, 'I'm not a rake.'

'Aye, ye are,' she yelled. 'You're terrible to women. Remember, I know ye were unfaithful to Lynn with that bint Marsha, and ye dumped poor, stupid Maggie for Lynn—'

Liam pointed in her face. 'You didn't even like Maggie,' he shouted, as if that was the nub of the matter.

'What fuckin' difference does it make whether I liked Maggie or not?'

'Well,' he said, noisily arranging the cups on a wooden tray, 'it mattered to me.'

'Bollocks,' said Maureen, to his back. 'The point is that you're horrible to your girlfriends and Siobhain's very vulnerable.'

'Oh, that's shite.'

'No, it's not.'

'Yeah, blame the guy, Mauri.' He opened the rattling old fridge. '*Cherché* the fucking guy.' He took out some milk, smelt it and put it on the tray. He was arguing the way he always did, evading the point, skipping sideways.

'If you treat her badly,' warned Maureen, 'if you fuck her about, Liam, I'll fucking kill ye.'

Liam held on to the worktop behind him with both hands, like a man standing on a precarious ledge. 'I'm not gonnae,' he said.

'How can you possibly know that?' said Maureen.

'She's ...' He hesitated over the wording, got flustered and waved his hand in front of his face. 'I really like her.'

'Liam, really liking someone isn't enough. This woman has a precarious grip on her mental health. It's not enough just to mean well.'

They looked out of the window at Siobhain and Leslie. Siobhain was bossing Leslie around the shrubs, getting her to crouch down near the back and pull out the weeds she couldn't reach.

'Just because she's been ill,' said Liam, 'that doesn't mean she never gets to go out with anyone, does it?'

'No, but it means she needs to go out with someone responsible, someone who'll be careful with her.'

'I can be those things,' he said, backing off across the kitchen. 'Anyway, she's allowed a life. She's allowed boyfriends. It's not like I've knocked her up or hit her.' He stopped and looked at his sister. 'It's a nice thing,' he said softly, 'a good thing. I'm not going to feel bad about it.'

'Would you have nipped her if she was still as fat as fuck?'

'Mauri,' he said, reproachfully, '*she* nipped *me*, and it all started when she was overweight. I didn't want her to go on that diet. I tried to get her to stop it.'

'Why would ye do that, Mr New Man?' said Maureen

tartly, knowing that all of Liam's girlfriends had been slim.

Liam smiled up at her. 'Take it from me, even love can't blind ye to methane.'

The kettle whistled to a pitch on the stove and Liam turned off the gas, used a tea-towel to pull the stopper off the spout and poured water into a teapot.

'I can't fucking believe you lied to me.'

'Tell the truth, Mauri,' Liam said playfully, 'ye can't believe I lied to you convincingly.'

He was right, and it annoyed her. 'Why did you lie?' she said, sounding accusing to cover her embarrassment.

'Siobhain wanted to keep it a secret. She was worried it wouldn't last.'

'Do you think it'll last?'

Liam glanced out of the window. Siobhain was getting angry, pointing at Leslie's feet and raising her voice. 'Well, it'll last for me,' he said. 'I think she's fantastic. She'd probably stay with me for the garden as much as anything else.'

He watched Siobhain through the window, and Maureen could see he meant it, he did care for her, but she was worried. Liam would always need to protect Siobhain, save her from hurt and harm. She foresaw his life, saw everything given over to looking after Siobhain. And when he failed, as inevitably he would, the recriminations and self-loathing, the acid self-blame. Liam was always looking after some poor damaged bird. First it had been her and now Siobhain. She wanted more for him.

Maureen carried the tray out to the garden and Liam brought out two more chairs. They sat in a little circle, sipping tea like visitors from a neighbouring plantation, as Siobhain talked them round the garden. She had planted the herbs near the back door so they could be picked easily in the middle of cooking. She'd put the virulent mint on the other side of the door, hoping to keep it away from the other herbs. It made such a nice smell and she hoped it would waft into the kitchen in the late summer, when it was better established. The shrubbery was full of weeds because the feckless neighbours let dandelions and nettles grow on their side of the fence.

Maureen thought ahead to the trial and wondered idly whether Siobhain might be in league with Angus. Perhaps he still had control over her and had made her leave the letters and parcels outside Maureen's door. She screwed up her nose at the thought, knowing what was prompting her suspicion. She was resentful at being so completely deceived and was not a little possessive of Liam. As Maureen listened to Siobhain talking, her sense of foreboding subsided and she could see that Liam and Siobhain might be a good thing. If Siobhain was allowed to take those chances maybe Maureen, too, could have a boyfriend, a normal boyfriend.

When Siobhain had finished her tea she took Leslie to help her finish the weeding by the far wall, leaving Maureen and Liam alone. The sun was sliding behind the house, a bank of thick shade sneaking up on them.

'So,' said Maureen, lighting a fag, 'what else have you lied convincingly about?'

'Nothing,' said Liam, savouring the last of the sun.

'You beat Tonsa up, didn't ye?' she said suddenly. Instantly defensive he turned to her, sucking his teeth in a hiss. He saw her eyes and dropped the stance.

'Ye cut her wrist, she could have bled to death.'

'I didn't cut her,' he said quietly.

'You did beat her up, though, didn't ye?'

Liam nodded faintly. 'Mauri, things happen some-times—'

'Did you hit her in the face?'

He wrinkled his brow as he watched Siobhain and

Leslie. 'Things got out of control. I'm not proud of it. I got into a situation …' He squirmed in his chair, avoiding her eye. 'I can see in hindsight … I got into a situation and there was nothing else I could do. I wish it had gone another way. I wish I was a better person and had never been in that position. But I'm not, I was there and there was a situation …'

'Did ye cut her?' she said.

'No,' he half smiled, 'I never cut her. There's a lot you don't know about Tonsa, a lot ye don't want to know about her. Tonsa's got a bad knife habit. She cuts herself and other people when she can get away with it. 'Member she was in the paper with her boyfriend when he got slashed? "Stop These Evil Men" headline? Well, it was Tonsa. Tonsa cut him.'

He looked at her, expecting relief or some sort of reaction, but she was staring at the ground in front of her, neck limp, thinking. She could see it all clearly now, proud Ella the Flash and Tonsa playing a knife over her hand, switching her skin, muttering threats not to tell, while Si sat and watched. She could have said something to the mortician at the time if she'd known, but Liam had lied about Tonsa. He'd been lying to her about Tonsa for over a year.

'I met Benny on Friday,' she said to hurt him. 'I had a cup of tea with him.'

Liam stared at her but she didn't look at him. She was waiting for him to shout at her that Benny was a bastard, but he didn't.

'How is he?'

'He's sorry.'

'Is that enough for you, that he's sorry?' Liam asked. 'Even though he helped Farrell fuck you over, after all he did?'

'No,' she said, 'it's not nearly enough. But I'm glad he's sorry. He asked after ye.'

'Did he?' Liam twisted his mouth, suppressing a smile, and turned back to the garden.

It was a long shot, she knew, but it was worth a try, just in case. 'You've lied to me about the baby, haven't ye?'

Liam drank the end of his tea. He put the cup down so carefully she hardly dared to look at him.

'Haven't ye?'

He sat very still for a while, one hand clutching his hair, the elbow resting on his knee. She touched his sunburnt back and he flinched. 'What is it?' she said, watching her searing white hand-print fade on his red skin.

Liam looked away from her. 'She's called her Maureen,' he said.

Maureen O'Donnell sat very still as the iron entered her soul.

40

From Hell

It was getting dark, a depth of darkness they hadn't seen for weeks. Clouds were gathering overhead and the heat was intensifying. The city was headed for a storm.

Leslie shook her head. 'Not there.'

Maureen knew she was right. They were crouched behind the hedge at the back of the house and could see Una sitting in an armchair in the kitchen. The baby was asleep in the white plastic carry-chair, sitting on the table. Her little arms and legs stretched and flexed in her sleep, as if in dreamy remembrance of a watery time before now. Una had been watching the television from her chair but her head was slumped forward now. They had been in the dark lane for forty minutes, crouched behind the hedge. The vomit spill Maureen had left there a few nights ago had dried hard.

'God, my fucking knees are gonnae snap,' said Leslie.

Maureen stood up and gestured to her to follow her out to the road. They walked round the corner to the bike, lighting badly needed cigarettes.

'Could he just be at home on his own?' said Leslie.

'Liam says he's not to be alone.'

'At Winnie's, maybe?'

The last time Maureen had spoken to her, Winnie said they didn't like him and hadn't seen him for a while, but she hadn't spoken to Winnie for a long time and didn't know what the state of play was. 'Mibbi,' she said.

'Come on,' said Leslie. 'We'll check out his house first.'

Ruchill was a wasteland between two rough areas. Damp housing thrown up in the fifties had recently been ripped down, leaving a Hiroshima landscape of roads crisscrossing empty rectangles of grass and rubble and a line of occupied tenements skirting the main road, like a Wild West film set. The devastation ended with a sharp dip down a hill to a deep burn. At the other side of the road the burnt-out tower of the old fever hospital, blackened and brooding, watched the road.

The entrance to Michael's flat was round the back through a narrow, open-cast staircase cut between the extended backs of shops on the ground floor, leading up to the raised back court.

Leslie turned off the engine and they sat and stared at the stairs. They didn't know which house was his and would have to climb up to the trap of the back court to find out. They got off the bike and stood looking around aimlessly. Above them, beyond the sharp railings, a clothes-line swung in the scorching wind. Leslie cleared her throat. 'You wait here and I'll go up,' she said. 'Stay with the bike.'

'No, I'll go,' said Maureen, insisting out of obligation.

'I'll go,' said Leslie. 'Ye can't leave a bike unattended in an area like this.'

But there was no one around to protect the bike from. As Leslie walked away Maureen noticed that she kept her helmet with her so that she could get away quickly. She watched Leslie engulfed by shadow then emerging at the top of the stairs. Leslie waved like an elated climber, then disappeared again.

Maureen looked around. Five hundred yards away a small estate of new buildings had lights on and windows open, the sound of Monday-night television wafting faintly across the flat land. The wind was coming from the east, bringing blistering heat with it, stinging her eyes. She looked above the tenement and saw the charred hospital tower. She could see it from her window. She remembered the winter past and how the tower had haunted her after Winnie told her Michael was staying up here. She had come up on her own and set fire to it, promised herself that she wouldn't let him take her down. She took a deep breath, remembering the cold snow on her face and the heat from the fire. Three days ago she couldn't think of Una's house without feeling sick, and now here she was outside Michael's. She thought of Una's baby flexing in the little chair and wanted to run back to the kitchen window to check that she was still there.

Leslie seemed to have been gone for a while. Maureen looked up just in time to see a head being swallowed in the darkness of the stairs. She didn't know who it was, didn't know who was coming towards her, and found herself moving behind the bike, holding on to the helmet by the mouth strut, ready to use it if she needed to.

It was Leslie and she was smiling. 'He lives on the first floor but he's not in. Why don't ye go up?'

'Naw, it's all right,' said Maureen casually. 'We should find him.'

Leslie put her hand on the handlebar as if she was touching base. 'Go,' she said. 'Go and have a look.'

Reluctantly, Maureen moved towards the stairs. The steps were steeper than they looked and the chill walls enfolded her, blocking the hot wind. She looked back to the bike from the dark. Leslie was resting her bum on it, ankles crossed casually in front of her.

The smell of rancid milk hit Maureen as soon as she reached the raised back court. Bags of rubbish were piled up by the back door, nipped and ripped open by nameless small animals. She approached the door and looked at the names.

Michael lived in the first-floor flat overlooking the court. Rusting bars covered his dark window. The kitchen window was broken at the top by what looked like a flying stone, a single, rounded incision with radiating spider legs. The living-room window was broken as well. Maureen felt elated to be so close to the site of Michael and not feel sick. She peered into the kitchen. Empty lager cans were gathering dust on the newly refurbished worktops. Soggy plastic bags were piled in the corners. The smell coming from the broken window was almost as putrid as the back court. How hard would it be, she thought, to take rubbish from in there to out here? He could almost have thrown it out of the window.

The living room was pathetic, the sort of room a corpse would sit in for months without being discovered. A single armchair stared at a wall. Sitting next to it was an old coffee table that she recognized as Una's, free local newspapers spilling off it on to the floor.

The jarring sound of a metal dustbin lid being smashed off the ground was so loud that Maureen started and jumped four feet back. Unsure whether the simultaneous flash of light was in front of or behind her eyes, she stood, her helmet raised above her head, ready to club whoever was there with it until they stopped moving. It felt like the tip of a whip on the back of her neck and she spun on her heels, then another on her arm, and on her shoulder and legs. A thousand cold licks hit her at once, switching the dust from her tired skin, pinching her awake.

Leslie looked up at the stairs just as Maureen emerged through the curtain of battering rain, walking slowly towards her across the street. She was grinning.

It seemed beneath them to hide now. They sat on the bike outside the pebble-dashed council house and Leslie suggested knocking on the door and asking. If Michael was there they'd leave; if not, they'd both go in. She looked at Maureen for a while, watching the watery veil slide down her helmet, dripping off the ledge on to her shoulders and her sodden T-shirt. Leslie stood up when the small nod came. She locked the bike, patted Maureen's knee and turned to face the wrath of Winnie.

It was a small cul-de-sac of houses and flats. The O'Donnells had moved in just a year after George and Winnie married, long after the fights started. They had grown up there, all of them. As Maureen watched Leslie walk away, stepping on to the concrete path, she saw herself and Liam coming home from school, Una and Marie through the window, watching telly, home ten minutes after the bell because their school was within walking distance. They could always tell by Marie's face what was going on in the house, whether Winnie was angry- or sleepy-drunk, whether George was making peace or had left for the evening. Leslie rang the bell.

After a while the door opened. An inviting spill of orange light caught the rain as it fell, making it look as if everywhere was dry but outside Winnie and George's door. Leslie turned back to the bike and gestured for Maureen to come.

Maureen walked nervously up the path. Winnie might be drunk. Worse, she might be sober, an alien, humourless stranger in Winnie's body with unpredictable rules and no common memory. Despite her apprehension Maureen's heart soared because, for the first time in seven months, she was going to see her mum.

George was wearing a pork-pie hat and carrying a copy of the *National Enquirer*, grinning so widely that the void of teeth at the back of his mouth showed, like an old horse. Behind him, standing on the stairs, tucking one edge of her dressing-gown into the other, was Winnie. She had just woken up and her face was shiny with night cream. When she saw Maureen the surprise made her foot slip and she sat down heavily, showing off her blue-veined legs, exhaling Maureen's name as if in prayer. Overcome, George dropped his magazine and opened his arms. Maureen threw herself at his chest, wrapping her arms around him, feeling his soft belly convulse as he cried through a grin. Wrapped in his arms she remembered standing on his feet to dance, remembered George slipping a fake Valentine card into her school bag and putting chocolate bars in her pockets when things were bad at home. She remembered late nights when he'd come home from pubs bringing wee vests and matching pant sets for her when she was far, far too old to wear them. They hung on to each other, crying and digging into each other, banging their heads together until George managed to push her away by the shoulder. He tried to speak but his face crumpled and he glanced at Leslie, mortified. He ran off into the front room, shutting the door after himself.

Winnie stood up, righting her dressing-gown, smiling and perplexed. 'Would ye like a cup of tea?'

She was a stranger. No longer the louche mother of yesteryear, Winnie scuttled around the familiar kitchen, putting the tea on the table and asking questions, quite coherent, politely pretending to remember Leslie being at Una's housewarming party when Winnie had been famously drunk and woke up the next day certain she hadn't gone.

'Ye probably don't remember,' said Leslie. 'It was a while ago now.'

'Oh,' said Winnie uncertainly. 'No, I'm sure I do remember ye being there. I remember ye from when Maureen was in hospital.'

Maureen waited for the conversation to turn sour: mention of her stay in hospital was usually a cue for recriminations and drama.

'What's that mark on your head?' said Winnie, kindly brushing over it.

'A bruise,' said Maureen, raising her hand to touch it. 'I've had it before and I don't know where it's coming from.'

'Will ye have some Dundee cake?' said Winnie.

Leslie nodded eagerly. Winnie set the tin on the table and proudly lifted out the cake. It was home-made, dark and heavy. Winnie smiled at Maureen. 'I made that,' she said, tapping it with a big knife.

Maureen smiled back. 'You're dead clever, you.'

Winnie nodded, shoved the knife in and watched the side crumble away, revealing dry clumps of unmixed flour, oily patches and hardened candied fruits.

'Oh dear,' she said, 'I've made a royal cunt of it.'

'Is it all right if I smoke?' said Leslie politely.

Winnie and Maureen laughed hysterically. Leslie joined in but didn't understand. She watched Maureen banging the table, Winnie crossing her legs and twisting away as if she was bursting for the toilet. When they finally calmed down Winnie explained. 'The sights this kitchen has seen,' she said. 'Ye can do anything but sacrifice a goat on the table.'

Leslie took out her cigarettes and offered them round but Winnie refused, saying she'd never got the hang of it. She picked up the packet and looked at the French health warning. 'Liam give ye these, did he?'

Leslie didn't want to get him into trouble so she shrugged. Winnie had been told during his dealing days that he managed bands, and Maureen didn't suppose Liam would confide in her now. Winnie rolled her eyes. 'At least he's not selling those drugs any more. That was a nightmare.' She looked at Maureen's open mouth. 'Yes,' she said, 'your old mum's not completely stupid. And I know he wasn't just selling mara-ha-joanna for pain control either, so don't try it.'

Maureen was astonished. During her drinking the one consistent feature of Winnie's behaviour was going for the jugular on any given day but she'd never mentioned Liam's dealing.

'Did ye always know?' asked Maureen.

Winnie smiled wisely. 'He told me last week,' she said, and got another laugh.

They were sitting quite cosily together now, Winnie and Leslie and Maureen. George came in and out of the room on various pretexts, smiling and giving Maureen the thumbs-up whenever he caught her eye. Maureen knew this might be the last time she saw George and Winnie, the last time they were ever really together, and she was trying to enjoy them. Winnie had given up the attempted pretence of being Homemaker of the Month and had settled for opening a packet of Jammie Dodgers.

'He's very ill, you know,' she said seriously, dunking a biscuit in her tea.

'Everyone says that,' said Maureen, 'but no one says what's wrong with him.'

Winnie put the sodden biscuit into her mouth and chewed it. 'He was taken into hospital today. Una says he turned up at hers in a mini-cab and his eyes were flickering about. She thinks he's had a fall and bumped his head. He falls over a lot.'

'He's a bit young for taking tumbles, is he not?' said Leslie.

'Oh, aye, he's my age,' said Winnie, adding, 'twenty-one,' as a weak joke. 'He's in some state.' She looked guilty.

'Is it the drink?' asked Maureen.

'I don't know what it is. Maybe he was always a bit

missing. He might always have been like that, sure what would I know? I was pissed the whole time I knew him. They've got him up in Gartnavel Royal for observation.'

'Are you still drinking?' said Leslie. It was a redundant question. If Winnie had been drinking they would have known all about it.

Maureen and Winnie looked at each other. 'I've no choice. They tell me my liver's gonnae explode if I drink again.' She reached across the table and took Maureen's hand, squeezing tight. 'You've made my year coming here like this,' she said.

'Mum, I missed ye,' said Maureen.

Winnie looked up and Maureen saw the angry questions in her eyes, asking why didn't ye phone me back if you missed me, why hurt me like that when I'm such a soul and the world's too much for me as it stands. But Winnie didn't say anything, just squeezed her hand again and made the best of it.

'Liam told me what they called the baby,' said Maureen, and Winnie blanched.

'What did they call it?' asked Leslie.

Winnie and Maureen looked at each other and Winnie turned to Leslie. 'Una called her after Maureen,' she said diplomatically.

'That's pish,' said Maureen. 'She didn't name her after me, she gave her my name.'

They sat in their makeshift beds in the dark living room, looking out over the city again, more peaceful than they had been the night before. Maureen thought about Michael's house, about facing it, and she knew she could do it. She felt a spark of sick excitement in her gut.

'She's very funny,' said Leslie solemnly, assuming that Maureen was thinking about the same thing as her.

Maureen smiled, feeling not a little proud of her mum. 'Yeah. I told ye.'

'I know. Ye told me loads of times but I never met her sober and at the hospital she was always, frankly, a complete arsehole. It's amazing that drink can change someone that much, when ye think about it.'

'The dark side of Winnie is a dark place indeed,' said Maureen, settling down into her bed. 'You seem calmer about Cammy.'

'I never, ever want to see him again,' said Leslie. 'In a way I'm glad it happened. I was worried that I hadn't given him enough of a chance. You should see Kate McIntyre – honestly, she's dead hard-looking, ye know? Wears tops open to her navel.'

Maureen put her hands under her head, and knew that she'd phone Mark Doyle in the morning. She had decided she was going to do it and nothing she did any more had repercussions. 'Leslie,' she said, sitting up suddenly, 'I've never told ye this because I didn't want to break your heart but I'm going to say it now. Cammy's a very, very unattractive man.'

'Is he?' said Leslie curiously. 'I thought he was good-looking.'

'No,' said Maureen definitely. 'He's a dug. And his chat was rubbish. And he was a sulky wee shite.'

'Oh, I know that.'

Maureen settled down again in her bed. 'A shite-talking dug.'

'From hell?' said Leslie uncertainly.

'From hell.'

Leslie sighed contentedly.

A car pulled up outside and a mini-cab driver hooted his horn.

'Goodnight,' said Maureen, already nostalgic for her old life.

'Goodnight,' said Leslie.

41

Democratic Demographic

It was cool outside the window. The rain had run itself out overnight but the pavements were still wet and the damp made the buildings seem more solid, as if their foundations had grown. She felt calm, very clear about what she had to do about Michael and Si McGee, but she wanted to check that there was nothing better they could do for the women.

On the phone Hugh had been snippy with her. He'd refused to come to the house to see her and wasn't there when Maureen turned up fourteen minutes late, which was out of character enough to be a deliberate slight. He'd suggested an international chain coffee shop in Sauchiehall Street. Maureen had bought a black coffee and had to break a tenner to pay for it, and only discovered when she asked for an ashtray that she couldn't smoke in the café.

'We didn't just make up the rules ourselves. We asked our customers if they wanted smoking areas and they said they didn't.' She had a blonde ponytail pulled through the back of her baseball cap and it swung when she spoke, flicking her shoulders, like a new device from those clever engineers at the Dandruff Be Gone company.

'Who did ye ask?' said Maureen, annoyed at the prices, the presumption and the pertness of the server. 'You've only been open for a millisecond.'

'Well,' she smiled, 'we didn't ask in here exactly. We asked in other shops.'

'In America?'

'And several in London,' she said.

'You asked people in America if I can have a fag and they said no and that makes it a democratic decision? It's not just a cynical ploy to get me to pay four pounds for a coffee then leave quickly?'

'I think you should leave her alone now.' Hugh was at her elbow.

They sat down on a plastic sofa by the back wall.

'I take it this is about the trial tomorrow?' said Hugh, looking stern.

'No,' said Maureen. 'I've discovered something and I want to know what to do about it.'

'I think you should just keep your mind on the trial, Maureen.'

'Yeah,' she said, 'I am, but here's the thing. Women are being smuggled into Scotland via an agency in Poland and they're being prostituted here. I've been told that if I tell the police they'll send the women home and refuse to prosecute the men who've organized this—'

'Wait.' He stopped her. 'Wait, you're way ahead of the game. Where are these women being held?'

'I don't know.'

'How do you know the police aren't dealing with this?'

'Is that right or wrong, Hugh? The police won't do anything about it?'

'You shouldn't interfere, Maureen. It's not a case of us being willing to do something, we do our best. We can only work within the legislative guidelines, ye know, we can't go about doing whatever we feel like.'

'I heard you'll just send them home.'

Hugh sighed. 'Probably. Look, we don't even have the interpreters available to question foreigners. In an ideal world there would be a special unit to do this but we don't have the resources or the authority to set one up.'

'You don't have the resources?' she said mockingly.

'Or the authority. We're not the fucking A-team,' he said, and she could see he was angry with her. 'You know, we might be ineffective in some ways but the public aren't always exactly helpful. D'you know that your neighbour has put in a complaint against the officers at Stewart Street for coming up to your door all the time? Did ye know that?'

'Yeah,' said Maureen.

'Did you put him up to it?'

'No,' she said. 'No, I didn't.'

'He's citing fourteen incidents and while the investigation's on-going we're on a warning.'

'Right.' She sipped her coffee. 'Want some?'

'You don't get it,' said Hugh, sitting very still.

'Don't get what?'

'If Angus Farrell gets out next week, and Joe wants an excuse to leave you there alone, it's perfect. You'd be completely unprotected.'

Maliano. She could almost see him, opening his front door, nipping across the close and leaving the letters. Two steps across and two back. Sober, she'd never considered him a genuine threat, but here he was, clearing the ground for Angus. He watched her all the time, knew the hours she kept, knew when she was at work. And if Angus knew someone like Benny there was no reason why he wouldn't know Maliano.

They said goodbye to each other and Maureen watched Hugh walk away. He turned back and waved. It was less like a goodbye than a dismissal. Maureen pulled open the heavy door of the public phone box, picked up the receiver and called Mark Doyle. To her surprise it was a pager service and she left a message with the woman on the switchboard, asking him to phone her back that afternoon.

*

When she got back to the flat Leslie was awake. Dressed in a crumpled silk shirt and shorts from her poly bags, she was sitting in the kitchen looking tired and drawn. She smiled as Maureen walked in, trying to hide how sad she was, and Maureen smiled back, doing the same. They made coffee and took it into the warm living room, kicking the bedclothes to the wall and sitting down on the settee. Maureen told her she had met Hugh McAskill and the police couldn't do anything about the women.

'All right,' said Leslie impatiently. 'Fuck them. They're not even fucking attempting to do the right thing.'

'What the hell can we do about this?' said Maureen, feeling lost.

'Plan B,' said Leslie.

'Plan B won't work, though.'

'It's all we can do.'

Reluctantly, Maureen stood up and went out to the hall, looking under the gas bills and junk mail on the floor for the business card. She looked at the number on the card for a moment before she dialled it.

Aggie Grey was in a noisy road with traffic hurtling past. 'Hello?' she hollered. 'Hello?'

'I've got a story for you,' said Maureen.

'Who is this?'

'I'm Maureen O'Donnell.'

Aggie had a smile in her voice. 'No, I'm Spartacus. How're ye, Nicky?' Maureen didn't know what to say. She was obviously a joke between Aggie and whoever Nicky was. 'What do ye want, then? Chicken and cashew nuts again?'

'Look,' said Maureen, 'I am Maureen O'Donnell.'

Aggie stalled.

'You were at the door, wondering what the fuck you were doing hassling nutters in their home?' said Maureen.

347

'Are ye at home?' shouted Aggie, louder than she needed to.

'Aye,' said Maureen, 'I'm at home.'

Aggie Grey sat on the settee smoking a cigarette, looking back and forth between them. She was as butch as a brick, very bright and very nervous. Leslie explained the story to her and asked if she would be interested. Aggie stared at Maureen. 'But not you?'

'No,' said Maureen, 'I'm not any part of the deal.'

Aggie sat and thought about it, as though she was considering doing them a very difficult favour. 'I can't take this story unless you give me an interview about Douglas Brady to bribe my editor with.' She blushed, knowing it was a lie and that she was being greedy, knowing that they knew it too.

'Fuck off,' said Maureen. 'We'll give the story to someone else. It's brilliant. You know it's better than the Douglas one.'

'No, it's a more important story, which doesn't make it a better story. Murdered married men having affairs is the best story. I could make it up, say I've met you and describe the house. Use file pictures.' She sounded terrifyingly professional. 'You've taken a chance inviting me up here.'

'Ye could do that,' said Maureen, 'but I'd write to the Press Complaints Commission and it would be bad for your career. The murdered-married-man story is better in that shitty paper you work for but this story could be printed in a different paper. You know it could. It would be good for you.'

'Will ye give us a picture of your floor?' she said, pointing at the bloodstains. It was all that was left of him.

'Fuck off.'

Aggie Grey looked at the cigarette in her hand and

348

thought about it. Finally she nodded. 'Tell you what,' she picked up her notebook, 'you're lucky I'm freelance. Very lucky.'

42

Yellow Doorway

Black clouds covered the moon, intensifying the oppressive darkness. The soil beneath their feet was wet and soft. She had never seen Mark Doyle so animated. The orange lights from the drive filtered through the dark trees, flickering across his face, obscuring the marks and scars. For a moment he seemed desperately handsome and dashing, the hero who would save the baby and make things all right. She thought of Pauline as a small girl and how strong Mark must have seemed to her, how clean and uncomplicated in comparison to every other member of her sordid family. Together they looked up the hill to Gartnavel Royal Psychiatric Hospital.

It had been built as a fortified containment facility in the Scots baronial style, with battlements on the eaves and solid turrets at the corners. The extensive grounds contained a complex of hospital facilities. At the bottom of the hill were nurses' dorms and Gartnavel General, a long slab of a building eight storeys high, looking like an airport hotel, separated from the psychiatric hospital by old trees. Although floodlit, the Royal seemed darker and sadder, hidden away like the mistakes and failures it contained.

She had desperately wanted to drink this afternoon after Aggie left and Leslie had gone to visit her mum. She'd wanted to sit and drink and contemplate her glorious behaviour tonight. She had to go for a walk around the town to stop herself and now she was trembling, weak from resisting the desire. Soon it would all be over and she could stop thinking and thinking and thinking about it.

'There's a door around there.' Doyle pointed, keeping his voice so low she had to strain to hear him. 'It leads into an old kitchen. The back door'll bring you out to corridor F. His ward's F4. It's off it, towards the back. They're shutting this wing down as well so they've not put any security doors or cameras in.'

'How do you know all this?' she asked.

'I checked it out this afternoon,' he said, reticent and uncomfortable.

'After I phoned ye?'

He nodded.

'That was very good of you.'

He glanced at her resentfully. 'D'ye wantae chat,' he said, leaning over her, 'or d'ye wantae fucking do this?'

'Yeah.' She looked back at the building as if she was paying attention and could be trusted. 'Let's do it.'

'Sure?'

'Aye. I want to.'

'It's not too late. We can turn back.'

'No,' she said, trying to look serious. 'I'm sure.'

She didn't feel serious. She felt elated that the moment was here and almost past. She was ready to do it, ready to make someone cleave to her will, to take a chance and change the future.

'Ye've got the knife I gave ye?'

'Yeah,' she said, patting her pocket. 'Got it.'

'Remember to wipe and drop it once you've done it, leave the knife there, don't take it with ye.'

'Leave it there,' she echoed.

'Leave it there. Come on.'

Still crouching, Doyle led her expertly along a track through the bushes. The soil was damp from the rain and muddy foot tracks from earlier in the day were still distinct.

'Look,' he pointed down, 'we're leaving shoe prints. Chuck your shoes after but don't go barefoot. A footprint's like a fingerprint. They can convict ye on it.' She had cheap imitation Timberlands on and they had recently moulded to the shape of her feet. She didn't want to throw them away. He led her round the perimeter of the building to an unlit area and stopped. 'This bit of the building's shut down already.' He pointed to a large ground-floor window on the corner. An unkempt bush was growing in front of it and it was almost completely covered. 'It's light in there but no one can see in. Even if a car came past. No one goes there. They'll not find him until morning.'

There were no bars on the window. The pane of glass was broken in the low corner but the disused wing was so long abandoned that no one had bothered to patch it up. She looked up and, framed in grey stone, saw herself tap Michael gently on the back, himself slipping gracefully to the welcoming floor and an end to all their troubles.

'You listening to me?'

'No one can see in,' she said automatically. 'They won't find him until the morning.'

'By which time you'll be rid of the knife and your shoes. What else have ye to do?'

'Get an alibi and make a phone call from home.'

'Don't say anything in the phone call, just chat about the court case tomorrow or something.' He raised a finger and bent low to look her in the eye. And don't mention me. Understand?'

'I understand.'

'Not to anyone. Ye haven't told anyone, have ye?'

'Not a soul.'

His fingernail was an inch from her eye and she understood it as a threat.

'Never tell anyone – anyone,' he said, jabbing the air. He tilted his head back, looking down at her like an impatient owner warning a dog. 'I'm here because of you.'

'I know.'

'Remember.'

'I'll remember.'

'Shut up,' he muttered, and turned back to the window.

To their left a car pulled up the drive, the headlights licking the jagged gravel path in front of them before it turned and stopped at the front of the building. They waited until the driver got out of the car, locked up and entered the building, heard the door click shut.

'When do ye take the knife out?'

'In the room, when he's standing in front of me.'

'Make sure he can't see ye take it out. He'll mibbi panic.' He turned and looked at her, a full-face stare, then nodded, pushing past her to lead her back to the path.

They parted without speaking. Maureen climbed out of the trees and walked towards the kitchen door, feeling more alive than she ever had before, hearing voices echoing up the hill from the open windows on the nurses' dorms, smelling damp soil, the coldness of the stone and lingering exhaust fumes. Doyle had jimmied the door to the kitchen earlier and it opened easily, fresh splinters of sweet-smelling wood pulling out of the lock as she slipped it open. She slid into the building and closed the door after her.

It was a large room, tall and long, smelling of dust and disinfectant. A black, empty patch of floor showed where the industrial cookers had been. Against the far wall a rickety stack of solid hospital wheelchairs gathered dust by the door. She hoped that Doyle had been sensible when he broke the lock and had worn gloves. She looked at her hands. She didn't have gloves on. It hadn't occurred to her to wear gloves, because it was hot, because she was leaving everything to Doyle. She'd have to be careful, watch what she touched the whole time, she couldn't leave her fingerprints all over the place. She stared at her hands, watched them shaking, and thought of what Doyle had said, that it wasn't too late. But it was too late: she'd imagined herself here too often before for another outcome to be possible.

Maureen lowered her hands and listened to the noise of the building. It was ten thirty and she would have to get home soon if she was to make a plausible phone call to anyone. The ceiling above creaked a low sigh and she heard a ticking in the pipes. She tiptoed along to the far door, leaving perfect prints in the dust, opened the door a crack and looked out.

The corridor was empty but brightly lit. There was a door off the corridor at the far end, and coming from it she saw a familiar yellow night-light. The door had a sign reading 'F4' on the lintel. She could hear men talking, their voices loud and joking, but she couldn't work out where they were.

She waited fifteen minutes, trying to pinpoint the voices and work out what to do. Finally she saw a shifting shadow in the yellow doorway and pulled the door in front of her closed a little. He had on a white nurse's shirt. 'Aye,' he said loudly, laughing back into the room. 'He did it an' all.' He walked down the corridor, passing close. She smelt soap and tobacco. He turned the corner at the far end of the corridor. The patients must be in a bad way in that ward, heavily medicated enough for the staff to shout at each other when they were trying to sleep. It occurred to her that Michael might be too deeply asleep for her to move him, and the possibility blossomed warmly in her chest.

Suddenly, the other voice came towards her out of the ward. He was fat, dressed in pale blue and holding a fiver, jogging with his heavy arms up at his shoulders, running after his pal, calling in a mock whisper. 'Hughie,' he said, 'Hughie, get us a couple o' Twixes.' He turned the corner, going after his pal. Maureen held her breath and slipped across the corridor.

It was a small room with four beds arranged two against each wall with the curtains pulled between them. A very old man was asleep in the bed in front of her, his hand lying limp by his side, a newspaper on his chest. She crept round the curtain. In the bed beyond, she saw Michael sitting bolt upright, wide awake and looking at his feet. She waited for a scream or a lunge, but Michael sat still, a small man in pyjamas. He had Liam's eyes and square jaw.

Maureen stepped forward and Michael turned to her, looking for guidance. He didn't know who she was. She pulled back the bedcovers and he swung his feet around to the floor, feeling for slippers with his toes. For reasons she would never be able to fathom, she helped him on with his dressing-gown before taking his upper arm and guiding him out of the room, across the corridor to the dusty kitchen.

It was dark and silent apart from Maureen's laboured breathing. She held his arm tight and felt her skin burning where it touched him. Michael didn't struggle or try to get away. He seemed to find her fingers digging into him reassuring, as if she was grounding him. He smelt of sour vodka and dusty cheese. The smell infected her, getting into her lungs, sticking to the moist membranes in her mouth. She felt Michael seeping in through her skin.

They listened to the fat nurse's feet as he came back down the corridor and went into the ward. The chair squeaked as he sat down. He hummed to himself and cracked open a paper. Beside her, Michael was still. She led him out of the kitchen, pushing him in front of her, afraid to let go of his arm in case she couldn't bring herself to take hold of him again. He followed her prompts compliantly and said nothing until they were two corridors away.

'Is it-it-it?' he asked, smiling nervously as though they had just been introduced.

Maureen heard it through the rush and roar in her ears. He reminded her of Farrell. 'Yes,' she whispered, walking just in front, reminding him to keep moving. 'Do you know this way?'

'Yes,' he whispered back, chopping a straight path with his hand, gesturing ahead.

'What are they doing to you in here?' she said.

He hesitated, unsure. 'Walking?'

'They're walking you?'

'Yes,' he said definitely. 'It's walking.'

He was watching her, reading her face, trying to work something out, who she was or why they were whispering. 'Do you know me, Michael?'

'Yes,' he said.

'Who am I?'

'A doctor.'

She stopped and looked at him. 'Who are you?'

'I'm ... mm.' He chopped forward with his hand again, forgetting what they were talking about. 'A doctor?'

'You're in a hospital but you're not a doctor. What are you?'

'I'm in. Nurses? Nurses? I make nurses?'

The burning in her hand subsided. He wasn't addled with medication: it always left a blurriness in the eyes. She heard the clatter of a trolley being pushed a long way away. They had to get out of the corridor.

As they hurried along she tried to remember what Doyle had said. Leave the knife, but wipe it first. Take the knife out when Michael was looking away. Phone someone when she got in, talk about the court case tomorrow or something.

Just as they arrived at the door to the disused wing of the hospital, she suddenly wondered how Doyle knew about the case tomorrow.

Maureen pushed open the door and stepped down into a fog of stale, damp air. Blinking to adjust her eyes to the gloom, she could hear her heart beat. Michael followed her, dropping the step to the corridor. He stumbled, letting out a little frightened exclamation. She reached out and caught him under the arms and wondered what the hell she was doing here, stealing this confused old man with Liam's eyes. He stood upright and she turned away from him. This wasn't the time to think, she'd been thinking about it for a year already. But Michael hadn't been real then: he hadn't been as small and he hadn't been confused. Don't look at him, she told herself, steeling herself against humanizing pity, don't think about it, just do it.

The room wasn't hard to find. Maureen followed the floor of broken tiles down to a window, looked left and right and found the corner room. She pushed open the door and ushered Michael in ahead of her as Doyle had told her to, reaching for the knife in her pocket. Doyle had been right about the room. It was bright but the window was covered by the fervent growth outside. The floor was covered in dust and rubble, crunching underfoot. It felt like the mental rehearsals of killing him, but Michael had been taller in the fantasy, stronger and scary, not this frightened and bewildered little man. He looked back at her for reassurance and she urged him onward, thinking of the baby: that was why she was here. She was doing it for the wean.

She pulled the knife from her pocket and stepped towards him. He was pointing at something on the ground, trying to ask about it but forgetting the words: 'Whatsits, it-it?'

She had the knife in her hand, raised the tip to his back and a chink of light caught her eye. It was outside the window, just outside, inches outside, a bit of glass catching the light. Mark Doyle was outside the window, crouching among the foliage, holding a small video camera to the hole in the broken pane and filming her. He had knives in his eyes.

43

Impossible Future

She was shaking so much she could hardly see. Needles of broken glass were stuck in her arm, each puncture demanding attention, each an urgent distraction. Michael groaned behind her and she spun, startled, almost dropping the knife. It was so much sharper than she had thought it would be, so much sharper than a normal knife.

She was terrified. She could hear her own breathing, in her ear, like a stranger's breath. It wasn't dignified, not a happy exit. She was afraid of herself. All her elaborate justifications had dissolved in the visceral reality.

Down at the burn, before the road, she washed her hands and cried at what she had done, rubbing her arms with the dirty water, working the glass deeper under the skin, the sharp pain reminding her that she wasn't dead. She took her squelching, bloody boots off and walked home barefoot, like a pilgrim, taking dark back roads. She left the boots a mile away, under a mattress on some wasteground. As she walked towards home she felt sure that the tangy metal taste of panic would stay in her mouth for ever.

When she climbed the stairs to her house she wanted to bang on Jim Maliano's door and apologize for what she had been thinking about him, give him a gift of something, take the packet of biscuits he had brought her from holiday and be gracious.

Following Doyle's instructions, she phoned Kilty the minute she got in the door and casually invited her over.

Leslie was sitting at the kitchen table, watching her in the hall, staring at her bleeding arm. When Maureen had said a cheery, 'Cheerio,' and hung up on Kilty, Leslie called to her, 'Mauri?' She looked frightened. 'Liam phoned for you. I told him you were asleep, like ye said.'

Maureen fell forward until her face hit the wall. She stood there, sobbing, terrified and disgusted, rubbing her forehead against the plaster.

Leslie took her into the bathroom and washed her face, then pulled her bloody T-shirt over her head and took off her sodden bra, made her drop her shorts and her bloody knickers. She took a poly-bag from the kitchen and wrapped the clothes in it, tying the neck of the bag tight as Maureen sat trembling on the side of the bath. She looked down at her wee bony body and saw that his blood was all over her, splattered on her calves, stuck in the wide pores on her thighs, smeared on her breast. Her forearms were covered in cuts, bits of glass glinting in the wounds like Mark Doyle's lens. The pain was all that was keeping her conscious.

Moving with what seemed like supernatural speed, Leslie stood her in the bath and washed her down with cold water from the showerhead. She brought some fresh clothes from the bedroom and got Maureen to hold on to her shoulder as she stepped her into the pants and shorts. She put the bra on wrong, pinching the skin on Maureen's left tit with the elastic, and pulled a fresh T-shirt on over it. She was tweezering the broken glass out of her arm before Maureen spoke. 'Leslie,' she whispered, 'I've done something . . .'

Leslie nodded at her arm, frowning hard. 'Were you careful?'

Maureen thought about it. She couldn't focus at all. She thought she'd been careful but she didn't know, she couldn't know. She shrugged, making Leslie lose hold of a long sliver near her wrist. Frustrated, she slapped her hand reflexively and Maureen jumped. Leslie looked at her and Maureen realized she was crying too. 'You better've been,' Leslie said, her voice terrifyingly shrill, her nose glowing red. 'You better not . . . Fuck.'

Leslie sniffed hard and went back to the tweezers. Salt tears dripped on to the cuts on Maureen's arms. Leslie cleared her throat. 'Mauri, I'm pregnant,' she said calmly, 'and I'm keeping it, and I'm gonnae need you to bring it up with me.' She started crying again. 'I can't do it myself, Mauri. I don't know the first fucking thing about weans.'

Maureen was stunned. 'Ye can slap me again if ye like,' she said.

By the time Kilty arrived Leslie had Sellotaped toilet paper over Maureen's cuts and dressed her in a long-sleeved top. They were both stunned, and pretended they'd taken a Valium each to calm them down for tomorrow.

'You shouldn't drink on top of Valium,' said Kilty, staring at Maureen's full tumbler.

'No,' said Leslie, 'it's all right. Ye can drink on top of these ones.'

'Well, why aren't you drinking, then? You must have finished your antibiotics by now.'

Maureen looked at her glass and wondered, for a moment, whether she'd done it to fan the fires of her self-pity, so she could keep on drinking. She interrupted Kilty's speculating to tell her she'd seen her dad in hospital but not to tell anyone because the family didn't want her to see him. She described the way he spoke, that he said he was a nurse and thought she was a doctor.

'That sounds like a wet brain,' said Kilty, pestering a cigarette, creating banks of smoke. 'That would explain the confabulation.'

'The what?' said Maureen.

'Making things up, I'm a doctor, all that stuff. Bits of their brain gets burnt out and they make things up to try and make sense of what they see.'

The skin on Maureen's forearms was burning. She had to concentrate hard to sit still and not rub the wounds or press the tissue.

'A girl in the detox unit's dad had it,' said Kilty. 'I used to take her up to visit him in hospital. One week he'd claim to be a sailor, one week he was a nurse, but he was always pretty cheery. Couldn't remember anything he'd done in his life. His family hated him, they were like these pent-up balls of fucking fury because he'd kicked the shit out of them and ruined their lives, but he couldn't remember it. So, there was this nice wee guy sitting in a bed smiling, and the family used to gather round him like angry vultures. I swear the mother used to hurt him when no one was looking.'

'Can ye get better from it?' said Leslie.

'Oh, guessing, I'd say the recovery rates are low. Most people die from it, I think. I heard something about vitamin B injections but I can't remember what it is.'

Maureen looked at her tumbler of whisky suspiciously. 'How do you get a wet brain?'

'Well, if ye drink heavily for years and don't eat. It's heaven for alkis, really, if you think about it. They drink to forget and then, one day, they finally do forget.'

Maureen nodded, ignoring the itching and trying not to touch her arms.

'So,' said Kilty carefully, 'are you ready for tomorrow?'

'Yeah,' said Maureen. 'Let's not talk about tomorrow just yet. Tell us about Josh.'

Kilty wasn't sure about him. He was nice and doing defence work because he thought it mattered, but he was a lawyer and she had a horrible image of herself wearing pearls and drinking Chardonnay. She didn't think it would work, really, but he was a nice guy and quite funny.

Maureen half listened, watching Leslie's face for visual clues about how to react. She kept thinking she was back in the dusty kitchen, watching the fat man running for a Twix, the sour smell of Michael as she caught him under the arms when he stumbled, the crunching underfoot, down by the burn. She understood the urge to drop away from life, walk into a police station and make a confession, to have the confusion and the terror over, to tell someone else, in detail, what had happened. But as she stood over the body she'd made a pact with herself: that her penance for this would be that as long as she lived, she would never tell anyone what she had done. And Sheila was right: it would always be the most important thing that had ever happened to her.

They lay on their beds in the darkness and gradually Leslie and Kilty's breathing deepened. Maureen lay awake, eyes open wide, staring at the ceiling. Headlights from occasional cars going up the steep hill rolled along the ceiling. Drunk people passed in the street, shouting or laughing, or staggered home alone. In the city below, sirens wailed and police cars rushed to avert crimes. Ambulances followed them or ventured out on their own.

She looked at her watch. It was ten to four and the sun was smearing the sky blue, waking the birds. Her arms were itchy, the Sellotape tugging at small hairs. She sat up and lit a cigarette, pulling her knees up to her chin and clasping them tight. If she didn't die from this, if the police didn't catch her, she was going to get away from here. She was going to sell up and go to St Petersburg and spend a month in the Hermitage, filling her eyes and her head with beautiful things and never waste a calm hour, never spoil a good meal with worry. The cigarette burnt her tongue, stripping it and making her mouth taste of metal tape again. She was getting pain spots in her lungs and couldn't laugh without coughing any more. She would go to St Petersburg and stop smoking and see beautiful things. If she had her time over again she'd stop drinking. In the impossible future she'd strive to be happy.

44
Afterlife

They woke up when the alarm went off at eight thirty and found Maureen sitting up in her sleeping-bag, a thin cloud of cigarette smoke hanging above their heads. They tried to make her eat something but she couldn't. They nagged her so much that she tried but couldn't swallow and had to spit the toast out into the bin.

Kilty had brought a crisp white shirt with an open neck and short sleeves for her to wear but her bloody arms would have showed. Maureen said she had already decided to wear a yellow top with long sleeves and the words 'porn star' printed on the chest. Leslie was ironing her skirt in the kitchen and shouted through that it was much better than the clean white shirt. Kilty watched them both curiously. Maureen changed in the bathroom. The tissue had dried on the blood, sticking to the wounds, but she didn't want to change the dressing herself. She put the clothes on and made an attempt with some makeup, using the last of the Dior mascara she had bought when she was flush, rubbing Touche Éclat into every crevice.

They left the house early, tripping down the stairs. The sun was splitting the pavement, filling the city with an unearthly white light. They walked in unison, barely talking, following the quieter streets down to the river. It was half past nine and the traffic was thinning after the rush-hour. Harassed-looking women in estate cars drove home after the school run and bus drivers, pissed off after the early shift, jammed the road on their way back to the station. Maureen was so tired she could hardly feel her feet on the ground, hardly see a hundred yards in front of her through the scalding light.

They walked along by the river, sweating gently, picking up the breeze as they passed the Sheriff Court on the far bank and followed the road round to the tail end of Paddy's. The settee was still under the bridge but the men weren't there. Maureen half raised a thoughtless hand, waving to where they might have been. Down the lane Gordon-Go-A-Bike thought she was greeting him and waved in response, pedalling slowly, going nowhere.

The High Court of Justiciary looked out over Glasgow Green, where junkie prostitutes, too down on their luck to look for drivers, relied on drunken pedestrians for their trade. Flanked by the city mortuary, the front of the building was a neo-classical string of ionic columns surmounting a set of stairs, topped off by a long pediment. Gathered outside on the stairs, four or five clumps of smokers made the most of the opportunity, puffing away and chatting to each other. One group was composed of lawyers, obvious in their expensive suits and easy manner. Another crowd wore cheaper suits and nylon skirts, smiling nervously and inhaling deeply.

Inside, through a revolving door, was a white lobby with a sparkling mosaic floor that ended abruptly in a set of plain, modern fire doors. At the side of the stairs a court official in a grey uniform was standing behind a black marble desk and police officers were dotted around, as if they were expecting trouble. The hall was full of people looking lost, wearing sombre outfits. At each side of the hallway, suspended from the ceiling, were television monitors, stuck on vibrant blue screens and Maureen saw the name: HMA – v.–Farrell. She approached the reception desk.

'Can I help you?' said the uniformed man pleasantly.

'I don't know where to go,' said Maureen. 'I'm a witness.'

'Do you know which case it is?'

Maureen pointed up at the monitor. 'That one,' she said, and showed him her citation paper.

A black-haired policeman in a short-sleeved shirt stepped forward from the back wall. The police had been watching Reception, waiting for her to check in, and now they were coming to arrest her for what she had done. Sweet relief washed over her. It was finished. She could tell someone what had happened, every detail, and hope for absolution. 'Maureen O'Donnell,' he said, pulling out a clipboard and ticking off her name. 'If you'd just like to come with me.'

Maureen smiled a consolation to Leslie, who looked worried, and followed the officer through a wood-panelled room off Reception and to the door of a waiting room. 'We need you to stay here,' he said, 'and give us notice if you have to go to the toilet or anything.'

It seemed like pretty lax security for a murder suspect but Maureen wasn't going anywhere. The police officer read the 'porn star' motif on her T-shirt and looked alarmed.

'Not really,' Maureen reassured him, smiling weakly.

He ushered her in and shut the door behind her. It was a small room. Cushioned metal seats were pushed up against the walls and sunshine poured in through a small, high window. He was in shadow at the far end of the room, his skinny ass taking up half of a chair, wearing a wide-necked T-shirt that slid off a shoulder, showing enough skin to be obscene on a woman.

'What the fuck are you doing here?' said Maureen, and Paulsa winced.

'Same as you,' he said, moving his mouth too much for the words, as if his lips were numb.

Maureen sat down heavily next to him, wondering why

he had been arrested. 'What have you done?'

Paulsa laughed, high and fast, like a, chimp in distress, and shot to his feet, moving across the room towards the door just as it opened again. The uniformed man stood aside to reveal Shirley, the blonde receptionist from the Rainbow Clinic, clutching a tiny handbag in front of her like a shield. When she saw Maureen, dismay shimmered across her face. The officer stood aside, holding the door open over her head, ushering Shirley into the room. She smiled a polite thank-you, ducked under his arm and sat down on one of the chairs. Maureen hadn't been arrested after all. She was there as a defence witness in Angus's trial and so were Paulsa and Shirley.

Paulsa and Maureen watched Shirley take a small cross-word book out of her handbag, a pencil and a roll of mints. She opened the book, pressed the pages apart and began to consider an important clue.

Shirley had been friendly when Maureen went to the Rainbow Clinic. They chatted during her visits there and when Maureen went back after Douglas died Shirley had talked to her about it. Something had happened in the interim. Something had happened that made Shirley now think that Maureen was frightening and disgusting. Paulsa, assuming he was spotting an ally in Shirley, went to sit three seats down from her. Too polite to get up and move, Shirley glanced distastefully at Paulsa's dirty tennis shoes and shifted the angle of her crossed legs away from him in a small, symbolic rejection.

Maureen's knees felt watery. She sat down, watching the door, and hoped the nausea would pass. Shirley would tell the jury that Maureen had been back to the clinic after Douglas died, asking questions about him, that she'd gone to see Angus. Paulsa would tell them that Maureen got the acid from Liam. Of all the people gathered in the witnesses' waiting room one thing was abundantly clear: Maureen was the bad guy and everyone knew it.

Nothing happened all morning. No one came to get them. They were allowed to go to the loo, as long as they told someone where they were off to. There were no-smoking signs all over the building but the toilet smelt of stale cigarettes and Maureen waved her lit fags around to disseminate the smoke in case there were hidden alarms.

All morning they sat, trying to find a place for their gaze that wasn't someone else's face, chest or groin. The room got smaller as the hours ticked by and Paulsa became increasingly agitated. He kept going to the loo and coming back, sitting down heavily and flicking the heel of a tennis shoe on and off. Shirley finished her crossword and moved on to another one.

Maureen felt sick with exhaustion. Tiny air bubbles made their way up her throat, popping in her mouth. The heat and sunlight in the room created optimum sleeping conditions and suddenly she stopped believing in last night or Michael or even the existence of Gartnavel. She was in the Hermitage wearing a warm fur coat, sitting in front of Matisse's *Arab Coffeehouse*, watching the goldfish turn and swirl. Bright colours fanned from their tails, falling through the frame to the floor and ceiling like sparks from a catherine wheel. Every drop of colour sanctified what it touched. She was smiling, smelling sweet cardamom and watching the world being cleansed with colour, when she turned her head and saw a flash. Mark Doyle was next to her, the pointed black tip of his tongue emerged from between red lips, turning into a roaring black cyclone, rushing, growing, opening wide to engulf her.

'Are you okay?' The police officer looked worried.

She had called out and somehow fallen on to the floor, banging her arm on the chair.

Paulsa had called the police officer rather than touch her himself. A red smut grew on her arm, seeping into her sleeve. Huffing with pain, Maureen looked up and saw Shirley, her legs crossed, a zigzag thread hanging down from the hem of her skirt and she knew this part wasn't a dream because it was too detailed.

'I fell asleep,' said Maureen.

She went to the loo and locked herself in a cubicle. She pulled up her sleeve and peeled back the tissue, ripping off the scabs, making them bleed. She wrapped fresh tissue paper around her forearm, salvaging two strips of not-very-sticky Sellotape to secure the ends.

Back in the witness room, Shirley continued with her crossword while Paulsa stared guiltily at the floor and patted his damp face with a paper tissue, leaving little patches of white fibre on his forehead. When the door opened every-one turned to face it desperately, as if the air supply had been cut off and suddenly restored. The policeman stuck his head into the room. 'Lunch. Back by one forty-five sharp.'

Everyone else seemed to know where they were going. Outside the room Shirley and Paulsa disappeared through the front door. Maureen stood outside the panelled room, feeling lost, and then she saw them. They were standing in a crowd, Winnie, George and Liam, Leslie and Kilty, Vik and Shan, all introducing themselves to each other and shaking hands. Even Leslie's cousin, Jimmy Harris, had made the effort to come and raised his hand, smiling. The rest of them turned in unison, beaming at Maureen like a homecoming dream of comfort and joy.

The small café in the basement of the court had been painted a grating shade of howling yellow. Maureen looked down the table at Liam, Vik and Shan, chatting, estab-lishing common acquaintances, and it felt strangely natural.

She had studiously kept them all apart in case Vik thought she meant to get serious. None of it seemed to matter any more. Leslie and George were talking, and Winnie was making Kilty laugh.

Liam seemed tired and jumpy. It hadn't occurred to her before now but there would have been a phone call in the night, bad news, someone needed to identify Michael. Liam was keeping it from her, protecting her. She caught Winnie's eye and saw the strain there, as if Winnie hadn't seen enough trouble in her life.

She reached forward to put down her sandwich and felt the twice-used Sellotape on her right forearm peel away from the skin. The tail of the tissue unfurled slowly, resting inside her sleeve. She put her arm on her lap and tried to remember not to use it.

'Mauri,' said Winnie, 'look. See them?' She dipped her head in a secretive manner, gesturing to a table behind her. 'That's his family,' she whispered. 'Don't they look mental?'

Two women in old-lady tweed overcoats were sitting at a nearby table, looking poor and slightly ashamed of themselves, carefully picking the salad out of their sand-wiches, laying it aside. One had a small elaborate growth on her chin, a bulbous lump of extra skin with smaller lumps on top. Next to them sat a gangly young boy in his early teens with the same uncomfortable look, dressed in a track-suit and T-shirt and highly polished brogues. Maureen could almost hear the conversation in the house before they left, the for-Godsakes, he wasn't going to wear that, oh, all right, then, but change the shoes at least. As Maureen looked at Angus's family she could imagine him having miserable Christmas Days in ugly houses, being a teenager and growing his hair long. The two women would have turned up at his every school play, been intimidated and ruined his graduation. She could see Angus trying to shed them as his income crept up and his tastes changed. He had a history, a background and a cause. Liam saw her looking at them and leaned across the table. 'Bet Hannibal Lecter didn't have to wave back to a family of hill-billy freaks at his trial,' he muttered.

Maureen smiled. Two women and no father. In the penny-dreadful version of the story those women would be the monsters who had turned him into a sexual predator and the missing man simply a source of sadness to him. She sat back, looking down the table at all of her friends. Still feverish with exhaustion, she imagined lifting them all away from here, taking them to a clifftop table overlooking a calm sea and having a lovely dinner together, a last supper. Winnie would be funny and George would be dear. Jimmy Harris wouldn't look so hungry and Leslie would have her baby in her arms. At the end of the night Maureen would retire with Vik and they'd cuddle each other and talk lazily about nothing much as they dozed off into a deep sleep. As she looked at them, Maureen felt she was in an idealized afterlife, where all was love and peace and everyone she cared about was looked after.

Liam finished his sandwich quickly and nodded her outside for a smoke. She was nervous that he might ask her about last night or following Michael. 'Why are ye wearing a top that says "porn star" on it?' he said, when they got to the steps.

'Cheer myself up,' she said.

'You don't look well.'

'I'm very tired,' she said, remembering to using her left hand to rub her eye. 'I didn't sleep last night at all.'

He looked at her curiously. 'Ye were asleep at ten o'clock when I phoned.'

'Oh,' she said stiffly, 'yeah, but I woke up then and I couldn't get back to sleep.'

The steps were busy with smokers. Three uniformed policemen stood at the bottom between the gates, comparing something on their ungainly utility belts. A crowd of well-dressed confident people were standing in a circle and laughing loud. Maureen saw nervous Aggie Grey hanging on the edges of the group and realized why they were happy. They had no interest in the case going either way, they were journalists. Aggie spotted Maureen coming down the steps and averted her gaze, smiling at the ground, making a discreet thumbs-up. Maureen did it back and when she looked again Aggie was smiling up at the building.

Joe McEwan was a couple of steps down from Inness, absentmindedly scraping the arch of his shoe on the stairs as he talked. He looked up and saw Liam and Maureen coming out of the door. He shot them a polite smile, pressing his lips together and looking away. Liam gave the same smile back and sat down a distance away, resting on a pillar to light up. The last time Maureen saw Liam and Joe together they had hated each other. She could tell they had seen each other in the meantime – recently by the looks of things. Joe would have told Liam about Michael. She could see Liam asking him not to tell Maureen, just until the trial is over, please, just until then. Neither of them had any idea that she was involved; Joe McEwan had finally decided that she was a victim of circumstance just when she stopped being one. Liam gave her a cigarette and she took it in her left hand, leaning over the match in his hand to catch a light.

'Are you Maureen O'Donnell?' It was one of the men from the group of journalists.

'No,' said Maureen.

'I think she's still in the canteen,' said Liam helpfully.

Maureen looked out over Glasgow Green, busy with

lunch-time sunbathers. Leslie and Kilty came out and Vik and Shan joined them all, and they sat on the steps of the High Court and smoked and were together.

The afternoon was shorter. Shirley had relaxed a little and answered when Paulsa asked her the time. Maureen went to the loo to have a fag every so often, just to keep herself awake. She found a newspaper tucked behind the cistern as if someone was coming back for it. She read an article about how television was damaging everyone in some indefinable way. Back in the waiting room she soaked up the sun through the small window and planned her night. She was going to have a bath, a long, hot bath, and she was going to drink whisky.

The police officer stuck his head round the door again and told them that the court had finished its day's business and they must all come back the next day for nine thirty sharp.

When she walked out into the lobby Maureen saw Elsbeth Brady and her mother-in-law walking down a corridor towards her, looking angry. 'You should be in the witness room,' said Carol Brady.

Maureen didn't say anything. She was tired and had no reason to apologize to either of them any more.

'I suppose you're enjoying this, are you? Being at the centre of it all,' said Elsbeth, with an unkind smile.

Again she said nothing but crossed her arms. A long, hot bath, whisky and peace. The women looked her up and down, read 'porn star' on her chest and brushed past her, walking down the stairs to the door. Leslie was standing beside her. 'Was that Carol Brady?'

'Aye,' said Maureen. 'And Elsbeth, Douglas's wife.'

'Douglas's widow,' corrected Leslie.

'Her nose has been running all day and she kept sniffing

really loudly,' said Winnie. 'I think she's allergic to not getting attention.'

Maureen didn't think they'd all be able to come the next day but she wanted them all to be together for just a little longer. She insisted that they go across the road to a café. She wanted to go for a drink but was afraid of putting temptation in Winnie's way. As they went into the café she saw Liam whispering urgently to Winnie. He gathered himself together and came over, telling Maureen that he had to go and get a part for the car. The guy wouldn't wait for him and he'd see her tomorrow. She knew he was lying. She knew that he had to go and see about Michael.

The Val d'Oro café had small seating booths in yellow, trimmed with red like a child's toy. They sat in adjoining booths, Leslie and Jimmy Harris with Winnie and George, Maureen and Kilty with Vik and Shan. They ordered drinks and rolls. Shan asked for two egg rolls and a roll with sausage.

'He eats all the time,' confided Vik. 'You've never seen a constitution like it. More food goes through him than Safeway's checkouts.'

Shan smiled, slow and easy, at Kilty. 'It'll just get me ready for my dinner.'

'Your mum's great,' said Vik quietly, so Winnie wouldn't hear.

'Aye,' Maureen said cagily. 'She's great sometimes.'

'How d'ye feel about seeing Angus again?' said Shan.

'I'm too tired to feel anything. What about you?'

'I wanted to kill him,' said Shan, a red flush rising up his neck, settling on his cheeks.

Back at the flat Maureen lay in a hot bath, watching her skin turn red under the waterline and bits of tissue disintegrate on her skin. The cuts were deep and red blood had settled into scarlet blackheads in the cellulite on her thighs. She heard Leslie out in the living room, watching a quiz show on the telly. They were going to have Leslie's baby together and it changed everything. They'd have to get jobs and stop being pissed all the time. They'd have to grow up. She sipped her whisky and knew she'd be asleep in ten minutes. When she thought about Gartnavel, thought past the shock and horror, she knew she'd done a good thing and providence would bless her for it. If only she hadn't put Liam in the middle of it.

45
Good One

Paulsa was agitated. He seemed not to have had his medicine that morning and was pacing the stuffy room, watching the door. Spontaneous droplets of sweat popped on to his forehead and top lip. He was licking them away, a habit Shirley found disgusting. Maureen could see her across the room, watching him, grimacing when he did it. Maureen wanted to tell him what Liam had told her, that they were defence witnesses, they'd be the last to give evidence, but the more upset he was the better it was for her.

Leslie had bought bandages for Maureen's arms and put them on her this morning, securing the ends with little elastic clasps. Some of the wounds were open, itching and festering. Leslie had washed them gently in salt water before vomiting in the sink.

Maureen went back to reading a newspaper she had picked up when she was buying cigarettes. It was a local newspaper and she hadn't noticed that it was a special sports edition. The back page crept towards the front, buffeting the central pages, and there was little for her to read in it. In the 'News In Brief' column she saw a headline that caught her eye. A body had been found up at Gartnavel Royal and police were treating the death as suspicious. The paragraph underneath gave scant detail, adding nothing to the headline but times and the fact that Stewart Street were conducting the investigation. Joe McEwan and Liam had definitely seen each other.

Maureen guessed that she wouldn't be called today. She began reading, dragging her eyes over a long article about football funding, and before she had digested half of it, they were called for lunch.

Kilty and Leslie were waiting in the lobby again with Winnie and George, Liam and Vik. Shan had had to go to work, apparently, but he'd be back in the afternoon. They went down to the canteen and ate sandwiches together. Maureen looked around the table and felt very lucky, having them all here, chatting to each other and getting on well. She saw Liam was looking tired and drawn and wanted to comfort him, but couldn't until he told her.

They were smoking on the stairs outside, Kilty and Shan were having a good-natured argument about Kosovo with Leslie interjecting supporting arguments for each side, when Liam took her aside. 'The night before last,' he said casually, 'what did you do?'

Maureen pretended to try to remember. 'I fell asleep and woke up and couldn't get back to sleep,' she said.

'So, you didn't go out?'

'No. Leslie was there with me. And Kilty. We all slept in the living room. Why are you asking?'

Liam looked down his nose at her. 'Just asking.'

She should push it: he'd be suspicious if she wasn't suspicious. 'It's a strange thing to just ask. Where were you?'

'At Siobhain's house,' he said, 'watching a video.'

They sat smoking and looking out at the sunny green.

'I really love her, Mauri.'

Mauri looked at him, at his curly black hair and straight nose, at the prematurely ageing skin beneath his eyes. 'I'm glad, then,' she said. 'I hope ye stay together for the longest time and are really happy.'

Liam smiled up at her. 'Really?' he said, touched and pleased.

'Yup.'

Liam grinned and stretched out a leg in front of him, looking away down the road and then back at her. 'I'm thinking about asking her to marry me.'

'Oh, fuck off,' snapped Maureen.

'Hey, you said you were pleased,' said Liam, raising his voice.

'You've known each other all of two minutes,' shouted Maureen.

Everyone on the steps was looking at them.

'We'd have a long engagement,' said Liam earnestly.

She found herself laughing. 'A long engagement?' she repeated.

Liam thought about it and laughed too. 'Yeah,' he grinned, 'a long engagement.'

'Who are you, the Duchess of Argyll?'

'You. Hello.'

Maureen turned and found Suicide Tanya staring down at her. She was wearing a grotesquely feminine Laura Ashley dress with a rosebud pattern on it, tottering in a pair of battered court shoes with a worn-down heel. Maureen suspected that Laura might have meant her to wear a bra with the dress: the cloth belt around the waist strained under the weight of her breasts. Next to her stood a pencil-thin myopic man wearing women's glasses, a dirty grey T-shirt and a Confederate soldier's hat. 'Suicide, how are ye?'

'Aye,' shouted Tanya. 'This is Reb. He's my partner.'

Maureen nodded at him. 'How're ye?'

Reb didn't nod back. His glasses were so thick Maureen doubted he knew where he was. 'This is my brother,' she said and, turning to introduce him, saw that Liam was at once enchanted and repulsed by Tanya and her beau.

'Hiya,' shouted Tanya. 'I've seen Angus.'

'Very good,' said Maureen. 'Were ye in the court, then?'

Everyone on the stairs was watching Tanya now. She was hard not to watch. As she turned to tug the elasticated sleeve from the groove in the fat of her arm, Maureen saw that the dress wasn't even done up properly. A couple of token buttons had been fastened but the waves of fat on her back tugged the material this way and that, leaving gaping holes of stretched red skin. Maureen realized she was witnessing the sexual awakening of Suicide Tanya. At the bottom of the stairs two young men in suits were sniggering at her, one covering his face with a fat hand, and Maureen suddenly felt precious about her. 'You look lovely, Tanya,' she said, inadvertently prompting a grin from Liam and some journalists standing nearby. 'Have ye been going out together for long?'

Tanya blanked the pathetic attempt to patronize her. 'Angus Farrell's a murderer and murdered Douglas,' she shouted.

'I know, Tanya.'

'It was in the paper. Reb telt me. Are you going to the court to look at him?'

'Dunno,' said Maureen. 'Are you going back in?'

'Yes. Later,' said Tanya, shoved her hand into Reb's and reeled away down the stairs towards the road.

'Who or what was that?' asked Liam quietly.

Maureen explained that Suicide Tanya had been at the Rainbow Clinic and had introduced her to Siobhain. She kept trying to kill herself and was something of a celebrity among the emergency services. The last time Maureen had heard of her, Suicide was being hoisted off a shed roof in Shettleston by the fire brigade.

'Reb seemed like a nice guy,' he said facetiously.

'I like Tanya,' said Maureen, raising her voice so everyone else on the stairs could hear her. 'She knows people are laughing at her, it hurts her. They put her on this medication to stop her killing herself and she can't control her voice and it makes her a bit thick.'

'Sorry,' said Liam. 'She certainly cuts a dash, though.'

Maureen relaxed a bit and watched Tanya leave. 'I've seen her wearing a backless gold halter-neck,' she whispered, and Liam winced. Maureen watched her undulating back disappear through the gate and reflected that even Suicide Tanya was sustaining a relationship with a man.

When Shirley, Paulsa and Maureen had gathered in the room again after lunch, the police officer came through and asked them to come with him. He led them through the lobby, past the door of the court Angus was appearing in, and along a corridor to a small door with the number '1' on it. 'Where are we going?' asked Shirley.

'This is the prosecution waiting room,' said the officer, as if that meant anything to any of them. Maureen and Paulsa nodded to each other, trying to show they weren't completely out of their depth. Shirley, who wasn't out of her depth, didn't bother trying to convince anyone of it.

It was a larger, windowless room with seats bolted to every wall. Overhead lights were muffled by a dropped panel. On each of the four walls hung an indistinct impressionist print in a thin gold frame. A smaller door at the back of the room had a stern notice on it, prohibiting unauthorized entry.

One hour into the afternoon Shirley was called to give evidence, leaving Maureen alone in the small room with fraught Paulsa. This, she suspected, was exactly what he had feared. As the door shut behind her Paulsa sniggered like a teenager on a frightening first date. Maureen pretended not to notice and went back to making up words that would fit into the spaces of the crossword. He sniggered again. 'Are you trying to get my attention?' she said, without looking up.

'Nut,' he said petulantly.

'What are they going to make you say out there?'

'In the court?'

'Yeah, in the court.'

Paulsa lifted his bony shoulders past his ears.

'Won't be good for me, though,' she said, 'whatever it is.'

'Doesn't matter,' Paulsa said, in a high voice. 'You're not on trial, are ye?'

'No,' she said, 'I'm not. Are you going to tell them Liam gave me the acid?'

'God, shit, no.' Paulsa moved across the room, sitting one chair away from her, leaning over confidentially. 'They're going to ask me about the acid you bought from me.'

Maureen lowered her paper. 'You're not mentioning Liam in your evidence?'

'No. Just about the acid you bought from us. They've got me on another charge. I haven't got a choice.'

She smiled at him, relieved. 'I understand that, Paulsa, I won't hold it against ye.'

'Liam will but.'

'Paulsa, Liam's retired.'

'But you're his sister. He'll fucking kill me.'

They were let go at half four and Maureen watched Paulsa slope off out of the building. Liam was in the clear, they weren't even going to mention him.

Minutes ago Angus had been no further away than through that door. Maureen remembered him listening to her describe the incidents with Michael, giving her cigarettes and tissues, telling her how not to die five times a day, handing her a future. He was a pragmatist, wasn't interested in connecting or empathizing, just focused on practicalities and problem-solving. He was through the door and it meant nothing to her. She went outside for a cigarette.

As the door opened to the green, Maureen smelt the sweet grass and saw the yellow sun dancing across the roofs of passing cars. The soft breeze caressed her face, brushing her hair back like a kind mother; the sun warmed her itchy arms and loosened her tired neck. Here she was, she thought, content and enjoying whatever she could, living her dream.

A man walked along the dark road at the top of the hill and turned into the park, hands in his pockets, shoulders hunched around his ears. Ten yards past the gates he disappeared into a thicket of bushes. A big moon hung over the blue city and Kilty, Leslie and Maureen were sitting very still, heavy hearts beating quickly, wishing they could smoke or drink or leave.

Liam had phoned Maureen at home, telling her that something had come up and he might not be in court tomorrow morning. He sounded stiff and strange but she didn't want to press him. It would be a complication to do with Michael and she didn't want to take in another shred of information. She couldn't stop thinking about Liam now, wondering where he was and what had happened, wondering whether she should have asked.

'That's forty minutes,' said Kilty, under her breath. 'Maybe they're not coming at all.'

Neither Maureen nor Leslie answered. They had both decided that they weren't coming but didn't want to leave yet, just in case.

'What if we—'

'Ssh,' said Leslie. 'Another twenty and then we'll go.'

'I need the loo,' said Kilty.

'Just wait,' said Maureen.

Another ten minutes passed and they were wriggling around, shuffling their numb buttocks on the cold step, when three cars and a large white van came round the corner, lighting up the Park Circus Health Club with their headlights. They stopped in the street and all the doors opened, everyone piling out and running up the stairs to the door. They didn't bother to knock, they had a big metal bar with handles on it and smashed the door open at the first try, shouting that they were the police and to stop.

In the hall a woman turned and ran, the yucca plant got knocked over and everyone was shouting, women screaming, doors being smashed in, orders to stop. All around, the genteel square lights went on and people came to windows to watch the furore, squinting out into the darkness. A woman at a third-storey window was holding a baby. She smiled and said something to a man standing at her shoulder. Two neighbours spotted each other at their windows across the square and waved.

Aggie Grey had tipped them off. The police had informed her of their timetable so she could get there with the photographer and do their media department's job for them. When she had passed it on she told Maureen it was top secret and she had to sit somewhere that the police wouldn't see her. She told Maureen to sit in the dark, not to move, smoke or do any bloody thing that would draw attention to herself. Everything Maureen had told her had checked out, from the agency in Warsaw to the Newcastle connection. Aggie said she had even found a file interview with an anonymous woman who had been through the network and managed to get away while she was in Dublin. She was still trying to source the interview but they had enough confirmation to run the story anyway.

Aggie was standing at the bottom of the stairs, a photographer at her side. He raised his camera in readiness and waited, setting off flashes as the police began to filter out of the club's smashed door, bringing with them skinny women in thrown-on clothes, one holding a bandaged hand in front of her. The body-builder had a surgical collar on and his massive arms cuffed behind his back. Two or three men were hustled into the back of the van, covering their faces or looking away.

When all the noise and bustle was done, when the cars had shut their doors and driven away and the van had left the square, when the neighbours had finished waving and shrugging to each other, the three women were left alone on the stairs. Leslie lit a cigarette. 'Good one,' she said.

46

Plummy Twit

Maureen was alone in the witness room. Paulsa had been called to give evidence and had been in there for forty minutes already. He had arrived this morning in slow-blink, tiptoeing mode. She couldn't imagine anyone managing to sustain a conversation with him for longer than three minutes – he seemed pretty off it and she didn't suppose he would make a very good witness. She was the last one, knew she would be the final witness and hoped she would be left until the afternoon. She didn't want the jury to come up with a verdict before Monday.

She was wearing a long-sleeved black shirt with trousers she had bought that morning, and felt grown-up and ready for them. She hadn't seen Liam before she came to the witness room, didn't know if he was out there or not. She suddenly thought that he might have been arrested for Michael, or something to do with Michael, but it was nonsense. She knew it was nonsense.

There was only an hour left until lunch when the door opened and the police officer gestured for her to come with him. She stood up, gathering her newspaper, breathless with nerves. He led her through the back door, along a narrow passageway and into an antechamber with an intimi-dating large oak door at one end. Next to the door stood a bald man in a black gown and bow-tie. He nodded to the uniformed man, acknowledging acceptance of the package.

He took the newspaper from Maureen, set it down on a chair at the side and opened the door.

It was very bright in the court, lit from above by windows in the ceiling. The body of the room was hidden behind a large wooden wall but she could hear a thundering silence, a man coughing, someone whisper. The usher pointed her up a small, steep set of wooden stairs and, as Maureen climbed, the room came into view.

It was grander than the small-claims court. The judge was sitting in a duck-egg-blue alcove above her, between two pillars and below a symbol of the crown, all ribbons and unicorns. Below the witness box, sitting at a large table, were the lawyers in their funny costumes facing the judge with their backs to the public. The overhead windows didn't extend to the public gallery and the benches were in shadow. Liam's face caught her eye. She went to wave, delighted to see him, but stopped her hand at her waist. Liam was looking worried and sitting next to Winnie. He seemed to be holding her hand. Winnie, she noticed, had not brushed her hair.

Straight across the room sat the jury, a mess of colour, body shapes and hairdos, a welcome injection of reality in the pantomime. They were in a little wooden pen, facing her on three benches of five, like a rollercoaster train dipping into the court room. She could tell by their expectant faces that she was billed as the finale. They were sitting forward, waiting voraciously. It was hot in the room and, high up in the booth, Maureen was hotter than most. She began to sweat furiously.

Angus was sitting to her left, in a wooden gallery, flanked by guards. He opened his eyes a little, like a pleasured child, and mouthed one word: Pauline. Maureen grinned at him and gave him a cheeky little wave. She saw the confusion and fear in his eyes and looked away.

The bow-tied man swore her in, holding out a Bible for her to put her hand on and she found herself taking the oath to someone else's God very seriously. The man told her to sit down on the wooden seat and went off, clambering down into the body of the court and up another small set of stairs into the judge's booth, standing slightly behind him.

A lawyer from the table went to stand up but hesitated with his knees half bent as the judge checked his watch. The judge nodded to him and he got up. He had a little black goatee beard, and wore a white wig and a gown. He walked all the way across the room and stood next to the jury, one arm laid along a dividing wall, his head tipped back affectedly. Beneath his gown his suit was expensive, his shirt well pressed. 'Missss O'Donnell.' It was a long hiss, a theatrical attempt to get everyone's attention and, she felt sure, malign her as unmarried. 'Could you tell us how you met Douglas Brady?'

Maureen cleared her throat and leaned nervously towards the microphone. 'I met him—' The microphone gave off a high-pitched crackle.

The bow-tied man came galloping over to her, leaning over the wall of the box. 'Don't lean in so far, stay back a bit,' he said. She sat forward a little and he winked at her. 'Super,' he said, his eyes twinkling. She watched him go back to the judge's box. His was the only friendly face she could see in the room and she wanted him to come back.

'Again, Miss O'Donnell,' it was the advocate, posing at the other end of the room, 'how did you meet Mr Brady?'

'I was leaving the Rainbow Clinic,' her voice echoed around the sound system, every syllable sounding legally significant, 'and I was waiting at a bus stop. He stopped his car and offered me a lift back into town.'

The advocate nodded, as if she was following his script.

'You were, were you not, a patient at the Rainbow Clinic?'

They were going to ask about her psychi history, she fucking knew it, they were going to make her discuss it in front of all these people. She paused and caught her breath. 'I was, yeah.'

'*Why* were you a patient?'

It was a big question. She paused to think about it and another man in a gown and a wig stood up, saying something about the question, and the judge nodded. 'Yes,' he said, 'I think you have to narrow that question down.'

They were all unbelievably posh. Maureen had never actually heard accents like that before, the wide vowels and rolling Rs. She had always thought she sounded plummy but compared to the lawyers she could be selling cockles and mussels from a barra.

'Very well,' the standing advocate resumed. 'Miss O'Donnell, how did you come to be attending the Rainbow Clinic?'

She decided to be straight about it. 'I had a nervous breakdown a year after I finished my degree,' she said. 'I was admitted to the Northern Psychiatric Hospital. After I left there I went to the Rainbow Clinic as an outpatient.'

The standing man was not pleased with this. He raised his eyebrows and furrowed his brow. She suspected that he had hoped she'd sound like more of an arse. 'But you weren't actually referred there, were you?' he said.

'No,' she said. 'I didn't like the psychiatrist I was referred to so I stopped seeing him and asked the Rainbow if I could see someone there.'

'What was wrong with the psychiatrist you were referred to by your doctors?'

He had been cold and disinterested but Maureen didn't want the lawyer to think she could be intimidated. 'He was a plummy twit,' she said.

On the back bench of the jury box a plump man in a purple shirt and a small red-haired woman snickered as though they had been trying not to laugh all day. The lawyer frowned. It took him a second to realize that the jury were enjoying it. Then he smiled as if this was a great joke they could all enjoy together.

'You certainly are quite a feisty young woman,' he said, objectifying her and robbing her of her dignity, 'aren't you?'

He waited for an answer, compounding the insult. If she agreed she'd look like a nutter, if she disagreed she'd look passive, so she compromised. 'Dunno.'

'Well,' he sounded sarcastic, 'you seem quite feisty to me, Miss O'Donnell, really quite feisty.' He paused to look through his papers.

'Is that a bad thing?' The voice echoed around the tinny sound system. It was Maureen, speaking when she hadn't been spoken to. The lawyers at the table looked at one another, the snide advocate looked at the judge for backup and the judge leaned forward. 'You're here to answer questions, Miss O'Donnell,' he said sternly, 'not to make conversation.'

'I'm sorry,' said Maureen, irked at being publicly ticked off by someone she neither knew nor worked for. 'I'm not a lawyer, I don't know the rules.'

The judge was not pleased with this. 'Then you ought to listen to me when I tell you what they are,' he said, and turned away from her to cut off any further exchanges.

'As I say,' said the smug advocate to the jury, 'quite feisty.'

It all felt very unfair. Suddenly from the public gallery came a drawling, angry voice: 'Don't you fuckin' talk to her like that.'

Oh, God. It was Winnie, choosing this above every other opportunity in her life to lift a drink and stand up for her daughter. Liam caught Maureen's eye from the public gallery, cringing, helpless to stop it. The bow-tied man gestured to someone. A uniformed policeman stepped out of the shadows at the back of the public gallery and removed Winnie from the court to the tremendous amusement of the back row of the jury box. Liam followed her out, carrying her coat. Maureen tried to smile as if drunken women were a big surprise to her too, but she couldn't pull it off.

'This is a criminal trial,' said the judge sonorously, looking around the room and addressing everyone. 'It will not be allowed to descend into a circus.'

For a moment everyone in the court shuffled in their seats and wondered what sort of rotten circuses the judge had been subjected to as a child.

The advocate gathered himself together, flicking through his papers and taking a loud, deep breath to get everyone's attention again. 'So, you chose to go to the Rainbow Clinic?'

Maureen said yes.

'And you went for how many sessions?'

'Two.'

'And,' he turned away from her, facing Angus, 'whom did you see when you were there? Who, in other words, was your doctor at the Rainbow Clinic?'

Maureen pointed at Angus. 'Angus Farrell.'

'Can you,' he turned to face her, 'point him out to us in this court today?'

The purple and green jurors sniggered audibly. Maureen pointed to Angus again.

'And what was Mr Farrell like during these sessions?'

Maureen was pleased that she had the chance to say something positive and overcome the impression that she had a grudge. 'He was great. He was kind and patient and very helpful.'

The advocate nodded. 'He helped you?'

'Very much so.'

The advocate pushed himself off the side rail and headed into the middle of the court. 'This is a little delicate, Miss O'Donnell,' he said softly, as if he gave a shit about her, 'but could you tell the court the nature of the problem you went to see my client about?'

Maureen cleared her throat carefully. 'I was experiencing flashbacks and bad dreams.'

This was not the answer he wanted. He tried again: 'Could you tell us what the cause of these symptoms was?'

She didn't want to tell them. She looked at the giggly jury members, at the table of lawyers and the haughty judge, and knew that not one person in the room gave a flying fuck. If she made a fuss they'd play on it. 'I was abused by my father when I was a child and this was the fall-out from it,' she said quickly.

The advocate nodded in apparent sympathy. 'And Mr Farrell was patient with you and helped you to get over it?'

She looked at Angus, sitting in the box between the two bored guards. His eyes were half shut, blank but creepy, as if he was about to pounce on her. She looked behind him and saw his ugly family, eating chewy peppermints, passing the roll between themselves. 'Yes,' she said, 'he did.'

'Did you see him as a father figure?' He waited patiently for her to answer.

'I don't know what you mean by that.' Her amplified voice rattled around the room.

'Did you see him as a father figure? It's a term in common usage.'

'I didn't see him as my father,' she said, knowing full well where he was going with it.

'You didn't see him as an older man who had helped you,' he said incredulously, looking at the jury, 'who perhaps had authority over you?'

'I don't see my own father that way, so, no, I didn't see him as a father figure.'

The advocate shuffled his papers. 'But he did help you?'

'Yes.'

'So,' the advocate addressed the jury, 'he was a good man.'

'He was good at his job,' said Maureen, quickly. 'I don't know what sort of man he was.'

'Miss O'Donnell,' said the judge, losing patience with her, 'no more interjections, please.'

'Sorry,' she said, a picture of innocence. 'I thought that was a question.'

The judge knew she was lying. 'Unaware of the rules of the court you may be, Miss O'Donnell, but you seem to have a natural aptitude,' he said, and the lawyers smiled at what appeared to be a thin judicial joke.

The advocate stepped forward, and continued to question her, making her tell the story of finding Dead Douglas in the front room. He got her to tell how she had written to the Public Registrar for a copy of Douglas's marriage certificate but wouldn't let her say that she'd done it because Douglas swore blind he wasn't married. And then he asked her questions about Angus, whether he had known that she was seeing Douglas and, if he had, would he have approved? Maureen said she didn't think he would because she was a patient. The advocate pounced on the comment, suggesting that Angus had tried to split them up and she'd fed him acid because of it. Maureen tried to contradict him and got into trouble again.

'Now, Miss O'Donnell,' the advocate went on, 'we have heard evidence about the state Mr Farrell was in when he was found on the Isle of Cumbrae.' He paused for effect. 'We have heard expert witnesses testify to the effect that he was very heavily drugged with lysergic acid diethylamide.'

Maureen nodded.

'LSD,' said the advocate, 'to give it its street name.'

It was hardly a street name. The red and purple jurors nudged each other.

'Furthermore,' he continued, 'we have, just this morning, heard evidence from Paul Cunningham that you purchased a large quantity of that substance from him before or around the time of the deaths of Mr Brady and Mr Donegan. Do you recall such a purchase?'

Maureen pretended to think about it. 'No,' she said.

The advocate turned on her. 'You don't recall going to Mr Cunningham's flat and buying a large quantity of LSD?'

'No,' she said certainly. 'I have bought drugs for recreational use from Paulsa before but I don't remember buying anything then and I'd never buy a big quantity. If you buy too much at one time and get caught you could be charged with dealing and sent to prison for ages.'

'"Paulsa" being Mr Cunningham?' he said.

'Yeah.'

'Angus Farrell, the man who helped you,' he looked up at her, 'has stated that after Mr Brady's death you came to visit him in the clinic and gave him a coffee. Mrs Shirley Evans has also testified to that. It is our contention that the said coffee was heavily laced with LSD.'

The judge intercepted to say something wry and the advocate conceded, looking at his notes.

'No further questions,' he said curtly and sat down.

The judge looked at his watch pointedly. He asked another lawyer sitting at the table if he would be long. The man said no. He was thin and nervous. The shirt and suit beneath his gown were cheap, and hung less well than the defence advocate's. He might have been a genius, but the slick, smug lawyer inspired more confidence. He stood up and shambled over to the same spot next to the jury.

'Miss O'Donnell?' His accent sounded less of a distant

speck on the social scale. 'You said you intended to end your relationship with Mr Brady?'

Maureen waited to make sure the question was finished. 'Yeah.'

'Why were you going to end it?'

'We were both pretty miserable,' she said, 'and he'd lied to me about being married.'

The prosecution's questions dragged on for a bit longer, covering the same ground about Douglas and there being no reason for her to drug Angus and how she liked him really. The judge started getting pissed off and looking at his watch. Finally, he asked the lawyer if he was going to ask any new questions instead of the old ones over and over and suddenly, after a small discussion between themselves, Maureen was dismissed.

47
Pineapple and Paint

A gentle breeze willowed across Glasgow Green. Empty crisp packets travelled around the flat grass like cigarette girls, scuttling between groups of people and static objects, lingering for a moment before cartwheeling off. Leslie, Maureen, Vik and Shan sat on the dry grass among the cigarette ends. Winnie, it seemed, had been drinking since the night before. She had turned up at the court in a black cab, had had a fight with the driver and was sneaking off to the loo for nips between witnesses. When the policeman on the door asked her either to stay in or stay out she told everyone loudly that she had cystitis. Liam had to take her home in a taxi to make sure she didn't try to break back into the public gallery. When Leslie told the story Vik and Shan laughed. They didn't understand that it was a disaster, didn't know about her history or her liver.

'You did well in there,' grinned Vik, kicking her leg. 'I liked the bit about the plummy twit.'

'Yeah,' said Shan, nodding seriously. 'Good crack.'

'When do ye think we'll hear the verdict?' said Maureen.

'Well,' said Shan, 'the polis on the door said they've got all the summing-up to do so the jury'll retire this afternoon or Monday. There won't be a verdict before Monday.'

'We should go,' said Maureen to Leslie.

'Should we?' said Leslie, squinting up at her.

*

'You should have made an arrangement to see him again,' said Leslie, when they got round the corner to the parked bike. 'He looked a bit upset.'

'No, he didn't,' said Maureen.

'He did,' said Leslie. 'You didn't even look at him.'

'I did so,' said Maureen, struggling into her helmet.

'He's nice, Mauri,' said Leslie seriously. 'He's a nice guy. He came and sat through that trial for you.'

'He wasn't there for me,' said Maureen, doing the strap under her chin. 'He was there for Shan.'

'Was he fuck,' said Leslie, pulling on her helmet. 'Where are we going anyway?'

'Estate agent's.'

'What for?'

'You'll see.'

When they got back to the house the answer-machine was winking a message. They left the pots of paint in the hall and went into the kitchen. Maureen made them a cup of coffee while Leslie took a celebratory pineapple cake out of the paper bag and broke it in half. She ate her half like a sandwich, sinking her teeth into the jam and icing centre, chewing and smiling to herself. She nodded Maureen to the other half.

'D'ye know, I actually don't like pineapple cake.'

Leslie spluttered through her mouthful. 'How the fuck can ye not like pineapple cake?' she said, guiding a rogue flake of pastry back into her mouth.

Maureen looked at the bright yellow cake, the clear ochre centre spilling out on to the white paper bag. 'Well,' she said, 'it doesn't taste of anything and it looks horrible. It's cheap pastry with jam and icing on it.'

'A peculiarly Scottish confection,' said Leslie pompously, and took another bite.

'Someone once said that all Scottish cuisine is based on a dare,' said Maureen.

Leslie opened her eyes wide and nodded keenly, as if such a premise would be a good thing. 'Yeah, I've been dying for one of these all day. D'ye not want that other half?'

Maureen looked at it and shook her head. Leslie was pleased.

'I thought you weren't supposed to get cravings until the third trimester?' said Maureen.

Leslie took another bite. 'Yeah,' she grinned, 'but I'll probably never get up the duff again so I might as well milk it from the start. Shouldn't you get your answer-machine?'

Maureen walked out to the hall and pressed the button. The message was from Liam and she was embarrassed that Leslie heard it because he sounded so vulnerable. He was phoning to say he was sorry for leaving a weird message last night. Winnie had been drinking and he didn't want Maureen to know, didn't want her to worry. He heard she'd done really well in the court today, even though that wee shit Paulsa had dubbed her up. Winnie was back at the house and asleep now and he thought she'd probably sober up tomorrow. Her liver was in a bad way, Mauri, really . . . The message trailed off into a sigh and he hung up. She tried phoning him at home but got his answer-machine and left a consoling message. She knew he'd be at Winnie's but couldn't bring herself to phone, not tonight.

They moved what was left of the furniture out of the living room into the hall and washed the floor. Leslie gave it a couple of tours with the mop and Maureen followed on her hands and knees with a scourer, getting into the corners. Douglas's blood turned the water brown. As she poured the contents of the first mop bucket down the toilet, Maureen said goodbye, goodbye to his sad eyes and his fervent hard-on, goodbye to his melancholy life. Douglas should never have been so sad: he had everything going for him, everyone rooting for him. As she reproached him for wasting what there was of his short life in ungracious dejection she thought about Suicide Tanya and knew that she had everything going for her too.

They left the floor to dry and sat in the kitchen, watching the start of the good Friday night shows on TV. Leslie ran downstairs and came back with a single fish, a haggis smothered in vinegar and a portion of chips. Maureen started eating the fish to avoid being nagged but it was delicious, fresh flaky fish in a sweet crisp batter. She ate some of the chips too.

They finished painting the floor at midnight. Leslie couldn't take the smell and went to sleep at her mum's, promising to come back in the morning to help tidy up. Maureen sat on the settee in the hall, touching the bandages on her stinging forearms, looking into the living room. The floor was pale blue now, a slick of shining, stinking blue, reflecting the lights rolling across the ceiling. The room looked enormous without the bloodstains.

She remembered when she had first bought the flat, standing inside the front door in the dark, afraid to be alone in a house that was hers. She remembered the things left behind by the people who had lived there before her: a cupboard full of empty ginger bottles, a saucer used as an ashtray and a recent copy of *Playboy* hidden behind a stack of folded boxes. She'd cried that night, knowing this was where things would get really bad because the flashbacks were getting so much worse. She remembered coming out of hospital and turning Beethoven's Fifth up loud on the stereo, smashing the mattress with a tennis racket until her palms were raw and she was exhausted. She remembered sitting out here in the hall, hunkered into a tight little ball, looking at Dead Douglas, trying to think her way to the phone, three feet away. She'd survived all of that and there wasn't a solitary doubt in her mind that she'd live through the aftermath of Michael.

48

Michael

It was one o'clock in the afternoon when Maureen looked at her watch. She had slept for ten hours and couldn't bring herself to get out of bed. She could tell it was a cloudy day from the grey light peeping in through the curtains and she was glad. The flat was full of the new-beginning smell of paint from the front room. When she got up to go to the toilet and climbed over the settee in the hall she was amazed at how different the living room looked. She checked that the floor was dry before walking into the middle of it. It was as if Dead Douglas had never been here, like the room she had known before he died.

She had a bath and soaked the bandages on her arms before peeling them off. The bit of glass stuck under the skin was aching and when she pressed on it yellow pus came out, but the other cuts were healing nicely. By the time Leslie knocked on the door she was dressed and sipping coffee on the settee in the hall. She reached over and unlocked the door. Leslie climbed across the back of the settee and looked in at the living room.

'Fucking hell,' she said, reaching into her bag, 'that's the business. Here, I brought ye a present.'

It was wrapped in pink tissue and when she pulled it back she saw that it was a half-bottle of Glenfiddich in a fancy presentation tin. 'I only got the half-bottle 'cause I know you're a bit of an alki.'

Maureen grinned up at her, opened the tin and pulled

the bottle out. 'What's this for?' she said, peeling the metal seal back.

'No.' Leslie grabbed the bottle and put it back in the tin. 'It's for Monday or Tuesday, when the verdict comes in.'

It seemed a cruel gesture to Maureen, to hand her lovely whisky and tell her not to drink it right now, as if Leslie was testing her. She must have known how hard it would be to have it in the house.

'Well, thanks,' said Maureen, and slid it under the sofa. She could buy another on Monday and pretend it was the same one when Leslie asked her to open it. 'My arm's going off.'

Maureen sat on a blue sea of the living-room floor where the light was best and let Leslie cut the skin with a sharp needle. The bit of glass stuck in her arm had worked its way back from the original wound and was pressing through unbroken skin. Leslie had already tried squeezing it forwards but it hurt like a bastard. Leslie's cigarette idled in the ashtray. Maureen looked at the top of her head as she bent over her arm, scratching at the skin. Maureen wanted a drink. Michael was over, Angus was almost dealt with, and Si McGee would never import women again. She didn't know how to have a glad heart without a glass in her hand but Leslie would give her a row. Even if she didn't give her a row, she'd look at her in a way that suggested a row and, because Maureen knew her so well, she'd have no trouble filling in the blanks herself.

'Should you be smoking?' said Maureen.

Leslie bent deeper over the wound. 'Fuck off,' she said. 'I haven't had a drink for weeks.'

'A mother's love's a blessing.' Maureen was glad it was hard for her too.

'Should you be winding up a woman who's sticking needles into your arm?'

The skin split behind the glass and a press of opaque yellow pus rushed to the surface. Maureen felt the release of pressure from the wound, and after a bit of painful poking, Leslie had the bloody splinter out and was holding it up between her fingers. She dabbed on some antiseptic cream that Maureen had found in the bathroom. It was a very old tube and the cream felt a little gritty but it was better than nothing. Finally Leslie wrapped fresh bandages around her arms and Maureen pulled on a shirt fifteen minutes before the surveyor arrived.

The photographer was half an hour late and didn't bother to apologize. Leslie tried to pull him up about it but he only spoke when she was speaking, cutting through her to say that his car had broken down. She was saying that they had intended to go out but he interrupted her to say that it was a Korean car, his wife's, actually, and it tended to break down. The conversation turned into a battle of wills, both of them refusing to stop their sentences and let the other one speak, like parliamentarians on a radio show.

'*Just*,' Maureen shouted over the top of them, '*take the pictures.*'

Everyone stopped talking and the man took his lens cap off, snapping the living room and getting them to move the settee back in from the hall. He left after ten minutes to take a photo outside and Leslie slammed the door on him.

They settled back in the living room, sitting on the settee and looking out of the window.

'God,' said Leslie, rubbing her tummy, 'I feel sick again.'

'Is it the smell from the paint?'

'No, I just feel sick. Tell ye what else, I've got tits like rocks.'

Maureen slid down the settee into a slump. 'What do ye think, then? A boy or a girl?'

Leslie took a deep breath, sat up and smiled. She had been thinking about it, enjoying thoughts of the future. 'Dunno.' She looked around the room. 'How much do they think you'll get for this place?'

'Don't know until the surveyor files his report. He reckons flats like this have been going for fifty grand. I'll just have to pray no one clocks that it's the scene of a grisly murder. Are ye going to tell Cammy?'

'I'll tell him if he tells me about Katie McIntyre. And he won't.'

'Ye sure?'

'Yeah.' Leslie seemed sad but resigned. 'Even after you've paid the tax and fees for a curator's course that'll leave you with a bit of extra cash, won't it?'

Maureen grinned. 'Yeah.'

'What are ye going to do with it?'

'Piss it up against a wall.'

The phone rang in the hall and Maureen stepped out to pick it up. It was Liam and he had been crying. 'Mauri,' he said, 'she's in hospital.'

The hospital complex was ramshackle and ill thought-out. It was getting dark as they drove up the steep hill. Metal chairs with canvas seats were abandoned around the grounds, left after a week of nurses and hospital staff taking the sun in their lunch-hour. Two ambulances sat outside A & E with their engines switched off, light spilling out of their open back doors, green-suited paramedics chatting, waiting for calls.

Liam pulled into the dark car park and turned off the engine. He sat, tapping the wheel with a finger, as if he was weighing something in his mind, before opening the door and getting out. Maureen climbed out and shut the door. 'Liam?' she called across the roof of the car.

He looked at her, suspicious and apprehensive. 'What is it, Maureen?' he said. 'Have you got something to tell me?'

'I want to ask ye something.'

He stood solidly on both feet and waited, and Maureen sensed that she was delivering a shocking anticlimax. 'Just I'm thinking of going back to college but if I do I won't be able to afford the house. D'ye think I could rent a room off you?'

Liam tutted, annoyed at her for asking such a frivolous question now. 'Aye.' He turned to the hospital.

Maureen trotted after him.

The pavement outside was covered in fag butts. They walked through two sets of consecutive automatic doors and entered the lobby. The A & E was dirty and faintly threatening. The receptionist was sitting behind a shout-proof, punch-proof, spit-proof glass wall, writing something on a sheet. Notices on the walls told visitors not to fight or throw things or splash blood around the place. A police incident room had been set up in a cubicle in the corner. A young officer was sitting inside with the door open, looking at a form.

Two old women were seated facing the reception area, watching it like a television. They smiled up at Liam and Maureen as they walked in, waiting eagerly to see what they were there for. The receptionist ignored them until finally Liam rapped gently on the window. She dropped her pen resentfully and slid a glass panel back to allow them five holes to speak through. 'I'll be with you in a moment,' she said tartly, slapped the panel shut and went back to her form.

'My mum's in here,' said Liam. 'She's in a bad way.' He turned red and covered his face, trying not to cry.

'That's a shame,' said one of the watching women.

'That is,' said her pal. 'That is a shame.' She leaned over to speak round Maureen and Liam to the receptionist. 'Go on, see to them. His mum's in there.'

'Aye, go on, it's the boy's mum, go on.'

The receptionist sighed and slid the panel back. 'Name?'

'Winnie O'Donnell.'

She looked at a sheet pinned to the partition in front of her. 'Wait.' She stood up and went to a phone on the back wall, dialled an extension number and turned back to them. 'Wait,' she said, pointing them into one of the row of seats.

They sat down and the old women turned back to look at them. 'Ye all right, son?'

Liam caught his breath. He blinked hard, trying not to cry.

'She's cheeky,' said one, gesturing to the rude woman, 'but she's a good receptionist.'

Maureen thought that not being a foul-mannered old bitch would have been an essential qualification for a good receptionist. She linked her arm through Liam's and gave it a little squeeze. She had never known him so brittle. Liam wrestled his arm away and sat forward, rubbing his face hard. A door at the far end of the corridor opened and Una looked out. She was not pleased to see Maureen there and focused on Liam, waving him towards her.

'There they go,' said the woman.

'Good luck,' called her pal cheerily.

Una was far ahead of them in the corridor. She turned at the corner to check that they were following her.

'How is she?' asked Maureen.

'Unconscious,' said Una, and disappeared round the corner.

'Why's she so angry with me?' muttered Maureen.

'She's angry with everyone,' replied Liam.

The room was lit by small, deflected lights, like night falling on a bright summer day. Winnie was lying flat on the bed under the sheet, wearing an oxygen mask, attached to a heart monitor and an intravenous drip. As the mask misted and cleared faintly, the sound of her breathing filled the room. George was sitting on a chair by her bed, holding her free hand, spent and desperate. He didn't look up as Maureen and Liam came into the room. Sitting behind him on a chair was Marie. She sat up when she saw Maureen come in, looked wildly around the floor and sat back, disappearing into the shadows.

'What happened?' said Liam, clutching his hair.

'Alcoholic poisoning,' said Una. 'She drank three-quarters of a bottle of vodka in two hours. Normally she could handle it but she hasn't had a drink for a few months.'

Liam stumbled over to George who stood up and offered him the seat. Liam took Winnie's hand and fell into the warm chair.

'What did the doctors say?' asked Maureen, lifting a chair on to the other side of the bed for George to sit in.

'Not good,' said George, smiling to hide his feelings. He sat down.

Maureen went out to the corridor, looking for a doctor, and Una followed her, catching her outside the door. 'She drank because of your trial, you know.' She spoke softly to hide the venom from Liam, so he would think she was just filling Maureen in on the details.

'I wasn't on trial,' said Maureen calmly, knowing Una was bullshitting, knowing Winnie's binge was about Michael.

'It was too much of a strain on her,' said Una, unreasonably. 'You should have kept her out of it.'

Maureen turned to look at Una. 'You are bitter and fat,' she said, 'and your new hairdo makes your face look like a bucket.'

Una raised her head, ready to retaliate, but caught herself, knowing Liam could see her through the door.

'And by the way,' said Maureen, 'Maureen is my fucking name. Find another one for your ugly baby.'

She stomped off to look for a doctor, feeling pleased with herself. Three men dressed in blue scrubs were inside what looked like a cupboard, two sitting on a table, one standing up, explaining something. They looked up when Maureen appeared at the door. 'Can ye tell us anything about Winnie O'Donnell's prognosis?'

The man on the furthest part of the desk leaned forward. 'Um, I'm afraid it's alcoholic poisoning. We'll just need to wait and see if she comes out of it.' He frowned at his watch. 'Should be within the next hour or so if it's going to happen at all.'

They brought in chairs from the corridor and arranged them around the bed. Marie was still trying to keep away from Maureen and wouldn't even look at her. The girls were trying not to fight for George's sake, and because Liam was so upset. He kept sighing and reaching out to touch Winnie with his fingertips, on the leg or arm, smoothing her hair back from her face. After half an hour Una stood up and said she was going to get a drink from the foyer. Marie got up and ran after her, bumping into Maureen in her rush to get to the door.

Maureen, Liam and George sat quietly in the dark room, the three of them as they had always been, watching and waiting for Winnie to do something they could react to. Her leg twitched at one stage and they looked at each other hopefully but she fell still again. Una and Marie came back in, less passive than they had been, making a noise and looking Maureen in the eye. They must have had a conversation in the lobby about what a cheek she had coming here. Marie brushed her jacket over Maureen's head as she passed and it felt like a deliberate gesture, as if she was showing that she wasn't afraid of her. She should have been, thought Maureen, she should have had the wit to be afraid of her.

A sudden snorting noise made them all look up simultaneously. Winnie hadn't moved but George was asleep in his chair, his arms crossed over his chest, his big hairy nostrils flaring as he breathed in. They laughed and the fragile silence was broken.

'To be perfectly honest,' said Una quietly, glancing at Marie for support, 'I don't think you should be here, Maureen. She hasn't seen you for months and her heart's under enough strain as it is. If she wakes up and sees you, it could be very bad for her.'

'I've already seen her, *Una*,' said Maureen, sounding petty and feeling vicious. 'I went to the house last week and had tea with her and George.'

Una's face tightened. 'When was this?'

'Last week. Last Monday.' She smiled at Marie. 'There ye are, Marie, ye can sell that story to the papers.'

'I'm gonnae kill the three of you,' muttered Liam, not looking up from the bed.

They fell quiet for a while, and Liam whispered to Una that Winnie's leg had twitched when they were out getting cans of juice. 'Good,' said Una encouragingly. 'That must be a good sign.'

Her hairdo was really awful. It was brown and blonde streaks, cut in jagged stringy bits at the back and short on top, like a Rod Stewart wig. Whoever had done it must have hated her. They watched Winnie again, hoping for a twitch, listening to George snore contentedly, when suddenly Marie spoke. 'You must be pleased about Michael,' she said softly. She was looking at Una, meaning to garner support, but it looked as if she was talking to her. Everyone was confused. Marie leaned forward and pointed a flaccid finger at Maureen. 'I was talking to you,' she said weakly.

Maureen shrugged and looked at Liam. 'She doesn't know about that, yet,' he said.

'Know about what?' said Maureen.

Liam sighed. 'I'll tell ye later.'

'Tell me now.'

'*I'll tell ye later.*'

'Tell me now.'

Liam sighed over Winnie's hand, holding it to his face, feeling the soft, paper skin drag on his cheek, and felt a ragged nail poke him. The hand was moving, the fingers wiggling, giving up with exhaustion and trying to move again. Winnie opened a sticky eye and looked around the room, at George asleep in the chair, at Maureen at the end of the bed and at Una and Marie.

'Mum?' Liam poked George's arm and woke him up.

They watched as Winnie struggled to lift her hand, straining hard, letting out exasperated sighs. Finally she managed to get the oxygen mask off, pulling it to the side so that it cupped her chin. 'You've ...' She stopped to breathe, shutting her eyes to concentrate. She opened them again. 'You've ... you've been a lovely audience.'

And Winnie coughed a laugh and fell back on the bed.

In a typical Winnie-esque fuck-up, despite having used her final words and written her epitaph, the doctors assured them that she would recover. They wouldn't be able to assess the extent of her liver damage until later or vouch for her future health if she carried on drinking. They could come in tomorrow to visit if they wanted but now they should go home and rest.

Una insisted that she drive George home in her big car and they all set off for the car park together. It was three in the morning and a yellow dawn was threatening on the horizon. It was very cold.

'Is anyone ever going to tell me about Michael?' said Maureen.

George put his arm around her shoulder and squeezed. 'We didn't want you to worry,' he said and squeezed again. 'Your dad killed a man in the hospital. He's never coming out.'

'George O'Donnell, *you*'re my dad,' she said, responding to the wrong bit of information. Liam turned and looked back at her. George squeezed her shoulder hard and let his hand fall.

Liam started the engine and pulled out of the car park.

'Who did Michael kill?' asked Maureen.

Liam clucked his tongue. 'A guy. Just a guy.'

She lit cigarettes for them and handed Liam his, watching the city slide past the window, enjoying the orange lights and huge navy blue sky. When she looked back Liam was watching her out of the corner of his eye.

'It wasn't just a guy, Mauri. It was Pauline Doyle's brother.'

She let it go.

'He was twice Michael's size,' said Liam, 'and he was young as well. He had a video camera with him but no tape in it.'

She wanted to tell him about the rush of blinding fury when she had seen the camera and knew, suddenly and completely, that Doyle was the other brother all along. She wanted to tell him about throwing herself through the window, her shoulder hitting Doyle as he hurried to stand. How, wrong-footed, he had toppled over into the bush and how she had used the knife without hesitating. She stood over him, watching the fountain of blood jet from his jugular like an early death in a slasher movie, heard him gurgle and, behind her, Michael trying to say something. She pressed his hand to Doyle's knife, took the tape from the video and left through the window. Doyle must have met Angus when he went to visit Pauline in the Northern and Angus would have given him the address for the pictures and the video. It was all so pat and clear she could hardly believe it hadn't occurred to her before. She wanted to tell Liam everything but she knew it wouldn't be fair.

'See Tuesday night?' Liam spoke again. 'When I phoned and Leslie answered?'

'Yeah.'

He took a draw on his cigarette and exhaled, the stream of smoke rolling across the inside of the windscreen. 'Were you asleep?'

'Yeah.' She wasn't lying very well, she knew she wasn't. Liam scratched his forehead, sucking his teeth and nodding.

'I got into a situation, Liam,' she said softly. 'I just got into a situation.'

He pulled the car over to the pavement abruptly. 'How did ye get Doyle to go up there with ye?'

If she told him Doyle was helping, if she told him she'd found out at the last minute and killed Doyle instead, he'd know what she'd been planning for Michael. 'Told him I had the tape and I could see his hands in it.'

Liam smiled. He liked that. 'And he came to get the tape off ye?'

'Aye,' said Maureen. 'He came to get it off me.'

Liam restarted the car after three tries and drove on, nodding sometimes, shedding the extra years as he took it all in.

49

Glass Storm

Maureen woke feeling happy but then remembered that she had no right to be. She had done unconscionable things that would change her life for ever. She made a coffee and sat in the kitchen by the window. It was grey and raining outside, small rain, getting into everything, making pedestrians grimace and hunch. No one knew she was up here feeling happy, no one could reproach her for it. She made another coffee and lit a cigarette, shut her eyes and imagined herself in St Petersburg, in a bland hotel drinking sour coffee and drying her face with scratchy towels. Walking along by the canal or river or whatever they had there, wearing a big coat. She saw herself going into the Hermitage, not seeing anything, just anticipating seeing things, and she opened her eyes. 'Shit.'

She went out into the hall and dialled the number for the hospital, got transferred to Winnie's ward and asked after her. She was stable, liver-damaged, but sitting up and talking to them all. Maureen could come in at half two if she wanted. The nurse had a Belfast lilt in her voice and Maureen could tell that Winnie was charming them all.

In the bedroom, she was dressing slowly and paused, looking around the floor at all the clothes. Taking three bin-bags from the kitchen drawer she bagged up all the clothes from the drawers and wardrobe that she hadn't worn for a year. She put all the extra bed-linen in a separate bag and leaned it against the wall. She checked her pockets for keys and money and took the bin-bags downstairs.

She had meant to carry them the two blocks to a charity-shop doorway but they were too heavy. She left them sitting in the rain at the foot of a lamp-post, pretending that she might take them round later, blaming the charity shop for not making it easier somehow to do the right thing.

Mr Padda Senior was working the shop today. He flashed her a smile and a 'Hello, dear' as she came in through the door. He had his gas fire on full and the damp shop was filled with a dry grain-store smell, making her wish for winter and the disinfecting cold.

Aggie Grey had been as good as her word. Billed under a headline as a major investigation, Si McGee was on the front cover of the paper, looking startled and guilty and sleazy, standing on the steps of the house in Bearsden. She could tell that his neck was shaking. There were action shots of the raids on the health club, the open door leading down the steps, men with their faces covered and a shot of a barred window. Even Mr Goldfarb couldn't miss it. She bought two copies of the paper for no good reason, a small packet of butter, two rolls and an overpriced packet of bacon. While Mr Padda was tilling it up she asked for a quarter of midget gems as well.

Back upstairs she read the article. Aggie's prose was emotionally flat and factual, as befitted the paper's style. The health club had been raided and the women were being detained prior to deportation. The paper even had a picture of the job agency in Warsaw. Tonsa and Si had been granted bail on Friday for a tiny amount. There was nothing much the court could charge them with, and Aggie's paper was calling for a change in the law. Maureen left the paper on the floor and went into the kitchen, turned the grill on and opened the packet of bacon. She felt fantastically happy. She was buttering the roll when it occurred to her that she shouldn't be feeling this good, that Angus's trial was finishing tomorrow and he might even get out, but she couldn't stop herself. It wasn't today and no one knew how good she felt. Maureen grinned at the rolls, thinking over and over to herself that she had got away with it, she had fucking got away with it, and even if everything turned to shit now, even if she got done for Doyle, even if Michael had to come and live with her for the rest of her life, well, fuck it. She was going to enjoy today.

She ran a bath and went to put some music on, remembered she'd given all her records to Vik and had to settle for the radio. She lay back in the bath, washing her hair as she listened to back-to-back disco toons. When she got out and dried herself she used up the last of the handmade lavender body lotion that had cost twenty quid and brushed her wet hair back. Her forearms were healing nicely. She pulled on her favourite ever dress, a cream cotton shift with big roses printed on it, and a pale blue cardigan to cover her arms. She sat cross-legged on the living-room floor and put on makeup, looking into a normal mirror, smiling when she caught her own eye.

The phone rang and through force of habit she let the answer-machine get it. Kilty asked her to pick up.

'Did ye see it?' asked Kilty.

'Aye,' said Maureen. 'Good old Aggie, eh?'

'My dad's apoplectic,' said Kilty.

'Ye can tick off all the goals in your wee book now.'

'I know,' grinned Kilty. 'Not much is going to happen to them, though, is it?'

'Well, ye can't have everything. Were you out with Josh?'

'Aye, well, we went to the pictures. He likes Michael Douglas. I've gone off him. I've got a date with someone else, though.'

'You're a quick worker, who's that?'

Kilty giggled with excitement. 'Your pal Shan Ryan.'

'Noo,' cooed Maureen. 'How did that happen?'

'After the trial.' She could hardly speak she was smiling so widely. 'I asked him out.'

'Oh, Kilty, what will your parents think of you going out with a black guy?'

Kilty laughed and arranged to pick her up at the house the next morning.

When she hung up, Maureen dialled Isa's number and found Leslie delighted with, the article. 'I love Aggie Grey,' she said. 'How's Winnie?'

'She's okay now. She was unconscious when we got there. She had alcoholic poisoning from drinking a bottle of vodi in three minutes.'

'Dear Roy, is this a record?' said Leslie, and tittered nervously.

Maureen giggled back. 'We're bad, aren't we?'

'Oh, God, aye,' said Leslie. 'We're fucking terrible.'

She had an hour to kill before leaving for the hospital and the half-bottle of Glenfiddich Leslie had given her was sitting on the table, winking at her, the colour changing from gold to amber to a pale, mesmerizing yellow. She put it in a cupboard in the kitchen, on a high shelf, as if that would make it harder to get. She sat in the living room, her mind in the kitchen, looking at the cupboard door. She couldn't stop thinking about it. When the noise in her head got too loud she got up and left the house.

She walked bareheaded across town, getting her face and legs wet with smirr. Her boots kept the rain out and, as she walked, she reflected on how great it was to be wet and have dry, comfortable feet, how good it was to be healthy. Somehow she came to think of six-stone Pauline with her poor ragged arsehole and she looked up at the sky and smiled. Behind the clouds, in deep yellow sunshine, Giant Pauline Doyle sat cross-legged, wearing a pretty dress and holding a golden string on one finger, a glass box suspended from it, twisting slowly. She was laughing, a light, uncomplicated laugh, and watching Mark Doyle trapped inside, covering his face against a snowstorm of shattered glass, his own knife at his neck, his death always imminent. Maureen stopped in a café half-way over and bought an ice cream.

Si McGee opened the door and slid into the hall, pushing it shut after his sister. The police had smashed it open and he'd had it replaced with a heavy, plain wooden plank. The joiner hadn't fitted the lock properly and he had to lift it up by the handle to get the door to shut properly. Si and Margaret turned and looked around the ruined hallway. It was quiet and dark: the only light came from the window above the front door. Cindy's desk had been put against a wall and the phone was smashed on the floor. Si turned on the overhead light and led the way down the shallow stairs to the basement.

'Why?' whined Margaret.

Si stopped and looked up at her. 'Because', he said, shutting his eyes with barely veiled impatience, 'if we find out which files they've taken we can work out what evidence they've got, can't we?'

'But why have I tae be here?'

'Because I'm here. I shouldn't have to do every fucking thing.'

Si turned and walked down the last few steps, Margaret following him. She was driving him mad. He was glad it had happened in a way, glad that he had reason to get out. The lawyer was sure they'd only get a fine and Si had saved a good stake for a new business, stashed safely in Jersey where neither the Inland Revenue nor the police would be able to get at it. He was getting out, away from mad, bad Charlie Adams, away from all the smells and horror of the present job, away from whiny Margaret and her Swiss Army knife. The basement smelt of stale pee and sweat. The police had left the doors open to the basement rooms, and the cumulative stench was disgusting. Si pushed open the office door. It was chaotic. Files and papers were scattered over the desk, the box files of managerial newsletters he had subscribed to since university were crumpled on the floor.

'I don't know anything about this,' said Margaret, picking up an overturned chair and sitting down.

'What did you do with your money?' He said it calmly, as if he was just asking an idle question.

'Fuck off,' said Margaret casually, lifting a copy of *Managers' Monthly* off the desk and pretending to read it. Her left hand fell to her shoulder-bag, the index finger sliding open the zip. He knew she had a knife in there.

'Don't be stupid,' said Si. 'I was just asking. Mine's in the Bank of Pakistan. They can't get it there.'

Margaret's hand moved smoothly, doing up the zip again. 'I don't know why I had to come.' She looked around the small grey room. 'I hate it here.'

'Look,' said Si, handing her a sheet of paper, 'they've left this.'

The door to the office opened slowly and Margaret stood up, her hand in her bag in a flash. Si could see the knife, the blade bared, and he was relieved that she was nearer to the door than him.

'Hiya. What's happening?' It was Kevin, still wearing his surgical collar and grinning as if he was welcoming them back from holiday.

Margaret tutted and dropped the knife. 'Fucksake,' she said, and fell back into the seat. 'What are you doing here?'

Kevin took a step towards her and shot Margaret Frampton through the back of the head.

Si watched his sister's face explode, her nose, her eyes, her forehead splash outward, red and black, like a carnivorous tropical plant bursting suddenly into flower. The force of the blast shoved her slim body forward slightly, making her nod before coming true and settling back into the chair. Si blinked and looked. It was nonsensical. There had been no noise. He blinked and looked again, forgetting to breathe. Useless dim-witted Kevin raised his hand again and shot Si three times in the chest. Si McGee slid to his knees, leaving a red trail on the wall behind him, tipping over a box file of *Managerial News*.

Moving stiffly so as not to jerk his sore neck, Kevin stepped across the office, feeling in Si's pocket. He found his mobile and lifted it out, flipping it open and pressing in a long number. At the other end the phone rang only once before being answered.

'Done,' said Kevin, watching Margaret's body slide down off the chair and land under the desk. He nodded. 'Yeah, everyone'll know it was for Doyle, no one'll fuck yees about up here.' He nodded again. 'Okay. Tell Charlie I'll be there.'

Kevin hung up, wiped the mobile and slid it back into Si McGee's pocket. He stepped across McGee's legs to the fire exit and opened the door, slipping out to the lane, leaving the door open just enough for some nosy bastard to find them.

50

Taunt the Sick

Winnie was in an open ward with the blinds drawn on the window behind her and the curtains pulled around her bed. She had the covers over her head. Maureen peeked under the blankets. Winnie's eyes were bloody and her face waxy white. She looked through tiny slit eyes and mouthed, 'Hello'. Maureen mouthed it back and withdrew.

A peculiarly gnarled-looking man and woman were standing nearby, chatting to each other. George explained that they were Winnie's friends from AA and had come to visit her at his request. Winnie was being sent to a drying-out clinic in Peebles as soon as she could stand, and her friends had offered to escort her there in their car. Maureen threw her arms around George and hugged him without his consent. He stood stiffly, bashful at showing emotion in front of strangers. He raised a hand to her head and patted it a couple of times. 'You're a good girl,' he said, but she heard him ask her to let him go, for Godsake, there were people watching.

Una arrived as if she was moving into the ward. She had the baby with her in a harness, a big soft bag of things, her handbag and a poly-bag of pills and food and magazines for Winnie. George was chatting to the gnarled couple so Maureen had to help her with the bags, tucking them under the bed. Una wanted to go round the bed and see Winnie's head and, with overplayed reluctance, let Maureen hold the baby. She stormed round the bed and lifted the covers abruptly, in a way only someone who didn't drink or under-stand hangovers could. She talked Winnie through the vitamins and magazines she had brought, speaking loud, making every muscle on Winnie's back and head contract.

The baby was tiny. Her fingers flexed in her sleep and tightened at the sound of her mother's voice. Her fist was the size of a thumbnail, perfect in every detail. Her pink lips pouted, her tongue rolled out and she opened her eyes. They were blue, pale, pale blue, just like Maureen's and Liam's eyes.

'Her eyes,' said Maureen, breathlessly, 'they're blue.'

Una looked up and her sour expression softened. 'All babies have blue eyes at first,' she said, 'but I think they'll stay blue.'

'She's not ugly at all,' said Maureen quietly.

Liam came, looking happier and calm. They all moved their chairs around the bed to Winnie's face and sat in a circle. George poked Winnie in the cheek and she groaned and tried to roll away from him but she was too sore and groaned again, then rolled back, a reluctant smile tugging at one corner of her mouth. George said see, she can move, look, she can move when she wants to. They taunted her, playing the hilarious passive-aggressive games that only truly dysfunctional families understand, laughing louder and louder because Winnie had the mother of all hangovers, asking Winnie what the food was like in here and did she have a trumpet the baby could play with. Even the AA people joined in, adding quips of their own. The AA man pretended to run out to the shops for some kippers and Stilton but came back, escorted by a staff nurse, who told them all to shut up and keep the noise down, there were sick people in here. And all the while Maureen kept hold of the baby, cradling it against her chest, cherishing it, hoping she would get to hold wee Maureen again and again.

She didn't even believe her own excuses any more. She wasn't drinking because she wanted to, it wasn't because she'd achieved anything or even because she was sad. It was compulsive and she couldn't stop herself. She unscrewed the cap from Leslie's half-bottle and drank it straight, greedily, as if someone might try to stop her, pausing for breath and refusing to think about what she was doing. And then the familiar blanket came down.

It was later and she was worried, falling down the close steps one at a time, holding on to the wall, clinging to her purse. It was light outside and she couldn't quite remember whether it was morning or evening. Outside now and evening, definitely evening. The charity bags that she had left under the lamp-post had been split open and three small boys had pulled her old dresses over their clothes and were laughing excitedly, pushing each other into a thick hedge.

Inside the shop and Padda Junior looking at her, making a joke, a man behind her laughing and Junior looking away. They were laughing at her because she was pissed.

It smarted for as long as she could remember it. A young boy and a stranger laughing at her because she was steaming and alone, as if she was Winnie, as if her being pissed wasn't completely different. She set the thoughts aside and realized that she was at last alone with a bottle with no one to ask her what she was doing. She toasted her reflection in the living-room window, a defiant fuck-them, and drank. The nagging realization wouldn't go away. Even Padda Junior had noticed she had a problem.

The walls of Maureen's mouth began to tingle, sending messages of alarm to her brain, telling her to run for it. Before she had time to think, she was on her knees in the bathroom, pushing the seat and lid up against the cistern, dropping her mouth to the water. Her chin smashed off the porcelain bowl and her head ricocheted back just in time to catch the rim of the seat as it fell on her forehead.

When she had finished being sick she stood up unsteadily and looked at herself in the mirror. She had an inch-long bruise on her forehead, one under her chin and a stripe of vomit on her cheek.

51

End Game

It didn't feel like the last day of her life. She had the immediate problem of a searing hangover to deal with. It was never usually this bad when she'd thrown up the night before. As she washed her face in the sink of cold water she began to remember Mr Padda's shop and hung her head in shame.

She took painkillers and watched the phone as she drank her coffee. She watched it and knew she'd have to do it some time, if she didn't want to end up in a hospital bed with everyone taking the piss out of her. She stood up and dialled Benny's mobile number. He wasn't answering and she was pleased. She left a message asking him to contact her, please. She thought she'd better do something about her drinking.

She got dressed with her shades on. Kilty would think it was strange that she was wearing shades in the house, so she put on her coat as well, hoping that she'd just look as if she was ready to go.

When she opened the door Kilty looked her up and down. 'Are you hung-over again?'

Maureen sighed. 'The shades are the give-away, aren't they?'

'No, not really,' said Kilty, pushing past her. 'It's the body, the face and the hair.'

'Shit.' She followed Kilty into the living room. 'Hung-over on a Monday, they'll think I'm a fucked-up waster.'

'Maureen, you need to address the—'

Maureen held up her hand and took a painfully deep breath. 'Please, Kilty, help me today,' she said. 'Please, I'm going to a meeting tomorrow.'

'Promise?'

'I do, I promise, I promise.'

'Okay, then.'

Kilty sat her down on the floor and took out a tiny makeup bag. She used concealer and blusher to draw features on to Maureen's face and put some eye-liner on her top lid to make her eyes look open, explaining that she wouldn't put it on the inside because her watery eyes would just make it run. By the time Leslie arrived the painkillers were kicking in, the blusher was doing its job and Maureen looked as if she was just having a slightly off day.

'Maureen's going to a meeting tomorrow,' said Kilty, as she let her in.

'Good,' said Leslie. 'Who're ye going with?'

'I phoned Benny,' said Maureen, wishing to fuck she hadn't told Kilty. She was bound to change her mind by the next day but knew they'd hold her to it.

'Right?' said Kilty. 'Let's go.'

A sharp wind hurled through the town, tugging the edges of their coats. They arrived at the court by eleven, which was ridiculously early because the jury would hardly have had time to sit down. Kilty chatted up the guard at the door and he told her to sit just outside and listen for a Tannoy announcement that Court One was coming back. They spent the next hour standing on the windy steps, smoking and waiting to hear. Kilty went down the road to a shop and brought back three takeaway coffees.

Forty minutes later Liam arrived, with a broad smile for Maureen and a nod for the other two. Angus's family turned up, dressed up for the photographs, and scuttled past them on the steps, knowing who they were now that Maureen had given evidence.

At twelve twenty a white van pulled up at the gates, followed by a black taxi. The side door on the van slid back and three men got out: a man in a slick suit, another guy with a furry microphone on a long stick and a cameraman. They hovered in the door of the van, fixing a large light to the top of the camera, while the smartly dressed man smoothed his hair. Whoever was in the black cab was talking to the driver. The door opened. It was Joe McEwan, wearing casual jeans, a leather jacket and a baseball cap. He glanced at the cameraman and walked past, coming straight for Maureen. He acknowledged Liam and looked at Maureen, nodding her over to one side. 'How are ye, Joe?' she said.

'The word is Farrell's getting out,' he said, 'and if he does, we think he'll be coming for you.'

'Oh?' she said, feeling as if he was being silly because the dark days were past now and this was just a tie-up, just a small detail that needed finishing off.

'I expect you've heard about your dad?'

'Michael? Aye.'

'He's a vicious bastard.' Joe reached out and squeezed her upper arm in a soldierly gesture of solidarity. 'I'm sorry.'

She was astonished. 'It's okay, Joe.'

'If Farrell gets out it won't be for long. The Fiscal's applying for an arrest warrant for the rapes right now.'

She nodded, wanting to get away from him and back to her friends, back to pretending that things were fine. The Tannoy warbled through the revolving door and Kilty called for Maureen to come. 'Ye coming in?' she said.

Joe shook his head. 'Look, we'll be rearresting him as soon as we can.'

She smiled. 'He might not get off.'

'If he does we'll meet you at your house, okay?'

'Okay.'

Joe pressed his lips together, and backed off down the steps to the waiting taxi.

'Come on, Mauri,' said Liam. 'It's time.'

They got good seats at the front, near the jury, and Maureen noticed that neither Carol Brady nor Elsbeth was there. The lawyers gathered around the central table, tense and nervous. Angus's lawyer was sucking a sweet. The ratchet noise of a lock being pulled back heralded footsteps on stone stairs, and Angus Farrell came up from the cells, escorted on either side by two guards. He was wearing a smart sports jacket in a small brown check and his demeanour gave nothing away. The bow-tied man came through a side door calling, 'Court,' and carrying a big metal mace with a little crown on top. Everyone in the room scrambled to their feet. Angus's lawyer crunched his sweetie into little bits and swallowed it. Then the judge came in and they were allowed to sit down again.

The bow-tied man disappeared through a side door and the members of the jury filed back into the court. The giggling man and woman had grown tired of one another's company or had fallen out. They weren't sitting together or looking at each other. The judge asked something and a juryman at the front stood up and unfolded a bit of paper. The case against Angus Farrell for the murder of Douglas Brady was found not proven, a verdict particular to Scots law, which meant that they thought he had probably done it but that there wasn't enough evidence. He was found not guilty of murdering Martin Donegan on the grounds of automatism.

*

The court was empty long before they moved. Too early. Maureen wasn't fit for this. She'd peaked too early. She couldn't find a shred of anger in herself. She was disappointed and irritated but she wasn't angry and she needed to be. She fell forwards, muttering 'Fuck,' and banging her aching head off the back of the bench in front, landing exactly on the bruise from the toilet seat.

'Let's get you out of here,' said Liam, taking her arm, and they all four stood up and inched along the bench to the door.

The foyer was busy. They had to struggle to get through the crowd of bodies to the door. They were almost there when Maureen began to see flashing lights and looked up. Angus Farrell and his lawyer were coming through the lobby, trailed by his shabby family. They were walking among a crowd of journalists barking questions and holding dictaphones up to Angus's modestly smiling face. The lawyer was talking and Maureen's legs went slack as they came past her. Angus was inches from her. He turned, quite casually, and spoke in a normal tone. 'I'll see you later,' he said to her, his fixed smile making the statement sound snide and lascivious. Maureen saw the lawyer hear him say it, she noticed that the journalists heard him say it, and her brother, Liam, heard him say it. But Angus didn't give a shit because Angus had a plan.

They had driven up to Balloch, fifteen miles away on the banks of Loch Lomond, in case they had been followed. Liam turned the car round and drove back to Glasgow, taking back roads to Garnethill. Leslie and Kilty had gone straight to Maureen's flat to let the police in. Liam dropped Maureen near the house, waiting to see if she got into the close and watching for Leslie waving at the window before he drove off to park the car discreetly. Hugh and Something

McMummb had already arrived and were waiting for her upstairs. She wished it had been anyone else. Hugh had gone off her, big-time.

Liam parked half a mile away and arrived back at the house with some bread and crisps, beer and whisky so that they wouldn't have to leave before morning. They sat in melancholy silence in the front room, sighing occasionally, getting up and looking out of the window.

Quite sniffily, Hugh asked Maureen to show him the back way into the house and she took him into the close and explained that the back court could only be accessed through a space between the buildings opposite. Liam thought maybe someone should sit and watch the alleyway, but Hugh pointed out that there were other ways into the back court.

Maureen's head was thumping, she had a rushing in her ears and couldn't break her mind from the circle of thoughts that Angus was out and Angus was coming. He had a plan, a clear plan of what he was going to do, and she couldn't fathom what it was. Her head was aching at the back, her jaw was sore and the skin on her forehead began to tingle with prolonged tension. She crossed her arms and pressed the sore skin on her arms to wake herself up. She looked up and found Kilty holding out a lit cigarette and a glass of whisky. Maureen took the cigarette.

'Don't you want this?' said Kilty, holding out the whisky.

'So fucking much you wouldn't believe it,' said Maureen, and turned to look out of the window.

Suddenly she heard a hard wheeze behind her back and spun round to find Kilty's eyes wide in shock. She was breathing out wide-mouthed. Maureen caught her breath. Kilty's lips were glistening, an amber, oily slick on one side of the glass. 'I don't know how you can drink that straight,' she said, looking sick, and wandered off into the kitchen, leaving Maureen taking deep breaths and trying to slow her heart.

Hugh came into the room and leaned against the wall.

'How long do I have to stay here?' asked Maureen, and he shrugged. 'Hugh, why are you in a huff with me?'

Hugh smiled a little and came over to her. 'That makes it sound very petty,' he said quietly.

'Isn't it petty?'

'No,' he said seriously, 'not to me. I've tried my hardest to help you. I've stuck my neck out and you've gone ahead and done whatever you wanted. I'd have to be stupid not to feel insulted.'

'Well, I'm sorry,' she said, apologizing because she wanted Hugh to approve of her, but she wasn't sorry at all. His tone brought her back to school again and the tyranny of the piteous.

In the street far below black cabs nudged up behind one another at the taxi rank like fat beetles, lunch-time pedestrians hurried by to get sandwiches or get back to work. It began to rain heavily, fat teardrops falling fast past the window. Outside, a mum stopped to zip up her child's coat, going back to push the empty buggy and letting the child splash along the pavement.

Maureen finished her cigarette, feeling sick and anxious, her heart racing. When she reached for the packet to take another she realized that she had one cigarette left. 'Liam?'

He was in the kitchen with Leslie, sitting at the table.

'I'm running out of fags, have ye got any?' He didn't, and Leslie only had three left.

'I'll nip home and get a couple of cartons,' he said. 'Don't drive,' said Kilty. 'He could pick you up at your house and follow you back here.'

The three watched as Liam got into a cab downstairs. He looked up and they could see him muttering curses at them as he waved them away from the window. Leslie and Kilty went back to the kitchen to watch for intruders.

Maureen lit the last of her cigarettes and looked out over the south side. Angus had a plan. He was smarter than any of them. Everything she'd done felt as if he had orchestrated it, giving him the acid, meeting Mark Doyle, being here now. She stood up. Being here now. He had planned this. He had written to her and threatened her and talked about her in hospital. He'd threatened her in front of journalists, on camera. He wanted her to know he was coming after her, to think he was coming after her, wanted her to stay in the house and hide, and wanted the police to protect her. She was on her feet, falling into the hallway.

'Leslie!' she shouted, grabbing her jacket and opening the door. 'Get the bike.'

Kilty and Leslie ran out of the kitchen. Hugh lurched to shut the front door but Maureen blocked it with her body. 'We'll take the bike.' She pointed at Hugh. 'Phone the police. Kilty, phone Liam. It's Siobhain. He's going to kill her. He's going to kill Siobhain.'

Angus Farrell had had a pleasant meal. He liked plain food, nothing that would repeat too much in the afternoon. After shaking off his ecstatic mother and Auntie Mima with promises to come straight over after lunch, he had taken Alan Grace to the DiPrano seafood restaurant. He ordered steamed cod with noodles and a fruit salad to finish. Grace ate quickly, Angus noticed, and asked for the bill before Angus had finished his coffee.

They parted on the pavement, pulling up their collars against the heavy rain, agreeing to see each other again soon. And well done, by the way. Grace's face withered into an uncomfortable smile. 'Go and see your family,' said Grace.

'That's exactly what I'm going to do now,' said Angus. He stepped out into the road and hailed a taxi.

The bike was skidding on the wet road and Leslie managed to slice through two imminent red lights without getting them killed. She took the motorway to avoid going down Duke Street. The splash-back from the fast cars was blinding. Maureen wondered how the hell she could see where she was going. Leslie ducked from lane to lane, skipping between the fast cars until she came to a large lorry and sat in the calm, dry vacuum behind it. Maureen held on tight, straining her head over Leslie's shoulder, as if that would get them there any faster. She thought of Mark Doyle and Pauline, thought of the state Siobhain was in when they first met her, thought of Michael and anything else that might make her really fucking angry, but all she felt was scared and weary.

The taxi dropped him outside a pub in Duke Street. It was raining heavily and no one was looking up at anyone else. For the first time Angus was glad of his broken nose, smirked as he thought how well it made him fit in with the hardmen and the bums coming out of the pubs and bookies'. He kept his head down and took a side-street, wishing he had worn a mac, hoping he wouldn't get anything on his jacket. It had cost three hundred quid, over three hundred, actually, three fifty or something, and he'd only worn it four times. He took his black leather gloves out of his inside pocket and slid them on to his hands, crossing his fingers over one another, pressing the soft calfskin into his knuckles.

Dennistoun from the motorway was a warren of one-way streets, designed to stop boy-racers from careering off the slip-road and taking the small back roads at seventy. Leslie did her best but ended up going the wrong way down a long one-way street for three blocks. She almost overturned the bike when they got to Siobhain's corner. They stopped, taking off their helmets as they sprinted up to the close door, leaving the motorbike unchained in a rough area.

The two concrete steps to the unsecured door were wet with footprints. Maureen ran at the door with both hands out, shoving it open. The damp footprints led upstairs, drying out on the turn to Siobhain's landing. Maureen dropped her helmet and bolted after them. The front door was lying open, a grey metal pick hanging in the Yale lock, still light spilling into the hall from the open living-room door. She listened for a second, knowing she'd hear him if he was there. Somewhere in the house Siobhain exhaled, ending with a tiny, despairing call from deep inside her.

Maureen ran down the hall, tripping over the doorstep, losing her footing and scampering on all fours. Her shoulder smashed into the door-frame. She pulled herself up and looked into the living room. Empty. She turned to the kitchen. Empty. She threw herself across the hall against the bedroom door and stopped. The facing wall was splattered with flecks of deep red. On the floor at her feet lay Angus Farrell, face down, staring under the bed, his broken nose in perfect profile against the beige carpet. The back of his head was a flattened, filthy red mess. Under the skin and blood, beyond the splintered brilliant-white skull, peeked a doleful blue. It was watery blue like the baby's eyes. Angus had lived long enough to touch his brain. His bloody hands lay by his ears, desperate handprints smeared on the carpet, grabbing red trails from retracting fingers.

Downstairs, the close door crashed open against the wall and Liam came running, screaming over and over for his Siobhain. The bedroom door next to Maureen quivered, making her stagger backwards in fright, and Siobhain

434

peered around the edge holding a cast-iron frying-pan, her hands and face speckled with red freckles.

They sat on the close stairs and waited for twenty minutes for the police to come. Liam held Siobhain on his knee, their foreheads pressed tight together, their hands intertwined. 'I thought I was being burgled,' whispered Siobhain.

Liam looked up at Maureen and Leslie, sitting close together, smoking the last of Leslie's fags. 'I didn't tell her the verdict was due today,' said Liam, 'I didn't want to upset her. Is he dead?'

'I don't really know,' said Siobhain.

'I think he is, actually,' said Maureen, and Leslie agreed, wrapping her arms around her tummy and rocking gently.

'Are you okay?' Maureen asked Leslie.

Leslie nodded over and over.

It took the police twenty minutes to get there because Kilty didn't know where Siobhain lived and couldn't remember her second name. Hugh had to call the police station and get someone to find the address in the files on Farrell's investigation. When they arrived the police made them all get out of the close and cautioned Siobhain.

Leslie waited until they were in the back of the police car and on their way to the station to give statements before she spoke. 'Is Siobhain gonnae be charged with murder?' she said.

Hugh turned to look at her. 'I doubt that,' he said gently.

Leslie sighed. 'I'm never gonnae be cheeky to Siobhain again,' she said, and looked out of the window. 'Never, ever, ever.'

52
Aye

There were four figures sitting on the ground, listening to the pipe player. They had no faces but the angle of a head, the drop of an arm showed they were immersed in the creamy moment, following the spiral of the music. In the foreground two figures, one lying, one sitting, were watching goldfish turn in a bowl. It was completely flat, the foreground and the background differentiated only by the size of the figures. Her eyes were drawn into the picture by the fish but then swayed through each of the characters, resting on a man with his head tipped back, enjoying.

She had been there for nearly an hour and a camp security guard with slicked-down hair and shiny buttons on his blazer was getting pissed off. She had tried to sit down cross-legged on the parquet floor in front of the painting but he stood over her, looking disdainful, and flicked her upright with an angry forefinger. She had to sit on the banquette by one of the three large windows. Matisse's huge canvas, *The Dance*, was distracting her from the *Coffeehouse*. The windows in the Winter Palace had net curtains on them. Every time they rustled behind her she smiled at the inappropriateness of it. She turned sideways and looked out through the milky curtain across to the chequered Palace Square and saw the sun glinting off the gilded onion domes of the Cathedral called The Resurrection On Spilt Blood.

She'd have to watch her time. There was only one English-speaking AA meeting per week in St Petersburg and it began in an hour. She hadn't been sober long enough to go a week without one.

He sat down next to her on the bench and took her hand lightly in his.

'All right?' she whispered, still looking out of the window. 'Are ye having a good time?'

'Aye,' said Vik. 'Oh, aye.'

THE END